NIREESWARAN

NIREESWARAN

V.J. JAMES

TRANSLATED FROM
THE MALAYALAM
BY MINISTHY S.

VINTAGE
An imprint of Penguin Random House

VINTAGE

USA | Canada | UK | Ireland | Australia
New Zealand | India | South Africa | China

Vintage is part of the Penguin Random House group of companies
whose addresses can be found at global.penguinrandomhouse.com

Published by Penguin Random House India Pvt. Ltd
4th Floor, Capital Tower 1, MG Road,
Gurugram 122 002, Haryana, India

Penguin
Random House
India

First published in Vintage by Penguin Random House India 2022

10 9 8 7 6 5 4 3 2

This is a work of fiction. Names, characters, places and incidents are either the product of the author's imagination or are used fictitiously, and any resemblance to any actual person, living or dead, events or locales is entirely coincidental.

ISBN 9780670096558

Typeset in Adobe Garamond Pro by MAP Systems, Bengaluru, India
Printed at Replika Press Pvt. Ltd, India

www.penguin.co.in

FSC
www.fsc.org
MIX
Paper from
responsible sources
FSC® C016779

To the stars in my solar system: Aswathi, Thara and Sooryan

—V.J. James

To my daughters: Sandra and Saundarya

—Ministhy S.

'Belief is one story and disbelief, another. Somebody prefers the former, and someone else the latter. But the truth is naked. It has no wrappings of either belief or disbelief.'

—Osho

Contents

Preface

The universe is a fascinating entity. The foundation of its very existence is based on duality. Positive-Negative, Hot-Cold, Joy-Suffering, Good-Bad, Belief-Disbelief: these have always been a part of our world and shall continue to be so.

Just like religion, politics, rationalism and atheism too start donning different guises based on the declaration of faith by select followers. The amusing fact is that everybody is dead-sure of their own viewpoint being correct and the rest being totally wrong! There is a constant tussle aimed at defeating the 'other' and obliterating it entirely.

For me, *Nireeswaran* was a humble attempt at rising above all such divisiveness of a combative world and viewing it from a higher perspective. *Nireeswaran* is neither a protest nor an appeal. The avatar originated from the thought that the truth is obscured by the hard shell of the human ego when it revels in arguments and shuts down all possibilities of dialogue. In order to write this book, I needed to travel to the interfaces where philosophical depths met the microscopic realms of science. I extend the same welcome to those who agree with what is exposited in the book and those who do not.

The great Indian heritage has always welcomed diverse views with open arms. If anybody feels that *Nireeswaran* is that unique truth which is beyond all names and forms, the cause of all differences and variations which manifests in man, animal, deva, asura and nature equally, let me submit that it is his or her freedom to think so.

I am humbled by the fact that more than 25,000 copies of *Nireeswaran* have sold in Malayalam, a small regional language, within a few years of its publication. To me, it stands as the sign of the generous love with which readers have accepted it. It took me almost five years to complete the original work. *Nireeswaran* is my third novel to be translated into English, after *Chorashastra* and *Anti-Clock*.

I wish to express my thanks to Ministhy S. for beautifully translating the novel. Much gratitude to Penguin Random House India for bringing out the book in such a wonderful manner. I would like to specially thank Elizabeth Kuruvilla, Saloni Mital, Vineet Gill and cover designer Devangana Dash for their immense contribution in creating this book. May Nireeswaran's benevolence grace everybody.

24 March 2022

V.J. James
Thiruvananthapuram

Translator's Note

When I read *Nireeswaran*, the richness of the subject matter, the mélange of characters, the depth of philosophy and science explored within the narrative, the charming simplicity of the interwoven village tales, and the detached, ironic voice of the unseen narrator left me fascinated. The book had won many prestigious awards in Kerala and many readers referred to it as a modern-day classic.

Having translated three novels of James, I was familiar with his erudition and proclivity towards scientific and philosophical musings. But *Nireeswaran* was a challenge in more ways than one. For example, you have a scientist conversing on mathematical conundrums and nuances of physics with an uneducated woman. And she understands what he says with clarity and probes further too! In Malayalam, the language is extremely, let me say, deceptively simple. And that simplicity set the standards of translation sky-high: how to capture every sentence with the same humility of spirit.

Every book transforms not only the reader but also the translator. It was a wonderful coincidence that I was working on the translation of the canto 'Aranya Kanda' (of Shri Ramcharitmanas) along with *Nireeswaran*. Suffice it to say that in my mind, the corporeal form and the intangible form of the Lord merged rather well!

In a world wracked with pandemic, upheavals and wars, we need books more than ever. I feel privileged to have translated *Nireeswaran*.

9 March 2022

Ministhy S.
Lucknow

Prayer

Now let us chant the glories of Nireeswaran.
And let us narrate the stories of the one,
Who is omnipresent and luminous!

A hymn for his compassion
That ensures the extermination of foes
And safety of the seekers.

For those unaware of his greatness,
For those who have not known him yet,
I shall narrate the saga of Nireeswaran.

Let him bestow me with grace
To elucidate his feats with elan.
Om Nireeswaray Namah!

ORIGIN

First Petal: The Germ of Thought

Since we know the word 'temple' as 'Eswaran's residence', if you object to the term 'Nireeswaran temple', kindly keep your misconception aside. Know that a place of worship, manifesting the notion of Nireeswaran, has come into existence. It is the chronicle of its origin that is narrated here, in honour of all virtuous souls. With the grace of Nireeswaran, whoever reads the story of this avatar with due sincerity shall have his internal grime cleansed and attain salvation.

A place of origin is usually referred to as 'Moolasthanam'. So, it is only after paying due respect to the street that was destined to be the Moolasthanam of the Nireeswaran should one embark on the story of that avatar. The street was known as Deva Theruvu, aka God's Street. From its very name, it was evident that even a blind man faltering about on that street would invariably end up in a temple. Among the populace living around the temple sans boundary walls, there was only one who couldn't see. The rest had sight, and a few possessed good insights too.

Speaking of insights, it would be pertinent to remember the three friends—Antony, Bhaskaran and Sahir—who were very different from the others in this regard. The trio, whose houses and minds were close to one another, lived in Deva Theruvu, maintaining untouchability vis-à-vis the temple and exhibiting open distaste for its rituals.

Their hot young blood, always bristling against something or other, was the force that bound them together.

Providing grist to that youthful proclivity to rebel were many topics, from religion and politics to the share market. Even so, if Antony, Bhaskaran and Sahir felt it wrong that the street, where different sections of people cohabited, had a name that smacked of a specific religion, there was something right about it.

The trio had already exhibited a genius in imparting an abrupt twist to straightforward things, even in selecting a name for their clique.

By picking the first syllables of their names—*A*ntony, *Bha*skaran and *Sa*hir—they had coined the term 'Abhasa Sangha'. In the local tongue, it meant 'the fellowship of the debauched'.

The stone platform around the tree on the roadside was the nerve centre of the Abhasa's operations. They assembled there every evening, and shared strong, tenacious opinions about everything under the sky and occasionally even above it.

Many of the natives frequented the spot to while away the dusk. It was a habit of yore. Groups of both old and young would seat themselves separately. Some would perch on the stone platform, while others reclined on the lush grass or chatted sitting atop the nearby boulder. Young children, hanging on to the forefingers of their grandfathers, would make their appearance and scamper around merrily. It was rather like a village park that came into being without any specific planning.

At the centre of the circular stone platform stood a peepal (al) and a mango tree (mavu), intertwined so intricately that it was impossible to differentiate one from the other. Their roots and branches had merged with each other like Siamese twins of botanical life, with inseparable bodies and veins. However closely you examined them, it felt that the branches of the mango tree originated from the peepal and that of the peepal from the mango tree. Nobody wanted to segregate the trees that stood as a single body, embracing and supporting each other. In common parlance, the natives referred to the blended existence of the al and the mavu as Athmavu, or the soul.

If the wind shook the mango tree, the strong arm of the peepal would hold it tenderly. Whenever the peepal swayed in the opposite direction, the mango would reach out and embrace it tightly. There was enough shade for any number of fellowships to flourish under the unison of the giant trees that shared joy and grief equally.

The Abhasa typically assembled at twilight, when the birds came home to roost. The jingle-jangle of the temple bells during the evening puja irked them immensely. It was Bhaskaran who first pointed out that instead of the much vaunted 'om' intonation, which the temple bells were supposed to evoke, the peels desultorily thrummed 'kom, kom, kom'! Through arduous exercise of their hearing acuity, first Antony and then Sahir corroborated that observation. Indeed, one misplaced inflection could turn the whole rhythm of creation, preservation and annihilation, the *shristi–sthithi–laya*, out of tune. For this reason and many others, the trio never cared two hoots about places of worship nurtured inside the compound walls of delusions.

The thought that the name of their street was based on the same belief system weighed them down profoundly. When the heaviness became unbearable, they thought of unloading it by obliterating all references to God's Street. It was a pity that though scientific temperament had grown to the skies and beyond, an eraser to wipe out such superstitious street names was yet to be invented. But then the dictum, even if espoused by another holy book, was 'Seek and ye shall find'. The forthcoming events shall reveal that the dictum turned out to be true for the Abhasa as well.

Antony, Bhaskaran and Sahir were certain that if people thronged places of worship even after the Gregorian calendar had flipped across twenty centuries, it was simply due to a lack of self-confidence. Such folks needed the glue of devotion to amalgamate. And their numbers were burgeoning to an alarming degree. Since they did not think rationally, the fellows did not understand the truth. Even if one were to distribute some truth freely to them, with their eyes and ears shut tightly, they would simply refuse to accept it. No wonder that one master had asserted that religion was the opium of the people. Why not trick the opium distributor using his own strategy?

Since direct combat had yielded nothing in all these years, why hadn't the realists tested some other intellectual manoeuvre?

There was no use in deploying strategies that had let down one's forerunners. Instead of blindly following the beaten path, the Abhasa started searching inexorably for something iconoclastic, bearing their own singular thumbprint. And during one such attempt, it was decided to alter the name of God's Street, as the first step—rather like a test dose before administering a penicillin injection.

However, it was not going to be an easy task. Though one could leap ahead in the imagination, the path to execution was rife with obstacles. Moreover, there would be intense pushback by the earnest believers against the name change!

'Listen! The best way to defeat an enemy is to try his own tactics!' Antony proposed. 'For example, what's the process of purification in a temple? If the astrologer augurs any impurity, a cleansing ritual, which purportedly increases the radiance of the deity, is carried out. But we should conduct a reverse purification instead! By removing the godliness from the street's name, we'll sanctify it anew.'

'But how?' Bhaskaran asked.

'No point in being poetically silent like the idealists! We should make surreptitious moves without revealing the sanctification ploy. If a street where the god reigns is called Deva Theruvu or God's Street, why can't the street where the Abhasa rules be named Abhasa Theruvu, the Debauched Street?'

'Abhasa Theruvu! There's oomph in it,' Sahir said with a guffaw.

'Don't laugh at it so soon!'

'I am not the only one laughing. Look at the peepal and the mango!'

The leaves of the peepal seemed to be chattering incessantly, like raucous kids racing upon hearing the school bell. And the mango leaves were bobbing along in agreement. Even when there was no trace of a breeze, the leaves of the peepal, possessing an extreme sensitivity, were receptive to the subtlest movement of air. Due to the virtue of constant companionship, the mango tree, too, had imbibed the habit of nodding, even when idling.

'Even if we rename the street, who will accept it? People will mock us openly,' Sahir objected. This was a perfectly justifiable comment.

Sahir found not only the temple bells but also the calls of the muezzin vexatious. The atheist in him refused to follow a life delineated by five sessions of prayer.

'I have an idea!' Bhaskaran piped up. 'Of course, we have to do it rather stealthily. Let us scribble the new name of the street on all walls. At first, folks might laugh, but over the course of time, the new name will start sinking in!'

Though the strategy did not have much potential, the duplicitous pleasure associated with its secretiveness amused Antony. Secrets intrigued him to the level of an obsession. He was of the opinion that sins committed clandestinely were doubly intoxicating. The moment an idea took root in his mind, Antony would tuck in his mundu and set about its implementation. Antony's body language was blatantly aggressive, like that of the macho superheroes of mainstream films, setting out to fight capriciously.

Though he was nearly forty years old, Antony had never worn any clothing other than shirt and mundu. His preference was for mundus with *kasavu* borders. One could say that he took after his daredevil father in many ways, including his preference for this attire. Due to him faithfully following his father's many secret penchants, the villagers had crowned him with the title of being 'born true to the progenitor's loins'. It was another matter altogether that the son, 'born to the father', was yet to sign any nuptial contract to become a father himself! The honest rumination, that marriage would not suit his way of life, was the reason. If anyone ever pestered Antony about the topic, he would retort, 'If lucky, even a priest can become a father!'

The next day, the village woke up to the humungous odour of debauchery. The name 'Abhasa Theruvu' had been scribbled on all the walls in the vicinity. The natives took the episode as a tasteless joke and shrugged it off with the contempt it deserved. Just because someone wrote something, could the godliness of the street vanish overnight?

But soon the black humour started getting its due. Through cold-blooded strategy, the Abhasa managed the changeover. Whenever they referred to the street in conversations, they intentionally spoke about Abhasa Theruvu. They started a spate of events by complaining in writing to the local electricity board office that the lights were not working in Abhasa Theruvu. It was another matter altogether that it was a deliberate act of insurrection which made the bulb conk off. That veteran of stone pelters, Bhaskaran, had accomplished the mission meticulously, incessantly chanting that 'the ends justify the means'.

The petty bureaucrats at the electricity board scratched their heads when they received the complaint about the outage. 'Abhasa Theruvu? Where the hell is that?' On mentioning the area, the officials laughed. 'Ah, you mean God's Street!' But the name blazed the passage of an electric signal in their brains, and when hearing of Abhasa Theruvu subsequently, their memories lighted up with the speed of electricity.

Whenever Bhaskaran, Antony and Sahir trooped to the city to booze and indulge in their other weaknesses, the trio made it a point to request for bus tickets back to Abhasa Theruvu. Though the conductor of the Sri Vidya bus found it amusing initially, when the bus rumbled to a halt near the street, he took a puerile pleasure in announcing loudly, 'Alight, all of you belonging to Abhasa Theruvu!'

Belonging to the debauched category himself and prone to venting his debauchery by rubbing against the young girls boarding the bus, the conductor took a liking to the new name. He started experiencing a verbal orgasm akin to rubbing against tender bodies whenever he hailed 'Abhasa Theruvu' on nearing the bus stop. It provoked him to announce the new name of the street more than was warranted. Since a hundred ears hearken when a tongue begins its job, the contribution of the bus conductor to popularizing the new name was indeed immense.

The participation of the lower strata of society was desirable in cementing the new name further. For that purpose, the trio singled out a male and a female. Maniyan, the barber of the land who shaved the citizens, and Janaki, the prostitute of the land who soothed their secret lusts, were the chosen ones. The barber's shop and Janaki were venues of commercial exchange frequented by all sections of society, the kind psychologically prone to yielding to monetary temptations.

Antony typically felt an engorged crick in his neck if he did not get his hair trimmed military-style by Maniyan every month. In the same way, whenever he felt a turbulence in his loins, it called to his mind Janaki's voluptuous curves. At the cost of a few extra rupees, Maniyan was glad to oblige by squeezing in the words 'Abhasa Theruvu' on the tin name board dangling above his shop entrance. Apart from the money, the Abhasa also offered to get the barbershop's ancient board painted afresh. Other than falling for the attractive bait, Maniyan's ready acquiescence was without much forethought towards its ramifications. The barber was oblivious to the fortuitous role he was to play in the imminent saga of the Nireeswaran.

Even without a board of her own, Janaki's business was prospering. As a result, she transformed into a board herself, advertising the Debauched Street.

Antony, Bhaskaran and Sahir made major efforts in launching operation clean-up in the street. They took care to plant many banners and boards at strategic places to reinforce their propaganda.

Over time, the execution of their secretive plans bore fruit, and the term 'Abhasa Theruvu' started being uttered by the common man's tongue rather glibly. To cut a long story short, after a brief stint of focused work, with the old name of Deva Theruvu being forgotten and the new name, Abhasa Theruvu, taking its place, the three hardcore materialists felt that the successful completion of their mission was the first major step of their great journey. After all, repetition of mundane habits is what life is all about.

Although they had succeeded in scrubbing the street clean of the name of God and making it depraved, their roiling blood did not settle into normal circulation. As the first instance of abuse provokes an insatiable thirst for more, the friends experienced a recurring friction within. Perhaps it was their flagrant youthfulness, or the fluctuations of minds yearning for newness, or the thrill of a different hunt—whatever it was, it made them feel that sitting beneath the majestic Athmavu, which possessed the dignity of the Bodhi tree, might enlighten them with ideas of a sky-high stature. Antony laughed that it could also be termed superstition. His was the blood which pined the most for novelty.

Antony's tough body was similar to that of a weightlifter. Unless he channelled his extra energy into some nefarious activity or another, he found himself struggling to restrain his manly desires. By positing something unique, Antony relished becoming the cynosure of all eyes. Maybe that was why, as he sat beneath the 'tree of knowledge', a new idea took hold in his mind. Analysed at depth, it was akin to a godly revelation dawning on the atheists. Truly paradoxical.

'They make these temples and churches with lifeless bricks and wood, don't they?' Antony asked, staring at the wind's thousand tongues fluttering above in the peepal leaves. 'Why not create a new god who is an antithesis of all existing gods? An Eswaran to face off all the gods?'

'When we are fed up with umpteen gods already, why create another Eswaran?' Sahir turned surly.

'There is a reason, Sahir! This god shall stand in opposition to all gods. And so, the name of the Eswaran that we create shall be Nireeswaran!'

'Nireeswaran, Nireeswaran . . .' Bhaskaran rolled the name around his tongue a couple of times. He had not tasted such a delectable word until then. 'I have heard of atheism but never of a Nireeswaran till now!' Bhaskaran relished both the meaning and the wordplay.

'There is real potential here! The atheist view is as old as faith itself. Wasn't Charvaka its exponent? Neither the Buddha nor Mahavira worshipped God. If we jabber like the rest of the rationalists that there is no God, there will be nothing unique about it. We must add a new dimension to it! Displacing one thorn with another, we should install a Nireeswaran in the place of Eswaran!'

'*Wah*! That is brilliant! To expose the absurdity of a place of worship, turn the concept on its head. As far as I know, nobody has tried such a thing till now!' Bhaskaran said.

'The Abhasa should be renowned for doing things nobody has ever attempted! Why can't we create a Nireeswaran for fun's sake? It will be much better than crying ourselves hoarse that there isn't any God.' Antony stroked the arches of his lush moustache left and right. 'We are stuck in some odd corner of this universe. Though we cannot shake up the whole world, there is no harm in attempting it, is there? At the very least, the village will be shaken, making our effort worthwhile!'

Though it couldn't be predicted if the universe or the village would experience any major turmoil, the Bodhi tree watched with interest as the seeds of a new idea were sown in the ripe fields of history. By dropping leaves down in the wind, it conveyed its best wishes for the plan.

It was an auspicious moment when the concept of Nireeswaran was presented for the first time, as an alternative to all notions of God existing in the universe. It was the instant when history stood ready to be split into two. Clearly, history must have reserved the ways and means to materialize the concept of Nireeswaran. To unravel them, one has to dig into this history. And so, only the seekers of truth willing to do so should continue to read from this stage onwards. The rest are welcome to voluntarily withdraw.

Second Petal: Body

'Easier said than done! If we wish to deify a Nireeswaran, he needs a shape, doesn't he? What sort of a form should we give him?' Sahir asked.

'Nireeswaran should be different from all conventional forms,' Antony opined. 'Deities usually resemble humans or animals, or the conjoining of the two, right? Nireeswaran should starkly stand out from the rest! Let us make a clay model first.'

It was Bhaskaran, adept at clay modelling at school, who was anointed for the purpose. Even before attaining adolescence, he had shaped a lot of feminine figurines from clay and indulged in many passionate affairs in his mind. Bhaskaran's replicas were based on the women he craved. He would gift their unseen curves to the clay models and strip them naked in his imagination. Vasanthi, Clara, Suhasini, Fatima, Reshmi, Lata, Mohini, Susanna, Raji, Sainu, Kannamma and even Padmavati—the teacher who taught him physics in the ninth standard—were given shape by his deft fingers. However, ridden with guilt, Bhaskaran had stopped sculpting his teacher's model midway. Consequently, that mentor's curse was reduced to an extent. Though his statues represented different women, their essential femininity was identical. His classmate Rahulan, gloating over his own status as a connoisseur, had chortled and said that this was due to Bhaskaran's lack of practical experience in the matter.

'Never mind! Once I gain experience, I'll recreate each with unique characteristics. That's how a true artist renews himself.'

'Yeah, sure! Recreation of female nudity. Bullshit! Can I borrow this statue for a day?' Rahulan asked.

'For what?'

'Oh, just like that.'

Bhaskaran sniffed a tightly coiled secret behind the loose talk. It took quite a bit of coaxing for Rahulan to disclose it. Apparently, Bhaskaran's creations had electrified Rahulan's senses! Each interaction Rahulan had with the statues was an experiment on the quantity of electricity his body could endure. When there were no more secrets between them, he persuaded Bhaskaran to be bountiful with the physical measurements of the formations. It was during one such attempt at enhancement that Bhaskaran became aware that creations converse with their creators.

Antony and Sahir were not convinced.

'No wonder people say that artists are eccentric,' Antony mocked.

'If that's true, he is a true artist,' Sahir said, adding fuel to the fire.

Only Rahulan stood stolidly behind Bhaskaran, fortified by his practical experiences. He testified that every creation did indeed speak to its creator. To establish his assertion, he narrated an episode. It was the tale of an orphaned artist who drank from the cup of sorrow, and of a girl who stepped in, with mesmerizing love, into the life of someone leading a solitary existence amid statues.

Sculptures are embodiments of love. When the heart is filled with love, figures accrue originality and radiance. Then, the statue declares freedom from the stone, which is as shapeless as the mind. Truly, the birth of each statue is nothing but the naked exposure of what was concealed. It is the completeness that remains, after every unwanted molecule that does not belong to the figurine is chiselled away—*a wholeness, where nothing could be carved and nothing could be added.*

One day, the sweetheart, who had renounced her near and dear ones, started living with the statues. It was the season when the tree of life burst into bloom. Colours, flowers, fruit, birds . . . since all the focus and energy were expended on one form, the earthly days turned heavenly. But the cost of a moment in heaven is the sum total of all sufferings in a human life. Hence nobody can experience more than one heavenly moment in a lifetime. That is why every love affair undergoes many trials, as if paying the interest due. Proving true that dictum yet again, when the maiden left her mortal existence, the artist went berserk. He realized that it was the woman by his side who had made him whole.

The sculptor started endeavouring to design his lover's full-bodied statue and give life to it. He sold off all his belongings to fulfil that dream. Days and nights of unceasing toil followed. As the figurine evolved into fullness, the creator started experiencing the presence of his lost love. In his solitude, she kissed him and inflamed his passions. In order to protect her from the blizzard, the sculptor wrapped her with his own clothes and blankets. He curled up, shivering in the bitter cold, at the feet of his lover. In the iciness that made even the trees shrivel, one day his neighbours saw him lying at her feet like a statue, frozen to stillness.

Hearing the story, Bhaskaran responded that every immaculate creation celebrated an artist's death. A pristine conception took life after sucking up the soul of its maker. Sahir, however, was averse to such deadly intimacies with the statues. What was the relevance of a statue when its maker became a dead mass? Though it was a rational query, Bhaskaran wasn't inclined to engage with it. Certain concepts could never be grasped, despite every effort to comprehend them. He didn't attempt to convince Sahir that a writer lived forever through his book and a sculptor by way of his sculpture.

Bhaskaran was now being tasked to create an iconoclastic statue. More than the spirit of selfless effort, the commitment owed to history was the point here. The artistic voice whispered from within that something would evolve from nothingness. Twisting some clay in his hand, Bhaskaran assumed a meditative pose. Nireeswaran was immanent in that bleak obscurity, untouched by time or its passage. If so, what was that shape? How was Nireeswaran going to take shape from the imagination of an ordinary human called Bhaskaran? Nothing occurred to him for some time.

Any alert artist would recognize that the ensuing moments were crucial. No one could predict which particular figure would take shape or which specific word would take life. When bestowed with bountiful grace, the artist assumes the role of a mere chisel, a paintbrush or a pen. Through him, a sculpture, a painting or a manuscript emerges.

When Bhaskaran stood fidgeting with the clay, his fingers, unbeknown to him, started working. Every twisting and swirling turned into a seeking. As the fingers searched for forms in the clay, something stilled them. It was a human shape—as is likely to crop up in any person's fantasy—which came up from the clay.

Sahir voiced his disappointment. 'I have heard that if a man imagines god, it will be in human shape, and if an animal imagines the same, it will be in animal form! But I never thought that if a man imagines an anti-god, it will still turn out to be human!'

'What can I do about it? It turned out this way. If you want, I can try once more.'

But Antony had a different perspective. '*God exists in human beings*—that is the way the argument goes, right? If so, the same is true with Nireeswaran. We should make an anti-god from this human shape. The first distinction between man and Nireeswaran should be that he shouldn't have a head. Let us chop it off now. With that, he will lose both his thinking power and intelligence. Isn't that the first quality a Nireeswaran should have?'

Since the words were sharp as a chisel's edge, no one murmured in dissent. Inspired by the cutting acuity of the words, Bhaskaran slashed the head off. It resembled a beheaded corpse.

'Now let us hack away at the arms! The ability to work will vanish. That suits the concept of Nireeswaran too,' said Antony.

Bhaskaran made no delay in severing the arms at the shoulders.

'For someone without head and hands, what's the need for legs? Nireeswaran shouldn't have the ability to move either!'

The legs were hewn at the knees.

Bhaskaran was drenched in perspiration, as if he had mercilessly mutilated and murdered a human being. 'Ouch! I feel as if I have committed some bestial crime,' he gasped.

Whatever the progressive views he espoused, Bhaskaran had within himself an artist's sensitive heart. He was used to sketching a human figure as per proportions, and so the cruelty involved in his nefarious deed was enervating. The artist within him had imagined a human shape in the clay. And when the figure was being dismembered, the sculptor experienced the deathly throes of a flesh-and-blood human inside it.

If the agony of mangling a lifeless statue was so extreme, how soulless must be those who chopped living beings to bits with their deadly machetes? Unheard by his friends, Bhaskaran whispered to himself that a creator held no rights over his creation. What had he set out to do, and where had it ended!

Yet, in a while, Bhaskaran overcame his inhibitions with the fortitude of one out to achieve a high goal even at the cost of shedding blood. Looking at the statue of Nireeswaran that he had crafted after maiming the original, Bhaskaran couldn't help commenting, 'Look, after cutting off the head and limbs, doesn't it resemble a Shivalinga? The statue of Nireeswaran should never look like that.'

'Wait, wait! This might be the appropriate look,' said Antony. 'Let people misunderstand it as a Shivalinga. After all, the foundation of faith is misinterpretation. Besides that, there is a symbolism involved, my dear artist!'

'What symbolism?' Bhaskaran asked.

'First we create a farce as attractive as a human being. By severing its head and limbs, we make it liable to misinterpretation. Then, to denounce such a misconception, we throw it into a canal!'

'What's the use of all that?'

'Manhood is all about indulging in unique activities. Where's the stimulation in leading a quotidian life, huh? Life should stand ramrod erect at all times! See, the psychology behind television advertisements is at work here—a trick which makes us purchase what we don't need in the first place! An advertisement that one sees frequently settles in the subconscious mind. If it lies there for some time, it will make the consumer unwittingly desire the product. He'll buy it the next time he sees it inside a shop. It is a capitalist strategy in a consumerist culture. Nireeswaran is going to work exactly like that. But this naughty guy in clay does not have the dignity of a statue. We should get it sculpted in stone!'

That was how the original figurine in clay was reincarnated in stone.

After moving from the seed of thought to the body divine, the next step was a worthy consecration. They needed to find an inauspicious day and ill-fated mahurat for the purpose. Nireeswaran, after all, was the god of everything inauspicious and ill-fated.

The Abhasa couldn't foretell the far-reaching repercussions of this silly deed that had sprung up from a joke. If they had, they would have contemplated thrice before attempting such a thing. Indeed, on second thought, they would have desisted from their plan.

However, history was waiting, having deposited secret treasures in clandestine places. Sometimes a tiny breeze can transform into a cyclone, capsizing the entire universe.

Third Petal: The Consecrator

At the next juncture, new apprehensions started emerging when the means almost collided with the end. Though it was Nireeswaran which was going to be installed, a priestly presence would elicit acceptance for the proceedings. Since many conventions were being challenged, there was a likelihood that expert archers were aiming arrows overtly and covertly from different corners. If shot directly, an arrow could be countered promptly with another, making a 'tshuum' sound, like in the television series *Mahabharat*. But what about guerrilla attacks? That was worrying Sahir.

Though he abhorred orthodoxy, Sahir was inwardly terrified of an enemy who never appeared directly. Unknown foes confronted him in his nightmares. Consequently, Sahir's sleep was as tumultuous as a battleground. For all his bravado, Sahir would wake up screaming in terror, unable to control his own dreams. If anybody else slept in the same room, he was sure to be scared out of his wits. If shaken awake, Sahir would mutter inanities and slip back into slumber. By then, the secret enemy would appear again from his hideout. In spite of his best efforts, Sahir could never vanquish the adversaries who wrangled with him in his dreams.

By mixing some Freud and Carl Jung together, Antony proposed a theory of psychology to interpret Sahir's dreams. There was no man born in that village who could topple Antony when it came to self-confidence. It was Antony who had delved, at least to some extent, into books expounding rationalism. Hence he was the best qualified among them to explain mysterious subjects, such as dreams that could mislead the human mind. His response to Sahir's nagging worry about the arrow went like this: 'What we are aiming is also a hidden arrow. The one felled will know only after his heart gets pierced! So, we have to install Nireeswaran in a common place, accessible to all eyes.'

'What is the logic behind that?' Sahir asked.

'Quick fame, what else?'

A bright idea illuminated Bhaskaran's brain. 'What about our own Abhasa Theruvu?'

'Aha! Nireeswaran in Abhasa Theruvu! It can't get better!'

There was another street that met Abhasa Theruvu, creating a fork in the road. It was at this busy tri-junction that the Bodhi tree had taken root and flourished, like an ancient witness. It could have been a historically anointed bird that had excreted the peepal seed on the spot decades ago. Either before that incident or later, some wastrel must have hurled a mango seed after ravenously sucking at the fruit. The trees must have grown up together, enamoured of each other. There must have been no man-made paths at that time, let alone any street. Later, when pathways took shape, the tree-loving forebears must have let the 'divine duo' thrive as one body.

The road turning its face away to the west was the main artery to the heart of the city. If one travelled four-and-a-half miles on it, one reached a bridge crossing a river, where the city's sins coalesced and churned. Though dark and scrawny in the summer, the water cleared and swelled during the rains. Men ventured near it only then.

Sahir had a soulful connection with the river. In his younger days, he had found it a pleasant experience to piss—'shrrr'—right into the river from the bridge. The rays of the sun falling on that spray would cause a rainbow to appear. Not a 'rainbow', but a 'urine bow'—his romanticism had prompted that particular nomenclature. It awoke the poet inside him. Afterwards, whenever he pissed into the river, Sahir found poetic inspiration.

If Sahir were to be asked about the relation between urinating and poetry, he would have vouched for their intimacy. Once, when he relieved his bursting bladder from atop the bridge, Sahir had felt the mysteriously pleasurable stirrings of poetry at the origin of the flow.

This was the time when Sudhamani had been consecrated in his heart. Consequently, like all love-struck teenagers, he too wrote poetry. But the sheer conundrum of grammar doused his hopeful efforts halfway through! Perhaps if Sudhamani hadn't shifted with her family to another district, Sahir might have blossomed into a renowned romantic poet. Cursing that literature should suffer an inestimable loss, Sahir set fire to the poetic dream within himself.

Years later, while urinating at the root of the peepal–mango combine, Sahir had recognized the stirrings of poetry again at his *mooladhara*. Consequently, he had a special affection for the kingly duo that had given a second birth to the poet within him. With the lush canopy above and the ground covered with fallen leaves, the precincts of the Athmavu were a perfect seating place for Nireeswaran. Since three roads merged at that junction, travellers from any of these directions, and even those who arrived directionless, would get a 'darshan' of Nireeswaran. There was the added bonus that Nireeswaran would face west, unlike the conventional east-gazing deities. When one was combating superstition face to face, the sword should be swung in the opposite direction.

The spot was fixed, but the priestly problem remained. Since they were attacking godly faith by destroying the very citadels of belief, it was questionable whether traditional practitioners would lend support to their mission. Though their ultimate goal was ridicule, they needed a pretension of spirituality to reach their destination. To deceive the faithful with opium, Antony insisted on getting a Brahmin priest. Only then would the real atmosphere of a deity's consecration be created.

'That is not going to happen. Maybe we can manage a fancy-dress priest. Which Brahmin will come to install Nireeswaran, eh?' Bhaskaran asked. 'The one who has known "Brahma" is the Brahmin. What if, quoting that logic, I become the priest?' he said laughingly. 'How else can we generate that hallowed-consecration feeling?'

'I have another idea,' Antony said. His gaze was on the sky beyond the canopy. He seemed to be foraging for something from nothingness. 'What if we approach Eswaran Embrandiri?'

'Eswaran Embrandiri consecrating Nireeswaran! Wow, it has a rhyming ring to it! But he is an ardent believer. Will he agree to our plan?'

'Not too hopeful about that! But that doesn't mean we have to be pessimistic either. Whatever happened in the temple ups our chances. That sort of fortuitous coincidence suits Nireeswaran perfectly!'

That was well said. Nature herself readies some synchronicities before the occurrence of certain phenomena.

Eswaran Embrandiri's devotion was like burnished sandalwood—it was not easy to say whether the fragrance or the shine was more attractive. Embrandiri's family tree had been transplanted into the southern village centuries ago from a Kannada Brahmin lineage. It stood sturdily, firmly rooted in the past. The role of the priest in the local temple was assigned to members of the Embrandiri clan by the erstwhile local rulers. However, even a family tree is subject to fluctuations of destiny, and that tradition was hobbled a few years ago.

On an inauspicious monsoon night, the divine ornaments of the deity were stolen. The circumstantial evidence was strongly against Embrandiri. On being accused of theft, which he considered sacrilegious even in his thoughts, the poor man collapsed weeping before the deity. But the closed door of the sanctum sanctorum did not open for the believer. He was arrested in front of the deity who slept with eyes tightly shut.

His daughter's engagement ceremony had been conducted just the day before. With the one who was supposed to place his daughter's hand in the bridegroom's himself handcuffed, the girl's *mangalsutra* was lost in an endless darkness. To determine an immoral connection between the wedding and the deity's ornaments required less-than-average police intelligence.

Embrandiri's soft-hearted wife died of a cardiac arrest caused by the insufferable humiliation. With her father in jail and her mother dead, the daughter lost her grip on her mind. By the time the real thief was arrested and the stolen material recovered, the earth had undertaken many irreversible revolutions. Under the auspices of a new priest, a special puja was being conducted in the temple at that moment.

Eswaran Embrandiri had turned his face away from the god who hadn't protected him in danger; he led a reclusive life with his mentally disturbed daughter. Though he was persuaded by many, including the new priest, to return to the temple, Embrandiri did not succumb. It was interpreted as his rebellion against the god who had let him down in a time of adversity.

Thereafter, Eswaran Embrandiri never crossed the temple's threshold. When a young man belonging to another caste asked for his daughter's hand, Embrandiri blessed the marriage—an indication that he was severing all connections with his heritage. His sole desire at that point was to entrust his daughter to a worthy man. Afterwards, he lived as a recluse, experiencing the all-pervading loneliness of his home and subsisting only on solitude.

It was certainly those circumstances that prompted the Abhasa to think about Embrandiri. The adversities a person encounters in life qualifies him for certain missions.

If a person, devoted to God all his life and backed by generations of worship, ends up facing atrocities, isn't he the best proof that belief in God is mere superstition? He was testimony to the 'living dead'. If ever there was a god, he should have protected the innocent Embrandiri. That simple argument seemed a smart way to market the idea of Nireeswaran. Who else was more eligible to consecrate Nireeswaran than Eswaran Embrandiri?

When they sauntered into the home of the erstwhile priest, the Abhasa fellowship knew that their logic might fail. Utter decrepitude met their eyes. Not a single object sighted there could claim perfection. Indeed, to separate Embrandiri from that decaying obsolescence was in itself a tough task.

It seemed as if no one had stepped inside that compound for aeons. The man was skeletal, subsisting on a few plants that grew in his yard, and totally cut off from the outside world. Embrandiri allowed anything that sprouted from the earth, including weeds, to thrive on his land freely. Every creature was welcome to live there without any hindrance. The house and its precincts had transformed into a natural dwelling place of creatures that human beings loathingly refer to as 'vermin'.

Embrandiri expressed neither warmth nor aloofness to the young men who had come searching for him. On hearing the word 'consecration', he appeared perturbed. Since they had anticipated a blistering explosion, this mild fire and smoke did not deter the Abhasa much. When they judged that Embrandiri was cooling down, the trio presented their argument tactfully. They were armed with questions capable of unbalancing a sensitive, fragile mind.

'If "Eswaran" means someone who pushes you into despair and turns his face away, what's the purpose of such a namesake entity? If a Nireeswaran appears in the place of an unreliable Eswaran, what is wrong with the idea? Neither Eswaran nor Nireeswaran can protect anyone in actuality. There is no one as suitable as you in communicating this message to the villagers. Now, even if you are not ready, we shall be going ahead with our mission.'

Embrandiri was bewildered. Were they applying their logic at an apposite place? To quench one's thirst, one should dig a well where the presence of water has been detected, or else rocks would crop up on the way, bringing the whole effort to nought. Viewed thus, the consecration of Nireeswaran would be fruitless.

For quite a while, Embrandiri had been questioning what God had intended to achieve through his life. Now he felt that he had the right to take a decision, being an 'Eswaran' himself. He had lived for years withdrawn into himself and was now yearning to reach out to everything; his conscience was prompting him not to discard something that he hadn't solicited but had come seeking him. Making up his mind, Embrandiri emphatically announced his decision, choosing to disregard any possible interpretations of it being an act of vengeance.

'I am ready for the consecration ceremony of Nireeswaran. Even if he is an anti-god.' Embrandiri spoke as if someone was making him say the words.

The Abhasa had never expected a boon granted so fast! It was overly dramatic, like a river making its way back to its origin at the mountaintop, after having descended through the valleys and merged with the sea. But then, given what was to follow, it was imperative that matters unfolded in that way.

Fourth Petal: Athmavu

There was nobody alive who could speak authoritatively on the history of the peepal–mango amalgamation. Even the doddering oldies confessed that it had existed even before they were born. Some were of the view that the Athmavu was eternal and it was sheer stupidity to search for its beginnings. Analogous to the logic that dialectical materialism arrived at about the origins of the universe, the Athmavu too reigned as a 'non-existent answer' to 'an erroneous question'.

In other words, the villagers were clueless about the creation, preservation and annihilation of the real *athmavu*, the soul. And those who knew, smiled mysteriously and lived ordinary lives, pretending that they knew nothing. Like other humans and animals, they ate when they were hungry. When they felt the urge to answer the call of nature, they defecated. On becoming lustful, they copulated. And so, those who did not know the Athmavu had no knowledge of those who did; or perhaps the markings (of enlightenment) were wilfully hidden from their sight.

The better half of the Athmavu—the mavu or mango tree—burst into millions of blossoms every year and became laden with fruit. But no one could climb the sky-scraping giant to pluck the mangoes. Since the trunks of both the peepal and the mango were joined, the bottom portion of the mother trunk, where it blended into the earth, was of extraordinary girth. If five men stood clasping their hands around the tree, their fingers could not meet properly. It was the favourite pastime of the village children to try to circumscribe the Athmavu by standing around it in a circle, with their arms stretched around the trunk. Their naive hearts believed that if they made that 'love-chain', the tree would grace them by shaking down many ripe mangoes. The tree, too, seemed to honour their innocuous faith. However, nobody ever dared to scale the Athmavu or reach its dizzying heights to pluck the mangoes.

The Abhasa was certain that all through history, superstitions had spread exactly like the faith of the village children. The logic was crystal clear: the credulous folks, when faced with something unfathomable, sought consolation in superstition.

On many occasions, the Abhasa had put forward such rational arguments before many. Yet, when the season of mangoes arrived, all the children, adolescents, youth and even the old stood staring lasciviously at the ripe mangoes dangling from the great heights, hoping that a passing breeze would shake a few down. During that time, all the birds of the universe, along with the squirrels and rats, would camp in the vicinity. The squirrel on the branch and the child on the ground would wait with equal alacrity for the mangoes to ripen. Since the only one who could access the ripe mangoes was the squirrel, the lone way to get the fruit was to inveigle the adorable furry creature with a song:

Ithhiripoovalan annarakanna

Enikkoru mambhazham thayyo . . .

Dear bushy-tailed little squirrel,

Drop me a mango fruit please . . .

Delighted with the song, the mild-tempered squirrel would snap at the stalk of the mango and generously let it fall.

Inside the hollows and branches of the peepal and mango trees flourished what seemed to be Kerala's entire family of crows, mynahs, parrots, greater coucals, Indian treepies and small green barbets, along with squirrels, rats, chameleons, civets and a million other creatures. The trees stood as a symbol of a balanced ecosystem.

It happened that once, a tribal hunter, a *mala-vedan*, proclaimed that he would conquer the Athmavu. He was visiting the village to sell wild honey and bear ghee. The hunter advertised that the honey was pure and had healing powers, having been scoured from a huge beehive on a gigantic tree inside the forest. Another claim was that if adolescents smeared the bear ghee on their faces, they would grow thick moustaches akin to that of local politicians.

Sahir had a physique and complexion resembling those of Mongolian lineage. There was only a smattering of bronze hair under his nose. Suffering from anxiety that his lack of a bushy moustache meant a lack of manliness, Sahir secretly purchased the bear ghee from the hunter and smeared it liberally under his nose, enduring its insufferable pungency. Though his misery continued for weeks, no hair grew. Sahir came to terms with himself and somehow managed to live with his smidgen of facial hair. For this very reason, he had an envious respect for Antony, who possessed a dashing moustache.

Though used to scaling many monstrous trees in the wild, the hunter was dumbfounded on seeing the size of the Athmavu. He swore that he hadn't seen anything like it inside the deep forests he frequented. He had chanced on some trees with interlocking branches but never the particular duality of the Athmavu, which seemed to have birthed dense branches in a moment of orgiastic ecstasy, when the two tree-bodies merged into one.

'Even then, I shall climb this tree!' the hunter declared.

The Abhasa was at the forefront of that venture. There were two reasons behind it. First, letting the mangoes go to waste affronted their socialistic beliefs. Second, they wanted to protest against the trees, which preened in the false dignity of a ridiculously mysterious name. Though the trees had no quarrel with the Abhasa, their majestic aura and the undeserving solicitude showered by the villagers on them aggravated the young men. On top of that, a prickly jealousy, typical of youth, against anything that was unyielding, incited them. They decided that it was time to vanquish the Athmavu. The hunter would harvest mangoes from it.

'This is a huge tree. So, the charge will be high.'

'How much?'

'Almost . . .'

'Huh?'

'Four hundred rupees.'

'For that price, one can purchase the best mangoes from Banganappalle in bulk!'

After much negotiation, a price of Rs 150 was fixed.

The hunter demanded a thick rope for scaling the gargantuan tree. He intended to lasso one of the branches in order to clamber up. Each of the Athmavu's branches had the circumference of a typical tree trunk!

Even after many hours had passed, the hunter, who had gone with the cash to purchase the rope, did not return. Fearing that he had made off with their money, the Abhasa was getting ready to chase him on bicycles when the man was seen sauntering back, a thick rope hung from his shoulder and a sharp billhook was in his hand. An enormous serpent seemed to be coiled around him. In order to fortify his self-confidence before vanquishing the gigantic tree, the hunter had gulped down copious volumes of the local arrack.

All the locals gathered to witness the hunter's brave exploits. Apart from Janaki, who had arrived rather early, there was Ghoshayatra Annamma, aka Annamma of the Procession, with her daughters in tow. Janaki and Annamma were two centres of female power who could turn the village upside down. Akin to a drunkard who, with each consecutive trip to the toddy shop, purges his body of the sense of the self, of 'I', Janaki had freed her body from all its inhibitions. She was acknowledged as the common property of the land, where nothing remained to be hidden from view or to be ashamed of. On seeing her in a crowd, most men, including Antony, would pretend not to know her. Janaki shrugged off that blatant indifference nonchalantly, as if granting a concession. She was aware that her existence was not the sort to be acknowledged in public. While becoming a witness for the hunter's adventure, Janaki kept her perspicacity well within the acknowledged limits.

But Ghoshayatra Annamma wasn't like Janaki. The villagers had christened her thus knowingly. The woman was notorious for daily bickering with her neighbours. Her enemies gossiped that she was not very moral either—an allegation that she paid little heed to. She had four fully grown young daughters. In her verbal battles with her neighbours, the girls joined Annamma's army and enhanced her prowess on the battlefield. It was because of the five women setting out to fight—as a procession—that the villagers had respectfully conferred the nickname 'Ghoshayatra Annamma' on the woman.

If her duel was with a woman, Annamma used the sharpness of her tongue to slash her foe. There were many who were mutilated or even destroyed by that long, twirling sword. Sometimes, when the feminine war reached its limit, the men joined the rival force. It was at those junctures that Annamma acutely felt the lack of male presence in her home. At such times, on realizing her physical vulnerability, Annamma, provoked to the extreme, typically adopted a lethal technique which had become pretty famous in the village.

She would pull up her mundu either to her waist or even higher! She had grown up seeing undignified slum fights where women adopted that dirty trick as the ultimate weapon. Though she had never expected to mimic those women, on one occasion, owing to the pressure of the circumstance, Annamma had to retrieve that memory. Thereafter, whenever she found herself at a loss, almost as if compensating for the lack of male support, she would heave up her mundu. Most of the men, usually thick-skinned, were thunderstruck by that exposure. Annamma felled many raucous husbands of the neighbourhood with this method.

Soon, the women around started realizing that it was better to concede defeat, as they felt jealous of the smooth, shiny thighs Annamma displayed before their husbands. Watching their men's elevated interest in the combat, with utterances of 'Let me ask her right now', the women finally decided to swallow their failure.

Consequently, Annamma had not had many opportunities to haul up her mundu in recent times and had even accrued an air of respectability about her. Now she was standing with her four daughters, wallowing in that new stature.

Everyone looked forward to witnessing something which had till now been considered virtually impossible. Sadananda Panicker, a veteran who had seen four generations growing up in his family, spoke to the hunter, who was checking the rope. 'You should not climb this tree. It is wrong.'

'Oh, what is this? Don't spout superstitions now,' Sahir countered.

'Why be like stubborn children? Let that poor man go. What if he slips and falls down?'

'I shall not fall!' the hunter proclaimed, his confidence triggered by the liquor. He sounded contemptuous, as if he had scaled trees far more monstrous in size.

'Can't you see? The man has no problem! What's with you now, grandpa?' Janaki joined forces with the Abhasa.

Miffed by that support, which bespoke a clandestine acquaintance, the old man muttered to himself, 'Do what you want! Unwanted avarice, indeed!'

Annamma, who was standing close by, quickly caught on. She felt that Sadananda Panicker must have some strong reason for being so specific about the matter. She whispered in the ears of her daughters, 'My mind tells me that something is about to happen!'

'What is it, Amma?' the eldest girl asked apprehensively.

'An accident is likely.'

'Will that hunter slip from the tree?' the youngest asked. She was the most beautiful and also the most pleasant among the daughters. The girl started praying to the Holy Mother to protect the hunter from any mishap.

The hunter was an old hand at his task. His finesse was on display, and he was boosted by the toddy he had ingested and by the intoxication of being the centre of attention. His first two attempts at lassoing a branch were not fruitful. On the third try, he managed to hook a branch with the knot. He skipped and primped, and tried the strength of the rope. The crowd of observers surrounding him pumped up his enthusiasm. Drawing energy from the audience, the man began ascending, with practised ease. As he started his journey to conquer the Athmavu, clutching the rope and stepping on the mother trunk, the thronging crowd, with the Abhasa in the lead, hooted and howled in encouragement.

The hunter observed that the teeming horde below was becoming smaller and smaller, reducing to the size of a colony of ants. He experienced a sensation of being freed from the laws of the mortal world as he moved higher towards the pinnacle. The man could not understand whether it was the liquor or the mesmerizing nature of the Athmavu that was quickly subjugating him. He had felt drunk-to-death highs in the past too. But today he was experiencing an enthrallment that no inebriant had gifted him till now.

The hunter no longer saw the mass below. The crowd watched him groping and crawling his way on to a branch. Like the first astronaut who stepped on the moon, and like Tenzing Norgay who stepped on Mount Everest for the first time, the hunter became their pride and joy. The man looked like an emblem on a flag hoisted at the Athmavu's mast.

Straddling the branch, the hunter watched the first mesmerizing mango dangling before him. Never had he lost himself so completely, even while conquering thousands of mango trees in the past. It shook him to the core to see that the mango was hanging from a branch of the peepal tree. Seated amid the dense foliage of the peepal and mango trees, the man touched the forbidden fruit for the first time.

The people on the ground could no longer catch a glimpse of the hunter. He was lost in the canopy and the thick branches overhead. Someone had seen him leaning over to pluck a mango. Then there was a fuzziness.

'Hey, what the heck are you doing there?' Bhaskaran shouted loudly.

'Hunter!' Antony joined in.

In spite of the persistent inquiries, the hunter did not respond.

He hadn't thrown down even one mango. What was the man doing up there?

'The arrack must have kicked in! He must be dozing off, I say!' Barber Maniyan made a sagacious sally. He cast a furtive glance at Ghoshayatra Annamma as he said this. The woman stared obdurately at the sky, trying to evade Maniyan's eyes. Her four daughters stood brushing against her, all looking up eagerly in the direction of the missing hunter.

'If the toddy befuddles him, won't he fall?' Janaki raised a pertinent question. The marigolds that she wore in her tresses spread their disturbing perfume all around.

Maniyan found an answer to Janaki's query, 'Could have ended up tangled amid some branches . . .'

'I warned him against climbing at the very start,' Sadananda Panicker reiterated his opinion. 'But the words of the old are derided these days!'

The small apprehensions soon snowballed into huge fears. Even after many hours had passed, the hunter did not descend. The Abhasa started panicking too. They were the ones who were responsible for stoking the fire of adventure in the hunter's mind.

'Better sneak away unnoticed,' Antony murmured.

'Shouldn't someone go up and check?' Bhaskaran asked tentatively.

'Why don't you try?' Sahir snapped.

'No way! I feel dizzy at heights!'

'Bhaskaran! You are adept at scaling coconut trees, aren't you? Why don't you climb up?' Sadananda Panicker asked.

Bhaskaran felt a sizzling sword pass through him, draining him of all bravado. He did not climb the tree. Nobody in the crowd dared to do it.

When the waiting progressed into the wee hours of the night, the crowd dispersed one by one. The next morning, they returned with great curiosity to find out if the hunter's corpse had fallen to the ground.

Only a section of the rope could be seen dangling from the pinnacle of the Athmavu, like a ladder winding its way to heaven. Never ever did the hunter descend it.

Fifth Petal: Friends

Thereafter the trees became renowned as 'the Athmavu through which the hunter ascended to heaven'. It was discomfiting to the Abhasa that their endeavour had only enhanced the divine halo around the tree. On hearing the word 'Athmavu', their minds filled with an abhorrence for something non-existent. How annoying it was to have the Athmavu flexing its muscles and openly challenging them!

'Where did that hunter vanish?' the villagers asked one another and their own selves.

'Most certainly he hasn't ascended the heavens!' More than a factual observation, Antony's words had emerged from a sense of obstinacy. 'As if heaven is situated on top of the tree!' he scoffed.

'Where has he gone then?' Sahir wondered.

'There is a rational and materialistic explanation for every phenomenon. We should rely on logic, not superstition.'

'Oh, tell us the logic which has dawned on you right now!'

'That hunter was tipsy with liquor when he climbed up. He must have felt dizzy at that height. Must have clutched on to some branch for dear life! And when he sobered up, the fellow must have climbed down the rope and scooted away.'

'If he descended, where on earth is he?'

'He could have left for the forest in the night itself, couldn't he?'

'Whatever!'

But the hunter did not drop in to visit the village—neither the next year nor in the subsequent years. The supply of honey and bear ghee, which used to arrive from the forest seasonally, ceased abruptly.

The hunter's history froze in the bewilderment of whether he was in heaven, earth or the land of Trisanku.

The rope dangled from the Athmavu for a long time, like an umbilical cord connected to death, holding the memories of the hunter. Little scamps used it as a swing, not realizing its historical significance. Eventually, its warp and weave gave way, and it broke.

Now, at the apex, one could see the fraying knot, the living testimony of an old legend. Possibly, if the knot too dropped off some day, future generations would think of the hunter as a mere figment of the imagination. The time for that seemed to be nearing fast. A woodpecker was regularly feasting at the grubs under that old knot. It was very likely that sometime soon, under the assault of its sharp beak, the last strand would give way and drop down.

Even after the hunter's vanishing act, the Athmavu continued to shower many ripe mangoes, and the children competed with one another to collect them. Yet, the good fortune of collecting the maximum number of mangoes went to the local prostitute Janaki. The reason was that her peculiar work hours necessitated her being near the tree during the odd times of the day when the mangoes dropped. She enthusiastically hovered around the Athmavu through the night. The sweetness of the fruit was unique, with a top note of the peepal in its delectable taste. Janaki found herself spellbound by the mangoes which, with their irresistible taste, pulled her repeatedly to the Athmavu. Having even a single mango freed her from all the exertions of sex work, including the burden of sin associated with it.

She started relishing the indulgence like a rite of holy confession.

The tree went on showering delicious fruit munificently; these were nobody's private property but meant for all the creatures around.

'Isn't this real socialism?' Bhaskaran jested, as if discovering a new idea. 'When nature herself is implementing socialism, there is no pillaging involved. The balance sheet of an outlook of equality, espousing that everything belongs to everyone.'

Words that he had specifically noted down while browsing through books, namely 'socialism' or 'outlook of equality', were all profoundly mixed in his pompous outpouring. He believed that catchphrases were essential for the survival of philosophy. After hearing such a spiel, the average person would not dare ask any further questions. Bhaskaran used to be astounded to hear gospel preachers reciting biblical passages learnt by heart. In his opinion, that in itself could steady a wavering mind by a good measure. He wanted his language to perform a similar role.

The Abhasa had decided that Eswaran Embrandiri would consecrate Nireeswaran's deity under the same Athmavu that stood with its 'socialist mangoes espousing an outlook of equality'.

Though he had verbally agreed, Embrandiri had not been impulsive about his decision. Before setting out, he had discussed the issue with his friends Arnos and Zaid. Now, if anyone feels that there is something amiss about Embrandiri deliberating the issue of idol consecration with those not connected with this matter, pay heed.

When the sea draws back, dropping a signal, before the emergence of sky-high tsunami waves, it is an effort to maintain the balance maintained over aeons. On close observation, one can see that, the circumstances entailing Embrandiri's question and its answer had been gathering shape over many decades.

Embrandiri, Arnos and Zaid had studied together ever since their forefingers were stained with that loamy soil where they had traced the first letters of the alphabet. Their initiation into learning had happened on the same day, at the same auspicious *muhurtam*, under Kunjukutty Asan's tutelage.

Although they belonged to different religions, Asan made them write the same words: *'Hari Shree Ganapathaye Namah.'*

Though a few relatives bickered with Thampan, Arnos's father, asking him why a Christian should get initiated into learning by hailing Ganapathy, he had trounced them by arguing that the enunciation of the word 'Ganapathy' could mean 'messiah' in some human language! Notwithstanding the differences across languages, like the word for 'hair' in Tamil turning into a cuss word in Malayalam, the belief had taken root in Thampan that when all the names and forms were forsaken, the same god would be discernible everywhere.

Apart from that, the numerology in the *shloka*, which introduced the learner to the fifty-one letters of the Malayalam alphabet, fascinated him. One should presume that the three little boys were touched by that incident, and that the seeds for a future inquiry into religion and spirituality had been sown in their hearts early on, a fact made evident by their life journeys. As children, they had decided to reach the pinnacles of their respective religions while remaining intimate friends.

'I shall become a top-shot cardinal,' Arnos said. At that age, that was the supreme position he could imagine. Ever since he had seen believers scuffling to kiss the cardinal's hand, Arnos had concluded that it was a post worth aspiring for. The child knew that the position of the pope was inaccessible to him. If he became a cardinal, he could visit Rome and be a part of the pope's selection process! Then he could see the massive cathedral at the Vatican. How impressive it was!

The other two, as ambitious as Arnos, also declared their goals loudly.

'I shall become a renowned sage,' Embrandiri said. 'Then I shall go and meditate on some snow-covered mountain. Most probably in the Himalayas.'

'I will become a muezzin,' Zaid ventured, rather hesitantly, about a role he was familiar with.

Children take many decisions like that. Some turn fruitful; most end up being forgotten. Rarely does anyone cast a backward glance on those paths. Still, there was something unnatural about three children contemplating godly pursuits. Also, there was a tinge of implausibility in these dreams, as seen in the historical chronicles on saintly lives.

The trio, who had written the alphabet together, joined a government school and scribbled their names on their first-standard classroom bench. By the time they crossed seven such benches engraved with their names, Embrandiri's father had passed away. Embrandiri bid goodbye to the eighth bench and joined the Mahadeva temple as the priest's helper. The dreams of being a sage and undertaking a Himalayan expedition were sidelined in the daily battle for survival.

It grieved Arnos and Zaid that Embrandiri had to quit school. Replacing him with another friend, named Indrajit, they continued being a trio. After school, they would meet Eswaran regularly. The trio, in effect, had become a quad.

Zaid, even in his youth enamoured of the holy words of the 'Mathnawi', joined the madrasa in the neighbouring district after passing his tenth-standard examinations. Thus, he started his journey from being simply Zaid to becoming Zaid Maulvi.

Arnos joined a missionary congregation after his Class Ten examinations and proceeded to a seminary in north India for theological studies. Indrajit alone kept himself free of religious shackles and entered 'Grishasthashram'. Though they had diverged on to different paths, owing to a spirituality beyond religion, they remained bound to one another. That bonding was beyond the ordinary nomenclature of 'fellowship' or 'friendship.'

Whenever Arnos returned from the seminary, Embrandiri, Zaid and Indrajit would wait for him beneath the Athmavu. By that time, the villagers had started addressing them with mock titles—Arnos as 'Arnos Pathiri', Zaid as 'Zaid Maulvi' and Embrandiri as 'Mukhya Tantri'. Indrajit used to joke that he had escaped a title because he wasn't associated with any religion. Right from his schooldays, he had been attracted by leftist thoughts that envisaged an equal society. Indrajit ingenuously believed that he would get to witness a perfect world in this lifetime, where wealth would be distributed among everyone equally.

These beautiful notions had entered his bloodstream from his father, who was a principled man. Permeated into one's blood in adolescence, some ideas can affect its very fluidity. In that blossoming period, any person with influence over a young boy can convert him into a believer, atheist, wastrel, insurgent or even a saint! In Indrajit, those ideas manifested as a disposition towards revolutionary ideas. When he was a student, he had contested and won the position of chairman of the college union, as a leftist candidate.

He did not forget to carry that left-leaning attitude with him even after he joined work. While cherishing red dreams inside, Indrajit continued his friendship with Arnos, Embrandiri and Zaid without any problem, following his father's benevolent outlook.

In those days, buoyed by youthful energy, the friends would debate for long hours while sitting under the Athmavu. Indrajit would stubbornly argue that the leftist ideology, which had sunk its roots deep in both Bengal and Kerala, would spread across India in a matter of mere twenty years; and with the passage of time, all the countries of the world would come together under the red flag. He would offer statistics and political viewpoints to substantiate his claims. Above all, these were the innocent and pristine wishes of a good heart on display. Indrajit trusted the ideal leaders who led simple lives much more than he trusted himself.

However, after getting married and becoming a father to two children, in a horrendous accident that slashed right through his life, Indrajit slipped into a coma. This was the aftermath of anaesthesia gone wrong; during a surgery to repair a broken arm, Indrajit had slipped into unconsciousness which lasted for twenty-four years.

Nobody believed that he would return to life. Medical science, too, had denied any remote chance of such an occurrence.

He didn't witness the fact that 'the ideal beauty of equality', which he had dreamed of spreading across the world, had been uprooted even from the spot of its existence, owing to mishandling by its practitioners. His friends used to discuss that if Indrajit ever came to know the truth, it would impact him powerfully.

Though his visits from the seminary reduced in frequency, Arnos attempted to maintain his relationship with his village and friends by writing lyrical letters in perfect Malayalam. But his letters went missing, caught in some tumultuous cove of life. The others were apprehensive of what might have happened to Arnos. But after an interval fraught with anxiety, Arnos unexpectedly appeared in the village, hauling a saffron rucksack and dressed in a *jubba*, which reached beyond his knees, and a loose white pyjama.

He had renounced his seminarian life.

Arnos never gave a direct answer to all the curious souls who questioned him. Something irreconcilable with his innate nature had caused that retreat. There are some who go back to a regular life just a day before accepting priestly robes. The natives presumed that Arnos had undergone such a phase. But the man who returned home was not ready to marry either.

Arnos, though, had the integrity to accept that all the failings were his own. Consequently, he never condemned either the congregation or his seminary. The insight that his way was different remained his lone source of strength. He found spiritual relief in returning to his lonely mother at home and taking care of her. The revelation that 'the one who discards his mother does not have an iota of spirituality' had dawned on him.

Though Arnos did not end up as a missionary, the natives continued to call him Arnos Pathiri. Arnos did not have any objection to being glued with the name of the priest who had authored the first printed book in Malayalam, *Samkshepa Vedartham*.

Finally, when his mother too embarked on a voyage, leaving her son alone amid the uncertainties of the world, Arnos Pathiri confined himself to the lonely homestead, gazing deep at the infinite sky within. Thus, the one who yearned to be a cardinal in his childhood ended up in his house, not even becoming a sacristan.

It was Christmas season then. It was also the time when Embrandiri got embroiled in the case of the missing temple ornaments. When the world showered Embrandiri with all its loathing and revulsion, Arnos was the only person to try and provide some solace. Though he consoled his friend that the diamond-like purity of his reputation would be restored when the real thief got caught, it did not do much to assuage Embrandiri's trauma. Embrandiri limited himself to his house, never uttering a word. Searching for the one who wished to be a sage, the Himalayas, with all its humungous silence, travelled from the north to the southern tip.

He did not see either Arnos or Zaid for a long period.

The madrasa and the *yateemkhana* associated with it were under Zaid's control. After spending a long time constricted by uncompromising routine, Zaid became affected by the monotonous orderliness of his life. It was not a rebellion against anything at all. When the mind raced like an arrow towards an 'understanding' which did not yield to definitions, it became impossible to focus on bookish knowledge.

The holy sayings, padlocked using words, pushed him towards an experience that transcended the book. But to float above, aided by insight, was also a grave danger. The orthodoxy which cannot keep pace would misunderstand. Though Zaid tried to persuade himself that it was his own shortcomings at play here, his mind did not agree. Seeing his confusion, Arnos intervened.

'Not everyone is destined to lie down in the same place. After waking them up, Allah shall beckon a select few to move forward. Prima facie, the person might think that he has fallen. But that falling can become a rising instead. If you fall into that centre of gravity which synchronizes every planet, why be afraid?'

Zaid was waiting for Allah to kindly send someone to take over the madrasa's responsibilities so he could accept his 'falling'. How beautiful it would be if the three childhood friends, who had gone their separate ways, could join together in their dotage through three 'fallings'.

It was during such a scenario that the Abhasa approached Embrandiri with the idea of consecrating Nireeswaran's deity. Embrandiri had emerged from the Himalayan silence of his home after a long while, stepping on to the small pathway and listening to the sounds of vehicles. He waited for dusk and started off only after darkness fell. The old man wished to avoid encountering people.

Arnos was astounded to see the reclusive man. And what he heard from Embrandiri was far more bizarre. Though he had been stunned on hearing about Nireeswaran, Arnos quickly regained his poise. In Arnos's opinion, spirituality was like a boomerang which returned right to its origin despite having been thrown in another direction. It was an attractive but wounding viewpoint. He sensed a similar, dangerous magnetism in the concept of Nireeswaran proposed by the Abhasa. Nireeswaran was also portending something unique, much like Embrandiri's unforeseen arrival.

'An idea as intoxicating as wine!' Arnos insisted that when an opportunity cropped up to challenge all existing orthodoxies and their hypocrisies, it should not be wasted. It was like a sign to mine the unrevealed secrets of religious texts. Rather, it was a sign akin to that rare alignment of orbital paths that enables a comet to whizz past. A sign that could be either good or bad.

Once Arnos gave his go-ahead, what was there to deter Embrandiri? Especially when it was going to happen under the mysterious, dignified Athmavu. Yet, Arnos murmured something about missing Zaid. It had been a while since they had got together. 'That fellow is very busy nowadays!' Embrandiri remarked.

Perhaps owing to the power of the word, Zaid miraculously appeared the next weekend. Words have such unseen power! Traversing uninterruptedly through the energy channels of the universe, they reach their destination. Those possessing an acuity of sense can catch the vibrations easily.

Zaid looked like a debonair middle-aged man, with carefully groomed beard and a white skullcap. Since his hair had started turning white, an aura of purity radiated from him. Those who approached him sensed in him a divinity, which was complemented by his natural serenity. Following certain Sufi spiritual practices, he had become accustomed to gazing inwards. That gave him a palpable charisma. He had just started experiencing the inner truth of the Prophet's saying: 'The one who knows himself, knows his Master.' Zaid was trying to emulate the illustrious Junayd of Baghdad, and Hasan of Basra, who had surrendered everything before the Lord.

Whenever possible, Zaid made it a point to travel to the dargah of Pir Muhammad Sahib at Thakkalai to revel in the holy, unseen presence of the saint. The hordes that thronged the place, irrespective of their religious beliefs, attracted Zaid. Each visit engendered in him a feeling that an empty tank was being refuelled. It was through such travels, undertaken neither to impress anyone nor for the sake of blindly following rituals, that Zaid understood the One praised thus: *Al-ḥamdu l-illāhi rabbi l-ʿālamīn*; praise be to God, Lord of the worlds.

The magnificent trees observed with interest the union of the three friends after a lapse of many years. An intense relationship of half a century existed between the trees and the men. Many a fruit that the trees had showered had merged in their veins as 'Jnanapazzham',[1] the fruit of wisdom.

'Look, friends,' Arnos spoke, seated in the cool shade of the trees. 'We were born to three separate religions. As per belief, Embrandiri will reach Vaikuntha, the abode of Vishnu, after his death. I shall reach Heaven. And Zaid will go to Allah. Our Indrajit is in a state which is beyond heaven or hell. So, we won't be able to see one another after dying. But I doubt how Heaven could be divided, preventing three close friends from seeing each other!'

'True,' Zaid agreed. 'Either all three concepts of heaven are ridiculous, or there is another explanation, where the three heavens merge into one.'

'Unity in tri-versity,' Arnos grinned and added, 'And so, Eswaran, go ahead with the consecration of Nireeswaran.'

'Which Eswaran did you hail just now?' Zaid wondered aloud.

'The original Eswaran Embrandiri,' Arnos said.

It was Amavasya seven days later. The (un)holy day destined for Nireeswaran's origin in the universe.

---

[1] The legendary fruit of wisdom which Lord Muruka had bestowed on Saint Awaiyyar.

Sixth Petal: Consecration

It's on those nights when the moon wanes that the most inauspicious things happen. When the earth lies immersed in deep darkness, unmitigated even by a sliver of light, demonic powers gain an edge over divine propensities. Humans and animals are transformed into bodily manifestations of lust. If you observe closely, you will see even the trees standing with their nerves stretched taut. Given a chance, the male tree might uproot itself and rush to overcome the female tree. The Abhasa were determined to install Nireeswaran's deity on a pitch-black night, when ominous forebodings reign supreme.

If they tried some glib marketing tactics, the event would also gain popularity. The Abhasa decided to adopt any means to fulfil their plans. Bhaskaran unearthed an old pull-cart from somewhere, repaired and polished it, and converted the contraption into a cinema-advertising cart of yore. With two cardboards placed like a tent, they evoked nostalgic memories of old theatres.

Bhaskaran remembered the poster of the actress Vijayasree, which showed her bathing while wrapped in a short *thorthu*. On observing Vijayasree being stuck on surfaces with a blue gum duly mixed with copper sulphate, Bhaskaran's hand had itched to smother some glue on the poster. On recollecting that memory, a searing heat spread through his body as if it had shed its skin; and the familiar serpentine motion was felt again.

'Control yourself, snake,' he scolded his kundalini and turned his attention to the adolescent boys hired to play the drums. It was Antony's idea that a drummer band should escort the cinema cart.

A more effective trick to enchant the crowds was yet to be discovered in the world. Accompanied by the clanging of the cymbals, the melee was complete!

There was a crumbling stone embankment encircling the Athmavu.

The natives referred to it as 'Athmathara', much like the common 'Althara' around banyan trees.

It was oval in shape, like a planetary orbit. Perhaps the originally conceived circular design might have convoluted into an ellipse. Or else someone's foresight had played a role. It was on that dilapidated embankment, where serpentine roots wildly intermeshed with broken rocks, that Nireeswaran was supposed to take birth.

As per the plan, the trio reached the spot at the designated time and stood on either side of Embrandiri, as if assisting him. It was the mentally disturbed Sumitran who first wandered there, lured by the goings-on. The village had anointed him as the first to arrive wherever a drumbeat rang out in the vicinity.

'I sense an omen in this fellow's arrival!' Antony said.

'What omen?' Sahir asked, averse to omens and their ilk.

'Sumitran's presence is appropriate to the facetious atmosphere of an anti-consecration.'

Bhaskaran readily agreed with the statement's veracity. Since he believed that 'god' was a foolish concept—something which never existed, did not exist and wasn't likely to exist—the only truth which remained was the bumbling half-wit Sumitran and the common populace, more intellectually retarded than him.

Besides, the initiation was being done by an eccentric Brahmin wilfully failed by the world.

A middling crowd thronged the Athmavu, as if a street magician or a nomadic performer had arrived. They had previously gathered there to behold the antics of the hunter. The Athmavu had made him vanish into thin air, gifting the observers a hallucinatory experience! What novelty was going to be on display today? Those who came near, fascinated by the drumbeats, saw a crowd and Eswaran Embrandiri in their midst, and soon became part of that mass. Nobody knew that Nireeswaran was about to appear in the world soon.

In the light of flambeaus, on that moonless night, the Athmavu assumed a mountainous stature. Regardless of social status, it welcomed everyone with equitable hospitality. Under it, there was Nireeswaran, devoid of expression, possessing an undistinguishable shape which could not be attributed to a human or animal; and nearby, Embrandiri, soberly engaged in the rites.

Embrandiri's hands moved deftly. In an unexpected moment, without waiting for any formalities or ritualistic traditions, he installed Nireeswaran on the stone embankment beneath the Athmavu. The Abhasa had not expected such rapidity. A few murmurs, a handful of gestures, a mystifying mantric enunciation . . . they were expecting something along those lines from the old man. But Embrandiri had dashed their hopes. Though it irked the Abhasa, it was destined to happen that way. On close observation, it could be seen that many incidents which upturned history had transpired without much ado. Their far-reaching consequences would surface only after a long period of time.

The Abhasa were bemused at the sight of Embrandiri standing with his hands atop the deity he had just consecrated, his eyes shut tightly. They didn't understand the relevance of that posture. Their mutually decided contract had no provision for such a stance. Maybe Embrandiri was praying, or breathing life into Nireeswaran. The trio contemplated jeeringly that the embryo of life would grow, allowing Nireeswaran to spread roots into the soil, sky and human minds.

They gathered some flowers and thrust them into Sumitran's hands. Another handful was given to Janaki. The butcher Moosa and barber Maniyan, too, accepted flowers, which they duly showered on the deity. Observing everything, Arnos stood impassively behind the crowd, wondering who was mocking whom.

Those who stay away are the closest ones. Arnos's gaze was fixed on Embrandiri, who stood like one possessed, oblivious of the surroundings. He had heard that Embrandiri used to go into a similar trance while conducting puja at the Mahadeva temple. It was like someone merging with the infinite skies beyond the clouds. Arnos often wished to witness the temple rites conducted by his intimate friend, but realizing that the hypocritic mass around would be dismayed by that attempt, he chose to see the puja in his imagination. Now, he was seeing Eswaran doing a puja of Nireeswaran with that same seamless merging.

If a desire sprouts in an unsullied mind, it will be realized at some time or other, irrespective of how impossible it seems. In other words, anyone who harnesses the mind can recreate the universe with steadfast imagination. This is the state of someone who realizes that the universe is a manifestation of the mind itself. Since Arnos was yet to ascend such heights, it might be construed that, looking at Eswaran that day, one of his mind's wishes had been fulfilled.

But the Abhasa took a different view. They had never expected Embrandiri to conduct himself with such sincerity over a mock consecration! For them, the old man was just a comic prop to create the suitable ambience of a farce. It seemed as if he was celebrating being the main priest, a status that had been harshly taken away from him. The man was considered partially insane anyway. It seemed as if that craziness had been stoked again. In one way, that was okay. Let the poor soul dwell in a world of fantasy at least for a day.

But the world of Embrandiri's fantasy was more vast than they had surmised. He kept meandering, with committed devotion, through the endless vistas of his mind's boundaries. He did a *danda namaskar* too before the deity.

The sight of the prostrating priest was like an electric jolt for Sumitran's brain. Without much thought, as if praying at a temple, he folded his hands and called aloud in his lisping tongue:

'Please, chave me . . . chave me . . .'

That was the lone prayer he knew—the only prayer his late grandmother had taught him, after struggling all her life.

Since the Abhasa considered prayer a ridiculous concept, it amused them that the supplication had originated from a half-witted person. The mentally weak was praying to the non-existing Nireeswaran! Wasn't it the same situation when the so-called intelligent folks prayed to Eswaran? Both were equally preposterous!

What Sumitran had sowed was a seed which would yield a golden harvest worth a hundred times' return. It was time to scatter fistfuls of that into the barren minds of many! Let the crop sprout and thrive! The moment the idea flashed in his mind, Antony bellowed, 'Keep praying, Sumitran. Pray loudly! Prayers have double the power on the day of the consecration! You shall be handsomely showered with blessings!'

Sahir seized the drift of Antony's statement perfectly. Rising to the occasion, he joined in with his pal, 'Nireeswaran, please turn this half-witted Sumitran into a sensible person.'

He threw a fistful of flowers on Nireeswaran, as if reinforcing the entreaty. Unable to understand that Sahir was actually mocking him, Sumitran joined in, showering the statue with more flowers. How interesting it was for him! He entrusted Annamma with some flowers from his collection. It was an attractive sight when the four girls started grappling with one another to snatch their share from Annamma's hands.

Janaki, too, had a handful of uthiri flowers. After tucking two into her tresses, she hurled the rest on Nireeswaran and felt the kindling of high spirits, much like Sumitran. Not just Ghoshayatra Annamma, but her daughters too found themselves amused by all that flower-throwing. Meanwhile, Janaki's attention strayed, with the audacity of a prostitute, and landed on the good-looking man standing aloof. He was a stranger to those parts. A prostitute is supposed to be alert at all times. When the next handout would come was unknown!

A crowd offers distinct things to different people. It grants a prostitute freedom to scout for customers, a thief to search for pockets to steal from and a drunkard to grab a sight to relish.

Listening to Sumitran's faltering prayer and Sahir's mockery-filled pleas, Bhaskaran felt a stir of wiliness too. Feeling that it was his turn to do something, he glanced at the horde around, searching for a reason to pray. His eyes fell on Parameswaran, who had been unemployed for almost fifteen years after getting his college degree. Seizing the opportunity, Bhaskaran prayed aloud, 'Nireeswaran, please help the unemployed Parameswaran to procure a government job soon!'

Even Parameswaran, who was an atheist, could not help shaking with laughter at that prayer. It was two years since he had crossed the age limit of thirty-five set for securing government employment. So many applications, umpteen job interviews—all to no avail. He had now given up totally. Consequently, he could relish the impossible supplication with its overtones of dark humour.

'Who else wants benediction? Ask without any hesitation!' Antony's voice was effervescent with the drink ingested at dusk and had the strength to lure the wobbling minds around. If the Abhasa were at the centre of the stage till now, it was the turn of the common people to step into the arena. An old, destitute woman, Kartyayani, uttered a prayer with much inhibition from the fringes of the crowd: 'Please help me find my lost gold chain.'

Though she had presented the same prayer to the main deity of the temple, there had been no favourable response yet. What was there to lose in praying to this new-fangled Nireeswaran? Investment: a few words! Gain: one chain!

Since everybody had their own reason for praying, Kartyayani's request was followed by many enthusiastic successors. Prayers started emerging one by one from the hitherto reluctant crowd.

'Please heal my husband's paralysis.'

'Let my son's Gulf visa come soon.'

'Help me pass my tenth standard exams!'

Antony, Bhasakarn and Sahir were acquainted with the mob psychology existing behind prayers. In a mob, people would lose their senses. And it was easy to influence those with no control over their senses. The Abhasa was of the view that certain religious organizations exploited mob psychology. The same technique had to be applied in reverse now, like administering an antidote for poison with another dose of poison!

Never in their wildest dreams had they anticipated such a spirited response. If the prayers piling up before any temple could be elicited before Nireeswaran, it was surely a redoubtable victory! It was just the first step in their guerrilla warfare. Making another calculated move, Antony looked at Nireeswaran and yelled: 'You'd better grant all these wishes! Or else we will conclude that you too are a mere piece of stone like the other idols!'

Janaki was struck by the logic of Antony's invocation. She was on the verge of securing a business contract negotiated majorly through surreptitious glances. It was then that someone from the back of the crowd, enthused by the multiple pleas being raised from all sides, submitted a naughty prayer.

'Please convert Janaki, the prostitute of our village, into a saint!'

The derision in that prayer was enough to trigger an avalanche of laughter from the multitude. Hearing that, barber Maniyan, trader Chettiyar, butcher Moosa, Ghoshayatra Annamma and her daughters, the Abhasa fellowship and even Eswaran Embrandiri burst into guffaws.

Wriggling out of that awkward spot into which she had been thrust, Janaki hollered: 'Who the hell wants to make me a saint? Go and convert your mother first!'

The ground of consecration turned suddenly silent. Nobody had any more prayers. Even the youngsters, used to cracking lewd jokes, were dumbstruck, recognizing the risk of battling Janaki. She in turn observed Ghoshayatra Annamma, capable of fighting with anyone, leave for home with her four fully grown daughters. All of them were strikingly pretty. What would poor Annamma do if these unmarried girls blossomed forth so resplendently?

The consecration ceremony had turned into a theatre where all the arrangements had been unexpectedly upended. As the drama proceeded, with the enthusiastic participation of the Abhasa, Janaki and the natives, Embrandiri began wondering about his present role after devoting a lifetime worshipping the temple deity. Arnos was also brooding on the same point. Both had the strong hunch that Nireeswaran was going to be the end of something, or the beginning of something else. If they were asked why, they would not have had an answer either. After all, it is when the unknown becomes known that joy is triggered out of the blue, right?

Seventh Petal: New Paths

Janaki reviled and opposed all gods. It was due to their lack of compassion that she had turned into a whore at the age of sixteen. Hence she really took a liking to the antithesis of god, the Nireeswaran. Bhaskaran had given her broad hints about their hilarious plans to challenge the divine. Once liquor filled his tummy, the lecherous parrot inside him would start prattling all secrets. It was after watching a few of Bhaskaran's performances that Janaki had understood the meaning of the phrase 'chattering like a parrot'. Though Bhaskaran pretended to be a brave rationalist, Janaki suspected him of being a coward inside.

As for Antony, liquor ratcheted up his daring. For him, even sex was an act of insurgency. Janaki had witnessed how religion and all the 'isms' abandoned a person when he was possessed by lust. She ruminated that the concept of Nireeswaran also had, more or less, the same sense of oneness as associated with sex. Indeed, there were no demarcating boundaries drawn by caste or religion when it came to both. Whether he was a believer or a terrorist, no man, when his body became aroused, cared for caste, religion or horoscope—nothing except the available female body.

Janaki never used to pray for any benediction. Even on the day when she satisfied seventeen customers, she sensed some unsated restlessness within herself. To assuage that, after wrapping up the seventeenth sexual union, when the time was past midnight, she sought out Damu. After offering him a share of her earnings and treating him with toddy, she lay subdued, immersed in the odour of his perspiration. It was that eighteenth union which aroused the woman inside her and glued her to a man. So many men, superior to Damu in their manliness, good looks or sheer brawn, had ploughed through Janaki. Their money or vigour could never arouse her. Or, rather, she hadn't allowed that to happen. Even while she yielded to their passions, Janaki safeguarded the purity of her soul, with an odd sense of faithfulness for Damu alone. No stranger could touch 'the woman' inside her body ever.

Janaki considered Damu's penis as a second personality. She even imagined a tender heart throbbing inside it! Even from afar, Janaki whispered to that heart. During those times, despite Janaki's absence, Damu felt himself stirring with lust and experienced an erection without any particular reason. Accepting the woman's touch, heat and kisses, he became utterly enslaved.

Damu spent his nights in the small nook under the makeshift box shop situated near the Athmavu. He did not have any regular employment. His activities included being a handyman in the neighbourhood—fetching water for the small shops and chopping wood for the kitchens. His nights were spent in solitude under the box shop. Damu, too, hadn't contemplated what his relationship with Janaki was. Beyond all thoughts and interpretations, he was essentially a man, and she, a woman. Except for Janaki, he hadn't known any other woman in all his forty-two years. Janaki gifted him with clothes and her body heat. At the clanging of the temple bells, Janaki would awaken before Damu. She would go to her house, and Damu went about his daily routine.

On the night of Nireeswaran's consecration, certain unexpected reinstallations happened in Janaki's life too. Though someone had tried to deride her with his lecherous remarks, the same mockery had paved way for another gain. Janaki succeeded in attracting a decently rich young man in the crowd that day. He was a stranger to her. If indeed there existed a deity called Nireeswaran, as Bhaskaran clamoured, she only prayed to gain that particular customer. It was unthinkable to demand a customer for the purposes of whoring from an upper-class deity. But Janaki remembered with a smirk that since

Nireeswaran was an anti-god, such boons could also be sought. Of course, she could have prayed for prosperity, a good husband and children too. But she wished only for an average customer who would ensure enough money for her to survive the day.

Janaki followed the man through the abandoned pathway which had been festive just a while before. An expensive fragrance wafted from his body. She had never encountered such a distinctive aroma before.

'Wow, what an enchanting scent!' Janaki gasped. That was a marketing gimmick, too, a ploy to understand the taste of the customer and to open the door for business. An interested party would bite the bait.

'Ah, did you like the perfume?' When the man asked her this, Janaki felt assured of a foothold.

'Is it very costly?'

'Yes, a bit . . . I can give you a bottle if you like!'

'Haven't seen you around before . . .'

'How could you? I have never been to this place before!'

Janaki felt that the guy was decent, as he made no frantic sexual overtures. She calculated that it would entail some deft manoeuvring on her part henceforth.

'What's your name?' the stranger asked.

'Janaki.'

'How do I trust you, Janaki?'

'What?'

'That you have no diseases.'

'Haven't felt sick ever! But no guarantee as well!'

'If you are unsure, then how . . .?'

'Let me go away then.'

'Wait a bit.'

The man took out some rupee notes from his pocket and extended them to her.

'What is this for?'

'Keep it.'

'Janaki never takes a payment without doing her job.'

'Consider it an advance. There is a job for you.'

Nobody had ever called her for work after paying an advance. Besides, there were many who cheated her after striking a deal, by never paying the dues. There had been instances when she was beaten up on demanding her compensation. A stinking drunkard had once shoved her into a gutter, growling that she shouldn't be aiming for profits from a business which demanded no capital. Consequently, Janaki was in a dilemma about the new offer. Probably the man read her face, because he interjected: 'Leave aside your doubts. I am a researcher.'

'Are researchers barred from having sex?'

'Not at all. But this money is not meant for that!'

'Then?'

'I am travelling through the path of a new research. Janaki, you might wonder at its nature on hearing about it. My research topic is smells. Not many people have explored that subject as yet, and I want to make a new discovery.'

'What has the whore Janaki to do with smells?'

'There are lots that a whore alone can find out. I am sorry, I should have desisted from using that term.'

'What's wrong in that? It happens to be the solid truth. Tell me more about smells.'

'Of course! Janaki, every object, be it a tree, a human or an animal, has its distinctive smell. You and I are distinguished by smells, and nothing else lends such a strong sense of identity. Even an object which seems odourless has its odour. Janaki, you have interacted with many men all your life and can help in my first stage of research into smells. I have never approached any woman before. I was wondering how to even start, when I happened to chance upon you!'

Janaki was bemused by the eccentric style of the man. Her nostrils caught the fragrance of sandalwood and aloeswood, which had wafted into the air at the time of Nireeswaran's consecration. She would not have cared about them had the man not made her aware of smells. The fragrances would have floated away, ignored like the bitter smell of despair in her home.

'Janaki,' the man said, 'you might not comprehend my scientific study totally. But there are certain experiments which should be carried out to confirm some hypotheses which I have. For that purpose, I need the help of a woman like you.'

'What sort of help?'

'Let me be explicit. Janaki, you share your body with many men, don't you? Every man smells different. What response do you have to each smell? Science says that each substance has its natural frequency. Smell might also be linked with this natural frequency at some level. For two persons to get attracted to each other, their natural frequencies and smells play a role!'

Janaki experienced the sensation of the Athmavu showering down both peepal leaves and mango flowers on her. As she was being baptized by the leaves, Janaki remembered Damu's smell. True, while the smells of other men filled her with revulsion, Damu's smell stimulated the core of her womanhood, instigating a union without any inhibitions. Janaki was sure that it was the smell of Damu's perspiration that had forced her to seek him out even after the relentless monotony of seventeen sexual dealings. It was her mind's intense desire to make herself believe that she too was a woman, and that had been actualized through that immersion.

Janaki had never experienced the stirring sensuality of a man's touch except through Damu.

'Sir, where do you live?' Janaki asked.

'There is a house beyond that turn. Rose Villa.'

'Oh, Rose Villa! I have played in that compound as a child. Wasn't it locked up for a long time?'

'Anything locked up shall be opened. That is called science. It is the house of my close friend. I am on a sabbatical from my research institute in Bangalore. You see, by the time I return after cooling my mind in this village, I wish to dive deeply into various experiences of smells and collate the maximum information. Janaki, whatever you convey will be included in that plan. Even so, all that will just be preliminary preparations for my real work.'

Janaki was nonplussed. All the men she had known had experimented with different sorts of oddness. But this experience was unique, with an equal mixture of farce and curiosity involved. For a prostitute, her body was just a rental object that cost money, to be handed over to lusty tradesmen or, just as well, to eccentric scientists. Janaki accompanied Roberto the scientist to Rose Villa with no other expectation.

However, when she headed back the next morning, Janaki hesitated to accept the money Roberto gave her. He had not even touched her body. She had opened up her mind, far more precious than her body, for his scientific studies. It was for the first time that Janaki had earned money by making use of her mind.

Some comradeships bud unexpectedly and spread roots in unanticipated directions, like two rivulets originating in the summer rain, flowing from east and north, and meeting each other to flow westwards in unison. It was only fair that on the day when the unique Nireeswaran came into being, many inimitable occurrences were taking place on earth.

Eighth Petal: Winds of Change

That night, the Abhasa celebrated their symbolic ridicule of lifeless idols with a boozing spree. They were of the view that a label saying 'wasted life' should be stuck on the foreheads of those who lived without purpose and died in vain. While young, a man should be gutsy enough to indulge in all possible adventures and leave the world flabbergasted.

Those would be the only anecdotes worth reminiscing about in old age! The memories might then partially return the youthful passions. There was something enthralling in walking the fire intentionally and boldly exploring wayward paths. That was exactly what the Abhasa had experienced recently and had pushed the village into experiencing.

Though it all seemed rather silly, their originality could not be ignored. The Abhasa had shown to the world that even the much-vaunted deity consecrations were nothing remarkable. They saw only the quotidian in the deity—something that could be easily uprooted and dumped the day after its consecration. On the day they hurled the statue of stone, incapable of fulfilling any wishes, into the river, they might kindle sparks in at least some minds. It might trigger a detonation in the angry youth who carried arsenals within themselves. Hence the Abhasa were enthusiastic about it all, as if they were choreographing a historic event.

To become part of history was no mean feat. Such stalwarts would be earmarked as ones who led great quests. What if someone digging up history encountered the names of Antony, Bhaskaran and

Sahir carved in golden letters? If the consecration of Nireeswaran ended up being as revolutionary as Sree Narayana Guru installing the Ezhava–Shiva, wouldn't those who were instrumental in the former gain recognition? It was what seemed trivial in the present that often ended up as a milestone in history.

Naturally, the fellowship resorted to expensive liquor to celebrate to the hilt. Nothing but high-end Scotch would do! They sprinkled the holy liquid on each other's head, hailing each as the divine installer of Nireeswaran. Cupping their palms and imitating the distribution of divine prasad, they sipped a few drops of liquor, murmuring 'Om Nireeswaray Namah' with mock devotion. They smeared the pickle, meant to be savoured, on their foreheads like religious marks. While they were concluding the final ceremonies of consecration thus, Antony felt his nerves stretch taut from the intoxication.

Whenever Antony's nerves tightened, rather than being a personal affair, it affected the entire universe. He then needed a means to satiate himself: either by picking up a fight with someone or vanquishing a female body. Since the chances of landing a fight were thin, he opted for the latter. 'Janaki or whoever is available! I need someone tonight,' Antony announced brazenly. This innate honesty was both his strength and weakness—he had no smokescreen around his character, neither the good nor the bad kind. One would not be wrong to conclude that Antony's wayward ways, pursued openly, were more credible than the secret dalliances of the outwardly moral lot.

Recognizing that Antony was in magnificent form, Bhaskaran chipped in, 'Me too!'

Bhaskaran was not visibly drunk yet. To use his own words, it was the period of 'shedding skin'. Once a year, he had to go through a compulsory exfoliation process, almost like an atheist's ritual. It was not exactly a disease but a very rare condition. First, the skin inside his mouth would shed. From there, it spread to the throat, proceeding to the stomach, to the small and large intestines. If he ate something spicy during this span, he felt as though heaven and earth had come together in him fierily. The period of skin-shedding, from his mouth to his orifices, extended almost to forty-one days, equivalent to the duration of penances for Ayyappa's mandala pula, and Bhaskaran would consume only tranquil green plants during that time. He would avoid liquor because it would burn him up.

His mother, an ardent Ayyappa devotee herself, sniped that for an unbeliever, who always mocked devotees undertaking penances for visiting the Ayyappa temple, to forcibly undergo a period of abstinence during the same time was owing to the Lord's displeasure.

'As if Ayyappa has nothing better to do!' Bhaskaran snapped back.

It was a peculiar body condition, related to the moisture and temperature around. Else, how could it occur annually during a specific season? His uneducated Amma did not have any knowledge of physiology.

Though he interpreted the phenomenon in many ways, Bhaskaran found it tough to keep away from meat and liquor. The only relief was that he did not have to desist from bodily pleasures. No wonder Bhaskaran had jumped in even before Antony had ended his comment about Janaki.

Sahir, the only one displaying an obvious distaste, kept aloof. He was never party to such adventures. A sensible eye, which made him look on these liaisons with contempt, worked inside him. In Sahir's perspective, morality was a means to disciplining oneself, beyond what religions and beliefs impose. Not even to shatter the so-called shackles set by religion did he indulge in liquor. Sahir also believed that a steadfast atheist should be deeply moral. If not, others would spread the calumny that non-religious folks could never practise self-control.

The village was already rife with gossip about Antony's wanton adventures. Apparently, it was because he had grown up denouncing the church and prayers! Bhaskaran was yet to be granted such notoriety. His occasional boisterousness was just to prove his worth among his friends.

In Sahir's view, a firm hand could easily persuade Bhaskaran otherwise. Bhaskaran's marriage with Veni would happen soon, and his distasteful stints would go up in smoke. Indeed, Sahir wished sincerely that his friends would lead more appropriate personal lives. However, all his feminine nature could express was a leniency towards their strutting male attitude. Hence his morality became a subject that provoked frequent teasing from his mates.

'Among the atheists, a sacred saint! Listen, these are all meant for real males.'

Declaring themselves 'real men', Antony and Bhaskaran would ridicule Sahir intermittently.

Sahir would shrug away these barbs. But once, provoked beyond tolerance by his friends, Sahir lashed out: 'Even bastards and vagabonds sleeping on the streets indulge in womanizing and boozing! Don't dare to justify it as the measuring tool for manhood. Real manhood is in refraining from unwanted proclivities.'

Though he did not drink himself, Sahir frequented all the liquor shops in the village and city with his friends. They mocked him openly but inwardly admired his innate goodness, like those who, being beyond redemption themselves, vicariously relish the lives that follow the straight and narrow path. Antony and Bhaskaran knew that true manhood meant the inner strength to keep depravities at bay. But admitting their own weaknesses was not easy for them.

'Holy One, please go home. Let these serpents dance around for a bit!'

Getting rid of Sahir, both headed out to Janaki's house. On their way, Antony sternly reminded Bhaskaran about the rules of precedence, 'Listen, elders first! You get only the second turn.'

That was part of Antony's intransigent nature. He always wished to be first in everything. Even when it came to visiting the loo! If anyone used it before him, he would be vexed the whole day.

'Please go ahead, big boss!' Bhaskaran acquiesced.

But the primacy demanded could not be executed. When they reached, Janaki was not home.

'Shameless hussy! Must have sauntered off for her night duty!' Antony kicked furiously at a wild sage plant in the yard. Its stalk collapsed, and the yellow flowers plunged into the sand. Antony assuaged his anger by pelting stones at the two dogs mating on the roadside.

'Just when one is at the point of no return . . . !'

Antony watched with malevolent pleasure as the dogs, unable to separate from each other, tried to scamper away in terror. 'Oh, lord! Imagine the plight of human beings if the situation was similar!' he muttered to the lord he did not believe in.

'Now, one has to rely on one's own self!' Bhaskaran said. 'I'm realizing the problem of not getting hitched in time!'

'Even after getting hitched, the real fun lies in jumping fences!'

'Don't expect me in your ventures after my wedding!'

'Some are a laughing stock before marriage. Some turn henpecked afterwards.'

'Oh, yes! Have seen tuskers getting tamed after their wedding!'

'Scram! Go and sleep, lying face down!'

'Order, order, sir!'

The next day, Antony woke up with a hangover at the peals of bells from near the Athmavu. Everyone in Abhasa Theruvu had heard it before him. They had also seen what was happening at the spot.

The half-crazy Eswaran Embrandiri was doing puja for Nireeswaran.

Sumitran was his handyman.

The Abhasa saw the sight when they came to investigate the sound. This was not part of Embrandiri's contract! Why on earth had that man indulged in such an act? Possibly, gaining a piece of the discarded stone must have made him recollect his heyday as a pujari in the main temple. Since there was no one to seek permission from, he seemed to have set off with authority at dawn. And what a henchman! Nonetheless, the trio was delighted at the sight of the partly mad and the mentally slow joining in the worship of the non-existent god! They sniggered, thinking how all rituals were equally empty of meaning.

'Please, chave me, chave me . . .' Sumitran stuttered as before, folding his hands before the disfigured form bereft of head or limbs. Never had he obtained such proximity and freedom to pray before the deity of the main temple. Whenever he had tried to edge closer, he had been pushed away to a far distance. Every visit to the temple had been a struggle to reach the sanctum sanctorum. In his half-baked consciousness, reaching the deity had become imprinted as the ultimate achievement. But each time, the temple functionaries barred him with a bramble fence of threats. They made sure that he never crossed that invisible barrier even unknowingly. His simple intelligence could never gauge why everybody was preventing him from reaching the god. He had longed to reach god's side one day, crossing all obstacles.

Sumitran was delighted that nobody prevented him from accessing Nireeswaran. He could even touch the deity freely! It thrilled him endlessly that finally he had a god, with no untouchable clause barring access to it. How long had he been yearning for a god whom he could touch like his own body!

Watching Eswaran conduct the worship of Nireeswaran with burning camphor, Sumitran stood reverentially, with folded hands. A few locals, attracted by the ringing bell, were present. The fragrance of incense sticks and aloeswood had created a temple-like ambience, and the worshippers had their hands folded in prayer, ignoring the deformities of the deity. Janaki came that way, carrying money that she'd earned, for the first time ever, without selling her body. She felt bemused thinking that Nireeswaran was the cause of that sudden windfall.

Observing the devotion-crazy fellows indulging in inanities early in the morning, Antony turned to Bhaskaran. 'Seems our ploy worked.'

'I would say so! Look at them bowing and scraping as if standing before a temple!' Bhaskaran chortled.

'Any ridiculous stuff sells fast in our land!'

After doing the traditional *aarti*, when Eswaran Embrandiri deposited the blazing camphor plate on the embankment, Sumitran did the *agni vandana* and touched his forehead devoutly. The motley group around unthinkingly followed suit. Some of them even put coins into the receptacle out of habit. Embrandiri stood gazing at those coins for a moment. The sight of the metal coins took him back to his temple days—a temple from which he had been cast out mercilessly so many years before. The breeze from the peepal, the scent of oil from the worship place of the Navagriha and the penetrating light of the sanctum sanctorum enveloped him. He felt a sudden jolt of awakening, as if he had abruptly returned to the presence of the divinity that he had served with consummate devotion, keeping his body, senses and mind in control.

But awakenings often end up touching some inner recesses of our being. The tears which erupt then are not salty like that of the mortal world; they taste like amrit. When he glanced through his amrit-like tears, Embrandiri saw the money that Janaki had deposited in the camphor tray and sensed a higher value in that gesture. The biblical anecdote of the 'widow's mites' suddenly struck him: 'This poor widow has put more into the treasury than all the others.' He never felt any contempt for that money, but believed instead that the offering of the prostitute was sacred.

'Watch that dirty hussy,' Antony bristled. 'She is busy offering money gained through her whoring!'

Embrandiri heard that comment. Wondering who was the dirtier of the two, he wryly smiled to himself.

Though he hadn't planned anything of the sort, Embrandiri found himself doing a puja the following day too, unable to resist the clarion call of his mind. He applied the ritualistic adornment of sandalwood and ashes, and drew the three stripes, the *mukkuri*, on the deity of Nireeswaran, rendering it radiant. After a long time, the concept of mukkuri, which his forefathers had taught him, seemed to have come alive. He wondered why he had drawn the three lines symbolizing Brahma, Vishnu and Maheshwara on Nireeswaran's deity. Why had he meditated on the three straight lines remembering Bhoomi, Swarga and Paatal? Why did he apply sindoor, symbolizing the inner eye, which removed Tripudi, all ignorance? He had no answer to these questions. Yet, following the instructions of his mind, he picked fresh flowers from his own yard—oleander, hibiscus and bauhinia—and, making a garland, adorned Nireeswaran. He performed all the customary rites and rituals.

Dawn was breaking. The falcon and cuckoo started their morning invocations to Nireeswaran from the branches of the Athmavu. Zaid and Arnos sat at a distance with minds of those undertaking a pilgrimage, observing Eswaran worshipping Nireeswaran and listening to the clear birdcall, purified through incessant practice. Zaid hadn't made it on the night of the deity's consecration. That was why Arnos and he reached the place before a crowd had started forming. He had to return to the madrasa that day. But he wished to catch a glimpse of Nireeswaran, though it was a mere piece of stone. Zaid, with an uneasy premonition, wondered aloud whether they would be able to sit together on that embankment again if Embrandiri continued his puja in that manner.

'What difference does the place where we sit make? These are all attempts to bind the infinite in finite space, isn't it?' Arnos asked.

'The finite spaces of infinity, good usage!' Zaid laughed.

'Ah, it caught hold of me last night! I touched infinity somewhere between my dreams and thoughts. Zaid, if there is a being which has no beginning, middle or end, what is wrong in calling it god, devil or Nireeswaran?'

'I don't know of such things, dear fellow! The most benevolent Allah creates souls and sends them to earth, so that they blend with eternity after death. But eternity eschews creation. Because creation implies a starting. But eternity is devoid of either a starting or an ending. So, if my soul was created at my birth, how can it become part of eternity after my death?'

'Eternity is cyclical, like a snake head swallowing its own tail. Hence if the soul is eternal, it couldn't have been created! The moment you say "creation", it is no longer eternal.'

'That would mean something which was always in existence and was never created. If so, Eswaran Embrandiri's Nireeswaran was not created yesterday. It was in existence but was discovered only yesterday!'

'Nireeswaran discovered by the Abhasa! I feel utterly thrilled. Let me drop a kiss on this hallowed ground!'

Without much ado, Arnos Pathiri bent over to kiss the dewy grass on the maidan.

'To humble oneself unto the earth is a grace granted by the divine,' Zaid said and touched his forehead to the ground, as if performing namaz.

'Let everyone think that us two oldies are busy doing morning exercises, eh?'

Both of them were in a childlike state of mind at that moment, possessed of an innocence which could not perceive any object as separate from another. Then, Arnos and Zaid heard Sumitran pleading with that same childlike innocence.

'Please, chave me, chave me!'

As usual, he was immersed in his singular prayer. He had no self-centred intelligence to demand food for satiating his hunger, clothes for covering himself or a shelter for his rest. Naturally, those who had such an intelligence denounced him as a dimwit.

Sumitran and Embrandiri reached early the next day. There were more visitors that day in comparison to the previous one. Proportionally, the offerings in the receptacle were more too. At least a few of the devotees seemed concerned about Embrandiri's poverty.

'Wow . . . it seems Nireeswaran is going to be a far bigger hit than our calculations.' Sahir was astounded.

'Well, if this trend continues, the offerings shall make Nireeswaran wealthy pretty soon!'

'Who knows whether miracles are also getting attributed to Nireeswaran?'

Thc three friends started howling with laughter.

No one knows at which moment Bhaskaran was prompted to utter those words. Literally, there had been a miracle! And Sumitran was the protagonist in that marvellous event.

This was how the whole episode unfurled. Seeing Sumitran scurrying around daily to help him, Embrandiri felt pity welling up within him. He had scolded him mercilessly when he was the priest in the main temple. Now Embrandiri felt regretful for his meaningless obduracy, which had obstructed the simple-minded fellow's innocent expression of faith. Sumitran would be the first to reach Nireeswaran's abode daily. He would also be the last to leave the premises. Embrandiri felt that Sumitran's prayer, which he uttered inarticulately as 'chave me, chave me', was far dearer to the Lord than the hypocritical prayers of others.

'Sumitra, it is not *chave* me. Say, *save* me . . .' Embrandiri tried to correct his enunciation.

Though Sumitran struggled to follow, he continued to make the same mistake.

'Try once more . . . save me!'

Sumitran tried but ended up at square one.

Unable to twist his tongue around the syllables, the attempts ended in repeated failure.

Arnos and Zaid, who were witnesses to the incident, were wondering about the stubbornness of certain words. They would not grant your wishes, even if you thrashed around wailing and pleading. The friends were touched by the kindness of the mentor, and they too wished that Sumitran be 'saved'.

Finally, when even Embrandiri was on the verge of giving up, the '*cha*' went away from Sumitran's tongue and, out of the blue, '*sa*' replaced it. A sea change took over Sumitran when the 'sa' came under his control for the first time in his life. The blessing of the words seemed to have elevated him to the skies. In a frenzy, he ran to Nireeswaran and started hollering, 'Save me, save me . . . !'

The prayer was so loud that everyone in the vicinity started paying attention. Both believers and non-believers could hear Sumitran's crystal clear 'sa'. Entranced, many moved to the embankment of the Athmavu. The nature of the crowd was like ants gathering around a piece of jaggery. The circumference of the circle increased as one followed another cluelessly.

In a matter of moments, the deity of Nireeswaran was surrounded by a sea of people. In their midst, Sumitran stood with folded hands, having turned 'cha' into 'sa'.

Annamma, who came running on hearing the news, gaped at the dimwit, who was now speaking clearly and praying to Nireeswaran.

'Sumitran!' she hailed him joyfully. Not having any sons, Annamma considered Sumitran as her own child. Primarily, he could be trusted around her grown-up daughters. Second, he was always ready to do chores. Sumitran also found it pleasurable to be with Annamma and her daughters, sharing simple home-made food.

When his own home treated him unkindly, the five women in the neighbourhood provided him succour. Sumitran strung the hibiscus and chrysanthus flowers from Annamma's yard in a thread of devotion and garlanded Nireeswaran daily. And lo and behold! Here was Sumitran speaking clearly!

Barber Maniyan was the next to step out of his shop. A 'head', tonsured halfway, waited patiently for a while inside the shop, and then followed Maniyan to the Athmavu.

By the time Antony, Bhaskaran and Sahir rushed to gauge why the world was suddenly turning topsy-turvy, the crowd around Nireeswaran had swelled in numbers, preventing them from reaching the spot. The winds of change started caressing their faces with its searing hands.

Ninth Petal: Dimensions

In the light of her new wisdom, Janaki tried to scrutinize Damu's mesmerizing male smell. The woman inside her felt embarrassed to admit that, despite being a prostitute, a man's smell enticed her irrepressibly. Janaki told herself that though a harlot is exposed to the public, there were certain things that should remain private.

Even so, she started following, with a novel scientific spirit, each smell that strayed into her nostrils. That search caused a new thought to sprout in her. It struck her that even someone like her, deprived of a middle-school education, could possess a scientist's keen eye. After Roberto had emphasized categorically that an education was not necessary for making scientific discoveries, Janaki started recognizing that someone unknown to her was residing within. In fact, Roberto had spoken about earth-shaking findings made by illiterate people. In the conjunction of observation and imagination, discoveries took birth.

On intensely contemplating the body parts which took part in sexual intercourse, Janaki felt like laughing at the maker's lack of imagination. How did the human race come to artificially cover these organs as if they were so despicable? Janaki wondered why this tendency to conceal—unknown to dogs, cows and gorillas, and never warranted by nature—was considered civilized behaviour? Why didn't man feel the need to cover up his hands and feet? The propensity to view the limbs differently from sexual organs was not something innate. A baby would never wear clothes unless someone dressed him up. The child would never feel the need to cover himself if nobody else followed the custom—something made evident by certain tribal communities that exist even today. How laughable that 'sex' was the word given to the furtive rendezvous of forcibly concealed organs!

The maker had definitely not conceived a simple process. He could have designed man and woman in such a manner that arousal and orgasm happened when their hands clapped against each other's. If so, Janaki's job would have been so much easier! In a crowd, she could have clapped her hands against a customer's and made some quick money. But it had one danger—that day and night the world would have resounded with rambunctious applause, much like at a cricket stadium!

If Janaki were given an opportunity to craft humankind, she would have tried something different. For example, when a woman opened and shut her left eye rapidly and the man responded with his right eye in a similar manner, both would have been allowed to reach the pinnacle of ecstasy. This would have been a recipe for disaster for all those sexual perverts who violated women! Indeed, there was a definite design flaw in the existing process!

If sex were possible through the eyes, Janaki could have satisfied customers by staring at them during the day, instead of waiting for the night to earn her living. Besides, by immersing herself in Damu's eyes at a convenient time, she could have gratified her own longing.

Almost immediately it dawned on her that in such a world, there would be no place for a prostitute named Janaki. If lust could be shared via the eyes, most of the so-called morally upright married women and men would droop exhausted during shopping trips and train journeys, and customers would stop seeking out women like Janaki.

'And so, Nireeswaran, let things stay as they are! Support the simpleton who toils with her body, by gifting her customers for sustenance.'

Even as her thoughts meandered, the exhilaration triggered by smells travelled along with Janaki like a budding infatuation. That was why she joined Roberto in his expedition to visit the Athmavu, under which Nireeswaran reigned, to discern the al and mavu using smells.

The natives looked askance at the scientist who was openly consorting with a streetwalker. Roberto never bothered to justify his reasons either. Eventually, the villagers accepted him as another unexpected aberration, much like Nireeswaran, who had popped up out of nowhere.

If every object had a natural frequency and also an odour associated with it, both the peepal and the mango, which constituted the Athmavu, should have those too. Roberto's first attempt was to differentiate the odours. It was possible that an object's frequency had no connection with the smell. Roberto had been burning the midnight oil, exploring whether any characteristic of an object could be related to its smell, so that he could devise an equation from which the exact proportions could be further derived. To make that possible, a database of all known objects of the universe had to be made and analysed. But how could one compare smells? For any comparison, one needed a fundamental unit for measurement, like metre for length, kilogram for weight and second for time. They all had universally accepted definitions.

To measure smell, one could configure a unit in the Malayalam language. For instance, give it the name 'Roberto' or 'Janaki'!

Roberto chose 'Janaki'.

If one assumed the fundamental unit as the fragrance of a jasmine flower:

1 Janaki = Smell of 1 jasmine flower

Now, one had to connect all the objects in the world to this fundamental unit of smell. Some smells might be equivalent to 10 Janakis; some others, half a Janaki.

Janaki started giggling at that explanation.

'I like it! After all, my life is based on one half of my body!'

'In truth, Janaki, when I am visualizing smells in correlation to you, I am getting some insights. I feel that I have been sent here to discover something new.'

'I also feel as if hurled into some new world! Smells being discussed over here, Nireeswaran over there . . . I am beginning to love this Eswaran who is not an Eswaran. What if we let Nireeswaran handle the smells?'

Roberto grinned. He had never felt the need to let anyone handle a matter and contribute to the results. Neither did he have a penchant for visiting any temple or church. For him, there was nothing to be gained from entering them, and nothing to be lost by staying away. It was possible to experience pure spirituality without visiting any religious places.

Since Nireeswaran had cropped up in this village as a concept more mysterious than his research topic, Roberto felt like simply obeying the dictates of a prostitute's mind, which was naive and unsophisticated.

'Leave the subject of smells to Nireeswaran.' All Roberto had to do was to play the fool, by locking up the arrogance of his scientific ego. There was a certain levity in standing before one's own consciousness occasionally like an idiot. All it required was simplicity and the humility to observe with a detached mind. That was when one could realize how surreal certain experiences could be!

It was while he stood near the Athmavu, devoid of the pull of ego, that a revelation dawned on Roberto, about a measuring instrument for smells, like those for electricity, light and speed! Another strange thought followed. Would it be possible to let a smell pass through the body just like scanning the inner body organs with an X-ray? It was a scorching thought. But how would he set about synthesizing a fundamental unit for further experimentation? Roberto decided to sit like a dunce on the embankment, hoping for another wave of intuition.

The scientist started feeling that sitting idly opened the door to a great universe of knowledge and that any know-how of the external world had to be realized internally first. His mind travelled to the possibilities of creating a new system using smells, analogous to bandwidths of sound and light utilized in ultrasonic scanning, and in X-ray and laser technologies. Many such ideas, derogated as crazy when proposed initially, had evolved into independent branches of science over the course of time.

In general, scientific inquiry emphasizes on the universal phenomena related to our five senses. Light is associated with the eyes, sound with the ears, touch with skin and taste with the tongue. Sound, light and touch are being used today for many non-destructive tests. Then why not use smell, much more subtle than those?

Roberto was perplexed thinking whether smell could penetrate a sheet of metal. Smells existed in bandwidths inaccessible to human capacity. Dogs, for example, have the ability of smell that is far more acute than that of man. Their noses are powerful sensors which enable them to track things at a distance of many kilometres by following the molecules of smell. The wind might have blown the scent far and wide. Yet they manage to sniff out the remnants and trace the origin. Dogs also respond to sounds which are beyond human auditory senses. Scientific instruments make use of those frequency ranges of sound and light which humans cannot sense. If these could penetrate dense objects and detect miniature defects in their structures, why couldn't those smells, undetectable by human nostrils, do the same and highlight even finer faults?

But that would require reaching that particular smell. Also, it would require the invention of an instrument which could measure it. As a precursor to reaching that remote possibility, Roberto was engrossed in conducting widespread research. He planned to codify his results and publish a paper first.

What were the fundamental differences between the smells which provoked headaches, invoked sexual feelings, made one unconscious, and those which soothed and healed? If every human had their own smell, what did it mean in reality? When one said that a dog has a strong sense of smell, what was the factor that made it possible? If that capability was increased, could one end up with an instrument which could perceive smells that even dogs could not access? Was there any relevance for a branch of science which studied how smells could penetrate material and depict the faults in the crystalline structure?

After all, what was not of relevance in the world? Roberto explained to Janaki what a stupendous phenomenon the sense of smell was! Apparently, there existed microscopic creatures which subsisted merely on smell.

'Creatures which eat smell?' Janaki was aghast. 'Where do they live?'

'Inside our nose, for example. They live on smell, and procreate. Janaki, have you ever thought of the travails a human being undergoes in order to ensure that his genes are carried forward to the next generation? He is born helpless, needs the protection of elders, should evade death by diseases or accidents and endure many adversities beyond his control.

'When he comes of age, he needs a suitable body of the opposite gender to ensure reproduction. When crores and crores of his sperms go waste, by a stroke of fortuitous luck, just one ends up successful. Imagine if instead of one sperm, another had merged with an egg! The child born would be a completely different person! Considered thus, each of us is the result of an improbable, spectacular coincidence! There are so many decisive factors which play a critical role in our existence, rendering us very helpless.

'But that is not the case for a single-celled microorganism which lives on smell. It doesn't need anyone to bring it up. No need for any mate from the opposite gender either. No need for water, air, light or food! It divides itself and replicates into two, four, lakhs and crores of progeny, thus recreating itself. How powerful and superior is that single-celled organism! When the number of cells increase, proportionally, the adversities increase too. Stating succinctly, the more complicated the organism, the more limitations it faces. Infinitesimal unicellular organisms reach a miraculous level of perfection. They will subjugate the macroscopic egos easily and survive!

'If so, imagine going to the nano level! The toughest antibiotic or even a nuclear bomb cannot destroy a microorganism which survives on smell. I am willing to call the micro level beyond that as "god". *The one fundamental micro state of every macro-level entity! An indestructible eternal state.* "Indestructible" implies never created too. And hence, Janaki, for me, you, Nireeswaran and the rest are all in a godly state,' Roberto said.

Having listened intently to Roberto, Janaki said, 'I could hardly understand anything!'

'And that is why our carpenter exhorted often, *He who has eyes, let him see; he who has ears, let him hear*!' Roberto grinned.

'Understood everything! I am thirsty . . . Can I get some water?' Janaki asked.

'Well, the same carpenter also said, *Those who drink the pot of eternal water I give, will never thirst again.* It was said to a woman with five paramours!'

'Wonder what will happen to those having more than five? Heard that the carpenter's closest disciple was a prostitute.'

'Those with eyes, see! Those with ears, hear!'

'Amen . . . Amen . . .'

PERPETUATION

Tenth Petal: Offering

The news that Sumitran was relieved of incoherence unleashed a tsunami of excitement in the village. The ripples set off from the Athmavu's embankment, the epicentre of the earthquake, and reached far and wide. People started visiting to check the veracity of what they had heard.

'See how superstition spreads!' Antony rasped bitterly. 'That fellow Sumitran used to stammer a bit and now speaks more clearly. But to hail it as a miracle wrought by Nireeswaran is rank stupidity! Some people habitually blow nonsensical stuff all out of proportion.'

Of course, there was sense in what he said. If certain syllables came tumbling out of a tongue, consistent practice also had a role to play in it. Following Embrandiri's advice, Sumitran had tried, ceaselessly, to speak well. The real wonder was that such extraordinary confidence had been instilled in Sumitran. After encountering him, Bhaskaran had been flabbergasted. Bemused, he asked Antony, 'One can justify this in many ways, but something out of the ordinary did occur in Sumitran's case, right?'

'It's commonplace for extraordinary occurrences to take place in the world! A mere coincidence, which has been inexplicably linked to Nireeswaran. Anyone can twist things out of proportion,' Antony said brusquely.

'The folks around are credulous. They will blindly believe whatever they hear,' Sahir opined. 'Why can't these scallywags realize that we did not install an Eswaran but a Nireeswaran? Oh, that inauspicious hour when we made the public appeal to Nireeswaran to sort out Sumitran's brain!'

'Inauspicious time? There is no such thing in a rational world.'

'I did not mean it . . . a figure of speech, that's all.'

'Things will be all right soon. Let us wait and watch for a bit. Then, we will execute the next step,' Antony said.

'What next step?'

'See for yourself! They are messing with Antony of all people! Let us enjoy the game for now. I can hurl that piece of stone into the river right away. But let it stay for a while. Isn't there a special thrill in tackling baseless faith when the stone causing it is still around?'

'I guess so . . .'

As the Abhasa waited for events to unfold, certain strange occurrences began to transpire.

A Public Service Commission memo for a government job arrived for Parameswaran, who had been unemployed for eighteen years after getting his degree. Having failed in umpteen interviews, he had plummeted to the depths of depression when the government unfroze a rank list from its predecessor's time. Parameswaran had a government job offer in his hands.

It was beyond Parameswaran's wildest fantasies that an examination he had written years ago, when the age barrier was still in his favour, would yield results so late. The missive with the government insignia made him weep with joy. The paper trembled in his hands—it had turned his whole life around with its stamp of authority.

It was around afternoon when the postman handed over the memo. The moment he opened and read the contents, Parameswaran planted an impulsive kiss on the postman's cheek and raced towards the Athmavu, shrieking 'My Nireeswara!' Muttering that Parameswaran should have tipped him Rs 50 instead of a sloppy kiss, the postman wiped his face and started chasing Parameswaran.

What the postman saw was Parameswaran standing with folded hands, weeping copiously before the stone at the Athmavu's base; there was no guard or fence around the idol, allowing access to anyone, anytime.

Let it be stated that Parameswaran gifted the postman an amount equivalent to two kisses there and then, as a reward for all that running.

The village was rattled once again. The natives had witnessed the submission of that prayer; no one had ever believed that it would be answered. But Nireeswaran was debunking all such scepticism. After Sumitran's gift of words, here was Parameswaran's gain of job.

'What's the big fuss all about?' Antony said. 'It wasn't just Parameswaran but every rank holder in that PSC list who qualified for jobs, right? How on earth could that be a miracle? And speaking of the PSC, they even send appointment orders to people who have died of old age!'

The dark humour in those words did not appeal to Parameswaran. The appointment order had changed his views, converting him into an ardent believer of Nireeswaran. The deity had granted a prayer that had been dipped in mockery, after forgiving the inherent scorn.

When one's whole life was being transformed, what was the point of wasting time on rational arguments? With the answer already in hand, all logic became irrelevant.

'Kindly keep your reasoning to yourself, dear friends.' Parameswaran smiled at the Abhasa. 'You see, I had long given up hopes of getting a government job. I even contemplated suicide after destroying my degree certificate! When the path has finally opened, my priority is not to denounce superstition! Indeed, I firmly believe that it is a miracle caused by Nireeswaran. It would never have happened otherwise!'

Bhaskaran was infuriated at how the caricature they had sowed and nurtured was fast acquiring a halo. The Abhasa had set out to oppose blind beliefs associated with religious rituals. And now, the fungal infection of superstition had spread to Nireeswaran too!

'Utter foolishness!' Bhaskaran hollered. 'Despite having degrees and proper education, you despicably choose to follow stupid beliefs.'

'Go ahead and say what you want! Each experience is relevant only to the person it is happening to. When one is suffering, not a single person who spouts idealism is around to help. Didn't your clique of three challenge the deity to grant me a job if he was powerful enough? Now that I got the job, why are you hell-bent on denouncing Nireeswaran? What is the guarantee that you will not eat your words at a later stage?'

'One stands by one's words, being a man! That stance is not for dunces like you.'

'What manhood? What stance? Tell me, what is the guarantee that the three of you are likely to be alive tomorrow at this hour?'

Hearing that, the hot-tempered Antony seized Parameswaran by the collar. 'Yes, a hundred times yes! But I am not too sure if you will be alive, you coward!'

Bhaskaran hurriedly separated them both. 'Let go immediately! What a shame that you are fighting with such a nincompoop!'

Antony's fair face reddened whenever he became enraged. His body burnt like the desert. His friends sensed these vagaries. Luckily, Parameswaran maintained his cool. Else, it would have led to a deep rift between old friends.

Sahir ruminated that such impulsive verbal duels often ended up as disastrous news items the following day. But he felt that Parameswaran should not have asked the touchy question, about whether they would be alive the next day. Hearing about death is an unpleasant experience for anyone, atheist or otherwise. Sahir had never been able to get rid of his fear of death by taking refuge in rationalism. Death implied a terror-filled uncertainty. Whenever he remembered the hushed prayers offered as a corpse was lifted for burial, Sahir's heart started to pound. Though he castigated himself that such anxiety was unbecoming of a rationalist, his attempts to overcome it always met with utter failure. What if Parameswaran's words had been pronounced at an ill-omened time? Let that not be true! Sahir's mental foundation was fragile enough to be swayed by so-called miracles. Mostly, he drew strength from the irrepressible audacity of Antony, who scoffed even at death.

The news of Parameswaran's job spread at the speed of light. So did the tale of Antony's revolt. Such news had the ability to proliferate by itself. With the addition of each recipient, the embellishments would pile up. Which land lacks folks who are not waiting for a piece of delectable miracle? Many of them now landed up at the Athmavu. When cohorts of fence sitters started joining in, the crowd thronging Embrandiri during the puja crossed the embankment and inundated the roads, affecting traffic. As an impassive Nireeswaran held court at the Athmavu, resplendent in the light of the lamp, a rather decent amount of money started falling into Embrandiri's camphor receptacle.

'Shame, it has become like any other church or temple. Can't tolerate it any more. Unscientific idiots!' Sahir complained to Antony.

'Let us uproot it and throw it away, just as easily as we installed it,' Bhaskaran pointed at the last resort available to them.

'Let it be so. By tomorrow, this divine form shall be annihilated.'

However, the Abhasa could not execute the plan the next day. A late-night phone call from Mangalore put paid to it. Antony possessed almost 40 acres of rubber plantation in Mangalore—a veritable paradise, consisting of hills, streams, trees and a variety of birds! Since he had a loyal caretaker, Antony displayed an indifference towards the management of that property. His hard-working father had procured the land for his son, but Antony hardly ever set foot on it. Indeed, his visits were rare, with Bhaskaran and Sahir often accompanying him. They would usually spend time in a hedonistic frenzy, gorging on wild meat and tippling liquor. The rule was to avoid even phone calls while bingeing on toddy brewed with cashew fruits and coconut flowers. The trio would return with new energy to indulge in fresh adventures.

However, a neighbour, whose land was adjacent to Antony's, was prone to disrupt his peaceful life. An unnecessary spirit of competition was behind that disturbance. The caretaker's frantic call forced Antony to immediately head off to resolve the situation. Since he had to leave at dawn, there was no option but to postpone the dethroning of Nireeswaran.

Sahir was grossly disappointed. 'Nothing works without you around, Acchaya!' Only when he was overwhelmed with affection did Sahir refer to Antony as Acchaya.

'Oh, I shall be back in a jiffy. Both of you take over administrative duties until I return!' Antony poked Sahir on the chin and set off for Mangalore. The poke on the chin was Sahir's exclusive privilege. He felt depressed at Antony's absence. Sahir would have gladly accompanied Antony to the estate reeking of wild meat.

During the rather insignificant duration that Antony was away, many not-so-insignificant happenings took place in the village. More news of prayers being answered started trickling in, as though in contravention to the Abhasa's scientific analysis and attitude.

Kartyayani's long-lost son, who had gone missing during the feast at Aruthunkal church when he was just three, returned home after eighteen years! Gafoor ended up getting a visa for the Gulf. Rumours were rife that Chomi's husband's rheumatism was getting better.

Sahir and Bhaskaran were dead set against any 'miracle' in the widely circulated news items. If one mixed truth with fantasy, even unremarkable events acquired an out-of-the-world aura. People would babble endlessly, and soon, the news would transmute to such an extent that it would be difficult to segregate the true from the false.

'Acchaya, you'd better return fast,' Sahir insisted during his phone conversation with Antony. 'We *must* throw away that stone! Under the present circumstances, we cannot do it without you!'

'Well, don't intervene until I come. See, I am needed here right now. But I will try to reach as soon as I can.'

'Who knows what new tales will spread by then.'

'Let Nireeswaran garner more powers, I say! When the foe becomes stronger, the battle gets interesting. Don't lose your morale. We installed a lifeless stone as a deity, didn't we? When the time comes, we will prove that a mere touch can demolish it.'

At the time when such assurances were being given, the Athmavu had become the cynosure of all eyes. And then, without consulting the main protagonists behind the consecration, certain undesirable tendencies started gathering force among the people. The first such was presented by none other than Parameswaran, whose atheistic world view had been toppled overnight.

'Next Thursday happens to be Nireeswaran's birth star. What if we make some payasam as an offering?' he asked Embrandiri.

Embrandiri did not find anything amiss about Parameswaran, an erstwhile atheist, turning into a steadfast devotee. Both were one in principle.

One could, after all, consider anyone who followed the religion of Nireeswaran as an atheist. Religion implied adherence to a certain viewpoint. From that perspective, the book of atheism was the holy book of its followers. If it were updated with a final chapter on Nireeswaran's consecration, it could become the doctrine of atheists.

But Embrandiri did not share his musings with anyone. It would have stoked ill will. And who on earth was going to pay attention?

But he was baffled about the sudden payasam offering. 'What do you mean by birth star?'

'Last month it was Vishaka Nakshatra, when the consecration took place. This Thursday, it is again the star of Vishaka.'

'Oh, that is how is goes.' Embrandiri's lips broke into a crescent-moon smile. How quickly had an atheist become trapped in the squares of the Panchangam—the Vedic calendar! There was but a thin barrier between the two paths of belief and disbelief. Some unbelievers changed course and became devotees, while some believers turned cynics. Both factions would crow over the latest convert and bombastically brag about the superiority of their path! They might even condemn the renegade as having lost his marbles. It was the same when it came to political affiliations. By stubbornly insisting that one's own path was exclusively correct, political adherents joined the ranks of the superstitious.

Well, it seemed that Nireeswaran was the one unwittingly born under the star of Vishaka. He was one lunar month old. After many dark years, Embrandiri was relishing the feeling of light-heartedness. Lost laughter was returning to the recesses of his heart. In the past, he had never cried openly. Now, he no longer laughed openly. Embrandiri realized that both laughter and tears originated from the same place. If one left them undisturbed, both would maintain an amicable relationship with each other.

Parameswaran agreed to be the sponsor of the payasam offering. As a token of gratitude to Nireeswaran, he was even willing to advertise his gratitude through a remembrance in the newspapers.

Embrandiri decided to appoint Gopalukutty Asan as the chef in charge of the payasam.

It was Janaki who informed Roberto about the latest development. Gopalukutty Asan, a blind man, was going to cook payasam for a Nireeswaran he had never seen! It was not the payasam but the unique phenomenon of smells associated with that cooking venture that interested Janaki. She thought that since the idea of an instrument to measure smells had taken hold of Roberto, Gopalukutty Asan would fascinate him immensely.

Gopalukutty Asan could assess the ingredients and the progression of cooking without tasting the dish. It was his inexplicable gift of smell that came to his aid. If the aviyal did not have enough salt or the rasam ended up bland, Asan could sniff it out! When Roberto heard that Asan had never tasted his dishes while perfecting them, it struck him that in close proximity of Nireeswaran was the human model of the smelling instrument he had been searching for! Seemingly unimportant and irrelevant prompts drive forward every significant discovery.

How could Asan's nostrils gauge the exact measure of salt, chilli, coriander and onion? How could a blind man, relying solely on the inner world of smells, control the systems of the external world? The instrument that functioned within Asan must be so powerful! If so, by imitating the smelling buds within the human nose one could develop sensors that would convert smells into electric signals; and by amplifying those one could eventually transform each smell into a form of data! That would enable comparisons and contrasts.

The next Thursday, both Roberto and Janaki presented themselves punctually at the Athmavu. They watched Gopalukutty Asan heave a huge brass pot on to the cooking stove made of three stones, and then, fold his hands at Nireeswaran, whom he had never seen and was never likely to see. There was a crowd near the site. On Sumitran's special invitation, Ghoshayatra Annamma and her daughters had arrived early. Sumitran was very protective towards the family. On seeing the mother and girls, it appeared as if five women of the same age were standing next to one another. Annamma was looking at how her goat's favourite couch grass had grown lushly near the Athmavu. She intended to hack a few sheaves later, with a sickle deftly concealed in a newspaper in her hand.

It was then that Bhaskaran and Sahir made their entry, ready to instigate a bloody revolution if needed. They had always been respectful of the unique smelling prowess of Gopalukutty Asan. Almost all the feasts in the locality were advertisements of Asan's cooking skills. But now, the young men planned to challenge him in an unscrupulous way. If Nireeswaran's first offering got messed up, it would dim the deity's glory.

It was with that ulterior motive that the duo turned up, all the while pretending to be innocent bystanders. Both were drenched in strikingly strong colognes. This was Antony's idea, and he had provided the technical advice for that stunt. If even dogs could be confused by applying scientific tricks, then what about a blind old gaffer?

The Athmavu's surroundings became suffused with the penetrating scent of the perfume. When the two young men came near, Asan's nostrils flared at the foreign smell. When his nostrils became stimulated, the old man quickly understood that a fragrant mutiny had been unleashed against him. To him, any odour other than that of his cooking was akin to a jarring noise during a classical concert. The concentration of the artist was at risk.

'Who has come wearing strong perfume? Not good at all,' Asan objected.

Bhaskaran and Sahir grinned, already celebrating their half-victory.

'We thought only dogs sniffed, Asan. As if we can wipe away the scent on our bodies!' Bhaskaran replied mockingly.

'Not just scent, one's innate character cannot be wiped away either! Well, we shall see!'

It soon turned into a duel between Asan and the Abhasa. Roberto felt annoyed about the young men tricking the blind old man. He became curious to know the aftermath of that battle of the smells.

What transpired afterwards was similar to a well-orchestrated musical concert. The rice was washed and deposited in the brass pot; the jaggery was boiled with meticulous alacrity; the amount of clarified butter was assessed by a mere sniff; and other ingredients were added after the cook had confirmed the perfection of the wafting fragrance . . .

While Roberto watched with great eagerness, Janaki interjected, 'I knew someone in my childhood who was like this blind person. He lived near my mother's family home. We used to visit every year for the temple festival: the *kettu kazcha* during Bharani celebrations. I used to wonder at the exhibits they made, as tall as coconut trees and pushed on rolling platforms to the display ground. But what stunned me more was the old artist who lived next to our home. I watched with my own eyes as the blind man painted lovely pictures of the gods and goddesses!'

'Lies! How can a blind man draw pictures? Janaki, you might have been mistaken. Or the fellow was playing you for a fool by pretending to be blind.'

'Not at all. He lost his sight when he was seventeen. Our grandmother told us that he painted only gods and goddesses because he could see with his inner eye. When we went near him, he would call us by our names, though he couldn't see! Shall this fallen woman suggest something which the scientist might not have thought of till now?'

'What?'

'Just as Gopalukutty Asan senses taste with smells, what if that artist saw sights using smells? What if a deaf man can sense sounds through smells?'

'Oh god!' Roberto was stunned. 'What an insight! Like the same electricity which activates the bulb and the fan . . . In reality, smell is not sensed by the nose, nor sound by the ear. It all happens at a distinct centre of the brain. One can visualize it as five different sensors attached to the same centre. That being so, it is highly likely, Janaki, that what you said is true! Using smells, one can see, hear or touch . . . Today, you have turned into a scientist! I owe all my further discoveries to you.'

'Forget such dedications . . .'

While politely dismissing Roberto's approbation, Janaki was recollecting her moments of solitude, when she could touch Damu remembering his smell. At any moment, Janaki could close her eyes and touch Damu. She could sexually provoke him from a distance. A strong current of Damu's body scent would penetrate Janaki at those times. She would melt with passion. Janaki could never comprehend that magical phenomenon which no one else could transmit to her. It was an indescribable experience. Janaki had not shared this even with Damu, tucking it away as a secret.

Meanwhile, Gopalukutty Asan had cleverly won the battle of scents started by the Abhasa. Nireeswaran's abode exuded the delectable fragrance of payasam, with top notes of sweetness and ghee.

'Let the first offering be served to the perfumed youth. After all, they put in so much effort!' Gopalukutty Asan quipped, taking sweet revenge on his detractors. The contempt in his words had impaled them; both the friends turned on their heels and left the place without tasting the payasam. They strongly felt the lack of Antony's commanding presence in those moments.

Roberto was amazed when the warm and wonderful taste permeated his senses. It was utterly delicious! Never had he tasted anything so enticing in his whole life. Indeed, it was unbelievable that a blind man had prepared the dish. The old man had opened a door to new vistas related to Roberto's research on smells.

Savouring the fragrance of the first offering at Nireeswaran's abode, the peepal and mango embraced each other more tightly and, turning into Athmavu, thrummed in perfect union.

Eleventh Petal: Awakening

Roberto had been yearning for a respite from the shackles of the research laboratory in Bangalore for a while. But he never knew that the desire was pulling him towards Nireeswaran's abode. One of his MSc batchmates, Arunjit, became the key player in the events. For a long time, Arunjit had been inviting Roberto with the promise of a vacation in his village, but work commitments had prevented Roberto from joining him. Dipping one's hand in superglue and touching different surfaces would summarize the predilections of official life. One became 'stuck' on to too many things.

In the workplace were many 'scientific seekers', much like cattle with nooses around their necks. The rope's hold would entrap them within the permissible limits. They were unaware of completing innumerable revolutions within the precisely delineated circumference. Though it appeared that they were moving ahead, it wasn't often the case. Many ended up as robots, losing the ability to feel emotions and experience beautiful moments of life. And some were snared by hubris and believed themselves to be superior to the rest. Roberto had often witnessed arrogance oozing out as pettiness from such people. And on the day of retirement, as they stepped out of the office gate, they turned into big zeroes! Unable to regain the lost human values or even live a proper life, deprived of the sceptre of power and the flummery of sycophants, most were driven to early graves. Nobody remembered them afterwards.

After many years in that environment, Roberto wished to detach himself and take up his friend's offer. Arunjit was working as a bank manager, having given up physics, the subject he used to study. Physics, *urja tantra* in the local lingo, had split into urja (energy) and tantra (system), and now he retained only tantra (strategy) for handling the daily life.

Spending all his hours with currency notes had made him sluggish. In life, there were certain times when these notes, albeit imprinted with monetary value, counted as mere bits of paper.

Arunjit, who had been Roberto's roommate in the hostel, was familiar with his peculiar lifestyle. Roberto could never sleep for more than three or four hours at night. His alert mind would wake him with a scolding, 'Enough of sleep, you oaf!' Their room was 'the empire where the sun never set'. Arunjit adapted himself to the situation by covering his head with a blanket and tying a knot, much like Gandhari's legendary one, over his eyes. Someone else in his place would have started bickering. Whenever Arunjit opened his eyes, he would see Roberto wrestling with heavy scientific tomes. Roberto tended to travel a hundred yards ahead of the lessons being taught in class.

'You will become a Nobel laureate one day! Robert Einstein!' Though Arunjit teased him mercilessly, he sincerely considered this a definite possibility. And he was still of the same opinion.

Roberto had no affinity towards any sort of dogmas. He did not feel the need for even conventional family life. Life was an unceasing investigation for him, gliding from one issue to another. Even when his clothes became old and tattered, there was no triggering of any 'caution' signal in his consciousness. He couldn't care less about what the world thought of his attire. It was usually Arunjit who ended up purchasing clothes for Roberto. Arunjit took good care of his friend—the extraordinarily gifted scientist leading the existence of an outlier—which helped Roberto's life from slipping into utter chaos. Although they parted ways after post-graduation, and Roberto joined work as a research scientist in Bangalore, both took care to preserve the warmth of their rare friendship.

During their college days, Arunjit used to visit his home every weekend. Sometimes, Roberto would join him. Roberto felt an uncommon freedom, not tangible in the city, during such visits. They relished the beauty of the simple local food, went for walks with their mundus tucked up and lazily pissed against the fences.

Arunjit's family included a father who had been in a coma for decades, a mother who had made it her life's mission to take care of him, and a younger brother. Whenever Roberto saw the corpse-like state of Arunjit's father—lying in a room at the west-facing end of the house amid a miasma of odours—he would try to imagine his condition. It was then that Roberto started exploring human consciousness and the subconscious mind in depth.

What was an 'unconscious' state? Was it mere lack of consciousness, or did the conscious mind travel elsewhere in that phase? Did our consciousness travel to the same place when we slept? If not, what was the difference between being asleep and being unconscious? If the travel between the conscious and unconscious states was the dance of similitudes, what role was Arunjit's father playing now?

Many such questions kept arising in Roberto's mind. He had an insatiable urge to unravel the secrets of any knot posed by physics or the life sciences. Of course, that was true of all the great scientists across history. Thus Indrajit, the unconscious human being, had forced Roberto's intelligence to commence several arduous journeys.

Many years had gone by. After Roberto started diving deep into research projects, his interactions with Arunjit dwindled. Roberto took up an offer of an international fellowship at the University of Michigan and returned after four years with a doctorate. But he never cared to affix the 'Dr' before his name. Occasionally, the thought would come to haunt Roberto, whether he was ignoring his best friend in his unremitting travels between different subjects.

When professional jealousy caused some of his colleagues to treat him as an outcast, he felt the need for a sabbatical and decided to return to the village where he had been a frequent guest years before. Arunjit's father was still lying comatose inside that west-facing room.

Though Arunjit insisted that he stay with him, Roberto felt that his unsystematic lifestyle would create issues for the brothers and their families. So, Arunjit arranged for Roberto's stay in Rose Villa, the house that his uncle had bequeathed as a gift to him. Because of the 'March rush', Arunjit was caught in a welter of work, often returning home very late at night. He couldn't even tune the dusty strings of their friendship. Arunjit sincerely wanted to take a fortnight's leave and spend it with Roberto. He wished to tie the Gandhari knot over his eyes once again and spend a night in Roberto's company. What had once been a chore now tempted Arunjit like a nostalgic memory. But his busy schedule inhibited his desire. Arunjit was yet to even catch a glimpse of the Nireeswaran that had created such a tremendous uproar in the village.

That was a destiny meant for Roberto from Bangalore. Whatever the truths or untruths associated with it, Roberto found himself relishing the strange creation of the three friends. It evoked a sense of affectionate curiosity in him. To install a deity in the name of a non-existent god was unheard of. Any institution that walked a different path usually had their trademark flags, memorials and symbols. But never had anyone created an abode for a non-god! Roberto could not ignore the trio who had dreamed up such a thing. The way they had christened themselves the 'Abhasa' was also enterprising. Hence Roberto took the initiative of meeting Antony, Bhaskaran and Sahir.

'You guys deserve hearty congratulations. What an innovative concept!'

The Abhasa swelled with pleasure at this adulation received from a modern-day scientist. They believed that science should be the basis of every new revolution. When they conveyed that opinion to Roberto, he responded: 'Science is not partisan to either belief or non-belief.'

'Does that mean we should denounce Nireeswaran too, just like Eswaran?'

Up in the sky, a dot-like jet plane was tracing a straight path. In the green verdure of the unity of the peepal and mango, the wind was gathering strength.

'Science is all about observation and classification. Now I am observing your Nireeswaran—with the eyes of neither an atheist nor a believer. If I take sides, my view will become prejudiced, though no one will admit that truth, of course. For true art or science, there is no leftist or rightist bias. It is like presuming that the straight line drawn by the jet's trail of smoke is dividing the sky into left and right. The notion of left and right depends solely on the one who looks. If the observer turns his body, what was 'left' becomes 'right' and vice versa. When both are the same, they were seen as different only because of the perspective!' Roberto said.

'Whom are you trying to trick?' Sahir objected. 'Your speech reveals a believer hidden inside! Though, of course, you pretend otherwise! If not, can you give a scientific explanation for those so-called miracles? Historically, too, there was propaganda that a man called Jesus Christ carried out miracles!'

'But friends, my thinking is that Karl Marx could also carry out miracles, much like Jesus the carpenter. But he made himself believe that he couldn't! Marx's belief was his disbelief in his own ability to herald miracles. A non-belief is also a belief. The belief that something exists and a belief that it doesn't are both beliefs. The one who believes he can speak well becomes an orator. The person who believes he cannot, fails to be one. The one who believes he can write, writes. The one who believes he cannot, does not. Life is all about beliefs, right?' Roberto laughed.

'Oh, so you are an idealist, eh?' Bhaskaran asked derisively. 'Just studying science will not suffice. One should have a scientific bent of mind too!' It frustrated him that a scientist from whom they expected support seemed unenthusiastic about their ideas.

'When certain concepts did not capitulate to one's intelligence, someone cleverly named it idealism. For everyone, what they believe in becomes their universe. Can you be sure that animals view all the objects of this world in the same size and shape as we humans do? Why, even you won't be seeing that peepal and mango in the same proportion as I do! Maybe Bhaskaran sees them a hundred times larger or even one-tenth smaller than I do? Don't we see that when a man is passionately in love, he speaks about his lover as being the most beautiful woman in the world? When hatred steps in, with those same eyes he looks at her as the ugliest.

'How many different sights the same eyes see! But that truth remains obscure. If I assert that billions of human beings have different perspectives, can you disprove it? Since the very measuring tools for unifying perspectives are also seen in millions and millions of ways, the differences will never be recognized.'

'A ludicrous theory!'

'Everything is ludicrous, including Nireeswaran. But I like it. What a brilliant idea!' Roberto said.

'Gaze to your heart's content! Shortly, there shall be another rite of hurling it into the canal.'

'Ah, I will get to witness that sight too before returning.' Roberto grinned.

It was natural for anyone researching smells to intrude into the zone of minuteness. Having reached there, Roberto could witness many truths, incomprehensible to normal people, opening up before him. The senses of sight, hearing and smell have microscopic vistas, which could be expanded with due practice. On diving deeper into the imperceptible nuances of objects and their natures, one reached infinitesimal levels. Smells can also be divided repeatedly to reach minuscule levels.

Then one reached an absence of smells. Smell was the grand total of *all absence of smells*.

Strangely enough, Roberto would expound his views to Janaki, who was totally disengaged from science. He knew that if any of the arrogant scientists of the Bangalore lab heard of it, they would howl with laughter.

'Discussing science with a whore? He is off his rocker!' That would be the response. And Roberto accepted that from their point of view, the conclusion might be right.

Once, even Janaki had wondered aloud, 'Where will this crazy research reach finally?'

Roberto's method was never to insist on any particular destination or even bother about it. Rather than spending his life searching for something, he believed in looking at life itself as a kind of search.

Mindful of that innate quest, whenever he went to his friend's house, Roberto would closely observe Arunjit's father for hours as he lay lost somewhere beyond the boundaries of unconsciousness. He was in a comatose state where one doubted whether the person even breathed, a condition where death seemed to have been willingly invited into life! Roberto would try to imagine the time and space where Indrajit's mind travelled.

Spending his time in that manner, Roberto found he was losing his grip on the surroundings. It was like getting entranced in an interesting, deep scientific topic. Whenever he faced inscrutable problems, Roberto would burrow into himself and emerge victorious. Many of the seemingly unanswerable secrets of science had emerged from the depths of mind when it lay still.

One day, while travelling deep through the mind, Roberto tried to recreate the inner universe of the comatose man. As if caught in a whirlpool, he felt himself getting sucked into someone else's consciousness. The human being called Roberto was lost to the world for some time. Hours later, Roberto awakened, and realized that he had forgotten himself and the universe around during that time.

Roberto faced the situation with extreme circumspection. In what emptiness had he lost those missing hours? There was no annihilation of his presence in those moments. His body was very much on earth, but his consciousness resided elsewhere. Roberto had a sudden insight that Indrajit's situation might not be different.

Just as Roberto had forgotten himself for a while, so had Indrajit been oblivious of his own self for decades. *If one consciousness collided with another, could a resonance occur, like it did for matching frequencies?* From the simplest perspective, the mind could be viewed as thought. And a thought was nothing but a vibration. If the vibration has a natural frequency associated with it, why can't a phenomenon similar to acoustic resonance happen?

Though he was not too well versed on the topic, Roberto continued attempting to shake awake Indrajit's consciousness with his own.

Since such an experiment had never been proven anywhere in the world, Roberto did not dare to share his thoughts about it with even Arunjit. Using his liberty as a close friend of the family and seeking special permission from Arunjit's mother, Roberto managed to spend many hours alone with the unconscious man. What began as a curious adventure soon acquired intensity and profundity. After a few days, Roberto found he could experiment even from a distance. His relentless efforts continued, and one day, turning the whole world upside down, Arunjit's father woke up from his twenty-four-year-long coma.

Twelfth Petal: Second Advent

After twenty-four years of unconsciousness, when Indrajit awakened to the world, he was alone in the room. His gaze fell on the annual Malayalam calendar. The red-coloured dates in close proximity confused him. It was the colour of blood, indicating the long holidays during the Holy Week commemorating the passion of Christ. Even when a fiery blaze kindled within, Indrajit felt a nothingness, as if his body had turned cold.

'Sudha!'

Though he meant to shout, only a murmur emerged. When the hailing did not reach the destination, Indrajit decided to get up from bed. But his thought lay trapped inside his mind, and the body did not respond. When his body continued to be immobile, like a rebel who had disregarded the mind's commands for twenty-four years, Indrajit, with a surging anxiety, frantically called out to Sudha again.

Then a face appeared at the door. An unfamiliar young woman. When their eyes met, many emotions flashed on her face with lightning speed. When she raced away, screaming 'Amma', Indrajit was really petrified.

Who was this stranger? When he glanced at the ceiling and the walls, he realized that those, too, were unfamiliar, and Indrajit shrank back in shock. The teak-panelled attic of his family home was no longer to be seen! Instead, a pink ceiling fan hung from a pristine white concrete plafond. Instead of being coated with distemper, the walls gleamed with shimmering new paint. There were light blue curtains dangling from the window. The room had a mélange of smells, including that of medicines. It was as if a ghoul had kidnapped him while asleep and shifted him to some other place!

Before Indrajit concluded his ruminations, there was a flurry of footsteps outside. An ageing woman rushed in panting and caught hold of Indrajit's hand.

In a tearful voice she said, 'Indretta!'

The liberty the old woman took with him irritated Indrajit. Vexatiously, he tried to free his hand and escape her touch, but he couldn't move an inch. Indrajit panicked, wondering what was happening to him. It was as if someone had pinned down his limbs and tethered his life. Who was this middle-aged woman clutching his hand? Her hair was greying, cheekbones protruding and face blanched. When he gathered his strength to push away that obtruding hand, she again pleaded, 'Indretta, it is me, Sudha!'

Indrajit felt a bolt of lightning pass through his spinal cord. After seeing one strange young woman when he had called out to Sudha, now a frumpy middle-aged stranger was peering at him! Was he still in the middle of an appalling nightmare? Why did the world seem topsy-turvy? Where were his sons, Arun and Akhil?

Indrajit heard the middle-aged woman instruct the young stranger, 'Ranjini, call up Arun! Akhil must be in his room! Do ask him to come quickly.'

Indrajit understood that the girl's name was Ranjini. He had never seen her before. But Arun and Akhil were very beloved names.

When the uncomely woman fondled Indrajit's hand, leaning close against him, Indrajit felt a slithering sense of revulsion move through his veins. When she caressed his forehead, Indrajit wished to slap her hand away. But his hand did not rise in obedience to the thought. Though he tried to trace any resemblance to Sudha in the face of the woman, his attempt failed miserably. As he struggled to move, his body continued to be rigid, as if tied to the cot. Indrajit did not realize that his body was in a state of inertia, unwilling to change its habit, having lain motionless for twenty-four years.

A young man came rushing into the room.

'Akhil, look! Your father has opened his eyes!'

Akhil.

Who was this youth with the name of his six-year-old son? He looked more than thirty years old. A well-built young man with a striking resemblance to his own self!

'*Accha*,' the young man, seated next to the woman, called out. 'It is me, Akhil!'

Unable to absorb what was happening around him, Indrajit felt as if something heavy was weighing him down. He seemed to be caught in the grip of some hideous nightmare which had trapped him in the labyrinth of its madness. As Indrajit lay motionless and aghast, as if he was the densest object on the face of earth, Sudha interjected, 'Indretta, see, this is Ranjini. She is Arun's wife. He is at work right now. We have informed him, and he shall be here soon.'

For a moment, Indrajit remembered his fractured arm. And he recollected going to the hospital in a taxi and lying on the surgical table. Eight-year-old Arun and six-year-old Akhil had waved at him as he was being wheeled in for the surgery. The last sound Indrajit had heard was the doctor's question: 'Indrajit, hope you are not scared?'

'Nah!'

Indrajit had pretended a nonchalance that he hadn't really felt. That 'nah' was the last word he had uttered before he became unconscious. The picture of Sudha and the children had filled his mind. Arun had been slightly jittery. Akhil's expression was one of childish curiosity. He was a shy kid. When a transparent mask was placed on Indrajit's face and he slipped away into a pleasant reverie, the faces of his children had been prominent in his memory. Now that he had woken after a brief stint of sleep, he seemed to be outside the operating theatre with a group of strangers.

A car screeched to a halt outside. The sound of a door opening was followed by hurried footsteps, and a fashionably dressed young man burst into view.

'Arun, dearest! Amma's prayer got fulfilled!'

'Amma!' the young man cried, and then he stammered, 'Accha!'

When he came running towards him, Indrajit lost the final vestiges of certainty. In the pleasant reverie into which he had slipped due to the anaesthesia, Indrajit had lost his sense of place and time. The eight- and six-year-olds had turned into strapping young men. Indrajit's twenty-eight-year-old wife had become middle-aged. Indrajit was yet to understand that a slight mishap had stolen more than two decades from his life.

The house became a festive ground. Joy abounded, as if someone beloved had been resurrected from death. As crowds started thronging, there was a commotion all around. Everyone gazed at Indrajit, as if he were some sort of marvel. Arunjit had called Dr Amir, his father's doctor. When the doctor arrived, he immediately controlled the stream of visitors and banned anyone from disturbing Indrajit. More important than the miracle of the return was the survival of the patient.

Dr Amir was aware of similar, albeit rare, episodes, having read about them in medical journals. But he was experiencing one at first hand only now. After twenty-four years of slumber, no human body was likely to be normal. Nothing could be said with certainty about the flow of blood in the brain. The slightest pressure inside the thin capillaries could trigger problems. Though the few cells which had been inflexible against the medicines were cooperative now, there was no telling when another emergency might arise. Such patients needed scrupulous attention. With proper medical care, they might regain their physical strength.

While the uproar around Indrajit progressed, Roberto stood as a bystander, simply observing. He felt an ineffable mental connection with the woken man. During his attempts to pat awake the consciousness of Indrajit, Roberto had become very close to him. Yet he was not confident enough to affirm that it was his inner journeys which had caused Indrajit's awakening. Indrajit was opening the doors of a wondrous possibility before Roberto, of one consciousness influencing another. An experience like the seamless merging of two seas. Though known by different names, all the oceans of the world were one great reservoir.

While Roberto analysed things scientifically, it was the news of a 'miracle healing' that circulated through the village—the juicy snippet that Nireeswaran had brought back to life someone who had been in a coma for twenty-four long years! A new association, which had taken root near the abode of Nireeswaran, came forward to boost the propaganda. They called themselves the Nireeswaran Prarthana Sangham, aka the Niprasa, aka the Association for Praying to Nireeswaran.

True to the name, the association worked as an intermediary for those who wished to solicit Nireeswaran's blessings. The claims of the Niprasa were rather simple. 'We shall supplicate before Nireeswaran on your behalf. The results could be validated by the petitioner.'

If someone had any doubts about the role of a go-between in prayer, the Niprasa had an answer to that too. There were many innocents caught in the rigmarole of daily life and hence unable to devote enough time to prayers. Due to sheer geographical distance, many seekers could not reach Nireeswaran either. Nireeswaran, however, wanted to help such souls too. The Niprasa was meant to help such applicants. The association vouched to work with devotion 24/7. In other words, they were a 'modern, money-back-guarantee prayer group'. The most attractive part of the deal was their guarantee that they would return the full deposit in money order if the prayer did not attain success.

Who would not be enticed by such a promise? When there was nothing to lose and everything to gain, even the cynics wouldn't hesitate to try. The Niprasa invitingly beckoned that fluctuating tendency of minds. When testimonies of wishes being granted started pouring in, the coffers of the Niprasa began to swell, much to the surprise of even its founders. Eventually, many sceptics who had raised an eyebrow at the Niprasa ended up as its members.

The truth of the matter is that neither Sudha nor her household had ever attempted to beseech Nireeswaran through the Niprasa. But Sudha never refuted the news that Nireeswaran was behind Indrajit's miraculous resurrection. Would anyone bother to argue who was behind the wonder, when someone who had been considered dead returned to life? Though she had never stepped outside her four walls with a prayer, someone had stepped in with a blessing.

Whether it was Eswaran or Nireeswaran, Sudha did not bother to confirm or counter any claims.

Indrajit thus became a heavyweight among the Niprasa's list of miracles. Without much delay, the Niprasa updated the advertising board of testimonies to their power, prominently highlighting the latest wonder.

Thirteenth Petal: 'The Niprasa'

Sudharman stood woebegone, beseeching, 'I have no work to do, Nireeswara!' when the thought dawned that 'prayer itself was work'.

Indeed, Sudharman would vouch that it was not his mind but Nireeswaran who had instigated the notion. Otherwise, would the mind get all tingly while praying? When he used to while away time on the footpaths, salivating after girls, such an idea had never come to him. Nor when he lay staring at the sky near the Athmavu, building castles in the air. When he set out to kill himself, frustrated at being denounced as the prodigal son, such a vision had not dawned. Now, fascinated by the tales of Nireeswaran's benedictions, as he stood imploring, albeit experimentally, instead of rebuking him with the words 'You oaf! Better scram!' *who* had provoked the insight that 'prayer itself was work'?

If the mind belonged to oneself, the thoughts should also be one's own. Yet, Sudharman refuted this logic and believed that it was the grace of Nireeswaran. Indeed, certain circumstances had serendipitously come together.

Sudharman's grandmother, Nani Muthassi, unlike her name 'Nani', which meant shy and reticent, was very forward by nature and would shamelessly utter whatever thought crossed her mind. She lived with Sudharman's uncle not too far away. With age, a debilitating knee pain took hold of Muthassi—a sensation akin to young serpents slithering up and down her veins! Whenever they crept through her body, Muthassi writhed in pain. It was when all the local cures had failed to abate the agony that Muthassi chanced to hear about Nireeswaran's prowess. She concluded that the fellow was rather mighty. Right from her youth, Muthassi had a predilection towards the mighty. On hearing the name 'Nireeswaran', apart from thinking that it was another 'Eswaran' like Parameswaran and Jagadeeshwaran, Nani Muthassi, like many others, hadn't mulled over the incongruity in the term.

Though Nani Muthassi wondered about the new avatar, there was no way she could pay a direct visit. Shouldn't the legs yield so that she could reach the place and submit her supplication? But they had declared a strike; only her mind was never in a lay-off mode. As per its whim, it would fly across the sky, reach Nireeswaran and have his darshan.

When Sudharman visited her one day, Nani Muthassi took him aside and pestered him with many questions regarding the big shot who had recently taken up residence in the village. Sudharman had not been a Nireeswaran fan in those days. Thinking on his feet, he had provided answers to his grandmother's ardent queries.

'Are you a believer of Nireeswaran too?' Nani Muthassi asked him with interest.

'Of course!' Sudharman fibbed glibly. Else he would have been drenched in a spate of unwanted probing.

'Did you pray for anything yet?'

'Yes, I have given an application.'

'What application?'

'For a job. Just like Parameswaran!'

'But he is educated! You failed in your tenth standard, you dunce! What job will you get?'

'Some job which a tenth-failed fellow can do.'

If he managed to placate his grandmother with clever answers, she would indulge him with pocket money. That would be good enough for a round of bidis, at least! Nani Muthassi's betel box would carry a few rupee notes at all times. Whenever her well-off children visited, they would tuck away some money in the box, saying, 'Amma, for betel and areca nuts!'

When Nani Muthassi opened her betel box during their chat, Sudharman's heart also opened up with hope. Retrieving two currency notes rather parsimoniously, Muthassi offered them to Sudharman. The Rs 50 note was meant as an offering to Nireeswaran. The Rs 20 note was Sudharman's fee for offering prayers on Muthassi's behalf. The remuneration was for working as an intermediary.

'If the prayer does not get fulfilled and my knee pain stays, you better return the money!' Nani Muthassi was ruthless about money matters. The huge golden earrings dangling from her aged ears swayed with the same intensity that could be sensed in her assertions. Due to the weight of the lead filling inside the golden globes, Muthassi's earlobes had elongated, carrying two huge holes. They were the remnants of a time when beauty was judged on the basis of the elongation of the earlobes! The holy reminder of a golden time which would never return.

Nani Muthassi was known for her sincere prayers and loving obstinacy. Unable to refuse her, Sudharman took the money and assured her that he would submit a prayer on her behalf. Indeed, he had been at his wits' end trying to make ends meet when his grandmother approached him with two currency notes and one prayer. The truth was, Sudharman had been eyeing Muthassi's golden earrings for a while now!

In all fairness, Sudharman did make an offering and pay obeisance to Nireeswaran. But with just one small change: the share meant for Nireeswaran and that meant for him were swapped. As per Sudharman, objectively speaking, Nireeswaran only deserved Rs 20. After all, the fellow was just sitting in one place as an immobile rock! It was Sudharman who had walked back and forth all that way. Since Nireeswaran was not habituated to smoking bidis and drinking tea, he did not have to worry about sundry expenses. Consequently, Nireeswaran was obliged to answer the prayer and forgive the embezzlement of Rs 50.

Though she trusted the newbie avatar, Muthassi continued to ingest ayurvedic concoctions, alongside the application of oils, unguents and prayers. Whether it was the salves and *kashayam* or Nireeswaran's blessing, there was a sudden relief in the pain. The serpentine slithering in her veins reduced drastically.

'Nireeswaran's a trustworthy deity! That is why he granted me solace,' Nani Muthassi swore.

Sudharman, meanwhile, was flummoxed by the outcome of the prayer, since the money for the offering had been smouldering away as tiny bidis between his lips. Nireeswaran, knowing full well that Sudharman was penniless, might have pitied him and granted respite to his grandmother. He felt like singing a paean, much like the Pentecost singers, as a tribute to Nireeswaran: *'How kind, how serene, how very caring about me, the saviour is!'*

Nani started giving free publicity to Nireeswaran, by enlightening those who approached her and actively seeking out those who didn't. She sagely advised other dowagers suffering from chronic ailments to approach Nireeswaran. Most were helpless old women who could hardly move an inch. Nani herself cleared the way ahead for them. A shortcut to Nireeswaran via Sudharman! The next time he dropped in to visit his Muthassi, Sudharman received seven applications and fourteen currency notes. As she handed out the payment along with the neighbourhood prayers, Nani strictly warned Sudharman: 'You'd better ensure that all prayers are fruitful. Else I shall make you pay back every single rupee!'

Obsequiously accepting his grandmother's instructions and deftly interchanging his share with Nireeswaran's, Sudharman managed to pocket Rs 350 in total. It was a virtual money-chain model of finance. Many more seekers approached him from here and there. Sudharman was munificent; Nani Muthassi had ignited a new fire in him.

When the number of the needy grew by leaps and bounds, Sudharman realized the need to form an association. That was how the Niprasa came into being. On hearing about it, Nani Muthassi said, 'Sounds all right! But if any prayer doesn't get fulfilled, make sure you return that money!' The golden earring heaved in Muthassi's long ears.

Sudharman caught a clue in his grandmother's warning. The trust instilled in customers by the tagline 'investment shall be returned, if venture is unsuccessful' meant a great deal in business. It would be considered a benchmark for the product's quality. The assurance that money would be returned if prayers went unfulfilled was bound to garner much attention. Anyone would want to bite the bait!

It turned out to be true.

With three friends, whose main job was also job-hunting, Sudharman organized the Niprasa, and it went from strength to strength.

Niprasa soon became a renowned prayer group. Many were persuaded by the advertisement, 'Out to help those with no time to pray or unable to submit prayer directly.' The assurance of a refund tempted many. Sudharman soon came to realize that the 'money-back guarantee' trend was more successful than he had imagined. It was a real smart deal.

His tenth-failed intelligence was sufficient for him to realize that most things happen by themselves, regardless of prayers. And those who didn't get their prayers answered would hardly turn up to pick a fight. Nobody ever came asking for their money. Those intoxicated with faith would never dare to do anything so bold. The trade secret of the Niprasa was simple: even if they returned the money to the dogmatic few who demanded it, the rest still added up to a resounding profit! What other business yielded massive profits without any investment? Everything was due to Nireeswaran's abundant blessings!

The sudden progress of the wastrel Sudharman, who used to loaf around in the barbershop and thereabouts, became a matter of public debate in the village. Indeed, the barbershop had played no small a role in showcasing the wondrous happenings. Anyone with hair had to visit the barbershop once a month. Barber Maniyan opened his bundle of tales during the haircutting sessions. If his tongue and scissors were to compete with each other on the basis of speed of execution, the scissors would have been spectacularly defeated. Even the cynics were trounced on listening to the exaggerated versions of

Nireeswaran's doings when Maniyan and Sudharman joined hands. Both had the gift of the gab.

'It was no mean struggle to help Indrettan rise again! Seventy-two hours of non-stop prayer!' Sudharman sighed, seated in Maniyan's shop.

'What sort of prayer is that?'

'No stopping for a sip of water even!'

'God! Wouldn't you die then?'

'We were bringing back a dead person, weren't we? Remember, he had been lying in a coma for twenty-four years!'

'Oh, righto!' Everyone nodded assiduously.

However, Sudharman's argument did not fly equally well at all places. The Abhasa attacked it with common sense.

'Didn't you read that a lady in Bombay woke from her coma after eighteen years? Was Nireeswaran in Bombay that day?'

When Antony posed the question with much irony, Sahir and Bhaskaran chortled in glee.

'Stop laughing,' Sudharman bristled. 'One day, you will end up praying too.'

'Oh, sure!' Bhaskaran sneered. 'Hey, listen, we are the creators of Nireeswaran! It means, we are the Eswaran of Nireeswaran! What if there is no stone for you to pray to?'

'As if!'

'One day the village will watch another miracle! The miracle worker's disappearance. It won't be long now,' Antony smirked.

Bhaskaran and Sahir had been waiting for such an emphatic reaction ever since Antony's return from Mangalore. They were crestfallen that their friend was persuading them to be patient and thus unwittingly extending Nireeswaran's lifespan. But they knew that Antony had some plan up his sleeve. He was biding his time for unleashing that cyclone. When Nireeswaran was sent off to Yama's abode, the nerves of the village would be thoroughly shaken.

Throwing Sudharman into deep anxiety, the trio stared challengingly at him. Their appearance was that of warriors who were already declared winners in an impending battle. Sudharman felt that they had drawn the battle lines against him personally. Soon, the great confidence with which he used to wax eloquent about Nireeswaran's miracles started abating.

Following the strategy that one's allies had to be informed in advance about an imminent war, Sudharman relayed the developments to Sumitran, who, in his turn, testified that he had a strong hunch about an impending catastrophe himself. When the creators turned into annihilators, who could stop the carnage?

Was Nireeswaran destined for a premature demise? If that happened, an obscure emptiness would swallow the whole village. Nireeswaran's name had taken root so deeply into the earth that it was impossible to contemplate such a possibility.

As he stood staring dejectedly at Nireeswaran, Sumitran heard the fluttering of a bird's wings amid the branches of the Athmavu. He was astounded at the stunning spread of colours! A peacock was staring down at them, its neck jerking spasmodically.

Sumitran wondered how a peacock, unseen in their region, could end up in the Athmavu. It must have lost its way. And now it was perched at the zenith of the tallest tree in the village.

'What if the divine vehicle of Nireeswaran was a peacock? Otherwise, why would it come and perch here?' Sumitran wondered aloud.

'True,' Sudharman agreed.

The peacock, however, did not confine itself to the Athmavu. Whenever it felt like, the bird flew around the vicinity. Swooping down on isolated places, it pecked around free-spiritedly.

One day, Sudha saw a peacock with its tail spread splendidly. The shimmering body, with its iridescent blue and aquamarine plumage, was eye-catching. There was a small crown on its head. The look in its eyes was all-knowing. The neck jerked intermittently, as if reacting to the sounds around. It was then that Sudha first realized that a peacock did not need rainclouds to spread its feathers.

When she threw a fistful of rice, it pecked around a bit before taking flight and settling at the pinnacle of the Athmavu.

Fourteenth Petal: Incompatibilities

Twenty-four years, what a long time that was! Two lifetimes of Vanvas. The universe had shed its skin multiple times in between and changed its hues. The years buried in sleep had inexorably alienated the man from this world.

Indrajit could not fathom what had happened to him. When he went off to sleep, he was thirty-two and the father of two young sons. When he woke up, his eldest son was thirty-two himself! It seemed that, overnight, the span of a generation had passed by and he had turned into a grandfather. The years of sleep hadn't touched either his body or mind.

When his grandchildren returned from school, they gazed with amazement at their grandfather, whom they had never seen awake. For them, until yesterday, Grandpa meant an immobile human doll. Their eyes curiously observed him, as if he were a doll suddenly brought to life with a battery. How interesting it was to see a doll start moving, overcoming stillness!

On seeing his grandkids, Indrajit recollected that his own children were the same age when he had gone off to sleep. They had grown up when he was comatose. He couldn't experience their childhood, adolescence or youth. The earth had used his sleep as the axis while completing twenty-four revolutions around the sun.

Here was his wife, who had made love to him just the day before, with all the enfeeblements and wretchedness of age. Indrajit could not make peace with the fact that he had turned into a fifty-six-year-old man overnight. Even after a quarter of a century, his mind remained the same. The exuberant vigour was all-pervasive, reinforcing his youthful identity.

Indrajit could not arise from the bed even after clawing his way back into consciousness. Twenty-four years of unremitting sleep had turned his muscles inert. Like a bird that had forgotten to fly, not having stretched its wings for years, Indrajit struggled and failed to transmit the command for movement to his limbs. When he lay like a dead body, unable to even open his mouth, there was no question of normal food. Fluids had been his only diet. All the lengthy tubes inside him might have shrunk by now! Yet, when he felt hungry, what Indrajit wished to have first was warm rice gruel. When Sudha fed him spoonfuls of salted rice water, he remembered his childhood and his mother's love.

'I . . . I . . . want to see Acchan and Amma . . .' Indrajit murmured weakly.

But the earth having revolved many times, that wish would never be fulfilled. His parents had passed away, carrying their never-ending grief over their son's pathetic condition.

Mother was the first to return. Till the end, Amma had sat beside him, hoping for a slight moan or a feeble movement. It was through incessant chanting of hymns, with a 108-beaded *rudraksha*, that she traversed the period.

She prayed incessantly that her son be spared and her life be taken instead. All those prayers had been submitted at the dais of the temple which was situated close to the home. There was no Nireeswaran at that time. Even if there were, Amma wouldn't have paid him a visit. She was an ardent devotee of Rudra and could not imagine any spiritual sojourn that did not include him. Her incantation of the Panchakshara mantra was such that she experienced the divine spots in the body where each syllable reverberated. The practice of *japa* eventually detached her from the materialistic world. Occasionally, she forgot even her son's state. And so Amma died serenely, as if she'd totally forgotten the vicissitudes of her life.

Indrajit's father was diametrically opposite to his mother. A tenacious idealist who refused to bow before any god, he firmly believed that man was the supreme being in the universe. But he was mature enough to never dissuade his wife from her beliefs. Both belief and non-belief had to attain ripeness in each individual independently. Namasivayam, Indrajit's *acchan*, never had any inhibition in venturing inside a temple, or even into the sanctum sanctorum if needed. Though Namasivayam knew that his name was incongruous with his atheism, he never undertook the radical step of changing it.

Namasivayam led an extraordinarily moral life. He never drank, smoked or looked at strange women with immoral intention. He would never raise his voice at anyone and remained serenely dignified. Indrajit's father was a true humanitarian, for whom serving humanity was serving God. The purity of his actions outdid that of any believer.

When his beloved wife died, Namasivayam took it in his stride, with philosophical calm. After conducting all the customary rites for her and forewarning that he needed none for himself, Indrajit's father followed his wife in a week's time. Namasivayam's demise exemplified his strong conviction that life was a bubble which floated upward and burst into nothingness.

In life, the brave rationalist had been perturbed only by his son's condition. Though he did not believe in miracles, Namasivayam had longed for his son to recover miraculously. By accepting the fact that life was nothing but the interspace between yearning and fulfilment, Namasivayam lived it out, and returned whence he came.

Truly, if any god existed, he would have been forced to descend in the heavenly chariot to fetch Namasivayam's soul. If a judgement was decreed after evaluating the account book of life consisting of right and wrong deeds, the unbeliever would have been escorted to Kailasa with chants of 'Om Namasivayah'.

Indrajit lay silent, not knowing that his parents had died within a week of each other.

But he could now recollect that even while sleeping, in his inert state, he had encountered his father and mother. Not as a dream, but as real as life! His amma was smiling at him sweetly. His acchan fondled his hair with infinite love and affection. Indrajit had felt the moist compassion of his father's caress. He experienced the fragrance of his acchan's presence, which always instilled a tremendous sense of security within him.

After waking from the coma, Indrajit couldn't believe that his parents were no more. He was sure that they had been with him while he slept. Did it mean that the unconscious contained another consciousness within? Since his experience was real, Indrajit could not denounce the inimitable presence of his parents. When he was in *that consciousness*, he hadn't known *this consciousness*. Now that he was in *this reality*, he was not aware of *that reality*. Indrajit was bemused: Which consciousness was true, and which one was to be adopted as the base to discern the other?

Indrajit was also unaware of the cases filed against the hospital during his coma. The specialists, comprising doctors, advocates and police officers, had often visited to examine the comatose patient. The court had finally ordered that he be shifted home, since keeping him in the hospital forever was impractical. Sudha was given special training to take care of a comatose patient. Her life became confined by the limits of the cot where Indrajit lay asleep.

Sudha's life became deformed in the protracted drudgery of taking care of her bedridden spouse for twenty-four years. She aged before her time, caught in a vortex of excruciating anxieties and woes. A lot of money had been spent on Indrajit's treatments. Though they tried every medical treatment available—allopathy, Ayurveda, homeopathy, Unani—nothing helped Indrajit. Since he couldn't ingest food, fluids were given through tubes to sustain his life. Sudha did all the chores by herself. In the past twenty-four years, never had anyone else been allowed to remove the excrement, clean her husband or feed him. She was adamant that nobody should ever feel Indrajit was a burden. For that, she limited her life stoically within the four walls of the room.

Never did the woman step out for her sons' weddings or any celebration associated with her grandchildren. Indrajit's body had eventually shrunk to a skeletal form. But Dr Amir, the family doctor, made an unnerving observation. When his consciousness was wandering, Indrajit's body slowed down. Now, even when he had aged to fifty-six, not a single hair had turned grey. His body cells were exhibiting the characteristics of a thirty-two-year-old. Dr Amir saw this as a wonder in medical science.

Whenever she gazed at Indrajit, Sudha felt that the seemingly sleeping man was celebrating an eventful inner life. It could be in the realm of dreams. Though the body existed in the mortal world, the mind was possibly traversing elsewhere.

Sudha's hair turned silver as time passed. Dark circles became visible under her eyes. Lines showcasing life's burden furrowed her forehead. Her cheekbones stood out prominently. Since she had carried more than her share of life's burdens, her body became weary and old. Though she was just fifty-one years old, Sudha looked nearly sixty-five. Yet these physical changes hadn't caught up with her husband. Except for the frailty caused by the lack of proper food, his body did not exhibit signs of even two years of ageing.

Since Indrajit was particular about shaving his face every day, Sudha had continued with that ritual all those years. She knew that an unconscious person did not need such fripperies. But she endeavoured to keep him as Indrajit would have maintained himself had he been awake. Even her sons would grumble at that daily shaving rite.

'As if you have nothing else to do, Amma! Do you think Acchan is aware of all this? Of course, you should take care of him. But what's the use of shaving a comatose man?'

'Am I troubling anyone? This is my decision. You won't understand,' Sudha would retort.

Sudha felt that Indrajit was conversing with her inner self. She would not even let her sons touch their father. Even if they were closely related, certain situations might incite in them repugnance for their father. She couldn't bear to think about such a state of affairs and took care to prevent them.

Every day she wiped clean Indrajit's body with medicated water. Whenever Sudha touched each part of the body that had once entranced her, she wished that the man, who would get aroused at her mere touch, would stir back to life. Steeped in that hope, she tenderly caressed him from head to toe, behind the shut bedroom door. She even lay naked next to the inert man, embracing him ardently. Since Indrajit had always been an extravagant sensualist, Sudha, swept in a bout of foolishness, fantasized that he would respond.

If anyone had an inkling of her doings, they might have denounced her as wanton. But such interludes triggered a resilience in her, motivating her to carry on with life. Sudha lived in the delusion that Indrajit was always with her.

Due to Sudha's meticulous care, Indrajit, unlike others in his condition, always had an exquisite freshness about him. But with every passing year, Sudha came to realize that she was growing older and that the distance between her and Indrajit, yet untouched by age, was increasing.

As taking care of Indrajit became a habit for her, Sudha stopped stepping out even to visit the temple. She would update her sleeping husband about the various stages of their children's growth, about Arun's wedding, the birth of their grandchildren and the rest. That, too, was linked to her belief that the sleeping man was listening to her keenly.

Sometimes, life is sustained because of such apparently irrational beliefs—a belief in destiny or God or any other notion.

The news about the miracles occurring at the Athmavu had spread far and wide. Sudha had never visited Nireeswaran's abode, nor paid attention to any propaganda. But she had seen the change in Sumitran with her own eyes. He was the handyman at her place, easily satisfied with food and a few currency notes. When he spoke with clarity one day, Sudha had been taken aback. Though she had heard about Nireeswaran's glories, sometimes in larger-than-life detail, from Sumitran and others, Sudha had reached the stage beyond prayers by then. She never probed for any clarification.

But now that Indrajit had unexpectedly opened his eyes and started talking, Sudha found herself equally delighted and horrified. In a few days' time, Indrajit could sit up in the bed. A physiotherapist came to train him to use his limbs. Eventually, he started to walk around. Both food and nutrition reached his cells and fortified them. On seeing her husband, freshly shaved and bathed, with a whiff of aftershave about him, Sudha stood thunderstruck.

That thirty-two-year-old male, bursting with vitality . . . with the same virile perfection that unendingly tempted her, the smooth-shaven face, the well-trimmed moustache, that intoxicating look in his eyes, his muscular arms and broad chest.

Was this her husband?

As if another young man of her children's age had stepped inside her home . . .

Standing before her youthful husband as his elderly wife, Sudha panicked, as though the roots of her existence were being brutally hewed.

Fifteenth Petal: Digambara

Barber Maniyan's salon was opposite Nireeswaran's abode, at the right side of the junction formed by three roads. Seeing the board saying 'Mani Cutting Saloon', which amply illustrated the language skills of the proprietor, many passers-by sniggered at the insinuation of getting one's balls snipped off, but Maniyan did not care two hoots. Out of the reach of the sarcastic laughter was Chettiyar's makeshift shop and, after a short distance, the toddy shack of Satyanesan. The liquor shop was far away from Nireeswaran; and many objected to the barbershop situated opposite to the deity. The term 'barbershop' itself had as much of the stink of a 'shop' as a toddy shop.

Maniyan inferred that Ghoshayatra Annamma was the one behind the gossip. There was no specific reason for Nireeswaran to be averse to a barbershop. Annamma, on the other hand, nurtured a grudge against the barber. The cause was a recent boundary dispute which had broken out between them.

Spending his lifetime's earnings, Maniyan had lately purchased a rice field adjoining Annamma's property. But Annamma's goat cared not a whit for the title deed stamped by the local sub-registrar. Due to the lack of cultivation, couch grass had spread lushly inside the field and on the bunds surrounding it. The goat wandered lavishly through the field, swam about in knee-deep water, pissed happily while swimming, feasted sumptuously on the grass and chewed its cud as if ruminating on the past. Although Maniyan was the main investor, it was Annamma's goat which harvested the crop. With its tummy ballooning out from gorging on rice saplings, the nanny goat waddled around with its heavy udders, haughtier than Annamma herself.

When Maniyan came to complain about the goat's illegal transgressions into his territory, not only did Annamma ignore the grievance by insisting that her goat would never indulge in such shamelessness, she also scolded him soundly. Maniyan did not give in either. When both started attacking each other like fighter cocks, Ghoshayatra Annamma's four daughters stepped out of the house in a procession as usual, to support their mother. When the verbal duel became heated to explosive proportions, the natives anticipated something eventful would happen.

Those who knew that Annamma had no other option but to pull up her clothes when pushed to the limits, loafed around unobtrusively. The four girls displayed a temperament that seemed to suggest that if the situation so warranted, they too would follow their mother's example. The mere thought of such a possibility caused much churning of youthful blood in the vicinity.

Maniyan was hollering louder than Annamma. 'Don't you dare play with me like the others! Edi, I am pretty bad!' he growled.

'I am even worse! Why don't you check around a bit?' Annamma did not give an inch.

'I can't be bothered to check the stinking status of any bitch! If the goat strays into my field again, I shall show you . . . !'

As soon as Maniyan said those words, Ghoshayatra Annamma, her pride wounded severely, spat out fire and brimstone. 'Pthbhu! I shall show you before that, blasted man!'

In a manoeuvre faster than her talk, Annamma hauled up her mundu. By the time her daughters wondered whether their mother's enthusiasm had overstepped the limit, Annamma's naked waist, above her fat, round thighs, stood revealed to the public. A lot of hisses and haws erupted from the mouths of the male onlookers, whether middle-aged and or in their dotage. The young men stood electrified, unable to breathe.

The spectators concluded that Maniyan had jumped into the battle pit without any idea about Annamma's tricks and would soon beat a hasty retreat. But sending them all into a tizzy, Maniyan freed himself from his own mundu and the rest of the restraints before stepping forth challengingly. 'Edi! Come let us do it right here!'

Annamma had never expected that sort of debacle. Gaping at his naked manhood, she scampered back into her house. Intermittently glancing back at Maniyan's Digambar avatar, her four daughters accompanied their mother in a procession. It was the first major defeat that Annamma had faced in her life. Indeed, it was the start of Ghoshayatra Annamma's decline and Barber Maniyan's ascent.

When the Nireeswaran temple gained popularity, Maniyan felt like a money tree had blossomed next to him. There were no specific rituals followed in the worship place. Hence Maniyan took the initiative of spreading the news that for attaining one's wishes, the shearing of one's hair was very propitious. During his pilgrimages, Maniyan had stood open-mouthed at the mountains of hair heaped near the Palani and Tirumala temples. If he too had so many 'heads' to 'chop', he might have turned into a *crorepati* himself!

'Eda, barber! Won't you stop shaving heads if you become a crorepati?' the Lord seemed to be asking Maniyan.

'No way, I shall never give up my assigned job,' Maniyan murmured slyly. Though it was Eswaran whom he had assured thus, it turned out to be Nireeswaran who blessed him abundantly.

The news spread that it was beneficial to shave one's head in order to appease Nireeswaran. Maniyan had facilitated it by tipping the Niprasa fellows handsomely. As a return gift, Sudharman ensured that everyone who came to seek their mediation was tonsured by Maniyan. No mean economist himself, Maniyan started a facility next to his barbershop. Entrusting a lad with the work, he started making some additional money.

After reaping the benefits at the shop, Maniyan went on to reap the harvest at his rice field. When the paddy heaps were measured, it was a golden crop. Maniyan felt that there were no limits to Nireeswaran's benevolence. Where on earth could you find a deity with its face turned towards a barbershop? When the thought struck him deeply, Maniyan started praying to Nireeswaran before setting his scissors to the first 'head' which came his way every morning. After touching the head, he would reverently touch his own forehead and close his eyes in remembrance of the deity. Like offering the first fruit of the field to the deity, he would inwardly submit the initial crop of hair before Nireeswaran.

Maniyan's barbershop was a provincial library of sorts, filled with spicy news and local publications with a flair for investigation. Then there were the voluptuous cinema magazines, with their seductive, scintillating pin-ups. These were the temptations which drew a lot of customers, before any sprouting of new hair, to 'Mani Cutting Saloon'. There were thirsty readers who never wished to miss an instalment of serialized stories with titles like 'Ammini's Golden Fruit' and 'Luscious Night'. Mani Cutting Saloon thus accepted the heavy responsibility of being a cultural centre, of fostering the habit of reading in the citizenry. Antony, Bhaskaran and Sahir, who were small-time readers, submerged themselves in serious reading bouts at Maniyan's barbershop.

Maniyan never banned political discussion in his shop; rather, he was titillated by modern politics himself. He relished watching how the ruling party and the opposition joined hands to create a theatre of the absurd. To the background tune of ever snipping scissors, Maniyan's shop was chock-a-block with political chatter. It was his father who had sagaciously told Maniyan that any customer becomes devoted to the barber who gabbles non-stop and would not miss his next appointment. Maniyan was also adept at head massage, which he practised selectively on meek customers; the consequent blood circulation ensured that they came in search of his barbershop the next time. By using both his magical fingers and gift of the gab, Maniyan lured his customers in for the next visit.

Whenever the ringing of bells was heard from Nireeswaran's abode, Maniyan would immediately drop his scissors on the table, untie his hitched-up mundu and, folding his hands deferentially, gaze in the deity's direction.

Antony, who shrugged away many peccadilloes of Maniyan, couldn't contain himself at that sight. He snapped at the barber, 'Huh! Have you gone mad too?'

'You three instigated this madness . . . and now you question me?'

'Maniyan! That was a mock consecration!'

'I have no idea. You see, I find times are good. So many heads to tonsure. Nireeswaran has been bountiful in his blessings!'

'Yes, you shall be anointed as the barber-in-chief when you ascend to *swarga lokam* after conking off!' Antony did not mince his words.

'But swarga belongs to Eswaran. Who knows about Nireeswaran's kingdom?' Maniyan countered spiritedly.

'Using the similarity theory, I propose *niswarga lokam* as an alternative,' Bhaskaran grinned.

Sahir remained silent all through that exchange. He had sunk into the depths of a woman's navel that could hold a gallon of oil. Extricating him from the film magazine would have entailed a pulley, one sturdy rope and the muscle power of four or five men.

It was then that Roberto strolled into the barbershop. Maniyan had granted a new lease of life to the reluctant Roberto a month before, with a shaving-and-cutting session. The scientist was not habituated to shaving regularly. In Roberto's view, there was no need to trim what was growing naturally. But Janaki insisted that he should shave at least once in two days and get a haircut every month without fail. When she opined that he would look human only then, Roberto couldn't help chuckling.

Someone had to remind him that he was human and, lest he forgot it, had to look like a human being. And that was how the miracle of getting a haircut two months in a row happened in Roberto's life. He indulged Janaki by allowing her to take such small liberties with him. Besides, the best place to gauge a village's pulse was its barbershop.

The moral police of the village suspiciously watched the scientist who interacted closely with the fallen woman. For Janaki, a self-declared whore, there was no need to feel any twinge of shame in being seen with Roberto. Besides, there was scope for honour as well! Meanwhile, Roberto treated gossip with the same indifference he had for cutting his hair and shaving his beard.

Considering the uncertainty regarding the time it would take for the research on smells to attain shape, Roberto immensely valued Janaki's contributions, which were helping him cross the initial hurdles. In the unbiased world of science, there was no difference between a prostitute, a murderer or a thief.

Hence he never felt the need to consider Janaki inferior in any way. But that remained an exclusive insight of Roberto's. It was different for the rest of people.

When Roberto sat down for his haircut, Antony, who was seated behind him, stared at the common mirror ahead of them and asked casually, 'What's up with your research? Any notable progress?'

'Ah, it is going on. Rather vast subject, isn't it?'

'How long will you be around these parts?'

'Can't say exactly! Maybe a few weeks . . . or even an infinite period.'

'Why such uncertainty? Isn't the Research Centre particular about deadlines?'

Roberto laughed. 'Yes, sure . . . there are some considerations. But if needed, one has to change those, right?'

'Won't it affect your job?'

'Living and discovering is the main job. The Research Centre cannot fetter one at all times, you know?'

That was Roberto's rather perilous perspective. He had seen many who had confused their lives with research, losing their own selves and unable to do anything else. After retirement, they had to fearfully start learning from scratch the business of living! Lacking any meaningful goals to hold on to, bereft of the status and privileges for which they had toiled relentlessly, they faced the predicament of having nothing to do and slowly rusted away . . . They had to begin their real life from that point onwards.

Roberto did not believe in such an approach. In his opinion, the flow of life should be uninterrupted even after retirement. And hence life itself was a search for him. It wasn't meant to be shackled by the four walls of the research laboratory.

'Looking at the way your research seems to be progressing, there is a chance of your settling here . . .' Antony smirked. Maniyan, who was busy chopping off hair, felt that Antony's words were sharp as his razor.

'Nah, there is no such plan.'

'Well, lapping up the milk with eyes shut usually prevents anyone from looking ahead. The villagers are watching your live-in relationship! That too with a degraded woman!'

Observing the sudden shift in mood as Antony aimed his weapon below the belt, both Maniyan and Bhaskaran were startled. A change of topic was not warranted at that juncture.

'Who said she is degraded?' Roberto asked peaceably.

'I say so! How many times I myself have degraded her!' Antony leered.

'Well, that's interesting! When you degraded Janaki, how come she alone was degraded? Since you were involved in the process, you too are degraded, right? But I won't bar you from entering my house if you come!' Roberto smiled.

'Don't act smart!' Antony blazed, with wounded pride. 'There are worthies here who have been questioning the goings-on!'

'Oh, moral policing? That is actually psychological anarchy. Good to know that such fellows exist too! When you get the time, do come around to check the goings-on.'

After paying Maniyan, Roberto stepped out nonchalantly. The haircut and shave made him look more handsome than before, like a serpent which had shed its old skin. Nobody ever expected such a strong rejoinder from someone who appeared naive.

Though he should have displayed loyalty towards Antony, Bhaskaran felt a deep admiration for Roberto. He had been disgusted by Antony's unreasonable attitude many times in the past too. But Bhaskaran never dared to voice his views.

When the temple bells clanged non-stop from Nireeswaran's abode, Maniyan hastily untucked his mundu and folded his hands worshipfully. Seeing him stand meditatively until the bells ceased to toll, Antony hurled the newspaper he was holding and stomped out of the barbershop. Looking at the way Antony had stridden away, Bhaskaran was worried that Antony would deliver a tight slap to Eswaran Embrandiri before seizing Nireeswaran's statue and dumping it somewhere far away!

As he hurriedly followed Antony, Bhaskaran called out, 'Sahir, aren't you coming?'

Grumbling to himself that the wrangling shouldn't have ended so soon, Sahir reluctantly extricated himself from the deep well with the gallon-worthy circumference and followed his friends.

Sixteenth Petal: The Search

Indrajit too was passing through moments of anguish. His greatest problem was that there was nobody around who could appreciate his experiences, with due gravity, while he was asleep. Arunjit had laughed it off as a mere 'hallucination'. Apparently, he had read in psychology texts that such flights of fancy were common during the suspended state between consciousness and unconsciousness.

'I have read many books too. But reality and books are two different things, Arun! If what I underwent was a hallucination, even our current conversation should be termed as one. Because I experienced those with the same clarity I feel talking to you now.'

Roberto, who was seated nearby, wished to intervene and stop the conversation. He knew that Indrajit's experiences were not to be slighted. It was foolish to discuss certain matters with men who could not appreciate them. They were limited by their intractable, thick shells and could not emerge from them. It was not their fault; the whole edifice had been designed thus. If an argument broke out, they obdurately stuck to their own viewpoint. That was why the ones who knew the truth preferred silence. The Tamil phrase *Kandavar minduvathillai*—'Those who have seen, shall not speak out'—served as its testimony.

Since Roberto felt it was wise to divert the topic tactfully, he did so. He decided to interact closely with Indrajit when Arun wasn't around and try to understand his angst in its wholeness.

It turned out to be a great relief to Indrajit too. Despite the significant age gap between them, Roberto responded to Indrajit's predicament with equanimity. And so, Indrajit afforded him the status of a good friend, as if Roberto were his contemporary. The man who had set about searching for smells had ended up at the edge of something more daunting! New knowledge appealed to Roberto like an exquisite taste in his palate—possessing both quality and value.

Though his sabbatical was coming to an end, Roberto decided to stay back longer. What Indrajit revealed was astounding! Roberto sent a formal letter to the Research Centre requesting for an extension of leave. Even if he were threatened with a dismissal, Roberto would not have swayed. That was why he remained Roberto. He informed only Janaki and Indrajit about his leave application.

However much a person tries, things will get revealed to an intimate friend, as true friendship has a mutual understanding much like a marriage.

'Nowadays, you are closer to Acchan than to me, right?' Arunjit asked Roberto one day.

'Why do you say that?'

'I mean, Acchan seems to discuss everything exclusively with you. And you seem to be hiding many things from me.'

'There is an element of possessiveness in all relationships, including friendship! Isn't there, Arun?' Roberto smiled. 'You are my best friend. And I hold your father in the same regard as mine. One fact is clear, Arun. There are some incomprehensible secrets behind your father's unconscious phase. Some arcane truths as yet unfathomable to mankind. Your father needs the support of a good friend now. That is what I provide to him. It would be easier for him to disclose experiences to me which he might hesitate to share with a son. Don't find fault with it, Arun!'

'I did not mean it that way!'

'That's fine. We go back a long way, don't we, Arun?'

The conversation ended there. Arunjit never again attempted to raise the topic. He was already entangled in weighty matters. The banking job required accountability. And alongside, he was balancing the rest of his responsibilities. He often returned late from the bank, on the verge of collapsing from exhaustion. It made Arun feel guilty that he had not found time for a heart-to-heart chat with Roberto as yet.

Friendships tend to rust away unless regularly sharpened. If stretched beyond the limit of elasticity, not only metals, but even friendships snap. Arun probably initiated that conversation with Roberto, owing to his remorse over the lack of time for nurturing their friendship.

Roberto found himself contemplating the odd equations involved in relationships. Nonetheless, his mind was also circling another intriguing gridlock. How come twenty-four years had left Indrajit untouched? Why hadn't his body cells aged?

Dr Amir hadn't been able to provide Roberto with a satisfactory answer. 'Such resurrections are very rare, and it could be another rarity that the body did not age!' That answer still demanded a scientific explanation. In Ayurveda there was a branch of treatment to regain youth and banish old age: Kayakalpa Chikitsa. But Indrajit hadn't undergone any.

'See, there have been many cases of patients falling into a coma due to the mishandling of anaesthesia. Most such patients die, after spending many years in a comatose state. Few have regained consciousness, once in a blue moon. But this man has upset the applecart of my knowledge.'

Though Dr Amir had discussed the case threadbare with many doctors, none could provide him with an answer to his satisfaction regarding the man who had woken up youthful after twenty-four years. The arrogance of medical science, that everything could be devolved into few formulae, seemed to shatter at some unknown point. It was all well that people spread tall tales about Nireeswaran's miracle, although Dr Amir felt no inclination to believe in such balderdash propagated by the Niprasa.

'Then how do we explain this scientifically?' Roberto persisted.

'I have no clue! Dr Roberto, do you believe in miracles?'

'Well, even if something is acclaimed as a miracle, it should still have a scientific reason. Miracles stay as miracles when we cannot interpret them in the language of science.' Roberto shrugged.

Roberto's nature was to adamantly undo the knots of a puzzle until it was solved. He had to discover a solution from within the universe of his own deliberations.

It was at this perplexing juncture that Dr John Kuruvila of the Lourdes Hospital offered a suggestion to Dr Amir. 'Why don't you discuss the matter with Dr Krishnan Ezhuthachan? I am sure he will be able to help you.'

Roberto had heard much about Dr Krishnan Ezhuthachan. He was an expert in parapsychology, and many internationally famous papers in the subject were ascribed to him. He was also a visiting professor at many universities worldwide. Dr Krishnan was renowned for effortlessly integrating the boundaries of science and philosophy. Now, having left behind the world travels, Dr Krishnan had settled in a solitary house situated on a hill. He was nearing eighty.

The trip to his residence was rather intimidating. After parking the vehicle on the nearest road, one had to walk through a forested region for almost 7 kilometres to reach Dr Krishnan's home. It was surmised that the inaccessibility and seclusion had been deliberately created. Since the visitors were few and far between, the old man enjoyed an unblemished tranquillity. A small house, a helping hand, a verdant jungle and lots of pets.

'If someone could light up the way, let it be so.' That was Roberto's motivation for searching out Dr Krishnan. The question roiling in him prompted him to set out on this quest. If food provided energy to the common person, Roberto obtained the same through the investigation of some mystery with no acceptable answers. He wished to have a companion in that adventure. However, neither Arunjit nor Dr Amir could spare the time. The only option was to travel by himself.

'The advantages of being single!' Roberto joked to Janaki. 'One can start off at any time for any place.'

'Yes, I understand. It is the same with me. Nobody to seek approval from!'

'Do you want to come along?' Roberto asked.

'To tell you the truth, yes. But I won't, even if you insist,' Janaki replied.

'Why not?'

'Women like me shouldn't be seen around with men like you. Your reputation will suffer.'

'Oh, my reputation has already gone for a toss! The hoi polloi is all saintly in nature if considered in totality. But if you catch them one by one, they turn out to be rascals! Let the moral police scream themselves hoarse. If you are interested, do come along. I have no issues, Janaki.'

'No, I feel it will be better for you to go alone.'

Nudged by an inner prompt, Roberto visited Nireeswaran's abode that evening. He stared at the board the Niprasa had put up. Roberto felt a tug of intrigue. The Niprasa had acquired much fame in recent days. Any incident of significance in the village was attributed to the Niprasa's unceasing prayers. When he stepped into the Niprasa's office, Roberto caught a glimpse of the huge list of their 'achievements' displayed prominently. Sudharman and his friends welcomed Roberto with folded hands and exaggerated politeness.

'Please come in, sir . . . What sort of prayer do you want?'

'Right now, I have no prayer to offer. Just wanted to look around.' Roberto smiled.

Roberto's eyes flicked across the list of marvels. To his utter surprise, Indrajit's recovery was also mentioned there. Roberto was unaware of anyone submitting such a plea.

'Of course, sir, someone did,' Sudharman protested vociferously. 'There is a girl called Megha that you do not know of! Indrettan was trying to save her when he met with the accident . . . then the whole rigmarole with the anaesthesia happened . . . Perhaps that is why she submitted the prayer rather quietly.'

That was news for Roberto. He hadn't heard much about the incident which had led to Indrajit's coma. Roberto decided to learn more from Arunjit later. Before leaving for his bank, Arun had arranged for a jeep to take Roberto to Dr Krishnan Ezhuthachan's place. Since it was a steep climb up, a jeep had been chosen for the journey.

It soon struck Roberto that the journey was going to be far more challenging than anticipated. Leaving aside the main road, the vehicle traversed the paths that twisted and turned through many unfamiliar areas. After consulting with the locals, he finally reached a point where the jeep had to be left behind. Roberto made friends with the lone shopkeeper while drinking a sherbet. He was informed about the distance to Dr Krishnan's residence. Roberto purchased a few paltry things from the shop, albeit unnecessarily, for fortifying the friendship. After entrusting the jeep to the shopkeeper's care, he moved towards his destination.

Roberto walked through a hill slope where goats were out grazing. A few streams cut off his path at many spots. They touched his feet and ran away gurgling, without looking back. The goatherds gazed at him curiously. They were mostly very young, poor boys.

Roberto saw the crown of the hill from afar. It took him almost three-and-a-half hours to climb to the small hut built with bamboo and palm thatch. The world-famous parapsychologist, much valued as a visiting professor in five continents, stroked his long, snow-white beard and smiled generously. His silvery hair grew long and curled against his shoulders. Except for the luxuriant grey hair, the body did not betray any signs of ageing.

'The second human face I have glimpsed in four months,' Dr Krishnan grinned. 'That might make you wonder about the first. Certainly not mine, because I don't keep a mirror! Though we see *with* our eyes, we never *see* the eyes, do we? We only know the sight, not the eye. Gopala . . . !'

When the old man hailed loudly, Gopalan, or Gopalakrishnan, came racing from the backyard.

'This is the lone human being that I get to see . . . Gopala, can you please fetch a tender coconut for the visitor? He must be tired after that long trek.'

When Gopalan went off for the coconut, Roberto started explaining the purpose of his visit. Dr Krishnan listened patiently, with his eyes shut. Maybe he was concentrating more on the words, or perhaps he was seeing certain sights behind the eyelids. After listening to the whole matter, Dr Krishnan's face lit up with that enchanting smile once more. He was wearing just a saffron mundu. His chest hair was curly and a pristine white. His face was radiant, and there seemed to be a silvery opalescence about him.

'It's a very peculiar case!' Dr Krishnan closed his eyes and seemed to be meditating. 'What happened to that man's twenty-four years? Did he . . . did he really travel that fast in his sleep?'

'Travel fast?' Roberto interjected.

'I will elaborate . . . Did you say that Dr Amir sent you here? He is a smart doctor. Above all, he is a truly altruistic human being. A doctor should definitely be caring. Indeed, that constitutes 90 per cent of the qualifications needed for a healer. The degree certificate carries just the remaining 10 per cent value!'

Dr Krishnan paused a bit.

'Few paradoxes strike me now. I hope you will not get confused further. Since you are a scientist, you will appreciate it better. The speed I talk about is a law in physics. Our lives have certain calculations connected to them. For example, we know about the number of seconds in a minute and the number of minutes in an hour and so forth. We calculate our age based on those rules. Time is nothing but vibration. Rather, the relative experience of vibration can be understood as time. Reflect on Einstein's theory of special relativity. Based on an object's state of motion, the time associated with it varies. It implies that time is elastic in nature. Am I right, dear scientist?'

'Yes, you are right,' Roberto said.

'When an object exceeds the speed of light, the time associated with it diminishes. Consider it this way: Suppose a man boards a flight which travels faster than light and goes for a space expedition. When he returns after twenty-five years, life on earth would have changed very much. The young people would have turned old, and many of the old people that he knew would have died! But the man who returns would not have aged bodily more than one month! Because his time would have moved very slowly. As an object's speed of travel increases, the time experienced by it reduces.'

'But how can Indrajit's condition be compared to that man? Indrajit definitely did not board a rocket and move at a speed faster than light, did he?' Roberto was sceptical.

Dr Krishnan smiled serenely. 'True, he did not. But we forget the intricate relation between the body and the mind. When we spend time in this mortal world, that relationship becomes flimsy. That is why the body cannot reach where the mind reaches! But in Indrajit's case, when his mind travelled faster than light, his body must have followed suit. An enigmatic challenge to our wisdom! Let me put it another way . . . When Indrajit was in a coma, did you check his breathing? How was it?'

'Very, very tenuous . . . I think he took a long time to breathe in and out. His heartbeat was very low too. One might even have thought that he were dead,' Roberto elucidated.

'Exactly! Now I see some light! The great souls have defined a human's complete day not just as twenty-four hours consisting of daylight and night, but based on the number of his inhalations and exhalations! To be precise, when a man completes 36,000 breathing cycles, his one day gets completed. A normal human in an ordinary day shall, on an average, complete that number of inhalations and exhalations. Now, imagine someone doing strenuous work and completing the 36,000 cycles in twenty hours. Then, his day happens to have been completed in twenty hours.

'In Indrajit's case, the diametrically opposite phenomenon happened! Due to his extremely slow breathing, maybe he completed 36,000 breathing cycles in a month's time instead of a day. That means a month became a day for him. One year turned into twelve days! Taken thus, twenty-four years equal twelve multiplied by twenty-four, 288 days.

'That means, the physical changes in him occurred only for a relative period of nine-odd months. Indrajit, who slipped off into a coma when he was nearly thirty-two years old, woke up after twenty-four years as a thirty-two-year-and-nine-month-old man.

'Of course, this might not have happened. To make things comprehensible, I am simply using some mathematics. You, dear scientist, are free to scoff at it.'

Roberto sat dazed at hearing those hitherto-unheard-of life calculations. Observing his amazement, Dr Krishnan Ezhuthachan continued: 'Haven't you read the Book of Genesis in the Holy Bible? "And the Lord God formed the man from the dust of the ground and breathed into his nostrils the breath of life." There is a symbolism in those words. When a person starts breathing, time starts its work within him. Breathing is movement. Movement is time. Do you know when a man tends to breathe hard? When he is furious or when he is experiencing orgasm. If any of these gets uncontrollable, the person will die an untimely death. A long life means a life detached from both of those. I have no idea how you, dear scientist, would accept what I am going to say further. When a man's breathing slows, and ultimately ceases, his time escapes the trinity of past, present and future, and becomes unitary. Even while alive, if someone can master his breathing to bring it to a zero-like stillness, he acquires Trikalajnana, the wisdom of all phases of time.'

'I mean, is that . . . ?' Roberto asked uneasily, 'is that even possible? Doesn't stillness of breath mean death?'

'Usually, when the heartbeat stops and the breathing stills, we declare that death has occurred. That is merely a clinical death. Biological death happens only when the last vibration inside the brain ceases. There are many cases of those declared clinically dead coming back to life. Listening to their near-death experiences will be hair-raising for the living. The places they travelled to, the people they saw, extra-sensory perceptions . . . so many things unthinkable for a common man. If you are interested, try to do research in that area. You will then realize that the words, "Seek and ye shall find;

knock and it shall be opened unto you . . . ," happen to be absolutely true. Indeed, the Carpenter said that knowingly.'

Roberto understood that the 'Clan of Carpenters' had not vanished yet. He started feeling that his mind was travelling faster than light.

Seventeenth Petal: Partition

Indrajit felt adrift, not having a single thing in his sight to relate to, and the feeling that he stood out like an unwanted appendage in the surroundings persisted.

The mind is the sum total of habits. If, suddenly, some people were to stand on life's way blocking one and assert that 'we are near and dear to you', the mind will refuse to accept it. Beyond logic and reasoning, it will tightly adhere to its accustomed ways and become intransigent.

That is why the peripatetic wanderer feels the pull of his home. It remains his abode of relief. Like objects being attracted towards the centre of gravity, the home beckons the man. Now what if, on returning, one finds that a few strangers have encroached on the home? Indrajit was, in a sense, amid strangers. Though his sons and grandchildren tried their best to establish warm relations with him, Indrajit struggled in reaching out to them and was at the point of giving up.

When he could walk around a bit, Indrajit stepped out of his house. The surroundings caused him utter bewilderment. The pathways were different. The veil of greenery that he was used to had vanished. Even the sky, having relinquished its pristine nature, seemed to be indifferent to the world. The newspapers thrown into the front yard early in the mornings were ostensibly filled with historical proclamations from some unknown country. The printed letters gave him the impression of a new language unyielding to him. Unfamiliar news, unknown people, baffling advertisements of strange products . . . the newspapers were strikingly colourful. It was as if a man who had been accustomed to a black-and-white world was suddenly hurled into a full-blown multicoloured universe!

Instruments and appliances that Indrajit could not even imagine in his wildest dreams took him by surprise. He found it difficult to adapt to the colour television, computer and the water heater in the bathroom.

Outside the house, the tarred roads and screeching vehicles hurtling past appalled him. Trying to cross the road, he hesitated often, intimidated by the traffic. To his surprise, little children, with school bags strapped on their shoulders, sauntered across the road without batting an eyelid. Indrajit felt awed at their confidence and courage. Finally, he managed to cross the road too. It was on the third day of stepping out of the house that he could achieve that milestone.

On seeing the cops, Indrajit hardly recognized them and struggled to reconcile his memory of the starched-and-ironed khaki shorts of yore with the new police uniform. Seeing the different types of soft drinks dangling in multi-hued bottles from the roadside shops, he recalled the lemonade of the bygone years. There were no sherbet shops any more. So many unknown automobiles of different makes were racing crazily down the road; most were foreign brands. With phones stuck close to their ears, people could be seen driving the vehicles with utter ease. Akhil and Arun both had their own cars. The monetary compensation for their father's lost years had proved to be a windfall in some ways. But the tragic forfeiture of Indrajit's life outweighed the gains.

Indrajit was overwhelmed with an abject helplessness. If someone had given him a choice about waking into such a fast-moving world, he would most certainly have refused. But life never asked for permission before proffering adversities. The misery made its appearance only when one shambled along with one's life, carrying it like a heavy burden, as others stared aghast. Life was not meant to be observed with a sense of wonder, but to be lived, moment to moment.

Whenever he saw his adult sons, he tended to instinctively retreat. Two more men at home similar to him! Arunjit, who had started balding, seemed older than Indrajit. When the children who used cling to his hands only yesterday stood in front of him as mature adults, how could he interact with them freely?

But Arun and Akhil did not encounter such a predicament. Though their father had been in a coma, both of them had experienced his presence in all their stages of growth. The twenty-four years hadn't created a fissure in their worlds. They were experiencing the wonder and joy associated with their father's recovery.

The fact that Indrajit hadn't aged was just a one-day wonder for them. The novelty soon lapsed into a casual acceptance. They were acquainted with Major Ravindran, whose hair was pitch-black even at the age of sixty. He was their neighbour and known for leading a very disciplined life. Consequently, Arun and Akhil did not find anything unique about Indrajit's apparent youthfulness.

But their father's condition was radically different. Indrajit was passing through the realization that being young could be troublesome at times. Despite his best efforts, he couldn't imagine himself as the father of two adults. While the heart yearned to see and cuddle the eight- and six-year-old sons, in front of him were two mature men whom he didn't even feel like touching! And when he tried to catch a glimpse of those tender faces in his grandchildren, as they hailed him as grandfather, he felt the call knocking at an unpleasant place within.

His interactions with Sudha turned out to be even more terrifying. What lingered in his mind was the pleasant scent wafting from his wife as she approached him with a hot cup of tea when he returned from office. But now, his wife smelled different. Could a body lose its fragrance over the years? When his mind obstinately refused to accept the woman in front of him as his wife, how cruel it was that her senescence reminded him of the lushly lived life twenty-four years before.

Sudha, having lost the loveliness of her youth, was herself going through an excruciating phase of life. The joy she had experienced when her husband woke from coma was outdone by the agony she felt seeing him regain his health. As Indrajit stood radiating his former youthful machismo, Sudha felt like shrinking away into the background in mortification.

The enticing smell of his aftershave, the throbbing veins in those muscular arms that used to lock her in an embrace with the ferocity of an unchained hurricane . . . Wasn't the same passion lashing around inside the man?

Hidden in his deep anxiety was an untamed, feral truth. Indrajit was thirsting for the intoxicating scent that used to spread in the bedroom when darkness fell. When his wife arrived, drying her freshly washed hair, the room would fill with the seductive fragrance of pala flowers. Once, he had impulsively blurted out that her beauty was that of a sensuous *yakshi*.

'Yakshi? But won't she suck blood?' Sudha demurred.

'All beauties suck man's blood,' Indrajit responded.

'Won't he die?'

'Yes, he does . . . in every union.'

Indrajit was passing through the pinnacle of youth, where such ecstatic deaths were celebrated. Though his name was Indrajit—the subjugator of the senses—in reality, he possessed no control over his senses. Every day, he would discover something new in Sudha to rouse his passions. Her nose ring with the sparkling green stone, a tantalizing drop of perspiration or the mole near her chin would turn him frantic with desire. All the passions of the world flooded in him, rising to mountainous heights. Like a fervent mountaineer, Indrajit would scale that challenging peak.

The devastating avalanche and landslide had happened during that phase. Now, there was no green nose ring or a crystalline drop of sweat to arouse him. Life became insufferably suffocating when they slept in the same room like two strangers. When his body yearned to rush out of the room for a gulp of enlivening air, Indrajit withdrew into himself to escape from the nerve-wracking tension.

Sex became a topic which neither of them could discuss or express. It hadn't been like that before. Anything could be shared at any time, any act of love was acceptable to both. Even an unexpected encounter ending in a passionate tussle had been welcome. Sudha hardly hailed Indrajit as 'Indretta' any more and knew the bloody, wrenching pain of letting go of this habit. How could she address someone who looked younger than her son as Indretta? Both tried their best to avoid addressing each other during their daily routines.

When her husband was comatose, Sudha had sworn to herself that she would never consider it as an accursed condition. She had a deep belief in the '*pativrata* dharma'. Sudha practised some rituals every day, confident that both nature and death would be subservient to a husband devoted to his wife and a woman who was faithful to her spouse.

Each morning, she would reverently touch her forehead against Indrajit's feet. Had Indrajit known about this rite before setting out on his unconscious pilgrimage, he would have staunchly opposed it. But Sudha felt it was a sort of pious observance. She would also drop a kiss on the temple of her husband, who was unaware of day or night, before going to sleep. The kiss and the touching of the feet were evidence of her naive conception of a committed marital relationship.

Ever since Indrajit awoke, Sudha found herself unable to exercise that limitless freedom. On discarding the habits that had been a part of her being for twenty-four years, both her mind and body became disturbed. It was analogous to a drug addict abruptly deprived of his daily dose.

As she lay on her cot facing the west wall, Sudha would be alert to the heavy silences hurled on her by the world. Her focus would be on the undulations of breathing arising from the nearby cot. Sudha could easily discern whether her husband was asleep, or even the stage of sleep he was in, based on her prior experiences. She would imagine Indrajit turning to his left or tucking his right leg in before falling into a deep slumber.

On such nights, when sleep heartlessly skipped off, Sudha ended up loathing her own womanhood. When her very life-spirit was just a touch away and she could not reach out to caress him, her simple, feminine heart found it an agonizing ordeal.

One night, unable to evade deadly temptations, Sudha sat up. Indrajit was fast asleep then. An overwhelming desire to see her sleeping beloved's face overwhelmed her. It was impossible to look into his face during the day. At night, since Indrajit couldn't look at her in return, she could gaze to her heart's content. Sitting in pitch darkness, Sudha braced herself by checking the rhythm of Indrajit's breathing. When she hesitated at the possibility of him waking up, Sudha found her own breathing quickening and, in an effort to calm herself, pressed her hand against her chest. Her timorous attempts to switch on the lights failed many times. At last, tremblingly, she managed it.

As Sudha had imagined, Indrajit was lying on his left side. His regular breathing indicated deep sleep. Gathering her poise, Sudha slowly walked towards her husband. As she looked at him with the deep thirst of someone who had just been granted vision, her woman's mind concluded that the sleeping man was the most handsome person in the world. With the same enticing good looks and well-muscled body of his youth, here, at arm's length, was her spouse.

For a moment, Sudha became a simple woman made of flesh and blood. As an unassuageable desire washed over her, in the freedom denied to her during the day, Sudha kissed Indrajit's forehead. Unwittingly, a teardrop fell, and he stirred in his sleep. Flinching like a thief, Sudha switched off the light and fled to her bed, holding back the sobs threatening to burst out. Her body was shivering, as if she had committed some grave sin.

That night, sleep wandered rebelliously as she lay forlorn in her bed. She was worried that Indrajit had sensed her impulsive deed. She abhorred herself, as if she had kissed a strange young man without his permission. What a torture it was to know that someone was hers, yet not hers.

After that, Sudha found herself unable to read Indrajit's breathing or perceive the stage of his sleep. Deep sighs rose from the other bed intermittently. Either her ability to gauge her husband's slumber had left her forever or the man lying in the next cot had lost the battle with sleep too. Sudha realized that the existential dilemma glaring at her in the darkness of the room was the most formidable ever. It agonized her to think about whether Indrajit was aware of that moment of vulnerability.

The way out of the problem was a forcible partition of the sleepless nights endured by two souls. Shifting her solitary cot to the room adjoining the kitchen, Sudha found a temporary sanctuary. It was a self-imposed boundary to prevent another bout of forbidden desire.

That poignant partition gave immense relief to Indrajit too. It was like a silent pact between them. A mutual understanding, without any grievance or worries. When both were in agreement, there was, of course, no cause for complaint.

But who had sinned against whom?

Though Indrajit felt relieved, he encountered severe mental stress too. Having lost forever the woman who had been close like his own heartbeat, he was to lead the rest of his life with a void inside the chest.

Eighteenth Petal: Body and Mind

Roberto returned after the meeting with Krishnan Ezhuthachan with the awareness that he was not just a 'Dr' but something much beyond. In certain parts of their conversation, the venerable old man had adopted long, secretive silences, as if determined not to expose everything.

If it had been for a matter open like the sky and earth, there would have been no need for Roberto to undertake such an arduous journey and approach Dr Ezhuthachan. Besides, both the earth and sky were prone to hide their real essence with facades. Roberto had learnt much, but much more was left to be learnt. Half-truths, he realized, could turn out to be the height of stupidity.

While he was on his way home, it struck Roberto that he had forgotten to ask an important question. He required an unequivocal answer about the experiments he had undertaken to awaken Indrajit's consciousness. It would have been worthwhile to listen to the profound views of the famous parapsychologist. Roberto was sure that their paths would cross again and they would then discuss it further.

Soon, during a conversation with Janaki, Roberto came to realize that matters often culminated inexplicably through those who were not in the least connected with them. Circumstances evolved as if dictated by time.

Janaki's curiosity had been stoked by the intimacy Roberto seemed to share with Indrajit and by his enigmatic visit to Dr Ezhuthachan. More than anyone else, she caught on that everyone looked at Indrajit as if he had returned from the netherworld. The village was celebrating his resurrection as if it was another of Nireeswaran's marvels. The ironclad arguments of the Abhasa opposing that line of thought were to no avail. Janaki had been witness to a shouting match between the trio and a group of believers.

In the duel between rationality and irrationality, though victory and defeat changed sides many times, the Abhasa appeared weak towards the end. Though the trio tried to dominate the situation by raising their voices when their logic failed to persuade, they had not been able to garner much support for their views. Antony justified the fiasco by expounding on how the number of people appreciating science and truth had shrunk to an extreme minority.

Indrajit became a topic of conversation between Roberto and Janaki on the same day she witnessed that battle of ideas.

'Isn't it a miracle to wake up as a strong man, after having slept for twenty-four years?' Janaki asked.

'Well, before that miracle occurred, I had gone on a mysterious journey, much like my quest for smell,' Roberto revealed. 'I don't know if it was right or wrong.'

'Mysterious journey?'

'A journey into the world of the mind, which is invisible like smell. In other words, after conceiving the mind as thoughts, and thoughts as vibrations, I attempted some crazy chess moves!'

Roberto elucidated on the experimental period when he tried to shake awake Indrajit's thoughts using his own. Janaki listened enraptured about that sojourn beyond the three-dimensional world. Roberto wondered how he could explain the concepts of vibration and frequency to an uneducated person like Janaki. It was a novel experience to adapt simple analogies to clarify complex phenomena.

'See, every object has a natural frequency associated with it. To put it simply, it implies how many times an object vibrates per second. Imagine a thin iron ribbon projecting out of a wall. If we press it hard and then let go of it, the strip will start vibrating with a buzzing sound, right? Its natural frequency would mean the number of times it shivers in a second. That is different for every material.'

'But what has all that to do with the mind?' Janaki asked.

'I'll tell you. If you place two vibrating materials possessing the same frequency next to each other, the strength of their vibrations intensify. It's like shaking something with full force! In science, we call it "resonance". Actually, I played with the idea of making my mind's vibration resonate with that of Indrajit. Janaki, I could actually experience that unnerving intensity! Could Arun's father have felt it too? Perhaps that is why, after waking up from his coma, he feels more comfortable sharing his experiences with me. Haven't you heard people saying "those two are of the same wavelength" when trying to explain an unaccountable closeness between two human beings? Sometimes, when you are thinking of someone, you get his phone call unexpectedly! One can conclude that a resonance of thoughts happened there too. In tranquil minds, it can be felt very intensely . . . See, I am not insisting that this was how the events rolled out. That's why I request you not to share this with anyone else,' Roberto said.

Even after his elaborate exposition, Janaki's expression was unruffled, much to Roberto's surprise. Let alone a sleeping man, Janaki was aware that even a wide-awake man could be made to pulsate using the mind. How many times had she induced convulsions in Damu from afar! But she was clueless about the science behind it.

Janaki found herself tongue-tied when it came to revealing the matter to Roberto. After all, in a life that lay openly naked, these few scraps were all that she could preserve tightly wrapped up. Though she dithered from exposing her secrets, she felt that she shouldn't create barriers in the lone relationship where she found herself free to discuss anything. And so, Janaki prepared to narrate the story of her own enigmatic journeys.

Roberto watched bemusedly as a sheen of shyness, odd in a prostitute, spread over Janaki's face. On hearing about the telepathy between Janaki and Damu, Roberto felt like slapping his own head, swollen with scientific wisdom, and saying to himself, 'You clown, there are scientific experiments going on in areas unfamiliar to you!'

'The touchstone of extrasensory perceptions cannot be the so-called scientific knowledge,' Roberto murmured, 'because science understands everything using intelligence. But it never understands the cause behind that intelligence! For doing that, one should be able to travel beyond intelligence and return with new insights. Using intelligence as a yardstick is much like analysing a house by studying the bricks which were used for its construction. It never reaches the soil, which was the origin of the brick. But the razor-sharp consciousness can penetrate depths beyond the mind and experience the primal cause behind the intelligence. Then the non-intelligence of the overhyped intelligence shall stand exposed! Janaki, I dare say that nobody in the Research Centre would have known science the way you have!'

When Indrajit arrived at Rose Villa the next evening, Roberto took special care not to discuss his visit to Dr Ezhuthachan. It might throw Indrajit into further befuddlement. The man was walking barefoot over paths strewn with thorns. Roberto was saddened to see the fifty-six-year-old ordained to live with the mind and body of a thirty-two-year-old. Indrajit was struggling to interact with his sons, who seemed to be his own age, and was floundering in a world comprising his elderly wife and young grandchildren. The loneliness in a crowd was more terrifying than death. Every man needed the space of a keyhole, at the least, to open his woes. Else, unable to find an escape route, the pressure would burst the walls of the heart, causing the loss of a precious life.

'Inside me, something is stretched taut to the point of snapping,' Indrajit opened the doors of his inner ruminations. 'I know what I am doing to Sudha is unfair. It is the mind which provokes all thoughts. Can a mind full of youthfulness be delighted with an aged wife? That's how I feel when I see Sudha.'

It was a rare occasion when silence was the answer. One could dive deep into an inscrutable scientific problem and try to untangle the knots. But here was raw human flesh, getting scalded in the steam of life! Roberto felt blinded and could only listen.

'Roberto, nowadays my body is aggressively demanding sex. I feel as if I'm going mad!' Indrajit confessed.

A helpless man who lost the battle with his own existence was unlatching his inner chamber, fighting a losing battle with his own existence. If a man was revealing his secrets to another, opening the rusty padlock after decades with creaky sounds, it meant he was seeking an anchor for hefting his burden.

When Indrajit opened his heart, Roberto was deeply touched. As barriers fall away, friendship is fortified. When facades, both internal and external, are removed, mutual rapport grows in intensity between friends. A loving bond is spun between the two with the weave and weft of give and take. But Roberto stood mystified, not knowing what was expected of him.

Sex was not a topic that interested Roberto. Consequently, he wasn't competent to offer any insight into it. But he knew that sex could assume both the gigantic proportions of Mount Everest and the disconcerting depths of the Pacific Ocean. Undeniably, sex could morph into the core question of man's existential crisis. Roberto could glean a picture of how the issue affected Indrajit.

For obvious reasons, it wasn't possible for him to discuss such matters with Arunjit. How could Roberto explain to him the quandary faced by his father, forced to sleep with an old wife?

At that juncture, Janaki unwittingly interrupted their exchange. She knew that Roberto loved to drink coffee made with goat's milk at around four in the evening. Never expecting any guest and suddenly catching sight of Indrajit, she felt like a thief who was caught red-handed, with panic writ large on her face.

Janaki had started enjoying the liberty of entering Rose Villa at any time—an unwritten pact between Roberto and her. When she served three hot meals to Roberto every day, Janaki enjoyed the feeling that she was well within her rights to do so. Ever since Roberto told her that it was food that formed a person's mind and life-spirit, Janaki had started implementing some corrections in her food habits too.

When he recited '*Annam vai manah; Annam vai pranah*', the words penetrated Janaki's subconscious mind, though she was untutored in Sanskrit. The innocence of the ignorant makes them adopt certain ideas with radical fervour. That is why the naive, as yet unburdened by knowledge, could be easily brainwashed to become a spiritualist or a revolutionary.

Roberto was not finicky about what he ate, the green plants growing in his yard being more than enough for his repast. Janaki felt that his eating habits contributed to his calmness. For some time now, Janaki had also been experimenting with this and feeling it in her body. Not only the body but the mind, too, felt drained of bestiality. It had begun to convince her that virtuousness in eating habits was the beginning of Mahayana, the divine vehicle. Sometimes Janaki perceived that it was food that materialized as body at the macro level, as mind at the micro level and as prana, the life-spirit, at a still minute level.

As Roberto had also mentioned that focusing could renew a person, Janaki found her mind focusing on the infinitesimal world. She observed that what Roberto said was true: whether good or bad, every thought was like inscribing a dot on a white sheet of paper. When many such 'dots' of thoughts were imprinted, they became 'visibly large' and eventually emerged as a habit. Since every action was ultimately the embodiment of a thought, if we put 'dots' of positive thoughts in the mind's sky, those would manifest as constructive habits. With utter sincerity, Janaki took to heart whatever Roberto said about the formation of habits.

Afterwards, whenever she started for Rose Villa, a pellucid mindfulness also accompanied her. Janaki had reached Roberto's home in the same state of mindful awareness when she caught sight of Indrajit and embarrassedly started retracing her steps.

'Stop, Janaki,' Roberto called out. But Janaki did not stop. Gesturing that she would come later, she hurriedly made an exit.

Janaki rebuked herself that the body she carried around was not one that could come and go as it pleased.

Indrajit sat bewildered at the unexpected arrival and hurried departure, not comprehending the story being played out before his eyes. 'Was it because of me . . . ?'

'Not at all. That's a poor woman who helps in the kitchen. She had to struggle a lot in her life.'

To avoid any hearsay later, Roberto gave the true picture of Janaki's life to Indrajit. He mentioned the fact that the hapless woman, who made a living by selling herself, was the main factor making him stay back in that village.

A breeze rustled in Indrajit's mindscape, and he saw a green sari splattered with rose flowers. A rose garden he had seen once coloured the body of a saree, creating a hallucinatory effect. Indrajit felt that his eyes were playing tricks with him.

'What's the matter?' Roberto anxiously asked Indrajit, who seemed to have lost his moorings momentarily.

'Nothing.'

Roberto felt that the man who was evading his question had many unspoken words bubbling inside him. Following that thought, unbiasedly looking at the cause and effect, Roberto travelled a long way, like a true scientist. An alarming insight dawned that Janaki might be the fitting person to discuss Indrajit's problems. It was a straightforward idea, that a prostitute would be an expert in an issue involving sex. Janaki would be a trustworthy partner in the effort to help Indrajit.

Roberto dared to engage Janaki in an uninhibited conversation because of the bond of trust they shared. When Roberto began to present the issue, in this context, of the conflict between the young and the old, though his inexperience on the topic was evident, Janaki paid attention. She was not just listening but also enjoying the fluster of an amateur handling a subject he was unaccustomed to. Finally, when she got to speak, Janaki astounded Roberto with her prescience. 'You see, I had foreseen this issue between them.'

'How?'

'Can we not be far-sighted in our area of expertise, just like scientists?'

'Definitely! Can you offer a solution to this scientific conundrum?'

'Some matters have no instant solutions.'

'Not even a temporary respite?'

'How?'

'Forgive me if I am wrong', Roberto said. 'Dismiss it as an idiot's query if you wish. Janaki, can't you help assuage that man's urges?'

As soon as she heard the solution proposed by the scientist, Janaki started shaking with uncontrollable laughter. Roberto was stunned by her response. 'Why do you laugh?'

'What else can I do? It is said that geniuses are often dunces in practical life.' Janaki felt pity for the pure-hearted man. After having laughed a bit more, she regained her poise. 'I am a body-seller. What you propose shouldn't matter two hoots to me. But wouldn't that be an injustice to his wife? She is a good woman. She sacrificed her whole life nursing him back to health. And now . . . ?'

'See, no one is at fault here. It is a battle between the body and the mind. All I can see is Arun's father's pitiable condition! The right and wrong of it is unknown to me. I just proposed an interim solution. Truly, I am caught in a despicable position right now. Playing the role of a pimp, no less! How quickly our lives turn topsy-turvy!'

Janaki did not reply. She had been ravaged by many unexpected occurrences in the course of her life too. The pathways of many lives had trespassed into the trail of her own. Sometimes, Janaki would sardonically indulge in the exercise of taking a count of those who had had her body. It was like sneaking around with a hidden camera in one's memory. Starting with the first unwitting step into the morass, she could recollect some of the initial ones and a few of the latest encounters. The ones in the middle were usually lost in a haze. Janaki could remember the butcher, the pickpocket, the bus owner, Antony, and Chettiar in that melee. She could not help but smirk at the thought that the body-worship had happened in hotel rooms, shops and even at the foot of the Athmavu where Nireeswaran's idol was installed. Janaki knew that she would never be able to count all those thousands of unions. Her life was similar to the mango fruit whose flesh had been feasted on by crows, squirrels and cuckoos, with only its skin and seed now intact.

One who had led such a life should expect anything to crop up at any moment. Even death. Indeed, what was the relevance of right and wrong then? The only option was to stand by indifferently as the next event unfolded, that was all.

Roberto gingerly put forth the idea of sending Janaki to Indrajit, even as his heart went against the thought. Certain things were prone to cause serious injury if not presented diplomatically. There were protocols to be followed while conversing with a man who was of one's father's age. Roberto justified it all by thinking that it was analogous to adopting a short cut in dealing with a mathematical problem. But Indrajit's response to his proposal confounded all his reasonings.

'Roberto, you failed to understand me. My problem is not mere lust for a female body! What I yearn for is sex where love is paramount! That can be shared only with one's love. Janaki is not the answer to that.'

Roberto stood drained of all his enthusiasm, blaming himself bitterly. A sinking feeling, that made him think he was the pettiest person on earth, took over his mind.

When she heard the news, Janaki said impassively, 'The power of his wife's chastity, nothing less.'

The physicist stood stunned on hearing the whore praising someone's chastity. The distant expression on her face reminded him of the Earth Mother who remained nonchalant even when her innards burned; had it been otherwise, all the green would have dried up long back, leaving the world a barren wasteland.

Nineteenth Petal: The Female Mind

Barber Maniyan's feat of having trounced Ghoshayatra Annamma spread like wildfire across the Malayalam-speaking land. He had shoved Annamma into an abyss of silence. Never again did her voice resound in the village. She became non-responsive, as if her vocal cords had been damaged. Annamma's daughters stopped stepping out of their home, either singly or in a procession. Annamma was like a tragic heroine felled by a curse, and her house was gripped by darkness. Nobody knew if she could come to terms with what had happened to her.

'Smart move, Maniyan! When everybody tightens their loin clothes before a wrestling match, you won by loosening yours!'

All the visitors to the barbershop showered him with adulation. As if partaking the profits of a great war, Maniyan spent his days intoxicated by the praise and soaking it in. The arrow tipped with vulgarity had not lacked in killing power. With the help of a small weapon, Maniyan had vanquished a formidable woman.

The next time Maniyan visited his farm, not even a glimpse of Annamma or her daughters could be seen in the vicinity. The barber scoffed that the female serpents had slithered into some hole inside their home, terrified at his sight. The realization that he had vanquished their arrogance, even at the cost of his loin cloth, made him strut and preen. Maniyan had no inkling that many females from the neighbourhood were casting lascivious looks at him. They were gems of womanhood who had become ardent devotees of Maniyan after being granted a 'darshan' of his uncommon manliness. It was good that the barber wasn't cognizant of his magical powers, evocative of Rasputin, which held them under his sway. Else he would have been party to many family squabbles in that locality.

Maniyan's investigative brain deduced, from the sheer lack of observable goat shit, that Annamma's goat hadn't strolled near his farm. Or the creature might be undergoing treatment for constipation. Not only were the rice plants near the embankments untouched, even the couch grass around was left pristine. Which meant, along with the female humans, the female goat had also been taught a lesson. That puffed up Maniyan's chest a little bit more.

On a Tuesday, which was his weekly day off, Maniyan sprayed Furidan to protect his crop from rice earhead bugs. Whereas the whole world enjoyed a holiday on the 'day of the sun', the barbers abstained from work on the 'day of Mars'. As he was habituated to doing things by himself, Maniyan had set out to spray the pesticide with enthusiasm. When he moved around the farm, wearing a face mask and carrying a cylinder strapped on his back, he resembled an astronaut. Though it was basic courtesy to inform the neighbours when one sprayed pesticide, Maniyan desisted from updating his sworn enemy Annamma. After all, he shrugged, anyone could see. And the stink of the deadly poison could not be ignored as it wafted around with the breeze.

Maniyan never expected that silly but intentional negligence to trigger a great disaster. As soon as the barber left, Annamma's goat broke free from its bondage and made for the fields. The creature's singular aim was the greenery of Maniyan's farm that had been tempting it sorely for a while.

Virtually invisible to the world, with no one to monitor it, the goat feasted to its heart's content. When it felt slightly dizzy, it dragged itself back to its ramshackle shed. The remnant of the snapped rope hung from its neck and trailed behind, like Yama's lasso. Unable to endure the wracking agony, the poor creature started bleating frantically and thrashing its limbs. Hearing the desperate bleats, first the eldest daughter ran out, followed by her younger sisters and eventually Annamma herself. In the throes of death, the goat gazed with tearful eyes at Annamma, who had nurtured it with jackfruit leaves, rice water and oil cakes. Annamma wailed dreadfully as she sat on her haunches by the side of her dying goat.

The lone source of Annamma's meagre income was the goat. During a financial crisis, she had to sell its pretty kid. Now the goat shed lay bereft of its occupant . . .

Under present circumstances, the goat's departure affected that household even more than a human being's demise would have. The five women were tossed into a whirlwind of uncertainty. Though it became evident that the goat had died due to poisoning, Annamma never attempted to wage a war against Maniyan over it.

It was only after many days that Maniyan got to know of the goat's death through Sumitran. For Sumitran, Annamma was like a mother, and he couldn't care less about the gossip about her. He was never considered a dimwit in that house. The rest of the villagers had started accepting him only after his speech became steady, thanks to Nireeswaran. But Annamma and her daughters had always made him feel at home. They had plucked wild jasmines and white orchids for stringing garlands for Nireeswaran. Sumitran had relished many cups of coffee brewed with rich goat milk from that house. It seemed as if the death of the goat had impacted Sumitran more than the owners.

When Maniyan was informed that the goat had been tied up but had somehow wriggled away to meet its death, a twinge of guilt pricked his conscience. He tried to ignore the feeling and focused on the snipping of hair instead.

'That harridan got her just deserts,' Dasappan commented maliciously. The proprietor-cum-manager of Daiva Sahayam Restaurant had once been grievously injured during a verbal duel with Annamma. When he had griped that she had added water to the goat milk, Annamma had openly challenged him, her shrewish tongue's onslaught making mincemeat of him. Dasappan had been moving around like a headless corpse since that incident.

'As you sow, so shall you reap,' Rayappan responded, not looking away from the newspaper. 'Well, Maniyan contributed to that reaping, that's all.'

'At last, she will stop queening it over others!'

Maniyan, usually garrulous, found himself at a loss for words. A sense of melancholy pervaded him. Though many visitors warmly congratulated him on his achievement, he received an unexpected reprimand too. It came from Roberto. Seated in the chair and staring at the series of reflections in the mirror, Roberto tut-tutted,

'You should not have stopped my daily coffee, you know!'

'What?'

'The milk came from Annamma's house. Now that her goat is dead, it has stopped.'

'I did not do anything knowingly.'

'Whether knowingly or unknowingly, the effect is the same.'

It was Janaki who used to procure milk from Annamma during her daily trips to Rose Villa. On the days she didn't, Annamma's youngest daughter would bring the milk in a bronze pitcher. Gorethy was as lovely as a film star, and her body language made it obvious that she knew it. Roberto guessed that her mother must have been very beautiful in her youth. He wondered how the five beauties had survived depending on just a goat. The goat's milk had been rich and creamy. He never felt that it was diluted with water. But the goat having died, it was time to search for another milk-filled udder. Janaki had already brought Roberto up to date with how Annamma and Maniyan had fought with each other like gamecocks, adding all the embellishments that the gossip network had provided. The narrative was as authentic as that of a local journalist giving a ground report without witnessing the incident.

'Would have been fun to witness that!' Janaki giggled irrepressibly.

Waves of laughter rocked Roberto on imagining the Digambar avatar of Maniyan. During such hilarity, one tends to ignore the sufferings of the victims. But after hearing about the goat's death, Roberto felt sympathy for Ghoshayatra Annamma.

Though Maniyan made routine visits to his rice field, there was deathly silence in the neighbourhood. The barber started wondering about the whereabouts of the erstwhile lionesses who had ruled the roost. Many well-wishers had cautioned him about the possibility of Annamma's reprisal. Hence, he was alert when he visited the farm. If there was an unexpected guerrilla attack from the five women, the magical amulet around his waist was not going to be of help. True, Annamma had been taken aback momentarily and retreated from the battlefield at their previous encounter, but even Nireeswaran couldn't help him if the five women joined forces now!

But Maniyan's fears were unfounded; no woman ventured to question him or even step out of the house.

When the farm started yielding milky white crop, Maniyan's affinity towards agriculture deepened. The weekly visits became daily, and he felt that unless he checked on his farm each morning, the day wouldn't be worthy. Maniyan found the smell of muddy slush exhilarating. Pulling out weeds, he would throw the roots into the canal and dump the leaves and stem in the field as compost. He would plug the fissures of the embankment with clay and caress the rice saplings tenderly.

On a beautiful morning, when Maniyan was busy unearthing weeds from his farm, there ensued an uproar from Annamma's house.

'Ammachi . . . !' the girls shrieked.

The barber stood dumbstruck for a moment.

Though he had never met or spoken to her after their naked encounter, prompted by an unalloyed kindness that existed within him still, Maniyan raced towards the origin of the uproar. He saw Annamma lying still, uprooted like a wild tree. Her daughters were trying to shake her awake, lamenting all the while, as if competing with one another.

'Get some water, quick!' Maniyan barked orders. Hesitantly, the eldest girl fetched water.

He sprinkled water on Annamma's exhausted face. Having lost all her former sensuality, the woman looked droopy and pathetic. When the water moistened her face like holy baptism, the woman, whose life had been shattered, slowly opened her eyes. Maniyan poured some water into her mouth. Even as she wondered whether to swallow or not, the drops trickled down her throat.

Annamma looked askance at Maniyan, wondering how the enemy had breached the boundaries of her home. The barber understood her bewilderment. 'I will fetch an autorickshaw. Let us get her to a hospital,' Maniyan suggested.

'I am all right. No need for all that trouble,' Annamma protested weakly.

Maniyan went ahead to search for an auto, thinking it was her confusion, at seeing her enemy coming to her help, that had triggered Annamma's reaction. It was time to shed all rivalry and help a person in need.

Luckily, an autorickshaw was making its way like a shy female on the route. Its name, 'Chattambi Kalyani', that is, 'Streetfighter Kalyani', was painted on its hindside. Annamma, supported by her two daughters, clambered into it. Maniyan shared the auto driver's seat. He was worried that it might have been a mild cardiac arrest that felled Annamma, and that it might foreshadow an imminent strike by the heart. Observing the unceasing tears of the poor girls, he felt miserable.

Maniyan had tried hard for a daughter but had ended up with three sons. They were lording it over back home in his native village, Attingal. Maniyan used to meet them once in a while. Since marrying a barber was against her wishes, his wife did not encourage him to visit regularly. A life full of compromises, regular supply of money orders, sporadic visits and three offspring due to the aforementioned visits—that was Maniyan's story. Nowadays, his trips to Attingal had almost ceased. And no one from his family complained, since the money orders were right on time. His sons had made it evident that it was a major embarrassment for them to have a barber as their father.

The doctor in the hospital examined Annamma's pale eyes and checked her pulse. 'Her body is very weak. Low blood pressure. I shall administer a drip and admit her,' he told the girls. On hearing the words 'drip' and 'admit', Annamma's agitation increased by leaps and bounds, and the girls restarted their wailing. There was no money at home to even purchase a mothball, and that was the real reason behind Annamma's fatigue.

It was then that Maniyan got a glimpse of their broken existence. He felt deeply guilty because of his role in causing their goat's death. The family had fallen into the grips of acute penury. Annamma's forlorn face made it obvious that her overtly aggressive demeanour had just been a facade.

'Don't worry about the hospital expenses,' he said while retrieving money from the waist knot of his lungi. A wad of rupee notes stained by male smell and perspiration. 'You can pay me back at your convenience.'

Ghoshayatra Annamma felt that her very life was drifting away from her. Her eyes, which used to sparkle like two suns in her glorious days, now glistened with tears. Through that moistness, like a distorted lens, the world seemed to be disproportional and dreadful. She did not attempt to wipe her tears and see the world for what it was. All her pretentiousness had collapsed like a tonne of bricks in a short time. All Annamma wished for was death. The woman would have willingly allowed the cherubs to carry her spirit away, forgetting that she would be leaving behind four orphaned daughters.

But nature was not willing to call back Annamma in that manner. With the help of the one who had brought her to her knees, Annamma outlived her sickness.

Two days later, seated in an autorickshaw named 'Thattalle, Chetta'—that is, 'Don't Hit Me, Bro!'—Annamma went back to her house. It felt like a homecoming after years of exile. Along with Annamma, the realization that 'an enemy can sometimes be of more help than one's relative' also made its entry into the home.

That afternoon, two lactating goats stood in front of Annamma's house and bleated for oilcake and rice water.

'Mmmeee . . .'

When Annamma and her four daughters came running to the door, they saw two nanny goats, beautiful like pictures in black and white. In the place of the one that was lost, two worthies seemed to have resurrected in the yard.

Maniyan felt it was the least he should do as a devotee of Nireeswaran. He had come to realize that the woman who had pretended to be so full of herself was a helpless soul in reality. To wage war against the helpless was a sin committed against Nireeswaran.

When he stood with folded hands before a solitary Nireeswaran that afternoon, Maniyan experienced something ineffable scampering inside his body. He felt it leaping out of him like a mischievous monkey and racing on the trees above, before merging with the stone idol, which stood detached and remote. There, as if finding eternal solace, it rested.

Hearing a sound behind him, Maniyan turned and saw two smiling faces, which reminded him of friendships that had flourished near the Athmavu even before the incarnation of Nireeswaran.

'Good work, Maniyan,' Arnos congratulated him. 'It was very good of you to purchase the goats for Annamma.'

'Such actions make us deserve the tag of human beings,' Embrandiri said. 'In fact, it is tougher to be a human than a god.'

'I never meant it like that . . .' Maniyan said humbly.

'Inside everyone lies a fertile field where the seed of goodness can sprout anytime. We can call it godliness or humanity, whatever we like.'

Embrandiri went near Nireeswaran and removed the faded jasmine garland draped around it. He turned to Arnos and asked, 'Don't you yearn to touch it?'

'Can I?' Arnos asked eagerly.

'You are the most deserving! And then, our beloved Zaid! Isn't this our own Nireeswaran . . . ?' Embrandiri smiled.

For a moment, the flow of time seemed to freeze inside Arnos. By then he had touched Nireeswaran. When both the friends together started decorating Nireeswaran, Maniyan prayed, yet again, with an overwhelmed heart, and made his way to the shop.

From that day, whenever Maniyan visited his farm, a cup of hot coffee, brewed with rich and creamy goat milk, awaited him on the ridge. Annamma and her girls ensured that not a single weed thrived anywhere in his field. Ripe crop flourished, making every onlooker envious.

The lasso of Yama turned out to be a ropeway connecting two sworn enemies.

'Look at Nireeswaran's tricks!' Roberto could not help commenting as he sipped the delicious coffee Janaki had made with the goat milk. 'The coffee tastes better than ever!'

'Well, I have used a magical trick for making everything tasty,' Janaki laughed.

'I know.'

Roberto contentedly sipped the overtones of sweet love present in both the milk and the coffee.

Twentieth Petal: Union

For a few days afterwards, Indrajit's feet refused to tread towards Rose Villa. Not only his mind but his body, too, cavilled at Roberto's effort to solve his problems using a woman's body. He felt shrunken to the size of a tiny seed. Indrajit did concede that Roberto had simply thought of a straightforward solution, without any wrong intentions. But some matters bruise the delicate layers of one's self-respect. Affronted, Indrajit had walked away from Rose Villa. Roberto, meanwhile, was chastising himself for that fiasco, fearful if it would affect their friendship.

The next day, overcoming the urge to visit Rose Villa, Indrajit walked through the path leading to the temple. He had been avoiding such journeys to escape the vexation caused by people gaping at him like he was a freak. Slowly, he was gaining the ability to handle such situations.

Both the path and the temple had undergone many changes. The unique coconut tree that stood bowing to the sun near the eastern part of the outer temple walls had disappeared. New coconut saplings had sprouted from the Kalpavriksha's apex, though it had never flowered in its life. From beneath, it resembled a parallel green world up above. That mixed-gender tree on which saplings sprouted in the place of coconuts had vanished and any sign of it having stood there was missing. Time annihilated many things, even removing the traces of their presence forever.

As he walked forward, Indrajit could not recognize the ostentatious buildings on either side. Yet the memory of the path lay embedded dimly in his memory like a previous birth. It led to the foot of the Athmavu.

There was a grizzled old woman, tired and weary, sitting on the sidewalk. 'Son,' she hailed weakly.

The woman held a walking stick in her bony hand, on which the veins stood out starkly. As Indrajit turned to her, she asked, 'Where is the temple of Nireeswaran?'

Indrajit felt utterly mystified.

Nireeswaran!

Though he had heard that word from many, the world of his own experiences was devoid of it. Yet, he said, 'I think you have to move further ahead.'

'Oh, Nireeswara!' the old woman sighed.

The sigh was evocative of the misery involved in walking further to the destination. She seemed to have come all that way, in the last phase of her life, with a serious grievance to submit before Nireeswaran. Even so, her exhausted body appeared to hold unlimited hope.

Slowly, the woman shuffled forward, aided by her stick, taking time for each painstaking step. Indrajit heard her mumbling, '*Nireeswaray namah.*'

He walked forward slowly but easily outpaced the woman. Retracing his lost years in his mind, Indrajit finally reached the Athmavu.

Twenty-four years had altered the tree. He remembered eating countless ripe mangoes as a child while gazing at the sky-high canopy. There had been a boisterous gang of friends to frolic with. The secret hideout of those carefree days loomed like a shadow-forest when he recollected the 'communist pacha', vazhana and kuppacheera that grew profusely in the vicinity. The sanctuary had been witness to many naughty tricks as the children played hide-and-seek. But now, the shrubs had all been cleared away. Instead, there was a carpet-like green cover all around.

Indrajit's gaze fell on the inconspicuous idol on the stone platform surrounding the Athmavu. So, the famed Nireeswaran, whose might was purportedly unparalleled, was such a tiny figurine? At first sight, it looked fragile, like a useless stone splinter. But Indrajit still remembered what Arnos had once quoted: '*The stone which the builders rejected became the cornerstone.*' That saying from the scriptures had been so entrancing. Arnos had said that seated on the same dais, and Zaid had also been there. Where had they reached, wandering through the passage of time? Why hadn't they come searching for him yet?

Indrajit was under the impression that no devotees would be around in the day but there was a girl near the deity. A beautiful girl, slender and slim. When their eyes met, something prodded Indrajit from within, reminding him of a familiar face. The other half of his mind immediately sprang in opposition. How could a fellow who had been in a coma for twenty-four years have ever met this young woman? She must have been born when he was in his anaesthesia-induced sleep. Or he might have seen her when she was a toddler! Was there anything more stupid than tracing the face of a woman based on that of a little child? Indrajit was trying to convince himself that it was another coincidence when realization dawned suddenly.

A presence, which accompanied him during the days of his unconscious state, suddenly started haunting him. It was as if someone had hurled incomplete vignettes before him! He could not link them, in spite of his best efforts. They triggered more agitation in him. Shrugging them off as figments of the imagination, Indrajit locked his gaze on the statue of Nireeswaran. It seemed to sparkle in the harsh sunlight. Then, flustering him further, the girl spoke: 'Indrettan, right?'

That was out of the blue. Suppressing a shudder, Indrajit nodded. Then, hesitatingly, he asked, 'And you are . . . ?'

'I am Megha. Remember the Trithazathel House?'

'Ah, Trithazathel . . . Madhavan's daughter . . . ?'

'Yes, you do remember, Indretta!'

Indrajt felt a sudden rush of memories, speeding backward with the swiftness of an arrow. The doorway to the unknown had opened suddenly. Was it just yesterday or twenty-four years ago that a demon stole his consciousness and hid it in the subconscious?

A picture emerged in his mind of a three-year-old girl stepping into his home, holding her mother's forefinger. Megha, that was her name. They were new in the neighbourhood. The little girl evoked the sense of listening to melancholic background music in a film where the hero had morphed into the villain. After sunset, maleficent howls would rise from the neighbour's house. The wild shrieks of the mother and daughter would ring out together. Indrajit had become aware of Madhavan, who would drink down a whole toddy shop and beat up his wife and child.

On a new-moon night, when their very lives were at risk, the woman had picked up her little child and fled. They came rushing inside Indrajit's home, weeping and begging for help. He remembered the terrorized look on the face of the three-year-old who kept looking behind her, struggling to breathe. The drunkard came staggering behind them and roared from the yard, 'Drive them out now!' Doing so would have meant certain death for the mother and child. When the man, whose brain was muddled with alcohol, did not listen to reason and tried to break into the house, the only way left for Indrajit was to defend them.

Madhavan had turned aggressive all of a sudden. Even before Indrajit could shield himself, Madhavan had swung an iron rod viciously at him. As Indrajit ducked instinctively, the rod struck his raised right arm, breaking the bone. By that time, the villagers had come to his aid and controlled Madhavan, thus avoiding a major disaster. After giving him a sound beating, the crowd had handed over the drunkard to the police.

Occasionally, Indrajit remembered the story and the characters. Sudha had mentioned that they were still around. He could not believe that the petrified little girl, shrieking in fear of her father, was the lovely young woman standing before him. His mind became disoriented while conjoining the pictures of a three-year-old and a twenty-seven-year-old, since those heartbreaking events, to his mind, seemed to have occurred just a few days before. How was it possible that he felt a closeness to a neighbour's daughter when he felt distant to his own children? But the girl reminded him of someone he knew intimately, during the life he lived while asleep. However, the tenuous strands broke off as soon as he attempted to recollect more.

'You must be furious . . . Everything happened because of us! I beg your pardon for my father's mistake.'

Pardon—a mishmash of two syllables! The word grinned shamelessly at times, not possessing the value of even shredded paper.

A life had been sundered into two, at its prime. No amount of effort could fix it back together. Indrajit stood helplessly, unable to find a tiny space for the word 'pardon' in between the fragments of life in chaotic disarray.

Twenty-four years was a huge span in a mortal life. When it all coalesced into one moment, he felt acutely suffocated. The impulse to move away took over. It had become a habit recently: his body moved mechanically, while the mind meandered aimlessly. Indrajit walked away without uttering a word.

Ostensibly, that reaction went against basic courtesy. Megha, looking pale, stared at his wake. She concluded that he was unable to forgive the past and that was the reason for his speechlessness. He had taken a wordless revenge by firing an arrow sharply tipped with silence. Megha was left regretting their accidental encounter.

After staring alternately at Nireeswaran, the witness to the conjoining of two eras, and Indrajit's retreating figure, Megha walked away towards her own uncertainties.

Indrajit started scaling the boulder, his mind weighed down by the meanderings to the past. Only after reaching the summit of the steep climb did he dare to cast a backward glance. The girl who had stoked embers within his heart had long disappeared from the world beneath. Indrajit found himself perturbed and wished that the girl hadn't entered his life to remind him of the episode of sin that was better off forgotten. He felt afraid that his very existence would be upended by the day's happenings.

Below him, the leaves of the peepal and mango intermeshed with one another. The canopy of the giant trees, coloured in shades of tender green and deep green, resembled a painting. One could watch the journey of the sun from east to west peaceably from the rock top. In his childhood, Indrajit and his gang of friends had scurried up and down this rock. At certain spots, there was a cliff-like sheer drop. The kids used to compete with one another, trying to clamber up those areas. Indrajit still remembered the terror that slithered down his spine when he first attempted the climb, wanting to impress his friends. When he was lost midway, unable to inch forward or backward, both Arnos and Zaid had egged him on. A mere slip would have meant his end. Yes, that would have removed any chance for a long sleep and the consequent barrage of problems. But he had clawed onto the rock and survived. Indrajit had transformed into the most skilled rock climber after that incident.

Twenty-four years had elapsed without leaving a memory behind. And Indrajit could easily recall the surroundings of the huge rock and the Athmavu as pristinely as if it was yesterday when he had last seen them. There were many small paths in the vicinity. Here, children had played soldiers by improvising guns and bullets using fruits called vedichinka. Since the Athmavu's surroundings were lush with shrubs, where vedichinka grew in plenty, even when it was not the mango season, the area used to be the favourite haunt of village kids.

Now the whole environment was different. The street was anointed with a crude nickname. The old cohort of friends hardly kept in touch, having scattered wide. Meanwhile, a hitherto-unheard-of divinity had conquered the land. In Indrajit's memory, which had no markings of his generation's rise and fall, only the magical rustling of the peepal leaves stayed pristine. Indrajit stayed until the crowd below had diminished. When the westering sun dipped, he gazed at it to his heart's content. It was the same sun, with the same fiery colour and undiminished radiance. Hearing the peal of bells from Nireeswaran's abode, Indrajit's attention got diverted. He had no idea that such a worshipful rite was conducted under the Athmavu.

Neither could he recognize his best friend Eswaran Embrandiri by the low glimmer of the lamplight. Indrajit would have found it next to impossible to imagine Embrandiri in such a setting. When twilight fell, he climbed down the rock and made his way slowly home.

When he reached home, Sudha raised an unexpected question, 'You saw her today, didn't you?'

'Who?'

'Megha. She has not been around for a long time. Guess there are too many problems for her to handle. But today she visited to raise a grievance.'

'I didn't say anything to upset her!'

'Didn't say anything . . . That made her upset! Poor thing, her mother died two years ago. Some say Madhavan kicked her to death.'

Hearing Sudha, who was usually terse, speak uninhibitedly about this subject, Indrajit felt a tug of anxiety inside him. Apparently, the murderer hadn't felt any prick of conscience in marrying a second time, without much delay. Megha had become an orphan, even though her father was alive. By working in the Aanganwadi, she sustained herself and lived as a paying guest in the neighbourhood. When that inauspicious event had occurred twenty-four years ago, Megha had been a small child. Both the mother and daughter used to visit the corpse-like Indrajit regularly. Sudha had loathed the very sight of them in the beginning, but their grief and love being genuine, Sudha had softened and eventually accepted them as part of her own family.

'They helped me to bring up our boys,' Sudha said tearfully. 'That girl used to pray daily for your recovery. Sumitran told me recently that she had even submitted a plea in their prayer group for you. You walked away in a huff when she met you, just after she'd finished praying for you!'

Though he didn't mean to distress her, Indrajit felt guilty that his response towards Megha was not fair. Sometimes it would be difficult to predict in which way the mind bent. And it was not possible for him to reveal his state of mind before Sudha.

An invisible barrier was erected between them, despite his best efforts to shake it off. Since he could not interact intimately with Sudha or even speak openly with her, being at home was a smothering proposition to him. It was to avoid staying in that he ventured out, searching for familiar places. Megha had made her entry in such a setting.

It wasn't long before Indrajit was forced to contemplate how this girl, who ought to have exited his life in the past, could have suddenly showed up in his present. An inexplicable experience at night was the cause of that. As he was on the verge of slipping into sleep, another life, as palpable as the real one, came searching for him. Though he had undergone such experiences before, never had there been this crystalline clarity. His sojourn was through a space hard to discern as either dream or reality.

During that journey Indrajit again met Megha. It was really an intense experience of a parallel life. Had anybody asked whether it was a dream, Indrajit would have sworn that it was not. It was an extraordinary state of his consciousness existing simultaneously in two lives!

When he lurched awake, Indrajit was pushed into a vortex of confusion. He yearned to share it with someone else. But he was certain that it would be difficult to convince any other person. It would only be judged as the wild fantasies of an unbalanced mind.

The strange experience prompted Indrajit to reach Nireeswaran's abode the next day. The warm remnants of the parallel life was still lingering inside him. His mind insisted that he should meet Megha again. Maybe it was triggered by remorse, or by an instinct beyond reason and logic. Though he waited for long, the desired one did not appear. That made his longing more intensive.

There was no information about Megha except that she worked in the Aanganwadi. The only recourse was to wait till the next day or until she appeared by herself. Another way out was to seek Sudha's help. But there was something clumsy about that move. Indrajit sat on the stone embankment thinking that if it was Nireeswaran's play that awakened him from eternal sleep, the deity could just as easily make Megha appear. After all, he had been told that it was Megha's supplication before Nireeswaran which had been answered.

Indrajit's attention wandered to Nireeswaran. The idol was striking in a bizarre way. At first glance, there was nothing attractive about it. He had no clue that it was the remnant of a figure which had undergone decapacitation and mutilation. Wondering about the number of miracles attributed to that unshapely figurine, Indrajit almost sneered. Perhaps due to it, or not, Megha did not appear that day.

When Megha appeared the next day, Indrajit did not pause for a preface and headed straight for an apology.

'I am sorry . . . was in a muddled state of mind that day. That was why I could not speak.'

A magpie-robin sang a *dhrupad* note above them. From the bird's sky, a few drops of rain showered on Megha, almost as if announcing the onset of the monsoon. Though the man had been asleep for twenty-four years, she knew him closely.

'No issues . . . I pray that you remain healthy and well.'

Now, Indrajit was getting more clarity. He was only thirty-two years old. It was as if he had entered a perfect universe, freed from all insecurities. He looked curiously at the stone figure on the embankment, at the one adept at playing games, wondering what else was being planned.

The man and woman watched the peacock flutter its wings from the green heights of the trees and descend. Indrajit gazed unblinkingly at the bird, longing to see the spread of its magnificent tail feathers.

Twenty-First Petal: Unseen Arrows

'The first father in the world younger than his own children,' Arnos murmured, soft like a mantra *japa*, when he met Indrajit after the decades-long interlude.

Indrajit's situation was strange, as though he were in some wonderland. To discern his childhood friend in the old man was an arduous task. The first instinct was a feeling of distance, typical of one's encounters with elderly acquaintances. As he stared, not believing his own eyes, the beloved youthful days they had spent together seemed to return. By that time, Arnos had locked him in a tight embrace.

'*Eda*, Indra! You look the same, even after twenty-four years. How fortunate to meet you again!'

The initial feeling of distance disappeared, and a great sense of relief took its place. Indrajit had been intensely longing for someone to interact with freely, swamped as he was with the vast universe which surrounded him. The lone person with whom he could open up, at least to some extent, was Roberto. But he did not belong to Indrajit's past.

The feeling of intimacy comes only with continued relations. It rarely gets generated in a new friendship, even though the growing intimacy with Roberto was definitely giving Indrajit much solace. But the man's ways were unpredictable, and he could return to his scientific adventures at any moment.

The chance meeting with Arnos gave him hope, much like finding an oasis in a desert. The tiny antlions, hidden in the loamy soil on which they had traced the first letters of the alphabet, seemed to be stirring again. The childhood friend, who would join Indrajit in blowing into the sand to uncover the furtive antlions burrowing beneath, was now hugging him again.

When the excitement of the reunion subsided a bit, Arnos asked, 'The time . . . Indra, didn't you know anything about it? Where did you spend your twenty-four years?'

They were sitting in the meadow near the Athmavu. The place was lush with couch grass. There were *muyalcheviyan*, *mukkutty* and *kakkapoo* in that mélange. Anyone searching for the *dasapushpa*, the ten local flowers used for traditional rituals, could easily discover nearly eight in the list right there.

'It was briefer than a moment. But it held a thousand births within. I can recollect a few of them even now. Some pictures appear, rather vaguely, when I am on the brink of slipping into sleep.'

Even as he spoke, a name floated in the ethereal sky of his mind, like a cloud spreading shade. He was facing the real experiences of his subconscious in the blazing heat of daily living. Had anyone mentioned such a possibility before, Indrajit would have been the first to oppose it. Indeed, he would have laughed mockingly at the sheer craziness of such a suggestion. Because for anyone standing with his feet on the ground, an out-of-the-world experience, beyond the grasp of gravity, was unreachable. And so Indrajit, during his years before the comatose phase, was unaware of such a possibility.

When his consciousness had been tangled with mysterious layers, a door had opened to a world of knowledge hitherto unknown to him. It was a futile exercise to convince anybody, since proving one's subconscious journeys in any scientific lab was out of the question.

There was a substantial crowd near the Athmavu by that time. Indrajit recollected that even in the bygone days, the natives would seek out that area to relax after a hard day's grind. Groups of aged folk, youthful gangs and playful children—all arrived at the Athmavu. Now they had all coalesced into one group.

Pointing at an elderly man amid the crowd, Arnos asked, 'Indra, any idea who that is?'

Gazing with abject attention, Indrajit found himself astounded. 'Isn't that Eswaran?'

'Yes. His destiny is another story altogether. He will come after the rush hour. How long has it been since we chatted together?'

The cold breeze, blowing gently, peeped into Indrajit's heart too. It was the breeze of yore that came gushing in, to push open the mind's door, which remained as yet shut. In the olden days, when Indrajit was with Arnos and Embrandiri, time never hinted the speed of its flow to him. Probably because he would be stinging with the pain of having been forced to drop school, Embrandiri would always enquire about the classes. That habit continued even when his friends reached college. They would part ways only when darkness gathered, fearing the rebuke of the elders.

Such a fellowship was probably rare at the time. Indrajit could now lay open the bundle of turmoil before Arnos and Embrandiri. Only those who were cognizant of the existence of the microcosm could appreciate the travelogues of someone who had crossed the frontiers of the mortal body.

'We often get together here,' Arnos said. 'Zaid joins us occasionally.'

'Ah, Zaid! Where is he now?' Indrajit asked.

'He runs a madrasa. His children are doing well.'

'Really?'

'He has gone to town. Will come running if he hears about you.'

'I want to see him as soon as possible.'

Indrajit was eager to know how the twenty-four years, which he had lived in a moment, had affected everyone else.

'In truth, we should have come searching for you earlier. No, let me rephrase it: we should have been the first to visit! However, we were waiting for Zaid's arrival, wishing to meet you together. Else something would have felt amiss. Meanwhile, you came searching for us . . .'

'Those destined to meet will do so. If not in this life, then in another . . .' Indrajit said. Then, looking at Arnos, he enquired, 'Who is there at home, Arnos?'

'No one,' Arnos said. 'Amma left. I did not bring anyone to keep me company. One takes care of oneself.'

Amma's death had left his house enveloped in an impregnable silence. Cohabiting with silence, relishing the joy of sitting around doing nothing, Arnos had retreated within himself. In the evening, he would seek out the motherly shade of the trees. Late at night, he would return, accompanied by Embrandiri. They would share a few words with each other, and by the time they completed half the way, their paths would diverge, symbolizing life's predicament.

Embrandiri would travel through the side path, turning from the shop beyond the bridge. Moving further, through areas covered with dense rubber trees, Arnos would return to his still and solitary residence.

Nireeswaran's abode had evolved to become the village's centre. On certain days, unpredicted turbulence was palpable in the air. The formerly dark and looming Athmavu now watched over a circle of humans lighted up by a flickering lamp, with the beaming Eswaran Embrandiri in their midst. The venerable old man had long reconciled to being forcibly called back to his religious duties.

When Embrandiri joined them after the rituals, Indrajit was enthused, as if recovering the lost heartbeat of his past. His friend had undergone an utter transformation. The golden-hued body seemed to have acquired a new shimmer. Embrandiri seemed to have taken a holy dip in some pristine, pure radiance! Since his hair was snow-white, he called to mind a divine, immortal character of the Puranic stories.

Sometimes if a locked door is shaken obdurately, its latch springs open, as if it were waiting for that to happen. That was how, in the twilight, as the peepal and mango stood witness, Indrajit attempted to share what had happened to him during his stint of subconscious timelessness.

While asleep, Indrajit had seen Kuncheriya, his playmate at school who had drowned in the river. Wearing the familiar belted shorts and white shirt, he was smiling innocently. When Indrajit revealed that he had seen his late parents and an aunt who had expired, Arnos wore his usual elusive smile.

'I saw another sight!'

'What?'

'In front of our church school, wasn't there a statue of St Antony carrying infant Jesus? I saw it clearly. The infant Jesus was smiling at me.'

In those days Indrajit used to stand indifferently before the figurine, even as Arnos, Zaid and Embrandiri bowed reverentially. His stance had been disdainful, unable to see divinity in a sculpture crafted from mud and stone. How could the same figure appear so full of life now, with a mesmerizing halo around its head?

'Maybe,' Arnos quipped, 'you might have seen Nireeswaran's consecration too, Indra. The foundation of both the conscious and subconscious minds happens to be the same.'

But what Indrajit told them afterwards was implausible. There were hints of an alternate reality Indrajit had experienced in the timelessness of his unconscious state. A parallel life was reaching out to him, beyond his reach in the world of the awake but accessible in the world of the subconscious. There were clear signs that Indrajit had enacted the role of a householder there. More than a recollection of a dream, it seemed to him like a memory of a lived past. While remembering a forgotten dream, nobody felt miserable about having seen fantasy characters. The memory of the children one saw in a dream didn't hurt so deeply either. But the past wasn't like that; it haunted one ceaselessly. A person could be traumatized by the helplessness of being trapped in it, as though in an enemy's dungeon, unable to return to his own country.

'Sometimes, I feel extreme agony thinking of my loved ones whose whereabouts remain unknown. It is a pain that's inexpressible!

I ask myself who are my real offspring—the children of this world in their thirties, or my little babies in that world? *Tell me, what is that world? Or, what is this world?*

Indrajit was flailing about in a mysterious time-phase which engirdled him. His friends were nonplussed; they had never known Indrajit to have ever been disposed towards such esoteric topics.

'Somehow, you intruded into a dimension that transcended the law of time. After all, "Indrajit" means someone who can transcend the senses,' Arnos murmured.

Arnos and Embrandiri were hearing about such a predicament for the very first time. It was a solemn reminder of the possibility that the consciousness spreads beyond the visible universe. It unveiled unseen worlds in deep sleep and dreams, as real as the gross world we experience in wakefulness. Usually, these worlds never met one another. But Indrajit's unconscious mind had travelled to the other world and brought back some remnants to the mortal world. For him, those were absolute truths.

A psychologist might resort to high-sounding scientific terms to declare Indrajit's state as a mental disorder, never having known deep sleep or *sushupthi* himself. He wouldn't even be able to contemplate *Turiya,* the fourth stage beyond wakefulness, dream and sleep.

How could one ponder about a state where all thought ceased? It was an absolute state devoid of all relativities, like sweetness experiencing sweetness. The state, where there was no distinction between the experience and the one experiencing it, was not something the brain could analyse with detachment. Hence psychology could visualize only at the sliver of sky above a narrow well. Even that glimpse would be dim, covered with clouds.

Indrajit felt trapped between this world and the other. And his friends could only sympathize with the one who had been ostracized from the normal experiences given to all.

'You will get the answer for that, Indra,' Arnos reassured him. 'There will be answers to everyone's queries. Because no question can exist if it doesn't have an answer. Else the disappearance of questions is the answer to everything.'

It was not an exact answer. Or perhaps it was the precise answer. On ruminating further, everything seemed like an absurdist play! How rightly it was said about life: 'A tale told by an idiot!' Now who was the idiot telling the story?

Even as the question, which was real and which was fantasy, remained unanswered, Arnos's gaze fell on another trio seated at a distance. The springing forth of this new trio of friends, like a re-enactment of their own friendship, had a curious precision and, further, a rare coincidence about it.

They were courageous young men who hailed themselves as the Abhasa and were like Young Turks who dared to encroach into the neighbouring country for attacking.

The Abhasa could view the meeting of the older generation only as a conspiracy. They suspected that a devious ploy against them was being brewed by Eswaran Embrandiri, Arnos and Indrajit.

It was nature's trick that the two fellowships were discussing diametrically opposite topics. Resorting to their rationality and logic, the Abhasa were hell-bent on shredding into bits every event that happened around them. They were confident of cogent scientific explanations behind the so-called wonders Parameswaran and Sumitran. But the fact that a man awoke from a coma of twenty-four years daunted them a bit. How had the man returned without a blemish on his youthfulness?

Somehow, Indrajit had burdened the Abhasa with the responsibility of finding a reasonable explanation for his return, which was also being touted as a great miracle wrought by Nireeswaran! The Abhasa sniggered about how the pits of superstition swallowed the gullible believers, when they happened to be the creators of Nireeswaran.

In childhood, it was a common pastime for them to dig deep pits, cover them with twigs and grass and lead unsuspecting people towards them. With an arm around the other's shoulder, pretending to be friends, one would treacherously trick the other into the pit. It was as yet unknown to the villagers that the Abhasa had designed Nireeswaran's consecration with similar plans, for the ultimate 'ditching'. At an opportune time, when the trio would slash at the magical hood of the serpent, it would topple over dead, and all the nonsense associated with the scintillating emerald it purportedly guarded would be exposed as humungous piffle.

The Abhasa had crystal-clear, scientific arguments explaining Indrajit's recovery. They were convinced that the villagers found a cheap thrill by attributing every coincidence to Nireeswaran. It had been an observed, though rare, phenomenon that some people woke up from coma after years. Hence, in the eyes of the Abhasa, Indrajit, who had entranced the naive minds of the villagers, was nothing less than a villainous figure. It vexed them to see him sit on top of the boulder. His mere presence was like a silent heralding of Nireeswaran's glory. They felt duty-bound to affix Indrajit's life within the sharply delineated squares of their logic.

'After all, every natural law has its exception,' Antony argued stridently. 'For example, the motion of planet Venus is against the general rule that all the planets in the solar system move from west to east. She travels from east to west. When the common rule is that metals are solid, isn't mercury both a liquid and a metal? There are many oddities in nature like this! Should we haw-haw that these are marvels? The man who feels nothing when 11 kilovolts of current passes through his body, fries an omelette on the heater kept atop his palm! Is that a miracle caused by any god? Sumitran and Indrajit are just the common aberrations of the natural world.'

'What was the need for this man to wake up after twenty-four years? Either he should have woken up a long time ago, or at least waited until we threw Nireeswaran into the canal,' Bhaskaran smouldered while dwelling on the sheer unfairness of it all.

'All's well that ends well. Let the dunces continue to believe! It will last only till we hurl the stone into the canal, right? When the miracle-doer sinks in the water, his powers will also vanish in thin air.

How can someone who cannot help himself offer aid to others? That will instigate a new line of thought. Let Nireeswaran continue to live for some more time,' Antony said.

'That's true,' Sahir agreed. 'By the way, I have to leave early today.'

A female serpent he had seen in a magazine at Maniyan's shop slithered seductively inside him and was coiling tight around his loins. He yearned to reach home to loosen that tension.

However, when it came to the larger picture, the tension was not to be assuaged; instead, more intricate knots were formed in the days to come. An infectious flu started spreading rapidly in the village. Antony and Bhaskaran picked up the virus and suffered severe cough, joint pain and fatigue. Modern-day flus debilitated their victims, leaving the patient no recourse but to be helplessly confined to a cot. The infinitesimal germs could tame the most powerful of men. Human intelligence, which gloated about its superiority, was forced to concede defeat then.

Only Sahir somehow escaped the conspiracy of the microbes. Apprehensive of his weak immunity, he avoided visiting his friends, and the Abhasa was shorn of the strength of their numbers for more than a week.

Sudharman, the founder of the Niprasa, was graced with a new revelation by Nireeswaran during that epidemic season. The moment the seed of inspiration sprouted, it spread like the microbes of the flu inside Sudharman. Unable to keep it to himself, he eagerly presented the idea before other devout Niprasa members, like Sumitran and Parameswaran. The subject matter entranced all of them.

Owing to Nireeswaran's benevolent glance, the Niprasa was flourishing; it had attained heights of popularity higher than even the peepal and the mango. There was nothing wrong in Sudharman's conclusion that it was the Niprasa's duty to assist Nireeswaran's elevation to higher pedestals. If anyone wondered about the need to boost a self-spreading entity, Sudharman had a definite answer.

A man's mind works through the organs of the body. If Nireeswaran is the unseen mind which is omnipresent, it can be deduced that the devotees form his body. So, it becomes the duty of the devotees to ensure that the "mind" is spread far and wide. Since Nireeswaran is a new god in the pantheon, certain rites and rituals have to be conducted to sanctify his divinity properly. Moreover, those rites should be reinforced with fitting interpretations. That will solidify Nireeswaran's legendary status in the years to come. Like the festivals of Onam, Vishu and Pooram, the legacy of Nireeswaran shall be exalted as part of the land's heritage for centuries.

It was edifying to note Sudharman's eagerness about the business opportunities that awaited the Niprasa in the event of a potential surge of Nireeswaran's popularity owing to newly constituted rituals. Sudharman proposed that three processions should reach the crossroads where Nireeswaran sat, starting from the three sideways. It would be like a grandiose proclamation about the deity to the world at large. Sumitran was entrusted with the job of getting a colour photograph of the festivities along with a four-column news item published in the vernacular newspapers. Nireeswaran was not born to wither away morosely, seated at the junction of three roads.

Eswaran Embrandiri could see the symbolism in that idea. He always preferred to follow the middle path, without expressing either antagonism or affinity towards anything. It was the truth-seeker's way: *the path came searching for the traveller, instead of the traveller seeking the path.* If the three side roads could be seen as symbolizing the past, present and future, the junction where they met was the apposite site for Nireeswaran, who was beyond the dictates of time. Truly a worthwhile notion.

In a short while, the idea was concretized. Three elephants made their way through the 'three time zones', carrying the replicas of Nireeswaran, accompanied by the animated *panchari melam*, the percussion ensemble complete with kombu, kuzhal, chenda and ilathalam. And a festive spirit was unleashed across the land.

Certain businessmen pitched in as sponsors for the various expenses associated with the celebrations, and soon it became more boisterous than the original consecration ceremony conducted by the Abhasa. The most disheartening fact was that nobody thought it fit to discuss anything about the festivities with the creators of Nireeswaran. Only Sahir, who had escaped the clutches of the perilous flu, ended up witnessing the confluence of the three processions at the Athmavu.

Listening to the clamour of the panchari melam, when Antony stretched his neck, he glimpsed the royal head of the tusker carrying the deity's image. He felt scalded, as if an intense bout of heat had enveloped the flu-ridden bed. His joints started aching viciously. It dawned on him that Nireeswaran had started upturning the lives of the natives. However, his body could hardly keep up with his mind. Else he would have ensured that the three tuskers carrying the divinity's image went down on their knees before him!

In his fury, Antony started pummelling the pillow. The smatterings of cotton burst out and spread in the air. His head hurt like hell, and Antony started fulminating against the world in general. He swore to himself that he would send the venomous arrow straight back to the initiators.

As the sounds of the panchari melam receded, Antony's temper also abated. He then came up with an idea: *Bide your time. The bugles of battle shall ring out soon enough! We shall expose all the dullards veiled by false beliefs!* Till then, let Nireeswaran garner strength and overcome, as it were, his childhood tribulations. When Nireeswaran entered the stage of youth after adolescence, Antony would engage him, at the acme of his strength, in direct combat!

Antony was sure that the opportunity was not too far away. As a precautionary measure, he suddenly felt the need to fortify his team with more like-minded members. If the Abhasa could attract those whose beliefs were in congruence with theirs, it would bolster their efforts in uprooting Nireeswaran for good.

Twenty-Second Petal: Peacock

There was an evergreen water reservoir on top of the rock. A small pool, its diameter less than a metre. Even in the bleakest of summers, it would be full of water. Tiny frogs lived inside, hoarsely croaking, 'Please don't dry up . . .' If the creatures accidentally jumped onto the sweltering rock, they would have been burnt to cinders. Indrajit felt that though twenty-four years had passed, the same little pond, the same frogs and plants were waiting for him on top of the rock. When everything else had passed him by, the ecosystem in the pond continued to exist like a parallel world in the present universe.

In that miniature world, among the algae and amoeba in the pond, the little frogs were gigantic creatures. Like the frogs trapped in the reservoir, Indrajit too was imprisoned by time. Whenever he sat there bleakly, enduring the abject misery of a prisoner, Indrajit felt that at the bottom of the tree, Nireeswaran was also experiencing the same feeling.

Inadvertently, a question would needle him: *What was the relationship between Nireeswaran and him*?

Indrajit was familiar with the phenomenon of small idols tucked into the crevices of rocks and giant roots of the banyan trees, transforming the site into places of worship. En route to the town, near the riverside, there was a place of worship for the primitive god Chathan. Also, a Vigneswaran reigned in the breach of a rock, appeased by the flame of a desolate stone lamp. Nobody from the upper classes ever worshipped that poor god, only the street vendors and slum dwellers. The priest, whose life depended on the scarce coins donated by the devotees, was destined to eternal penury.

Here, near the Athmavu, everything was different. Indrajit was mystified while contemplating whether Nireeswaran had angelic or devilish proclivities. Imagination could be boundless in its reach. One could fantasize about a ten-trunked elephant or a fire-spitting bird coloured in a hundred different hues! But what was the validity of a fairy tale in the real world? At the stone embankment where Nireeswaran stood, the boundaries between fantasy and reality had blurred, much like ridges after a furious flood.

Indrajit had no answers when it came to responding to the propaganda that it was Nireeswaran who had performed the miracles in many lives, including his. Megha herself had confessed to having made such an entreaty. So was he subservient to Nireeswaran's benevolence too?

Indrajit found himself loath to follow that trail of thought. Well, he slept. Then he woke up. There was no need for either Eswaran or Nireeswaran to partake of the credit. He could generously accept that Megha had made him a subject of her prayer, without seeking anyone's permission. But it was worrisome to reflect that a girl bearing her image had cohabited with him in the world of sleep. Indrajit would argue with his own mind that those were senseless thoughts.

Soon, he would find himself descending into a morass of guilt, that his own ability to differentiate between fantasy and reality was at fault.

Many questions would spring up in his mind:

1. *Who was that girl?*
2. *At which point in time did she take shape in his subconscious mind and set up a home?*
3. *What was the reason behind the mesmerizing force field which was radiating from her?*
4. *If her presence was creating an unworldly ambience, what was the connecting thread between him and her?*

Indrajit was aware that there was one and only one answer to all those questions. But certain matters turned out to be delightful and baffling at the same time.

A hardcore atheist had woken up from a deep sleep with new insights. Words like 'god', 'prayer', 'wonder' had never touched Indrajit all his life. If his mother was radiant due to her faith, his father was self-enlightened with materialistic ideas. Indrajit had a bias towards his father's materialistic outlook rather than his mother's unquestioning faith. He had indulged in bitter verbal disputes with Arnos, Zaid and Embrandiri even while maintaining cordial friendliness with them. However, now, his own experiences were posing a challenge to his sturdy common sense.

Indrajit found it paradoxical that Eswaran Embrandiri, who was a devout believer, was now worshipping Nireeswaran, the antithesis of his beliefs! Yet, his mind was prepared for an amicable compromise now, as Nireeswaran was making Embandiri's life prosperous with coins of offerings.

Above all, Indrajit had realized that one's consciousness could not be measured exclusively through what one experienced while being awake. The wakeful state of mind was but a small part of the intellectual capacity. Like evaluating a house just by its outer appearance, there was a limitation in understanding it. Only by entering inside could the variegated sights be seen.

He came to the conclusion that it was sheer stupidity to denounce the truth by looking at the outer shell alone. Though everyone visited the same place every single night during their sleep, the seven barriers of forgetfulness hid the journey soundly. Only on returning, with full consciousness of having reached there, shall the awareness arise.

Till then, each life was a 'frog in the well', mistaking that the piece of the circular sky glimpsed above was the complete sky. Having traversed through both the states, Indrajit could identify the distinctions between the finite and the infinite.

An alarm went on in his mind when Indrajit started yearning to spend more time with Megha. Sudha was being relegated to the position of an ancient relic. A woman who had once satiated his body and mind had lost her personality and disappeared into oblivion.

Indrajit felt pity for the woman who had sacrificed her life in safeguarding a man's sleep. And he knew that his mind's travels were through a treacherous path. Cruel might be a more appropriate word than treacherous. But Indrajit was no yogi who had overcome the limitations of body and mind.

The body demanded everything desired by a healthy physique. If one were to approach a man in his prime and ask him to relinquish all his earthly desires, how would he respond? Enforcing such a command would be like chaining the unconquerable hurricane of life. Indrajit had always been a connoisseur of life's pleasures. A man who never wasted a single opportunity for celebrating life. Now, a callous judge had issued a harsh verdict, banishing every pleasure from his life.

Indrajit tried to analyse the attraction he felt towards Megha.

In age, she was younger than his own children. Her approach was always free of blemish. Consequently, it was disconcerting for Indrajit to confess that Megha had been intimate with him in his subconscious world. It would be perceived either as the blurting of a crazed mind or a fantastic story cooked up for enticing her. The realization that his experiences did not seem in the least credible only made his existence more unbearable.

Sudha could instinctively sense every kind of turbulence, both physical and mental, in Indrajit. She knew that he could desist from anything but sex. Though there was an invisible distance between them, making any discussion impossible, Sudha could sense the intensity of Indrajit's cravings. But her husband had never given her any cause for complaint in any respect. It was his need and right, and it would be an injustice to make him abstain from his yearnings.

Who was pointing fingers at whom now?

When Sudha caught a whiff of Indrajit's feelings for Megha—through certain responses of his—it was as though a crystal vase had crashed inside her heart. The girl had started visiting them frequently. Her interactions were open and irreproachable. Megha was clueless about the new equation between the husband and wife. Every time Megha visited their home, and Indrajit visibly perked up, Sudha felt the sharpness of the double-edged truth.

Sudha knew that the consequences could be far-reaching if she mishandled the situation. Since new deities for worship can easily be installed in the chimerical human mind, the girl whom one considered as a daughter could instantaneously transform into a competitor overnight. Therefore, Sudha's responses to Megha became stilted and inhibited. Perhaps the inferiority complex as a result of losing authority over her husband had brought about such a transformation. The woman who had once cried at the sight of her sleeping husband started weeping over a man who was wide awake. Sudha felt that while praying for Indrajit's recovery, she should have added the condition that he should wake up as an old man.

Soon enough, Indrajit got indications of his home life becoming choppy. He was extra alert about anyone digging out the secret besmirching his mind. The only recourse was to avoid confrontations. That was how he ended up becoming a regular visitor to Nireeswaran's abode.

'When I stand beneath the shadow of the intertwined trees, I find a serenity not found anywhere else,' Megha said one day with a smile, casting a glance at the lush natural awning overhead.

'Same here,' Indrajit agreed. 'I feel so light-hearted as I stand talking here.'

'But you have so many people to chat with at home, don't you?'

'I am like an orphan surrounded by many people.'

Indrajit stood listening to the flutter of a solitary bird atop the Athmavu. He understood that the cast-out bird was a mirror image of his own self.

What could be the desires of that poor creature? Did it have a home, young ones, a shared love? Were the losses churning inside the bird like memories of a past life? The very churning of the 'ocean of milk', where both demonic and godlike passions were subjected to turbulence! For the bird separated from its mate and incarcerated in another world, life must have held only solitude. The panic of having woken up in an utterly strange land was reflected in the bird's eyes too.

A few ripe peepal seeds fell on the ground, as if supporting Indrajit's ruminations. Tender green leaves rustled, signalling the imminent flowering of the mango tree.

'I can be called an orphan . . . But what about someone with a home full of loving souls?' Megha wondered aloud.

Indrajit stood flummoxed, unsure how to handle the quandary he was thrown into by the innocence in her question. Theirs was not a relationship where the soul could be laid bare. Yet, he ended up murmuring, 'I have lost many things, including Sudha.'

The pointed words were a bolt from the blue. It was enough to fluster a woman's mind. 'Even to think so is a sin! The way she took care . . . like a penance! Sacrificing all the pleasures of life . . . no other woman could have done that!'

'I know how virtuous it is. But it is just one half of the virtue. Sometimes I feel that I shouldn't have woken up from the coma! Fate is unjust to certain people. Doomed to isolation, with nobody to understand them . . .'

Megha was unaware of his problems or their nature. If there was any solution, it would be with Nireeswaran, who had brought about Indrajit's awakening. The only recourse she had was prayer, which did not entail any investment. If the true nature of prayer was a meeting of the minds, then underneath the Athmavu, where Purusha and *prakriti* merged as one, before the stone figurine, she could pray with a concentration not found elsewhere. It was a form of intimacy, as if she was conversing with her own self.

Megha and Indrajit met many times near Nireeswaran's abode. Some were coincidences and others were self-created. But neither of them realized that they were being watched, and the village considered them as transgressors of forbidden boundaries. They had no inkling of being depicted as tarnished characters in spicy gossip sessions in the countryside and in the interiors of homes. The gossipmongers started sharpening their hidden arrows. The weapons multiplied manifold and sped towards the man and woman.

Antony was thrilled on hearing the salacious news. If the one whom Nireeswaran resurrected became the cause of an earthquake, it would be great fun witnessing the unfolding of events! He had been scouring for a new weapon against Nireeswaran ever since the procession. Apparently, the 'Adi–Madhya–Antha'—the beginning, the middle and the end—had merged that day. He snickered to himself that by now the beginning and the middle were over. All that remained was an ending.

Though the original plan of the Abhasa was to remove Nireeswaran's idol in a ceremonial occasion, as riotous as its consecration, the new turn of events made them rethink. They decided to keep a close watch on Indrajit. Since Indrajit would be instrumental in their scheme of casting aspersions on Nireeswaran, the trio decided to support the erstwhile enemy's actions.

When the three gathered near the Athmavu for further deliberations, the peacock started screeching from the branches, as if cognizant of all the goings-on. The bird had been around for weeks, and it showed no signs that it wanted to leave. Most of the villagers exhibited genuine affection towards it. Since peacocks were rarely sighted in that region, crowds thronged to catch a glimpse of the solitary bird which had got lost from its muster. Some hoped that it would grace them with a dance. Certain devotees started seeing divinity in its walk and strut. Antony found it absolutely abhorrent.

'We are habituated to seeing godliness in animals and birds!' Antony seethed at the peacock's conceit. 'One day I am going to catch it and put an end to all that bilge!'

Antony's style was to assail everything that exhibited haughtiness, whether animals, birds, humans or ideas. Possibly sensing what was in the air, the bird kept from crossing dangerous boundaries. It pecked around only in select yards, mindful of the time of the day and place.

One day, the peacock swooped down near the Nireeswaran idol and spread its beautiful tail feathers. After consuming the offerings left behind by the devotees and shaking itself thoroughly, the bird took flight and, moving from tree to tree, made a landing in the yard of Antony's house.

On seeing the unexpected visitor, Antony told himself that the bird had come searching for its own death. The poor creature wasn't aware of the man waiting with a ready noose. It merrily pecked around, unaware of the ominous threat looming nearby. Antony tossed the lasso with the skill of an expert bird-catcher. The noose ended up around the peacock's neck like a wedding garland, since the creature was not agile enough to fly off instantaneously.

When Antony attempted to tighten the death-knot, the peacock freed its neck from the noose with unbelievable flexibility and flew away screeching to a nearby branch.

Livid at the way the creature had escaped death by a hair's breadth, Antony hollered, 'If not today then tomorrow, I shall finish you off!'

Bhaskaran was relieved that Antony had failed in his bird-hunting expedition. Since there was both an artist and a naturalist inside him, he wasn't willing to declare solidarity with Antony in such matters. He even showed courage to oppose him a smidgeon. 'Don't try to catch it. The poor creature did not steal anything of ours, did it? Birds also have a right to live.'

'Mankind comes first, and the rest of nature should be subjugated to us!'

'That is an outdated idea. All have equal importance. Birds, animals and even trees—nothing should be harmed. Nature's rhythm gets upset even if one plant is uprooted.'

'As if! One day, I will catch the peacock and cook it for dinner!' Antony challenged.

'That is a crime! Can get you jailed for more than seven years,' Bhaskaran warned.

'Then I will kill one more in the eighth year!' Antony smirked. Taking umbrage on hearing that even man-made law was on the peacock's side, Antony stooped to pick up a stone and aimed it at the bird. It briskly evaded the throw and hid itself among the profusion of leaves in the heights.

But something happened the next day, making one suspect if the peacock had extracted its revenge! From its beak, a venomous snake slipped and fell right in front of Antony. Since it was impossible for a snake to fly across the sky, Antony leapt back petrified, losing all poise. The stunned snake slithered quickly into the serpentine roots of the Athmavu and vanished from sight.

Sumitran, who was a witness to the incident, issued a cautionary warning to Antony. 'You'd better be careful. Can't say from where ominous signs will come!'

Though the warning was for Antony, Sahir felt dizzy on hearing those words. He was scared to death of snakes. The stories someone had narrated in his childhood, highlighting the vengeful nature of serpents, still haunted him.

One such tale was of Garuda with a king cobra in its beak. During its sojourn through the skies, the snake had fallen on a man's head and bitten him to death! Garuda swooped down on the snake again as it lay on the ground, proving the infallibility of death. The death that descended from the skies before going back to the skies . . . it was a story that stoked great horror in Sahir. Dreaming of Takshaka, the snake which could assume the form of both microbes and anacondas, he had ended up screaming that night too.

The heat intensified over the land. As the water in the reservoir on the rock top started boiling and swirling, the little frogs lay low, half-dazed, expecting death.

ANNIHILATION

Twenty-Third Petal: Opposition

A starkly peculiar ecosystem of manners evolved around Nireeswaran. He was easily accessible to anyone. There were no dogmatic rituals or written rules. A person could light a lamp, a candle, an agarbatti or even blow out the flames! It was decided that nobody would object to any form of worship, thus creating an eclectic aura around Nireeswaran. Those who pulled the strings to implement the protocols preferred to remain anonymous.

Arnos and Zaid felt that their friendship of yore, cutting across religions, was again stretching its tender hands towards them. It was the continuation of the thoughts which had germinated inside them as they wrote their first letters together. Any notion which was deeply rooted in the mind would inevitably manifest one day. That was why Tathagatha said, 'You have become so because of your thinking.'

Now their thoughts had found an embodiment, a sanctuary open to anyone, at any time. Nireeswaran was not biased when it came to doling out his blessings to the lamenting needy. Indeed, he seemed to have signed a bond of assurance with the devotees on a blank paper.

Theresa, Sarojini and Rashid had obtained grace in the same measure. When the news spread that caste and religion were immaterial for receiving Nireeswaran's benediction, the deity took on an image that transcended any form of discrimination. If they so wished, a parish priest offering eucharistic sacrifices or an imam paying obeisance would have been welcomed at Nireeswaran's abode.

The blessing of Nireeswaran was in ensuring that no category or section of people could claim an exclusive ownership over the deity. A concept which cleaved through religious discrimination had incarnated by itself as per the requirements of the time. None of the existing religious texts had introduced a Nireeswaran in corporeal form. If at all anyone could lay claim to Nireeswaran, it would have to be the clan of atheists, aka the Nireeswaravadi—the name closely matching with that of the deity. But that lot shrugged away Nireeswaran as just another non-existent god. That was the quandary faced by Antony, Bhaskaran and Sahir now.

When the entourage of Nireeswaran's followers from various religious backgrounds grew by leaps and bounds, a bevy of 'out-of-the-box' thinkers put forth a new proposition. The Nireeswaran who showered such bountiful blessings on his devotees was not to be subjected to rain and shine beneath a tree. He definitely deserved a royal seat and an elegant roof above his head!

Although it was a simple protective roof that was initially thought of, it soon attained the form of a temple. If the rich folk took up the resolve, it would hardly take time for any idea to solidify into reality.

The news of an imminent temple construction greatly provoked Antony, Bhaskaran and Sahir. Now was the time to act! Until now they had silently watched it all, biding their time to unleash a powerful retaliation. But if a temple for Nireeswaran arose in the vicinity, everything would slip from their hands, and the problem would assume a monstrous shape. Determined to stem the flow, they hurried to meet Eswaran Embrandiri.

'Heard that discussions are on for building a temple here?' Antony's tone was cutting.

'I too heard about it,' Embrandiri gave a noncommittal reply.

'What stupidity is that!' Sahir, usually averse to jumping into the fray, became enraged. 'Build a temple around a lifeless stone? The very mention of the word temple makes us allergic!'

Looking at Zaid who stood nearby, Sahir pointedly asked, 'Even you would be opposed to a temple, wouldn't you?'

Zaid had arrived in the village after a long break. He had wanted to see Indrajit ever since he got the news of his recovery. However, the responsibilities of running a madrasa left him with little spare time. When Allah was kind enough to give him an aide, Zaid had rushed to the village immediately. After many decades, all four of them had met under the Athmavu.

Now, the Abhasa had posed a question to him, whether he would have objections to a temple being built. Sahir held on to the obnoxious belief that Zaid, being a Muslim, would blindly oppose the temple construction.

'What obscenity is there in the word temple for you to feel allergic to it?' Zaid asked solemnly. 'The word means "a place". A temple can also be interpreted as a body, and the deity as the power residing within it. Thus, if you are allergic to the notion, the problem does not lie with the temple but with yourself.'

Sahir had never expected such an answer. Since he did not have the gift of the gab like his friends, he struggled to find an appropriate response. As he fumed, Embrandiri interjected. 'Children, now it is no longer a simple stone. It is the very nerve of the village. Like the intellectual nerve, *medha nadi*, of a body, every land has its own nerve.'

'You crazy priest, while spouting gibberish, just remember whom you are talking to! We are the ones who dressed you up in the buffoonish role of a priest to install Nireeswaran. It was to oppose superstition. Now when the whole kerfuffle has turned into another superstition, we cannot stand by and watch!'

Antony's vehemence reached its acme. When matters were not to his liking, his blood flow would instantaneously surge. A similar gushing occurred, albeit in a different guise, whenever he glanced at a female body. In Sahir's words, Antony's blood 'was a wee bit too fluid'.

'I am a crazy priest, agreed! But when I conducted the initiation ritual of Nireeswaran, my role was clownish only in your minds. I never considered it a mock consecration. Irrespective of anything said, or by whom it was said, I affirm that Nireeswaran is my concept of God. What is important is not the name or the ritual, but the faith and the dedication. If needed, you atheists can also pray. Even if you denounce all known gods while praying, it would still attain fruition.'

'Stop preaching to us. We are not nincompoops!'

Even when Antony raised his voice, Eswaran Embrandiri remained serene. 'I have seen the world. And stayed away from it for long too. You forced a man who had conducted puja for Eswaran since birth to worship Nireeswaran. I have witnessed umpteen times in my life, how, on becoming established, the movements against any sort of evil turn into a replica of what they were trying to oppose! No difference whether it is a political party or religion. Nothing ever attains perfection.

'Those who join these outfits in the hope of perfection eventually learn to turn a blind eye towards many aspects and compromise. Some honest souls relinquish both politics and religion and become impassive.

'Is there any idea more beautiful than the exhortation of loving one's neighbour like oneself? Forgetting all religions and politics, if we simply implement just that idea, wouldn't all the problems of the world get resolved? The minds have to be accustomed accordingly.

'Force begets more force. You wished to oppose Eswaran, didn't you? Now you are driven to battle Nireeswaran instead! How quickly your goal shifted, without you having an inkling! The Nireeswaran, whom you oppose, is now the land's hope!'

'If so, we will rout that hope very soon! If we could install a stone here, we can very well hurl it into a stream!' Antony threatened.

'Your fervour is laudable. But I fear you've erred in your decision. Children, what was a mere stone before consecration has now transformed into Nireeswaran, affixed to a firm foundation! Perhaps the one controlling even you!'

'We shall see who is controlling whom! See, this dirty piece of stone was dug up from my compound. It was Bhaskaran's handiwork and was sculpted into its present shape. He crafted it with the skill which he uses for moulding naked feminine forms! We spent money to install it in this place. Apart from the three of us, who has any claim on the statue? After negotiating the rates, we anointed you a buffoonish priest! Now we are planning to jettison the whole damn thing. Haven't you studied science? The denser object sinks into a less dense one. Watch the strength of the stone vanishing when it sinks into the river water,' Antony fulminated.

Indrajit, who had been a silent onlooker, wondered who was fighting whom and what might be the purpose behind the brouhaha. It was as if the strife of his sleeping life had been carried into this world. Even as he stood, unable to distinguish between right and wrong in the ongoing argument, Arnos looked on impassively.

Nowadays, his focus was on shielding his mind from what was happening around him. Practising wilful detachment, he attempted to be imperturbable amid the fiery fights and tempestuous scenes. He wanted to reach a stage where he could remain undisturbed even if a bomb were to fall on him, or if he were to plummet right into an avalanche. Here was the perfect training ground for him. A tranquil state of idleness inside the crashing, mad wave of the roaring sea!

'Children, you are right,' Embrandiri spoke without losing his cool. 'At that point, Nireeswaran was within the boundaries of your mind. But now it has expanded through thousands of minds and has enfolded you within its own mind. To be precise, Nireeswaran is now part of the *one supreme mind* of the universe.'

'Aha! Supreme mind! Bilge! There is nothing like that.'

'Yes, there is. It is akin to the water reservoir formed when many small wells conjoin. Even a dry well can curb its thirst from that source. It is impossible to drain it off. Nireeswaran is also like that now. You do not have the willpower to combat it right now. Without the inner strength to overcome Nireeswaran, you shall never be able to destroy it,' Embrandiri said.

Antony's blood boiled to the point of evaporation. He yelled fiercely, 'Then watch me fling away that Nireeswaran right now! All that huffing and puffing shall be exposed in a jiffy. That is what we want to show too! To prove Nireeswaran is no different from any fake god and is equally stupid. Watch the live demonstration!'

The Abhasa saw Nireeswaran as an egregious obscenity among the flowers and lamps. Their hands itched to dethrone it from the arena adorned with candles and agarbattis. Even Arnos found himself wavering for a moment. Surrendering his determination to control himself, his eyes went searching for the deity too.

It was the moment when Nireeswaran was going to be obliterated from history, once and for all. A shameful retreat for an unexpected birth. As the god of all miracles stood like an orphan, the creators set out to annihilate its existence for all eternity. Indrajit was sardonically wondering whether it was that piece of stone, about to be tossed away, which had given him back his life.

The Abhasa rushed forward. But when the three pairs of hands reached out for Nireeswaran's statue, a formidable shout stopped them in their tracks.

'Don't you dare touch it!'

Petrified by the warning, the trio turned and were stunned again. It was Sumitran, with an intimidating aura of power around him! The lumbering halfwit, who used to mumble 'chave me, chave me', had turned into a fearsome figure forbidding them with unequivocal clarity. Antony, Bhaskaran and Sahir found their masculinity debilitated. How did such commanding power resound in Sumitran's voice?

'If you touch Nireeswaran, none of you will go back alive!'

They wished to mock him and say, 'Go away, lisper!' But it was impossible to utter a word. Sumitran was not a lisper anymore but a living miracle.

Seeing them vacillate, Sumitran spoke again, 'Just take a look behind you, before you venture to touch the deity . . .'

The Abhasa saw a milling crowd forming behind them. As if one man had multiplied into many, they were watching with flaming eyes the malefactors in front of them. The crowd was increasing in number by the second . . . Not tens or hundreds, even more! A human wall of protection was being built around Nireeswaran.

The three were dumbstruck at the sight of hundreds of villagers seemingly up in arms.

'Look, their mind is Nireeswaran's temple. They have built a protective wall around the deity with their bodies . . . If you want to destroy Nireeswaran, you have to destroy each one of us first,' said Sumitran.

Most of the milling crowd had been attracted by the hubbub and were not hostile to the Abhasa. However, the trio didn't know that. Their mental state was such that they saw even an innocent bystander as a formidable opponent.

Amid the unexpectedly gathered crowd, Antony, Bhaskaran and Sahir lost their composure, and their enthusiasm and vigour drained away. They were not burdened by the desire to redeem the world anymore. Their grandiose, messianic aspirations soon dwindled, and they began looking for a way to wriggle out of the mess, much like any other ordinary creature acting on its survival instinct.

'Well, one thing is evident,' Sumitran snarled. 'You are Abhasa, not just in your name but also in your deeds! Know that you are spared only due to the kindness of Nireeswaran, whom you wished to destroy. And you are forbidden from entering these precincts from now on. Consider it as Nireeswaran's command!'

When a hum of agreement arose from the crowd, the Abhasa, defeated and unnerved, dragged themselves slowly away.

Behind them arose the tinkling of the bells, announcing a special puja for Nireeswaran.

It sounded like the death knell for the trio.

Twenty-Fourth Petal: 'Raajasa'

To escape from the extreme chagrin and disgrace, the three friends crushed the neck of a liquor bottle.

Emanating the sound of the life-breath escaping through the head, the cork popped. Antony filled his glass with great intensity, like he was setting fire to each of his peeves. As he swallowed the burning liquid, discarding the formality of the usual 'cheers', in a voice sharp as the tip of a sword, he spat out, 'I shall destroy everything!'

He truly meant what he said. The shards of humiliation had pierced deep inside him. Antony believed that he was perfect, with hundred per cent markings of masculinity. When he stood with his chest puffed out, he cut a rather impressive figure in any crowd. He passionately denounced all flimsy beliefs, slithery like earthworms. Had there been anybody else in place of Antony, the Abhasa could not have claimed such an aura of manliness. Everybody respected the trio because of Antony's family legacy and commanding power. But today, for the first time, his trumped-up machismo had been outrightly questioned.

And it was that infernal halfwit who had paved the way for that fiasco. It was too tense a situation for a direct fight, otherwise Antony would have slapped him soundly and tossed away that dirty piece of stone. A stupid stone had grown sky-high, mocking their unique intelligence; instead of destroying it, they had been forbidden from even stepping close to it! But that did not mean the defeat of the Abhasa. If a door closes, another shall open. They believed in the dictum 'survival of the fittest', and got immersed in their attempts to find ways and means of tricking the genie back into the bottle.

The Abhasa used to assemble under the Athmavu to seek a way forward in any adverse circumstance. But now, the Bodhi tree, which had provided a roof for their thoughts, had been confiscated from them. From its sanguine presence, which used to elevate their minds, they were now huddled in the confines of a narrow room.

Bhaskaran and Sahir became worried at seeing Antony getting drunk. The natives were yet to meet a tippler with his capacity. Even after ingesting seven pegs, Antony's bearing would be unflappable and his speech steady. Bhaskaran's limit was three pegs, whereas Sahir's was zero. Thus, when it came to liquor, Antony followed extremism, Bhaskaran moderatism, and Sahir was devoid of any isms.

During an emotional outburst, when Antony stepped into the extremist zone, his behaviour would become unpredictable. If he had to exact revenge, be it against his friends or parents, he would promptly set out to do so. Considerations of consequences were irrelevant. Even if there were thousands of onlookers near Nireeswaran's abode, the extremist Antony would have seen them all as specks of dust. But he had not had the support of liquor when Sumitran had thrown down the gauntlet. His manliness had suffered a setback. How would he walk through the village, daring everyone, from now on?

That was what terrified Sahir and Bhaskaran. If Antony was muttering frequently that he would destroy everything, it was the portentous sign of doomsday. The only uncertainty was regarding the way in which he would finish the world.

The rush of blood, instigated by the endless bout of drinking, provoked Antony to explore a varied path. He needed a female body to let go of the tensions accumulated throughout the day. His nature was to sadistically imprint his stresses and strains on the feminine form. Usually, he doused this fire in a town hotel, with the help of a high-priced call girl. The hired women would typically allow him to practise degrading and even cruel acts, tempted by the money he would offer. The intensity of sexual pleasure that Antony derived while inflicting pain on his partner was enormous.

Though he was nearing forty, Antony abstained from marriage. His parents were afraid of putting restrictions on their son, who ridiculed conventional ties for the sake of following a precarious lifestyle. The fear was more when their son turned up drunk. Antony had relished his liberty to the utmost, right from his youth. His vehement ideas, that the world did not require any systems and that no one should control the inherent chaos, had made him an atheist. He avowed that it was man who decided his own destiny.

Sahir's and Bhaskaran's habits were slightly different. They were twenty-five and twenty-six, respectively. Antony provided them not only with friendship but also a feeling of security. Being a follower of the Middle Path, Bhaskaran's concept of sex was diametrically opposite to that of Antony. Bhaskaran was engaged to his cousin Veni. He had never dared to fantasize about her, except in the much maligned missionary position. Employed in a cooperative society in the next village and subject to small-time political leanings, he was supposed to step inside the laboratory of missionary positions in the forthcoming Onam season. And poor Sahir was destined for his dreams turning to horrendous nightmares.

On that 'extremist' night, the town was too distant for Antony to head there for his appeasement. The only compromise was Janaki. When Scotch was not available, an exhilarating local brew would suffice. So he ventured forth in search of Janaki by himself. Nowadays, she was not to be easily found loitering near bus stops and footpaths. The youthful scientist Roberto had apparently made her his private property. Where else in the world could one watch the fun of a rich scientist hiring a whore as a research aide? Were all scientists eccentric by nature?

Whatever the answer might be, Antony was adamant on having the local dish tonight. Intentionally separating himself from his friends, he went looking for Janaki. When Bhaskaran and Sahir expressed their willingness to accompany him, Antony became forbidding in demeanour. Controlled by the rajasic powers of alcohol, Antony swaggered forward like a *virat.*

He sighted the small tiled house from a distance. Since there was no boundary wall, those who wished to plunder could enter from any direction. Apart from Janaki, there was only an old woman in her home. She was a distant relative who had wandered to the place, bearing the bundle of her orphanhood. Janaki was bold enough to live by herself. She was not safeguarding any dignity in herself, which could be invaded by someone at night. Also, there were no valuables inside the nondescript house to attract thieves.

Though her face was pretty and body shapely, Janaki could not progress much in life because she was just a village whore. Occasionally, Janaki would think, self-deprecatorily, that she would have been a respectable rich lady by now had she practised her trade in the town. Nowadays, that stale thought made her brood pitifully rather than laugh with mirth. Janaki would ponder philosophically at times that everything, including her mind, had surpassed her.

By the time Antony reached the house, Janaki was asleep, having quit playing games with her mind. However, men would often wake her up, with the urgency of someone approaching a doctor at unearthly hours during an emergency. At those times, an ethical impulse, along the lines of medical ethics, would drive Janaki, and she would usually assuage the patient's burning needs. Antony had come calling tonight with the overbearing arrogance of his 'right' to do so.

When Janaki opened the door, she saw an extremist before her.

'Edi, what's with your pomp and show nowadays? Have you increased your rates like film stars? Both involve acting, isn't it? Tell me, how much for a full call sheet tonight?' Antony leered.

Janaki disliked that blatant bargaining. 'Today I cannot . . . feeling unwell,' she replied.

'No sickness is permissible for women like you. Can a train stop its run because the track is unwell?' Antony guffawed, as if he had cracked a classy joke.

'Go away, Antony. I told you I am unwell.'

Janaki knew that it was not merely the matter of being 'unwell'. Janaki had started looking nauseatingly at her body. She had no clue how the idea had germinated within and grown. Perhaps certain words of Roberto, spoken unsuspectingly, had taken root within her. Even he would not remember them now.

Since her mind had revolted against her body, Janaki wished to shut the door in Antony's face, but he pushed it open.

'A whore is the common property of a village. The spunkiest man there shall rule over it!'

'Spunky!' Janaki broke into derisive laughter. 'You have not seen as much manly mettle as I have! Nobody like a whore to classify men, is there? Most show-offs turn out to be paper tigers in reality!'

'Don't include me in that flock. Today, Antony will show you his spunk!'

'Your spunk! Aren't you ashamed to use that word again? The whole land witnessed how spunky you three were in front of Nireeswaran! What happened to your spunk when you scurried away, with tails tucked between your legs? If you had hurled that stone away, uncaring of anyone, that would have been spunky indeed! But now, I am awed by that piece of stone which you could not touch . . . I am impressed by Nireeswaran.'

'I shall destroy it . . . most definitely I shall . . . but I want you tonight,' Antony barked.

A fury stoked by shame has the power to turn the world to ashes. Janaki knew from previous experiences that he wished to hurt her with everything frothing inside him. He was a man who unleashed tempestuous passions, enough to shatter the universe, through sadistic sex.

'I quit that job.'

When Janaki spoke straight to his face, Antony did a double take. 'Don't try to escape by lying.'

'This is not a lie! I have stopped the business of selling flesh.'

Even as she uttered those words, Janaki wondered whether she was fibbing, caught up somewhere between decisions and ruminations. Still, this was a temporary respite, at least.

'Even if you wish to stop, do it after tonight. Like Nireeswaran's consecration, we will have a huge celebration in the village. I shall arrange the percussion players . . . *Dum dum diddle dee! Janaki stopped her business, woe me! Dum dum diddle dee! Janaki stopped her business, woe me!* Wow, that will be spectacular! Afterwards, you may transform into the sainted figure inside a glass enclosure!' Antony jeered.

Gesticulating vulgarly, his hand grabbed Janaki. Antony's long arms extended beneath his knees. He could easily clasp anything in his reach. Now, his right hand was brutally vanquishing Janaki's left breast.

Janaki sensed that Antony was traversing through the extreme phase of his drunkenness. He felt exhilarated while imparting pain. In that fiery journey, he would use his teeth, nails and brawn as weapons. Those were occasions of excruciating torture for Janaki. Strangely, she wished that Damu had given her such pain in Antony's place. Through what enchantment could the same act, agonizing when unleashed by Antony, turn intoxicating when carried out by Damu!

Janaki pushed Antony away with all her strength, and he ended up smashing against the wall. She did not know where that power came from. Nor did she recognize the darkness into which she fled through the open door. The old woman, who was fearfully watching everything from her room, tightly bolted the door.

Antony let out a belligerent yell. The day which had given him a second mortification was accursed and damned. He controlled his twitching hands by hurling an old chair into the front yard. Twisted and broken, it lay like the remnant of some horrible accident. The small insects which had nestled under it buzzed around in terror. One expressed its protest by sinking its sharp stinger into Antony's handsome face. The spot started swelling uncontrollably, like a scrotum filled with seminal fluid.

Twenty-Fifth Petal: Transformation

Out of breath, Janaki sought refuge in the house where the roses, with worm-eaten petals, waited like ancient souls. Even the half-dying light in the sky was dimmed by the clouds. Roberto, stumbling along some unknown pathway of science, was startled to see the unexpected guest.

'What . . . what happened?'

Janaki forced herself to remain silent about the physical abuse. 'Oh, nothing in particular.'

'Heard there was quite a mayhem at Nireeswaran's abode. Did you end up there by any chance?'

When she merely shook her head, Roberto suspected that something was amiss.

Janaki's dishevelled appearance suggested a recently concluded business deal. That was not a topic which troubled Roberto. As with labourers toiling in the slushy farms, there were beads of perspiration on Janaki's body. The face was that of a soldier who had lost a war. Roberto surmised that what Janaki needed at that occasion was a cooling of both body and mind.

'Want to take a shower? There is a bathroom right there.'

Janaki longed for one. Her body had been brutalized many times in the past. She was used to randy men who obtained sadistic pleasure from her. Janaki had stood weeping with bloodied nipples and nail-scarred breasts. She wished to wash Antony away from both her body and mind. A shower wasn't available in her house. In certain hotels she had taken a shower, either alone or with a companion.

When she was with men who enjoyed such wet overtures, Janaki too had savoured that spray.

Standing under the shower, Janaki examined the areas Antony had assailed. She felt nauseated at the rosy swelling. A hatred for her own body, hitherto unknown, overwhelmed her. Recently she had been feeling that the body's true potential blossomed not when it was exposed but when it was enwrapped.

When the water cooled her nerves, Janaki slipped into a reverie about her childhood spent amid the luxuries of Rose Villa. She used to accompany her mother, who worked as the housemaid there. Her body had been pure as a glass enclosure with a saintly presence. Nobody had trespassed it. The residents of Rose Villa included Indrajit's uncle, who had retired from a foreign job, and his wife.

The first thing the childless couple did was to set up a large rose garden in their compound. The resplendent blooms usurped all of their parental affections. They granted membership to all the locally available varieties as well as to hybrids imported from across the seas. The couple found happiness in cross-breeding the roses to produce new species. The offspring of their research were baptized with the names reserved for their unborn children—Jishnu, Sitara, Radhika et al.—and they babbled happily with those tender buds.

'Look, Sitara is in full bloom today!'
'Jishnu is a real charmer . . .'
'Why such a long face, Radhika?'

Each rose plant received their love liberally. Though Arunjit's uncle and aunt could have minted a fortune from their garden, they never looked at the flowers with a greedy eye. Hence it was an eternal spring in their yard. Butterflies and bees were regular visitors, and buzzed around inebriated after sipping the honey. When rose researchers visited the place, they felt as if the heavens had descended there. Many students of horticulture stayed as guests at Rose Villa, fascinated by the ambience. The house, traditionally called Mamangalam, was thus rechristened Rose Villa.

Indrajit's uncle and aunt had converted their never-flowering togetherness into an everlasting rose-season. Neither could imagine even one of them leaving the house of roses. They always prayed that they would leave together. And it came true.

When the husband died, even before the body was cremated, the wife too packed up her life-bundle. The woman was cremated in the same pyre that had been prepared in the backyard for the man.

Janaki reflected on their intense love for each other, which had made such a joint departure possible. 'Those whom death cannot part' was a common saying. But the sight of the couple, draped in white, lying together in the same room, had been heart-rending. Even in death, they were proclaiming to the universe that true love was a form of commingling.

The world had no clue about the reason behind the couple's childlessness. They kept it secret while alive and took it securely along with them as they departed the world. That was the only thing they carried on their journey out of the mortal world.

Since the couple did not have any children, they gifted Rose Villa to Arunjit, who was related to them by blood. It was he who had taken care of them during their twilight days and also lighted the pyre like a son. Until the house changed hands, Janaki had been a regular visitor with her mother, helping in drawing water for the plants and adding fertilizers. How she had relished the kozhukatta, cooked by Arunjit's aunt. Little Janaki was attracted by the temptations of such delicious tidbits and used to spend many hours playing with the butterflies.

'Each rose needs the care due to an infant. Or else it will fade away.' Listening to what the lady of the house said frequently, Janaki too had started visualizing a baby's face in each of the roses. She would gaze at them for long, trying to read their minds. It was through such assiduous effort that Janaki mastered the art of differentiating between the male and female flowers at first sight. Whenever she extended her cheek towards them, taking care to avoid the thorns, the roses would lean in and plant a kiss on her face.

Eventually, like all seasons of bloom, the flower season of Mamangalam, too, retreated. Most of the roses wilted, following the fate of those who had taken care of them. Now, as if completing the full circle of destiny, Janaki had ended up in the same place. As a continuation of what her mother did, she dusted and cleaned the house. She watered the few roses that had survived the withering, and accepted payments from Roberto.

Janaki was unaware of what connected her with the scientist who had come to stay in the house of her childhood memories. Clearly, it would not fall under the usual classification of a man–woman relationship. Neither lust nor love were the ingredients of that association. Janaki's limited knowledge failed in comprehending the bond they shared.

One thing was sure, whenever she was lost, like an ant seeking a peepal leaf during a deluge, Janaki's feet would invariably take her towards the sanctuary. She knew even the exact number of steps she had to walk to reach Rose Villa from her own home. Though in her frenetic pace while fleeing Antony, the number of steps appeared to have reduced to half.

The worry that nagged at Janaki was how long the house would remain accessible to her. Time would banish her back to that wretched loneliness. Janaki would be forced to return to the cannibals, who, on sighting a woman's body, only saw flesh to be devoured. The whole night Janaki tossed around restlessly, weighed down by her uncertainties.

Before the break of dawn, Janaki prepared Roberto's breakfast and started for her home. Since it was the mango season, she wanted to gather the succulent, sweet fruit, made slightly bitter by the peepal. The Athmavu, through which the tribal hunter had ascended to the heavens, stood laden with ripe mangoes; nobody had ventured to harvest it as yet. Those who came seeking it would be its owner.

When Janaki reached the spot, she found that the atmosphere was very different. There were some people sleeping on the stone embankment and the nearby meadow. First, she assumed that they were gypsies. However, on not sighting any bundles or vessels, another thought struck her. These were volunteers who had come to guard Nireeswaran, considering the threat to the deity. The men had gathered to prevent Antony from executing another revolution in the night. The leading soldier, Sumitran, had wrapped himself head to toe in his lungi.

Janaki felt like giggling. If all that talk about Nireeswaran being high and mighty had any vestige of truth, what was the need for an army to protect him? Janaki remembered the anecdote about a popular political leader known for his wit, who had once queried, 'Why does God need security?' His dignified better half had been an ardent devotee!

If anyone were to ask her, Janaki would have contended that divinity never needed any watchman! The only irrefutable logic was that the one incapable of protecting himself could never watch over others.

If need be, even Janaki could have easily removed that piece of stone. The brawny guards were in deep sleep, dead to the world. The security being merely a facade, Nireeswaran had better find his own ways to protect himself! Janaki felt that if humans stopped complicating matters, the universe would carry out its business in simpler ways.

In the following days, the village got polarized. When certain progressives joined the Abhasa, the natives were cleaved into dual factions of those who supported and those who opposed Nireeswaran. In order to defend against guerrilla attacks, a Nireeswaran Protection Council was formed in the blink of an eye.

'We should warn those daring to fight us!' Sumitran challenged sneeringly. 'For that, let us carry out a procession with flambeaus through the village!'

The members of the protection council joined hands, and the torch procession, which started auspiciously from the trijunction, moved into the side lanes of the village, emitting the stink and smoke of burning tires. That boisterous march showcased the indivisible unity of the devotees. Punching their fists, they filled the air with their nerve-stirring slogans. When the crowd of Nireeswaran supporters passed by the houses of the Abhasa, the shouts ratcheted up into a crescendo.

'If you touch Nireeswaran, you shall be burnt into cinders!'

Sahir was intimidated. Bhaskaran refused to step out of the inner room. But Antony, who was proud to a fault, could not restrain himself any longer. He had just endured humongous humiliations. Disregarding his parents' pleadings, he tucked up his mundu and rushed towards the gate. 'Who the hell wants to mess with Antony?'

The sloganeers had never anticipated such a blazing comeback. The combined power of their vocal cords depended on the false bravado of mob psychology; individually, each of them was timorous. Antony, on the other hand, did not care two hoots about the consequences of his actions.

What ensued was a kerfuffle, involving vigorous pushing, shoving and cuss words. If some sensible members of the protection council hadn't intervened, the public road would have turned into a battleground where Antony and Sumitran would have torn each other to shreds. Even after being forcefully held back, both were trembling like aggressive fighter cocks. It was evident that if not today, then tomorrow or in the near future, one would peck the other to death. Sumitran seemed to possess demonic powers nowadays.

When hard-shelled egos clash, it is deadlier than a nuclear explosion. News became rife that the opposite factions were heckling each other and encounters were often ending in fisticuffs. When the Nireeswaran Protection Council members started taking turns to keep guard over the deity, the villagers concluded that a reprisal was likely at any moment. Nobody could make out whether the reports floating around were factual or invented.

The Abhasa had not expected such a dramatic shift in the climate, full of storm and thunder. The fact that they were barred from accessing Nireeswaran, of whom they were the progenitors, was more disgraceful than a slap on the face. Their get-togethers became clandestine, as if they were a banned organization.

'Didn't I insist much earlier that we should throw away that stone?' Sahir's fair nose reddened with rage as that of a circus clown. 'By delaying it for some more time, where did we end up?'

Antony was aware that the sharp edge of the accusation was pointing towards him. 'I shall say the same again! Let us bide our time. Don't you know that my aggression only increases with obstruction? I shall definitely destroy it!'

'But now the circumstances are against us.' Bhaskaran did not hide his anxiety. 'It had been an ideological fight till now. But today, the demand is for physical action. We had never planned for such a contingency.'

'To establish an ideology, an armed conflict might be necessary after a stage! Such occurrences are common throughout history,' Antony intoned like a grave philosopher.

Sahir stared at him, aghast. 'What's the use of establishing ideals by killing and getting killed? I don't want to perish in a fight. Can't we tactfully remove that stone and avoid a combat?'

'Of course! That is inevitable. I shall find a way. What's the use of living otherwise, eh?' Antony ground his teeth.

Looking at the way the word spread around, a petty stone was assuming the position of a boundary stone demarcating life and death. A paradox of the smaller than the smallest turning into something bigger than the biggest! The object was so fragile that a mere flick of one's finger could easily topple it. Now, a tactical move mightier than an elephant's pull was necessary to remove it. A few days passed in devising the tactics.

Having created two factions, whose thoughts were caught up in a blaze, Nireeswaran continued impassively, devoid of any burdensome thoughts himself.

As for Janaki, she was delighted at seeing the fragility of the Abhasa and their inability to touch the indifferent rock. She had never cast either a devoted or a resentful look at the deity till now.

For her, it was just another trip to the foot of the Athmavu. However, an invisible compound wall seemed to have sprung up in the vicinity.

One day, after taking a luxurious bath, using a fragrant soap and donning her best attire, Janaki approached Nireeswaran's abode. Since she had liberally used the scented talc and perfume given to her by Roberto, the fragrance floated around, creating a new world of smells. Her goal was not to entice men. In fact, she herself was not sure of her aim. Janaki knew that there were certain rotten smells staining the word 'human' which even the best perfume could not remove.

Like the needle of a weighing balance, an emotional surge oscillated within her, between the words 'pure' and 'impure'. It happened while she was at the foot of the Athmavu. It was an attempt to find the touchstone pivotal to both purity and impurity. Her search was for the steady state, wherein both the left and right became a matter of perspective.

Immersed in the search, Janaki ended up at Rose Villa again.

Roberto was astonished at the sight of Janaki all dolled up. An enigmatic grin spread across his face.

'What's behind that meaningful smile?' Janaki enquired.

'You are all decked up today!'

'What's the problem with that?'

'I am the problem! Because science is in my veins, I can see everything only through scientific terms.'

'What do you mean?'

'We are all caught in a rat race, right? Competition for improving production, for gaining better quality, for grander sales . . . The market value shall increase only on obtaining an ISO certificate.'

'I can hardly make out a word.' Janaki felt intimidated.

'Well, even your profession is not free from competition. Why isn't prostitution practised at the ISO level? How come we don't have a hooker with an ISO certificate? The target of the prostitute should be complete customer satisfaction. For example, when a customer steps in, a prostitute should welcome him like a new bride by embracing him coyly and kissing him. Of course, quality has to be emphasized, through the display of a health certificate. She should gauge the sort of play the customer is interested in and provide him service accordingly! When he leaves, she should proffer a sweet or a kiss and murmur, "Do come again darling!" You know, one can get a customer feedback form filled to assess the level of satisfaction and instructions to improve the services further. A prostitution service in accordance with ISO standards. It goes without saying that the returns should be commensurate with the services rendered! Tell me, how is my idea? I have formed it scientifically, keeping you in mind. Janaki, you shall become the first ISO-certified sex worker from India!'

As soon as Roberto finished his lecture, Janaki stepped forward and landed a resounding slap on his right cheek.

After that totally unexpected assault, Roberto stood still like a wax statue, his nerves all frozen. Whatever was fluid in him, including blood, solidified.

His breath escaped his body for a moment and hovered around the head. On regaining it, Roberto observed that Janaki was sobbing bitterly.

Unable to comprehend why she had become so incensed, Roberto ventured timidly, 'What . . . what's the matter, Janaki?'

Whatever had been suppressed for a lifetime burst out, spurting lava and sulphur in its wake. In between sobs, Janaki whispered that she could never live by selling her body again. 'I cannot . . . I cannot!'

A supplication, which was also a scabrous joke, proffered to Nireeswaran, unspooled like a court jester's scroll in Roberto's memory. In it had been a request to transform the village prostitute into a saint! Roberto had discovered Janaki after hearing that entreaty, and they had journeyed together till now.

'Eswara! Nireeswaran is indeed a class apart! If it proceeds like this, wonder how my topsy-turvy research is going to end!' Gingerly touching his swollen cheek, Roberto mumbled, 'Cannot stop anything from coming!'

Janaki observed the pale petals of her finger marks on Roberto's fair face. She remembered a male flower from her lost childhood, which had stood gazing at her in the same yard. While caressing the softness of its petals with her tender fingers, she had murmured, 'How much I adore you, beautiful flower!'

Wondering over the karmic leftovers that flowers were born with, Janaki swung in the gallows of her own destitution.

Twenty-Sixth Petal: Searing Joys

Barber Maniyan, Ghoshayatra Annamma's erstwhile nemesis, had ended up slicing her life into many pieces before sticking them together. After getting to know the family closely, Maniyan became convinced that the villagers were spreading salacious slurs against Annamma and her daughters. Sharp barbs of guilt prodded his conscience, because he had indulged in such gossip too.

Enmity is a sort of blindness. Once it infects a person, the diseased eyes can't see even a flicker of goodness in the object of hate. In the quest to trounce the opponent, nobody pauses to think that the foe is also built of flesh and blood. Maniyan felt mortified that his actions were no different. Why had he pierced the women's hearts with a vicious thorn?

Like the impoverished Kuchela, who had offered his meagre share of flattened rice to Krishna, Maniyan submitted his bundle of remorse before Nireeswaran. In doing so he found a bit of respite, as if some long-vanished clan god had made a benevolent comeback.

Nireeswaran had turned into a raging tempest shaking up the very spine of the village. And Maniyan was among the first members of the Nireeswaran Protection Council. He regretted the distance he had to keep from the Abhasa. Though Antony, Bhaskaran and Sahir were dear to him, Maniyan could not support the trio when they were set to annihilate the deity.

Meanwhile, the time came to harvest the paddy field. This time, it was in Annamma's yard that Maniyan stacked the rice stalks and set up the threshing ground. A bamboo structure similar to a goal post was erected, and the women labourers held on to the cross bar while threshing with their feet. Heaps of grain piled up on mats woven from palm fronds. Annamma and her girls managed everything, so Maniyan did not have to shut his barbershop and supervise the threshing.

After a very long interval, Annamma's kitchen was filled with the fragrance of newly harvested rice being cooked. They served Maniyan a sumptuous feast on a freshly hewn banana leaf. A man was having lunch inside that house after what seemed like aeons. Annamma's eyes became moist in nostalgic remembrance. Her *chatta*, the upper garment, became speckled with blue continents of dampness.

'What's the matter, Annamma?' Maniyan asked anxiously.

'Oh, nothing . . . I was just remembering the past,' Annamma replied tremulously.

Her daughters wondered about the remarkable change in their mother, known for her shrewish temper. Annamma's mind was off on a pilgrimage, crossing many previous decades, towards a faraway village surrounded by hills. Certain trials of life, which had led to her present life near the green fields, were calling out her name. 'Anna . . . !' they affectionately hailed the wide-eyed teenage girl of yore.

It was a time when a certain Johnny, a gymnast adept at 'cycle yagna', had made his appearance in the valley. Everybody addressed him as 'Master'. Johnny Master never got down from his cycle, as if pedals were naturally attached to his legs; he kept on cycling. The whole village thronged outside the circular rope barrier, gaping at him. It was here that, at the tender age of sixteen, Annamma watched the marvel called 'record dance'. It was a rumbunctious dance, with old film songs playing on a gramophone in the background, conducted by three members of Johnny Master's troupe—one female and two males. The penurious female dancer's body, with jarringly protruding bones, did not have an extra inch of flab. The spittoon-shaped loudspeaker announced that her name was Vijaya.

Since the woman danced very intimately with her male teammates, even embracing them during some moves, some jealous souls started a rumour that she was actually a 'he', though Annamma believed otherwise. Vijaya's sinuous movements excited hot-blooded young men. Even the sixteen-year-old Annamma felt the impact of those openly lusty thrusts. During the dance, Johnny Master would rest his cycle against the pillar-like structure made of a coconut trunk in the middle. He would touch the ground with his feet only for the scintillating finale, for which he spent twenty-four hours under the earth. For that duration, a standby would ride Master's cycle.

As he went around in a cyclic motion, Johnny Master's gaze would fall on the jostling circle of villagers. His eyes grazed abundantly on the spots where lush female beauty abounded. Johnny Master was born with the skill of knocking out women with a mere look. Women would flock around the cycle-yagna spot at twilight, their arms laden with eggs, plantains, coconuts and tapioca from their homes. When they hurled these multifarious objects towards the cycling man, he would seize each with utter ease, twisting and bending his body in marvellous poses. Lying on the moving cycle, he would enact the Shavasana posture. He would move the pedal with his right hand intermittently.

The cycle carried Johnny Master like a devoted and faithful pet, looked after by its owner for years on end. There was an ineffable fusion between the two—each seemed an inseparable part of the other. Many feared that the cyclist would topple over, especially when the cycle went on a dizzy spree balanced on a single wheel. But Johnny Master never fell. He emulated, though with more finesse, many special items previously exhibited by outsiders such as Dindigal Ponnuvelarasu and Hyder Ali.

As each day passed, the intimacy between the villagers and Johnny Master grew. By auctioning the donated plantains and eggs, Johnny Master's coffers grew heavy. Annamma had listened with astonishment when her close friend Radhamani giggled about Johnny Master spending his nights astride his cycle.

'What about pissing and shitting? That too happens on top of the cycle, you mean?'

'Huh! If you don't believe me, why don't you take a peep yourself?' Radhamani retorted tartly.

Though she wished to, Annamma did not attempt any peeping. With the passage of days, she realized that Johnny Master's piercing look was penetrating her heart and not her eyes. It began to vex Annamma when his glance fell on anyone but her. Every day she dolled up before visiting the arena. To allure the onlookers, the troupe had many gimmicks up its sleeve, such as magic shows, dance, Kalaripayattu and even circus items.

An unhealthy competition erupted between Annamma's house and that of the neighbour on the matter of supplying milk for the performers' tea. The desire to hear the names of their respective households being announced as the major 'contributors' to the cycle yagna had sown the seed of mutual rivalry. Annamma was made to rush with frothing milk in a bronze pitcher even before any upstart from the neighbouring house ventured forth. Johnny Master would still be astride his bicycle when she reached the place. The rest of the troupe stayed in a makeshift camp.

Soon, along with the exchange of milk early in the morning, other things started changing hands. The door to Annamma's heart was invitingly open, and anyone could enter without knocking. For Johnny Master, it was rather easy to enter through it. In the evenings, he started exhibiting new-fangled items with great enthusiasm and fervour. His smile was enticing. Before the cycle yagna could wrap up the ninth day, the pedalled feet touched the ground. When Johnny Master disappeared along with his cycle and Annamma, the villagers manhandled the rest of the troupe.

The young men did not waste the opportunity for 'dealing' with the female record dancer who had been tantalizing them with her hip movements. Though the girl tried to wriggle free inside the tent, most of the youths around were attempting to extinguish their desires to the utmost, and it was in that process that they discovered that the 'woman' was actually a man. The fact that the feminine mystique which had aroused their passions wasn't that of a woman upset the men terribly. Even after knowing that it was a 'Vijayan' rather than a 'Vijaya', a few of them decided to go ahead and get to know Vijayan better!

That was how Annamma ended up in the energetic, animated world of cycle yagna. Though Johnny Master had been adept at seducing women during his earlier jaunts, those flings were limited to descending from the cycle only to conduct his 'yagnas' with the female bodies. However, after eloping with the smart-as-a-whip Annamma, Johnny Master became the proverbial bellowing bull tamed with a rope through his nose. During the forthcoming shows, the 'night adventures' were next to nil. Four daughters were born, one every year, into that cycle family. Their journey led the family to the present locality. With their limited resources, all they could purchase was the little compound adjacent to the paddy field.

However, Johnny Master could not live in his new home even for a full year. After the completion of his masterpiece item—of spending twenty-four hours under the earth—when they dug out the pit, they found a stiff body. Though he had taken enough safety precautions, death had invaded that enclosure. The corpse was lying aslant in the pit, hand on heart. Handling a cardiac arrest inside the pit had not been a part of his training.

Johnny Master's lifelong ambition was to break the world record of Bombay-wallah Hyder Ali, the icon of all cycle gymnasts. The adulations that met Hyder Ali, who had cycled non-stop for 106 hours in Kozhikode's Mananchira Maidan, where the district collector had gifted him a handsome sum, had inspired Johnny greatly. Johnny Master wished to perform a glorious event like that and make good money for the upbringing of his four daughters. But all the castles in the air were shattered when he went under the earth.

Annamma did not want to return to her native place or seek anyone's support. When she had severed connections with her kith and kin, Annamma had never anticipated such a catastrophe. She toiled on farms and fields, carried stones at road construction sites and bravely brought up her daughters by herself. Even now,

Annamma was unsure of the crises awaiting them. Her daughters, with hardly a year's age difference between each of them, grew up fast to a marriageable age, and it was to protect them from unwanted attention that Annamma intentionally acquired the moniker of 'Ghoshayatra Annamma'. But Maniyan had ruptured the false hardness of that outer shell.

Maniyan, too, was acquainted with the bleakness of an isolated life. For his single meal in the day, he was forced to visit Dasappan's Daiva Sahayam eatery in the neighbourhood or request for food to be delivered at his place. The barbershop, suffused with the stink of hair, also doubled up as his residence. Amid the sacks stuffed with hair, Maniyan would lie like another lifeless sack. Often, he would wonder about the meaning of his life. A detestable life filled with lice and dandruff! In a world where people baulked at an unsightly strand of hair, was he not insignificant like a louse among millions of hairs? The dangerous and depressing nature of that realization made him chop off his ruminations at that juncture.

Nowadays, at frequent intervals, Maniyan was getting wholesome food at Annamma's house. In fact, he had begun to appreciate 'taste' in food for the first time. He started regarding the four girls as his own daughters. It surprised him that he could feel that way. He burned in self-reproach, recollecting how he had humiliated their mother by his display of obscenity before them. How paradoxical that the action that had once made him swagger was now a source of guilt!

One day, Maniyan dipped into his savings and took five simple gold chains to that house. When the mother and daughters started weeping and hugging one another, almost as if the Grim Reaper had come calling, Maniyan stood utterly bewildered. Tears, which he thought had dried up a long time ago, returned to his eyes, and the barber hurriedly stepped out without a farewell, not wanting anyone to see him cry.

Barber Maniyan realized that certain joys were more searing than death. That night, when he turned towards Nireeswaran's temple with folded hands, Maniyan felt the whole world rushing to fill him up; or maybe he was expanding to fill the whole world.

Twenty-Seventh Petal: Inner Chambers

Though Roberto had made some progress in his research on smells, he was not satisfied. He needed to separate the wheat from the chaff, and organize the results. A free and serene ambience was necessary for writing a paper establishing the solid foundation of his research. The atmosphere in the laboratory was entirely different. In the mechanical surroundings, one could not focus on writing, as the mind was easily distracted.

When it came to writing, even when it was a research topic, Roberto tended to be lazy. Due to that inherent laziness, many world-class papers, which should have been presented at reputed seminars, did not see the light of day. Excellent articles, which should have featured in international journals, never made an appearance.

Many of his crafty colleagues were a step ahead Roberto in this regard. They had precise calculations about how to garner the attention of the scientific world. It was as if some were researching on the subject 'How to Inflate Trivial Concepts to Marketable Research Papers'. With the help of some facts gathered by browsing the Internet, preparing a seminar paper wasn't arduous. The yardsticks for excellence at many research centres were the total number of seminars where the papers had been presented and the number of journals where one's articles had appeared.

Roberto was a colossal failure in that regard. The number of papers published under his name were few compared to those authored by his colleagues. The main reason for this was his lack of interest in transforming his research into published work. There was also something distasteful in defining himself vis-à-vis the number of papers written.

However, Roberto was adamant that he would classify all his findings about smells scrupulously. In his view, even if the papers were few in number, the content should be both solid and significant. That was why he had opted for a sabbatical. By keeping away from the research lab, he could conquer his tendency to procrastinate.

Roberto's research findings, revitalized by insights from the quotidian life around, were evolving into a unique paper. The progress had been surprising even to himself. He was confident that before long, he would arrive at a method for classifying smells. A random thought, emerging from the blue, had made him optimistic in that regard. Whenever his mind meditated for long on a subject, Roberto would unexpectedly get answers from within. And hence he believed that no question would be left unanswered in the universe.

Science merely helps unveil some of the laws behind nature and never creates even the slightest law by itself. In the interminable 'hide-and-seek' game played by time, nature simply uncovers her face sporadically. At that stage, those indulging in the search become gleeful like infants, as if they have discovered something momentous!

Both scientists and rationalists are ignorant when it comes to comprehending how the eternal laws are executed with clockwork precision. Shrugging them away as phenomena that have occurred from time immemorial, on which one need not wrack one's brains, they either bury their heads under the sand like an ostrich or pretend not to have noticed them. Ergo, even when science explains *what* is happening, it is silent about *why* it is happening.

When it came to that conundrum, Roberto had found himself thinking that even rationalists clung to philosophical realism which they had denounced till then. The lackadaisical approach that 'for an erroneous question, no answer exists' ended up as a mere play of words.

Roberto was on an honest quest, seeking answers to these questions. That was how he started digging deep into seemingly ordinary phenomena. For example, consider how a tiny seed lay hidden under the earth, sprouting when the conditions turned amenable, eventually growing into a great tree. What was the 'intelligence' which detected the suitable condition and triggered the germination?

What 'intelligence' worked behind the body's immune system getting alerted when an injury happened, causing the blood to clot and the wound to eventually heal? Where in the universe did that wisdom dwell which decided 'to act this way, so that things happened that way'?

Even when one set out to interpret things using one's own intelligence, science had no explanation for the workings of that same intelligence. There was no clarification about how the genetic codes, as explained by the genome mapping project, got inscribed so perfectly inside the genes. The lackadaisical argument that we just happened to evolve in that manner was as flaky as a superstition.

When a disaster happens, mankind tries to survive by facing it intelligently. Sometimes, it is prone to making mistakes. But nature displays a 'super intelligence' which handles universal phenomena without the slightest mistake! Science has no answer about how nature accomplishes that with perfection.

Some gave the name God to that illimitable entity, attributing to it form and characteristics present in their own imagination. Nireeswaran, as per Roberto, was the final link in that continuum. The newest god in the universe and also, simultaneously, the oldest.

The rarest among the rare venture beyond names and forms, in their quest for that unique truth behind everything, and end up experiencing it. The universe percolates inside them as omnipresent consciousness.

It is an awakening, that what appears as the smallest 'vignettes of consciousness' are all part of the singular body of the 'supreme consciousness'. Similar to how the little finger, face, heart and reproductive organs are part of the same human body, all the apparently divergent and contradictory matter join together to create the distinctive body of the universe.

Only those who can access the 'unified consciousness' of the universe can experience it as his or her own consciousness. For the rest, it stays beyond comprehension, like an incredible fairy tale.

Captivated by the confines of one's own petty consciousness, it is akin to limiting oneself to a little finger, heart or reproductive organ alone, and abstaining from experiencing the whole body.

And so, answers have to be sought not inside the paltry arrogance of an individual's mind but by stepping with bowed head into the vistas of the infinite intelligence. Roberto had been able to decipher answers to many mysterious truths in that manner. He was traversing the world of smells using the same approach.

But he was expected to validate the insights using the common measuring tools of physics. Roberto had in mind some specific experiments for that purpose. If Roberto's trials were successful, the scientific world would be turned upside down by smells! Just like sound, light and touch were being utilized, smells too would be used in different fields of science.

Even as the world of smells possessed him with greater urgency than ever, Roberto was being forced to respond to certain unfamiliar circumstances in his immediate surroundings. Although he was used to seeing hypocrites in the research laboratory—who would shower praises to his face while surreptitiously watching with envious inner eyes—the reactions of the three young men in the village were starkly different.

Roberto was bemused by the reasoning that had made the Abhasa regard him as their arch-enemy. It was primitive and atavistic to consider those in disagreement with one's idea as adversaries. Nature encompassed all sorts of diversities. Even hard-to-digest perspectives had their own space. If defecation as such was disgusting to think about, the related organs had a vital role in the body's functioning. It would be extreme stupidity to assume that by chopping off the urinary tract or the small intestine, one could expurgate them.

To Roberto's mind, the ability to tolerate dissenting opinions was the measuring tool of one's cultural evolution. The primary step towards cleansing the world was to scrub and clean oneself. Or else, with vanishing mutual respect, the world would become messier through protests and discord, and humanity would not move forward even an inch.

Though the Abhasa kept him at a distance, Roberto was fond of Antony, Bhaskaran and Sahir. He found it stimulating that their youthful blood boiled with a sense of purpose. But they were unsure of the proper means of attaining the ends. Perhaps their mentors hadn't guided them well.

To Roberto, Nireeswaran was undoubtedly a fascinating concept. The concept of 'Beginning, Middle and End' not being applicable to Nireeswaran, it was untouched by the notion of time. In science, the 'state without origin' was claimed exclusively by energy, which could neither be created nor destroyed. It didn't need a place to exist, nor was it dependent on time.

Roberto was unaffected by the stubborn belief that everything unfurling around Nireeswaran was a miracle. But he felt that the laws of force were intricate. Why wasn't the fact that the world could be reduced to ashes by releasing nuclear energy be seen as a miracle? Had it been announced a hundred years ago, it would definitely have been regarded as a wonder! Is it not true that new discoveries would be made some day about the explosive power of the mind, which was nothing but subtle matter?

Who knew whether the explorers, who ventured into the laboratory of the human mind, had already discerned it as having the brightness of 100 crore suns? Since only experience led to conviction, it was another of nature's marvels that except for the person who had sojourned within, neither society nor a research lab nor the intellectual faculties of a great scientist could perceive that illumination.

It is easy to denounce such thoughts as mere figments of the human imagination. However, those who allow for any possibility are found to be more open-minded than others. The inflexibility that one alone has exclusive insight into the universal mysteries, with a pronounced tendency to look down on the rest as ignoramuses, is not indicative of wisdom but of hubris triggered by ignorance. The seeds of pure wisdom would germinate only in the fertile fields of humility. How true was the saying that 'the hallmark of wisdom was nothing but humility'!

Roberto was aware that two close associations of his vexed the Abhasa. The first was the ineffable bond he shared with Janaki. The community could not come to terms with the nature of that friendship. The whole issue here was that an object appeared different depending on the onlooker's perspective.

In his relationship with Janaki, Roberto had come to realize that one's personality could be very different from what people perceived. The poor prostitute was more dignified than many so-called respectable citizens of society. Roberto had no intention of changing anything in that friendship till he returned to Bangalore.

The second irritant to the Abhasa was Roberto's closeness with Indrajit. There was hardly any reason for three boisterous young men, thriving in their present circumstances, to resent a hapless man who had just woken up from decades-long sleep. But in their view, Indrajit was the main reason they had lost their grip over Nireeswaran, since the noteworthy miracle of his awakening was attributed to the deity.

It was pitiable to think of Indrajit, who was forced to sleep when the world raced forward. Like a passenger struggling not to fall on his face in a motionless vehicle which suddenly accelerates forward, he was fighting to keep his balance. Since Roberto's presence handed him that 'holding bar' he could grasp, Indrajit shared even the trivial thoughts of his mind with the young man. He could not have existed without confessing matters to someone. That was how Indrajit ended up speaking about the girl affecting his very existence.

The revelation did not make Roberto flinch. He had already been apprised of the matter. Megha had, by then, turned into a topic of furtive whispers within Indrajit's home. Certain news never entered a home through the front door; it could be incendiary and end up scorching lives.

One day, with burning innards, Arunjit had spoken to Roberto. 'I need your help.' Arun's face was sombre due to the internal strife.

'What on earth is the matter?' Roberto asked.

'I need you to intervene . . . and convince my father.'

'About what?'

'The villagers are gossiping . . . We are so worried.'

'Why can't you ask directly? What's the need for a mediator?'

'I can't do that! Acchan has woken up after twenty-four years. I cannot afford to annoy him.'

That was the problem Roberto, too, was facing. Before delivering a judgment, one should evaluate all the circumstantial evidence with due care. Having known Indrajit's very heartbeats, Roberto could not look at him with the same eyes as the villagers. Some measure the weight of objects within the gravitational field of earth, others at the surface of moon. One cannot be adamant that both the weights should be the same.

'Your father is a good man,' Roberto said. 'But there is one thing we cannot fathom—the human mind. How can we assess the way it works? Are you aware of your father's real problems?'

'What problems?'

The east wind was sultrier than usual. The Aquarian sun had thrown open its furnace. If a summer rain did not offer a respite, a harsh stint of drought was very likely.

'There are certain matters which a father cannot discuss with his son,' Roberto clarified. 'Now, I have no other recourse except to tell you. Let me ask you something sensitive! How cosy is your marital relationship?'

'Very.'

'You have a compatible sexual relationship, I presume?'

'The only remaining greenery, I'd say!' Arunjit commented.

'What if you are asked to chop off that greenery from today?'

'What nonsense are you talking? Impossible. Neither of us is prepared for that.'

'How easily you said *impossible*! Now, let me ask you another question. Tonight, you sleep with your beautiful wife. Tomorrow morning, when you wake up, you see an aged woman beside you. How would you feel? Such things can happen in Wonderland or Arabian tales. But what if it were to happen in real life? We were all overjoyed when your father returned. Do you have any idea what his life is like now? He is an unfortunate man whose bodily needs are denied. Your father is not the lucky man who woke up from sleep, as everyone perceives.'

Arunjit stood dumbstruck. There had been no cause for him to analyse the imbalance caused in his father's life by the spate of events. Indrajit's situation was similar to someone trying to rein in a wild stallion with a flimsy string. And on its path was placed a delicate crystal vase labelled 'family', liable to be shattered at any moment. If a strange girl was becoming the reason for imminent devastation, it was imperative that she be removed from the scene.

'I understand, Arunjit,' Roberto consoled him. 'Let me talk to your father.'

'Mere talking won't do. Forbid him strongly from meeting her again.'

'Selfish, isn't it?'

'A bit of selfishness is excusable when it comes to one's family.'

'Well, your father is also part of your family, right?'

'Roberto, how come you are being so stubborn?'

'I am saddened by that man's condition. Well, I shall try to speak to him . . . today, if possible.'

'Don't say "if possible". It is possible! Our family is on the verge of collapse.'

Even when such tremendous upheavals were occurring in his house, Akhiljit, Arunjit's brother, remained an unruffled spectator. Akhil was laconic and self-possessed by nature. His state of mind was harmonized with the aphorism about Dakshinamurthy: 'Silence is exposition.'

Right from childhood, Akhil was obsessed with engines and motor vehicles. It would have been best had he trained to be an engineer. But Akhil found the barriers too high for him to surpass. The red marks on his answer sheets made him only an ordinary graduate. He became a supervisor in a private company.

The various machines on the shop floor delighted him. He would watch assiduously whenever engineers visited to troubleshoot machines by dismantling them and rectifying the faults. Meanwhile, Akhil would have internalized the architecture of the machine like a veritable photocopier. He could skilfully repair the machines afterwards, all by himself. The company had complete faith in him due to many such incidents. Even without an engineering degree, Akhil ended up heading the machines department.

For him, machines were not mere machines. He imagined a mind inside the metallic body. When certain breakdowns happened, due to their complex structure, it was difficult to analyse the exact cause. Akhil would resort to intelligent guesswork and followed his intuition. With utmost humility, he would carry out a dialogue with the machine. He would plead with the machine, requesting it to reveal its faults. The machine always ended up accepting his earnest requests. Using that singular approach, Akhil could diagnose problems which others could never gauge.

'If you had actually done engineering, you might have reached the top!' his co-workers would shower him with such praise.

Akhil, however, thought things were better the way they were. Had he mastered engineering, he would have lacked the humility needed to converse with machines and would have ended up as another human robot.

Perhaps because of his proclivity for rumination, Akhil tended to be silent. He did not offer opinions about the burning issues at home. It was unthinkable for him to waver in his affection for his father.

For a man who could communicate with a machine's heart, connecting with a human heart was all too easy. Who could claim that the inner chambers of the human heart weren't actually visible to Akhil? It was not to the erudite scholars but to the pure-hearted illiterates that the hidden worlds opened themselves up. 'The pure in heart shall see God.' Akhil believed that the saying carried nuances much deeper than the literal.

Tumultuous waves not madly crashing around the surface of his mind, such a person could clearly see the rubies and pearls on the bottom, and experience the truth of the saying that the kingdom of God is within.

Twenty-Eighth Petal: Gospel

When matters went out of hand, the Abhasa was caught in an imbroglio. Their effort to scuttle existing traditions and to create a new one was not only unsuccessful but had also triggered contradictory outcomes.

Nireeswaran's fame was surging every day. Its dwelling was being enlarged, from the 1-square-foot platform at the base of the Athmavu to an immense temple. The construction was to be planned without causing any disturbance to either the Athmavu or the deity. Since the enemies were sure to attempt some form of retaliation, jeopardizing Nireeswaran's growing reputation, security became a major concern.

It was a tough task to mark out enough space for a temple at the tri-junction. So it was proposed by some that Nireeswaran be relocated, somewhere in the interior of the village, away from the main road. However, the majority decided that it was better to let the deity stay at the place of its origin. What if the uprooting caused a deterioration of its powers?

The major issue in extending Nireeswaran's seat had to do with the redesigning of the streets based on the place of worship. The junction of the three side paths would end up inside the boundary wall of the temple. The streets would be pushed behind, and newer spaces would have to be carved from the neighbouring compounds.

After deliberation, the aforesaid suggestion found acceptance. The only confusion was about the land involved in the extension project. Who would be willing to give up his property for the sake of faith? But when the efforts started, there were none of the anticipated troubles, and the results were even faster than expected. The whisper went around that every fistful of earth contributed for Nireeswaran's temple would augur good fortune for the donor. The temple work started in a jiffy and progressed at a rapid pace.

The street's appearance underwent a drastic change. When the temple's boundary wall and surroundings were painted afresh, all the names, scribbled or painted, vanished from sight. Abhasa Theruvu, that ill-omened term, lost all relevance and was soon forgotten.

The Abhasa, though wrathful, could only watch as the street draped itself in modern adornments. Unable to put a stop to it, they felt dejected and wretched. Of course, it never meant a complete retreat from the battlefield. It was inevitable that they would have to begin sharpening another deadly arrow. It would be their final assault, bereft of all regrets.

Around the vicinity of the new Nireeswaran temple, first a tea shop and then a variety of smaller establishments came into being. Soon after, guest houses and hotels sprang up. Then, buses carrying pilgrims started arriving from various places, and the crowd increased proportionally.

When the old signboard 'Daiva Sahayam Hotel' was replaced by 'Dasappan's Nireeswara Sahayam Hotel', it encouraged many others too. Nireeswara-brand incense sticks and Nireeswara-brand camphor packs made an entry into the market. Following that, Nireeswaran made an appearance on candle packs. An assortment of lockets inscribed with 'Nireeswaran' and finger rings embellished with that name became available. These holy objects were sold at a revolutionary pace. Caps and T-shirts saying 'Nireeswaran' became very popular among the youth.

The land was filled with Nireeswaran's aura. A mofussil place, never before seen in any map, was scaling the heights of fame.

The astounding fact was that Maniyan's workplace flourished amid all these transformations. The barbershop was the closest to Nireeswaran! Imitating Dasappan's example, Maniyan too modified his name board from 'Mani Cutting Saloon' to 'Nireeswara Cutting Saloon'. He scrubbed away the name Abhasa Theruvu, which he had scribbled on his shopfront, tempted by the few coins offered by the Abhasa, and replaced it with 'Nireeswarapuram'.

It was a name that encompassed everything, both the good and the bad. Maniyan was apprehensive whether Antony would come heckling him about the money he had spent on the old board. But Maniyan was now prosperous enough to throw ten times that amount at Antony's face! Though he mentally prepared himself for such a contingency, the trio did not appear to bicker with Maniyan. Had they started visiting a new hair salon? The feminine navels in the film magazines had been pining for Sahir for several weeks. In Sahir's absence, those navels had been fingered by many men and had transformed into major gutters that could swallow a few two-wheelers easily!

Roberto was watching with interest the rapid transfigurations happening in the village. The man who was once censured as a thief, accused of stealing god's ornaments, was now the main priest of the Nireeswaran temple. His daughter, who was pilloried for having married a low-caste youth, was now held in high respect by society. There was no caste discrimination in Nireeswaran's presence, no distinction between scholars and illiterates either. You could attain serenity by reading the Holy Bible inside the precincts of the Nireeswaran temple or read the Holy Quran and purify your mind. You were free to read the Holy Gita and enjoy an immersive experience. If you wished to do nothing, that was possible too; you could just wander around without being attached to anything at all. Otherwise, you could attain salvation by reading Karl Marx's *Das Kapital* or the voluminous *Vairudhyathmaka Bhauthikavadam* or *Dialectical Materialism*. Indeed, they could all be seen as eulogies to Nireeswaran's ways.

It was not just the Abhasa who lost a sanctuary when the architecture of the Nireeswaran temple changed. Janaki's beloved Damu, who used to spend his nights beneath the box-shops raised on makeshift platforms, was adversely affected too. When the streets were shifted, the stalls were demolished. When the new shops and new ways came into being, Damu lost his space. Uncertainty crept into his life.

Janaki had stopped visiting him in the recent past. Except when she sought him out, Damu had never approached Janaki in her house. Though both were partners, this relationship had always functioned as a sort of one-way track. Roberto could not understand why Janaki was getting away from that relationship.

'Janaki, why don't you have a life with Damu?'

'No need.' Janaki's answer was resolute, holding the entire power of a full stop. Her facial expression was intriguing—very different from the non-verbal cues that Roberto had picked up during his scientific sojourns.

'I liked his smell and manliness,' Janaki explained. 'I loved him with my unblemished soul even when I was selling my body. That was because I was a prostitute then . . . But now, I am not.'

Janaki had sufficient reasons for liking Damu when she was a prostitute. If she had insisted, Damu would have married her too. But that would have made her lose the grounds for her love. When she was a prostitute, they could have an association just as a woman and a man. It was that unconditional love-making that Janaki had liked and desired. After marriage, when they lived under one roof, many conditionalities would creep into their relationship. Janaki would lose the erstwhile Damu and vice versa. If he married her, even on a whim, Damu might feel a sense of shame later.

'Why should I murder my old Damu and become the wife of a new Damu?' Janaki's voice broke.

'I cannot understand you, Janaki!' Roberto said.

'Even I can't.'

Roberto stood dwarfed before the sky-high perspective of a poor village prostitute. It was true, Janaki was getting fazed by her own self.

'My days here are getting shorter. Have to start the real experiments after returning to the lab. All I have done till now is collate some data for that effort.'

Janaki smiled even amid her tears.

'No marvel of Nireeswaran is as wondrous as a village prostitute becoming the friend of a big scientist. When are you planning to return?'

'Very soon. But I shall come back occasionally. To see you, Janaki, in the presence of Nireeswaran . . .'

'You might not find such a Janaki then.'

'Why not?'

'Don't know how to answer.'

'Planning to convert from a whore to an ascetic?'

'Won't it be a mere change of dress? Even when I was a prostitute, I felt like an ascetic.'

'I concede defeat. In this village, every single thing is paradoxical! Nireeswaran is Eswaran. A whore is an ascetic. Definitely, as per scientific laws, the phenomenon of absolute zero is taking place in this locality.'

'I am a poor erstwhile whore. Your absolute zero makes no sense to me.'

'Well, as one of our carpenters espoused, the truth shall be first revealed to whores and children. His close friend was a prostitute from Magdala. So, my dear erstwhile sex worker, the theory is rather simple. When we learn to count, we do it forward: one, two, three . . . If it increases in that manner, we will reach thousands of crores and more, uncountable numbers . . . eventually extending to infinity.

'In the same manner, we can count backwards from zero. Minus one, minus two, minus three, which shall stretch to minus infinity! If you join a positive one and a negative one, you end up with a zero. The same happens when you add a positive hundred with a negative hundred. Now when you put a positive infinity with a negative infinity, you end up with a zero again.

'In short, if you add all the positive and negative numbers in mathematics, the grand total will be an unprovocative, calm zero. A similar situation exists in all natural phenomena and not just in mathematics. All happiness and sadness, when combined together, is zero. All light and darkness commingled, again zero. And when Eswaran and Nireeswaran come together, it is a zero. This round zero is the salvation of us scientists. It was discovered by our own Aryabhatta. Janaki, did you understand anything?'

'Oh yes, when the round null takes over the brain, you turn into a nut,' Janaki giggled.

Roberto burst into hearty laughter.

'Well, that's news for me! Nut must have been inspired by null. Those who cannot recognize the significance of null, can only refer to those who can as a nut. It is very logical; an eternal truth, like zero. But one should be careful while playing with zero.'

'What do you mean?'

'The one who appears inert is to be feared the most. Because when you try to disintegrate zero, the energy released can destroy the entire world. If we provoke the peaceable zero inside an atom, an atom bomb is created. The zero always yearns to remain zero. That is its state of existence. If someone adds a ten to a zero, it will create a minus ten to balance it out. Hence, in nature, for every joy, an equal amount of sorrow gets generated.

'Modern science says that there exists "anti-matter" to balance out the "visible matter" of the universe. And so, my dear prostitute, it is a matter of good fortune that even when you indulged in physical relationships with men, you did not immerse yourself in sexual delights. But each of those men will endure an equivalent amount of unhappiness dictated by the zero's yearning for balance! Religion might pronounce it as the "punishment for sin".

'Let us not get snared by the circle of religions. Neither should we be terrified of sins or salvation. We should appreciate it as a simple science of the cause-and-effect relationship, leading every action to its natural result. It is Newton's third law of motion, which works everywhere. Just a matter of understanding, transcending religion.'

'But this poor prostitute had enjoyed uniting with Damu!' Janaki confessed.

'An equivalent grief shall definitely balance the delight. The pain of separation from Damu, which you now endure, having renounced prostitution, is nothing but that. A person who knows how to balance every action can be called, if needed, "the Buddha" or "the Enlightened One". Or even a lunatic . . . What's in a name anyway?'

'Oh, Nireeswara!' Janaki called out loudly. 'So this is the gospel addressed to prostitutes!'

'Every gospel evolved like that. I will tell you another bit of science, Janaki. Just like we use the kilogram to weigh matter or the metre to measure length, there is a real measuring scale for assessing human beings too. It is neither money, nor status and might. When measured on that scale, the apparently respectable citizens and rich men of society might be lagging far behind. There, among the forerunners, would be an erstwhile prostitute called Janaki.'

Roberto got up slowly. Moving near the innocent soul of the former prostitute, he gently touched her for the first time. Planting a tender kiss on her forehead, he murmured, 'You are not a prostitute but a saint.'

Janaki's eyes overflowed with tears. A wail, as deep as the serene sea, started inundating her.

As if entangled in the perfect heart of zero . . .

After that, Janaki never visited Nireeswaran's temple. Neither did she go to the Eswaran's temple. When both existed inside her, where could she venture? How could someone who was already at home go home?

Twenty-Ninth Petal: The Bull

Parameswaran had been deliberating for a while about the ceremonial offering of a bull at Nireeswaran's temple. He had sighted many bulls which had been presented to the Thirunakkara Thevar, roaming around with full liberty all over the town. Everyone treated Thevar's bulls respectfully and fed them lavishly. Parameswaran decided that Nireeswaran deserved a bull of his own. The natives would revere such a bull and also remember the devotee who had offered it. He was exuberant over the idea of the villagers thinking of him often, even if it was by means of a bull.

What Parameswaran daydreamed about, he implemented very soon. He offered Nireeswaran a frolicking young bull. Seeing its shimmering smooth skin, many were tempted to fondle the creature. Though it was magnificent in appearance, the bull was a passive animal. It wandered around the village, happily grazing near the Nireeswaran temple, consuming the banana skins offered by the shopkeepers and chewing the cud while lazing around under the trees. The young bull trespassed wherever it wished and lay down to rest irrespective of the place. No one dared to say a word due to the local belief that the bull's entry anywhere was auspicious and its earthly existence regal. After someone fondly called him Nandi, the name stuck.

'Trust that bull's luck!' Antony would sardonically remark on encountering the creature.

Though it was 'enslaved' to Nireeswaran, Antony found Nandi's majesty, bodily beauty and masculine self-assurance striking.

The untrammelled liberty with which it wandered wherever it pleased was rather impressive to him. Antony might have developed a sympathy towards the animal since he saw himself as an unbridled royal bull. Why else would someone, who viewed any object connected with Nireeswaran as an abomination, become fond of such a creature?

'This animal love of yours seems to be new!' Bhaskaran teased him.

It was difficult to fathom the reason for his fascination. Then, Antony had the sudden brainwave that he could turn Nandi into a weapon against the deity himself.

'How will you do that?' Sahir was flummoxed.

'Let us bide our time. A path shall make itself known.'

For the past few days, Antony had been saying this quite often: 'A path shall make itself known.' It really meant that he was seeking out a path himself. Ever since his humiliation at the Nireeswaran abode, a niggling frustration, of the kind he had never felt before, had been haunting him. In addition to that, the disdainful treatment meted out to him by Janaki had challenged his manhood. The flambeau march and the construction of the new temple had also been scalding experiences. The three friends decided to lie low for a few days.

They set out for Mangalapuram, where Antony had a hideout faraway from prying eyes. Though the plantation, with its green and bubbling springs, soothed their frayed nerves, the festering wounds in their hearts did not heal. Yet that sabbatical was invigorating. It was when they returned, having amassed the energy for battle, that the young bull caught Antony's eye.

Nandi was graced with the freedom to step anywhere at any time, and he used it to the hilt. The bull became a regular visitor at Ghoshayatra Annamma's home. The main attraction was Ammini the cow, which had been gifted her by Maniyan. It was Maniyan's idea that a cow would bring in more returns, since the goat breeding was becoming profitable. Annamma's daughters were all in agreement.

That was how Maniyan purchased Ammini, who had a spotted tail and a pretty mark on her forehead. Like Annamma and her daughters, Ammini too was gorgeous.

It is unknown whether animals have a consciousness of beauty like human beings. Nevertheless, Ammini's shed became Nandi's favourite haunt. Perhaps they were conversing in their own special tongue. Annamma found the bond between the two creatures perfectly acceptable. Some of her neighbours suggested that since Nandi belonged to Nireeswaran, his presence would usher in good fortune.

Even otherwise, Annamma had a big heart, and she was stirred by her inherent compassion towards animals to share a portion of Ammini's bran gruel and oil cake with Nandi. She found it heartening to watch the two bovines slurp the rice gruel from the same vessel, like a loving young couple. The pleasant memories of a cycle gymnast rose in her heart. Annamma gently stroked Nandi's shining young body.

Though they interacted intimately, no one ever caught either Nandi or Ammini indulging in amorous activities. Even so, with the passage of time, Ammini gave birth to a calf. The newborn male calf was as handsome as Nandi. It scampered all around the compound and circled Nandi and Ammini affectionately.

Annamma did not have the heart to tie a rope around the tender neck of the naughty little creature. Relishing that unbridled freedom, it ran around the whole place and made its presence known. Sniffing curiously, rubbing against Nandi's body and frolicking with abandon, the little one made the whole place come alive. However, it was an invitation to disaster. A scooter, travelling through the side road, knocked down the romping calf one day.

The little one lamented 'Amma, Amma', thrashing around in pain. Ammini lurched forward on hearing the wails. Even the strong rope around her neck could not restrain the mother cow. By the time Ammini, grunting and keening, rushed to her young one, the calf had breathed its last after having bleated out the final 'Amma'. On hearing Ammini's incessant wails, Nandi, followed by Annamma, her daughters and a few villagers, rushed to the spot. But the errant scooter driver had vamoosed by then.

Ammini's udders did not yield a single drop of milk afterwards. Maniyan fetched the butcher Moosa to skin the carcass of the calf. Some old-timers had advised that if a replica of the dead calf was created by stuffing hay inside its skin, the mother cow would produce milk when the 'hay calf' brushed against her udders. So Maniyan attempted to trick Ammini. But human intelligence had utterly failed in understanding the animal. Ammini did not yield milk even after that effort.

The cow also started getting rattled even at hearing the distant sound of a scooter. When the noise came near, she would break free from her rope and rush ferociously towards the source of the sound. Once she knocked down a Chetak scooter which was going down the side path. Without harming the rider, she attacked the vehicle with her horns. After watching the torn and mutilated seat of the scooter for a while, the cow retreated lowing wretchedly. When Ammini started attacking every scooter that happened to move through that road, people stopped riding scooters down that path.

The villagers were not aware that an animal could carry such deep emotions in its heart. They had assumed that Ammini would soon forget the demise of her progeny. But grief haunted the mother like the aftermath of a terrible calamity.

Yet Sadananda Panicker, the doddering old man of the village, had a different perspective. 'Animals are not like humans. They remember their earlier lives.'

'So what?' Shashankan asked curiously.

'These creatures don't see humans as humans and animals as animals! For them, there are only relations. Ammini cannot bear the loss of the calf because of that feeling.'

'What bilge!'

'Not at all,' Sadananda Panicker asserted strongly. 'The cats and dogs which you see near our houses are beloved souls from past lives. They know the truth. But we do not understand it. Due to different "karma" they end up as such. And we throw stones at them, refrain from feeding them and even beat them up at times!'

'Please stop this drivel! It gives me the shivers,' Shashankan retorted. He had the habit of throwing stones at stray dogs and cats.

'Can't you stop harming those poor creatures? Feed them a bit, if you can! Who knows whether you are stoning your own beloved son from a previous birth?'

Shashankan was dumbstruck by that observation. He was deeply attached to his son.

'Have you ever looked deeply into an animal's eyes? The poignancy of that look will touch your heart. Once imprinted within, the moistness brimming in that glance will never leave you. The wretchedness caused by its condition, of knowing everything and being unable to communicate it, brims forth in that look!'

To check whether Sadananda Panicker was telling the truth, Shashankan furtively approached an orphaned dog lying in an overrun compound nearby and stared into its eyes. In the gaze of that creature, forlorn and neglected for years, was a penetrating pathos. The look stabbed Shashankan's hard heart like a sharp-edged chisel. He shrank back, as if his heart had been cleaved into two. Unseen by anyone, Shashankan fetched some rice and fish curry and offered it to the animal. Not in the least bothered about the food, which was not expected of a starving dog, the creature once more gazed into Shashankan's eyes. On observing tears welling in its eyes, Shashankan choked with emotion.

After that incident, Shashankan stopped harming animals. He looked at Ammini, breaking free from her rope, with deep compassion. One look had led him to many other looks.

Such a look awaited Arnos too.

It was during a casual walk to the Athmavu's surroundings with Indrajit that he first observed Ammini's fury. The enraged cow was chasing a scooter with lowered horns. Caught in the frenzy, with the terrified rider and frantic Ammini coming straight at them, Indrajit flattened himself against the fence, while Arnos froze in his tracks, forgetting to move. He escaped by a hair's breadth.

After following the vehicle for a while, Ammini stopped, as if accepting defeat. As she gazed after the scooter and heaved in its exertion, Arnos picked up its broken rope as if by some impulse. And Ammini followed his lead obediently. Reaching Annamma's yard, Arnos tied the cow to the trunk of a coconut tree. Then he offered some hay to the animal and caressed her tenderly. Ammini stood peacefully, immersing herself in calmness, the moistness of her eyes lovingly reflected in Arnos's own.

Following that episode, whenever Ammini chased a scooter, she would stop abruptly at the very instant Arnos hailed her, as if a switch had been flicked on inside her. He would always feed her with some grass, leaves or hay. On seeing that sight, Sadananda Panicker's conjecture about a previous life's connection seemed plausible. When a few people raised that query, Arnos simply smiled in reply.

However, it was not possible for Arnos to be present there at all times. On one such day, another tragedy occurred. A mini lorry filled with sand struck Ammini as she chased after a scooter. The poor creature started lowing frantically; her leg had been broken. By the time Arnos reached her side, Ammini was lying on the ground, unable to bear the pain. Nandi was standing nearby, tears flowing from his eyes.

The villagers managed to hoist Ammini on to a handcart and hauled her to Annamma's yard. Arnos stroked Ammini ceaselessly. Tears flowed continuously from the cow's eyes. Nobody understood that she was crying more due to the mental torment than the physical agony.

The veterinarian said he was helpless. The business-minded butcher proposed that slaughtering the animal without delay would be profitable. He was willing to offer a deal.

For a few days Ammini lay in the same posture, unable to move its limbs. Vicious little bugs started assaulting her in her helplessness. Ants swarmed around the watery discharge from her rheumy eyes. Annamma and her daughters could not bear that horrifying sight. Though Arnos painstakingly removed the ants, he knew that far more would soon gather. After caressing Ammini for the last time and before taking his leave, Arnos commented, 'Better let her go before she suffers more.'

Though the proposition was financially lucrative, neither Annamma nor Maniyan had the heart to sell Ammini to the butcher. For them, she was a family member. They decided to bury her in a corner of the compound.

When Chinungan arrived to dig the animal's grave, Annamma and her daughters did not step out of the house. When Ammini's breathing almost ceased, Chinungan dragged the ant-covered animal into the pit. The pit was filled with mud to prevent more ants from invading it. After a few minutes, the top layer of mud shifted a bit and a few fissures appeared on it. That was the last of Ammini's writhing. Only Nandi, standing faithfully by the heap of soil, noticed it.

That evening, with a saffron-coloured cloth bag slung over his shoulder, Arnos went to the Athmavu and met Embrandiri.

'I am going on a journey.'

'Where?' Embrandiri asked.

'Don't know.'

'When will you return?'

'Don't know.'

Reaching the town's madrasa at night, Arnos spoke to Zaid. 'I am going on a journey'.

'Where?' Zaid asked.

'Don't know'.

'When will you return?'

'Don't know.'

'Won't we be seeing each other again?'

'Aren't we seeing each other all the time?'

'You are right. Let Allah be with you,' Zaid said.

'Let Allah be with you,' Arnos replied.

As he had done when he had renounced the Christian assembly and returned to the village, having discarded his possessions, Arnos took off and headed towards the magnificence of the mountains.

Thirtieth Petal: The Laws of Motion

In his next trek up the rocky hilltop, Roberto purposefully accompanied Indrajit. His goal was to create an ambience of privacy so that he could fulfil his promise to Arunjit. From the peak, one could touch the vast emptiness above. The world lay bruised down below, but one seated so high would feel a sense of liberation from all the woes. And if one were to witness the sunset, it would rejuvenate the mind.

Sometimes strong western winds would blast through the heights. Those standing on the pinnacle felt that the wind would abduct them to the heavens. One had to sit alone at the top, under the light of the full moon, to experience a sense of illimitability. Only then would one's senses be able to capture the nuances of nature. Certain souls who were cognizant of all this would visit the rock top during full-moon nights.

When they sat staring into the glories of the west, Roberto casually introduced the topic of interest. The gusts of wind were yet to gather strength. A few crows were winging it home, croaking twilight wishes. As if emerging from life's own feverish body, heat waves were rising from the boulder.

'I apologize if I am stepping into delicate territory,' Roberto cautiously pitched his preamble. 'See, my outlook is different from that of others.'

'I know that,' Indrajit interjected, 'and that is why I express myself so freely with you. Many consider me to be a little loony! Maybe they are right?'

'No way.' Roberto smiled, shrugging away that tentative suggestion.

'I would have to emphasize the same point again. I knew that girl, whom everyone is pointing fingers at accusingly, in my unconscious state. We were together. And we continue living together,' Indrajit enunciated.

As usual, when the conversation reached that point, Roberto's composure was disturbed. And Indrajit was quick to discern his discomfort. The ability to read another person's mind was a curse that had accompanied him from his decades-long sleep. He could astutely catch the thoughts flashing past in another mind. But Indrajit had kept it hidden from everyone, including Roberto. It would only make people wary around him. What was more dangerous than someone's camera-like eye watching one's mind?

Observing the man who was stunned by his words, Indrajit asked, 'Roberto, don't you feel that you are talking to someone in an abnormal state? Then tell me: What is the normal state?'

'I am yet to come to grips with certain aspects of it! Listen, all I am saying is, I am not able to understand it. No truth-seeker can afford to condemn as incorrect what he finds incomprehensible. If you say that a living person of this world was with you in another lifetime or is still with you, that will confuse me no end.

'I have read about research conducted by Dr Raymond Moody on near-death experiences. Now those were based on people who underwent clinical death but returned to life before their biological death. Indeed, I have carefully studied both supporting and opposing interpretations.

'I am aware of my own Valiyammachi's experience. You know, she and I were very close. When I was studying in college, Valiyammachi suffered a heart attack and was admitted to the ICU. The doctors declared her dead. The caregivers were asked to inform the relatives. But, out of the blue, Valiyammachi's heart started beating again.

'When I reached her side, Valiyammachi smiled at me. By her facial expression, despite her inability to speak, I could make out that she wished to tell me something. Later, she confidentially disclosed her experiences during her "declared-dead" phase!

'Valiyammachi apparently had an out-of-body experience. While she was outside her physical form, she noted every incident in the hospital room. She knew how the doctors tried to resuscitate her in vain. Valiyammachi was on her way to a different world then. She did not wish to return from that joyous world. I still remember Valiyammachi saying that she met me in that world! So, you could be right. That's why I am not confident of disregarding all your experiences as hallucinations.

'You see, Valiyammachi revealed some other secrets to me, which cannot be shared with anyone else. Some of what she said has come true. And some things are yet to occur. I cannot discuss more than that. No one will ever believe me! The listener will only say that the speaker is abnormal. Therefore, I don't dare to refute that there are other worlds as tangible as ours. Rather, our world is as abstruse as the rest!' Roberto shrugged.

'Oh,' Indrajit said, 'what a stroke of good luck that there is at least one person with whom I can freely converse in this world! Roberto, your Valiyammachi could visit that world once and return. My fate is to go back and forth without respite at times!

'I shall say that your Valiyammachi is existing along with you in another world at this very moment. That is the truth. Now, I don't know if Roberto has a dual or multiple existences. But I know of more than one Megha. How devastating that knowledge is!

'I can vouch, with the same clarity of being alive now, that human consciousness can navigate many worlds. Roberto, after waking up from my sleep, I realized it more starkly. When I was in a coma, perhaps my consciousness travelled to such unknown places. I can't imagine anymore that this reality is the only one! In one such world, or even more, I have known Megha closely. She is my greatest solace. Why is this world finding fault with me for meeting her?'

'The world does not see the way we do. Yours is a forbidden relationship in their eyes.'

'Which world's cautions should I accept? Who is shifting me sporadically from the free world to a world full of restrictions? Let everyone call me crazy! But this is my truth, and I cannot deny it.'

Indrajit became emotional. Though he could not observe Indrajit's face in the looming darkness, Roberto could read his feelings.

'I shall never denigrate what you spoke about parallel worlds. As a scientist, I will only enquire into the rationality of the interpretation. The common belief, that time travels only in a straight line, is getting questioned here. While studying the theories of physics, I have often thought that time has spherical dimensions.

'It is similar to the possibility that one can draw an infinite number of straight lines from the centre of a sphere. When our consciousness is confined to travelling in one single line, we experience it as our truth. *But if our consciousness happens to hit on, say, another line of the infinite possibilities, the life experienced in that timeline shall also feel true.*

'If so, our meeting now is simply one of the infinite millions of probabilities. There is also the probability of our meeting each other at another place in some other time, or even the probability of our never meeting at all! All these possibilities are co-existent. However, since our mind can perceive time travel only in a straight line, we cannot experience all these multiple likelihoods at the same moment. That is how severely constricted our sensory world is.

'If someone escapes from straight-line time travel and moves into a parallel existence, he might experience the veracity of life therein. Maybe that is the explanation behind your meeting Megha, or Valiyammachi meeting me in another world. The exceptional situation where consciousness escapes straight-line time travel! Of course, I have no idea if anyone has officially reported such an incident till now,' Roberto concluded his musings.

'Does that mean I am a mere guinea pig now?' Indrajit asked dejectedly.

'Not at all. Your experience is not something which can be proven in any conventional laboratory. In this world, we are bound by certain physical laws. But when you go deeper into the nanosphere, the laws of matter become inconsequential. Science is yet grappling with particles like neutrinos, and black holes that can swallow even light.

'The human mind being enigmatic, I presume it has powers that enable it to go beyond neutrinos and black holes. Even now, I don't know about the laws that are applicable there. To put it metaphorically, what fascinates me in the path of scientific investigation now is Shankara's monistic philosophy.

'*Brahma satyam, jagat mithya*: the philosophy that asserts absolute consciousness is reality and the world is an illusion. Though certain people misunderstood it as a *mayavad*, an unrealistic argument, anybody studying science minutely shall perceive the eternal truth in it.

'For example, suppose that hundreds of films starring a popular hero and heroine are running at different theatres simultaneously. Though the same people feature in the films, they appear as different people of various ages in each film. The hero might be twenty-five years in one, seventy-five in another; a soldier in the first, a sanyasi in the second, even a murderer in the third! All these are the same person at the same time!

'In the material world, seated in one of the theatres, the viewer watches the movie and identifies totally with one role: weeping, laughing, loathing . . . and experiences the whole gamut of emotions. Without differentiating that it is a mere movie, the viewer's consciousness merges with the movie. Life is similar to that movie experience.

'Misunderstanding the sensual world as reality, we laugh, cry, loot and kill! By forgetting that this happens to be mere acting and the real essence is something else, we are getting entangled in illusion. Life is also experienced as the linear continuation of one and only one movie. Totally immersed in it, laughing, crying and fearing, we pull on . . . Since we cannot access the parallel lives, the different movies starring our own selves, currently playing in many other theatres, remain hidden from us.

'You have travelled to parallel worlds. But there is no guarantee that those worlds are real either! The original actor is not a part of any of the movies. The state of his various characters does not influence him ever. Shankara's "*Brahma satyam, jagat mithya*" should be scrutinized from that perspective,' Roberto explained.

'Yes, as Shankara said, the truth is something else to me too. This visible world is not my world for sure. Advaita might be useful for argument's sake, but it will not help with ordinary flesh-and-blood life.' Indrajit sighed.

Roberto said, 'Every theory, including that of relativity, was a mere hypothesis at first. Ratifications came much later. Shankara's darshan, that everything is a manifestation of the singular truth, has scientific backing, in my view. The objects in this world may appear different from each other but are actually constituted of the same fundamental particles.

'Everybody knows that the mountain, the human being, honey and poison are all made up of elementary particles like electrons and protons. Even though they are made of the same constituents, poison kills while honey heals! But the molecules of both contain the same particles in different proportions. Now, science is chasing the even minuscule "God Particle", called the boson, to identify where the transformation of energy to matter occurs. Science is searching for the missing link between the theory of general relativity and quantum mechanics now.

'These things fascinate me, like they would any other scientist. But now I've started thinking seriously that the world's greatest laboratory is a human's inner universe. The "God Particle", and the stillness transcending the emptiness, can only be found if you search there.

'I am mesmerized by that phrase "*Satakodi suyryaprakasham*", the light of a hundred crore suns. Nobody can describe, based on any wild fantasy, the light of a billion suns created when infinitesimal particles undergo fission.

'To summarize, careful analysis makes one conclude that one single truth manifests as innumerable entities. Some experience it. And they identify everything as the one and the only one truth. If you rephrase "Brahma satyam, jagat mithya" as the scientific notion "*urja satyam, vastu mithya*"—that is, "energy is reality, matter is illusory"—aren't both the statements same?

'If you look from the level of energy, there is no matter, only energy! And if you look from the level of matter, and perceive using your senses, energy cannot be comprehended. Imagine crafting figurines of humans, animals and trees, from say wheat flour, and depositing those back into the flour itself. The world is like that. The flour is the truth but the shapes are illusory. Those who cannot comprehend that truth keep moving from one illusory experience to another relentlessly.'

When Roberto finished his expatiation, two leaves, one of the peepal and the other of the mango tree, floated in the breeze and landed near them. Picking them up, the scientist looked at them intently. 'See, nature has sent these to reveal the truth.'

'What truth?' Indrajit enquired.

'These leaves, as we know them, are atoms when viewed under powerful microscopes. On further magnification, only the electrons and protons become visible! Beyond that is the world of quarks. And further on, the state of energy in its pristine form. This is true of the rock we are seated on and of the air we are breathing right now. The particles that the leaves are composed of are also the same that make up the rock, the air and us. The living and non-living things, and the air—all are extensions of the same energy. I am right, aren't I?

'In the sensory world, what we perceive as different objects are fundamentally the same energy. That is Shankara's Brahman! Matter remains as energy and energy remains as matter simultaneously. From the construct of our senses, it appears as an object but when viewed through a powerful enough instrument, it appears as energy. The result is different, depending on the state from which you perceive it,' Roberto elucidated.

'How . . . how can that be true? The universe and all these objects . . . how can they be an illusion? These sights and sounds . . . how can they be non-existent?' Indrajit was confounded.

'Humans can see, because our eyes reflect the light waves constituting the limited range of the electromagnetic spectrum. This spectrum also consists of gamma rays, infrared rays, radio waves and many others. A camera, or an animal, with eyes attuned to those frequencies, will see the same objects differently.

'The same is true for hearing too. We humans can hear only those sounds that fall in the frequency band between 20 and 20,000 hertz. Since dogs can hear sounds beyond that range of frequency, their sonic world is different from ours. Who knows whether they see sights inaccessible to our eyes?

'Some creatures cannot see colours. Theirs is a black-and-white universe. Certain other creatures see in two dimensions what we see in three dimensions. Precisely speaking, this world which we see as "real" is merely a "feeling" triggered by the limitations of our five senses functioning in restricted frequencies.

'For those species that view the world in a different form and shape, the "truth" might turn out to be totally different from our truth. Instead of light, if someone sees using another radiation, their sense of sight will be very different! Who can assert which sight is real and which an illusion? The obduracy that "what I see is the sole truth" is actually the result of our own severely limited sensory perceptions, isn't it?

'The intelligence which searches for the causality behind everything, employing these very senses, is also constricted. Only that which is free of all relativity can be called truth. It is nothing but energy. Therefore, I don't dare to reject the logic of experiencing different worlds through different sights! Rather than deny anything, I humbly admit my ignorance.' Roberto smiled.

'But . . . what about one's own consciousness? What is its role in such a scene?' Indrajit persisted.

'Just like anything shaped from wheat flour remains wheat flour, everything is consciousness! In other words, energy itself is consciousness. There is nothing other than energy in the universe. If you imagine the universe as an ocean, all objects can be considered as icebergs. Though an iceberg has a distinctive shape, it is nothing but water. The heavily dense air, just above it, is saturated with water vapour.

'When our awakened consciousness touches the macrocosm, it is like an iceberg. When our consciousness touches the microcosm in a dream state, it flows and spreads, like water, having no specific shape. In a much deeper sleep, our consciousness spreads everywhere, like water vapour. In all three states of matter, the essence remains the same. Just as the iceberg is both water and vapour, every object is composed of the same energy. The rock, the air between us and Nireeswaran—a continuum of the infinite energy that can neither be created nor destroyed,' Roberto summarized.

'How easily said! But whatever philosophy says, life remains a harsh, solidified truth. Wounds and hurts are so real and true while we experience them. As far as I am concerned, Megha is also a truth,' Indrajit said.

'Of course, I don't deny it. When the consciousness traverses in the materialistic world, we are bound by the world's rules. But one should be able to transcend everything. In that phase, where all differences vanish, Megha ceases to be either a relationship or a bondage. Yet one cannot attain those heights while remaining within the laws of this world. If you ask me, I am personally not against your relationship with Megha. Nevertheless, I cannot convince others. It is an unforgiving situation,' Roberto said, expressing his helplessness.

'I wish I had not woken up! Then, I could have existed in a world which was not bound by the laws of this one. Stayed as water vapour and not as an iceberg . . .' Indrajit retreated into silence for a while and then asked, 'Roberto, they assigned you to counsel me and help rectify my path, didn't they?'

'What is there to rectify in this matter? After all, to rectify something, one should know what is right! There seems to be no solution in the offing. I heard that Megha's father is a rogue. Wonder how he will react to the gossip,' Roberto replied.

'I am not bothered about all that now,' Indrajit protested.

'So long as you live in this world, you should be bothered about it. No amount of justification of "another world" or "another life" would suffice. Shall I be frank? When you confess that you cannot stay away from Megha, what do you mean? You want to live with her?'

Indrajit gazed intently at Roberto. The truth was that he could not provide a satisfactory answer. Inside him was an image similar to the union of peepal and mango. Who was anchoring whom . . . ?

Indrajit looked at the setting sun silently. Darkness was falling, with the gaping mouth of the sky ready to swallow the last ray of light.

The tête-à-tête was ending without any clear resolution. Roberto had nothing to offer to Arunjit, in spite of his diligent efforts. Some matters necessitated a lot of patience. And even if nobody did anything, events were set to follow their course naturally, as per the laws of motion.

Roberto observed with curiosity as Indrajit picked up the leaves of the peepal and mango. Even when they parted ways, Indrajit held the leaves close, as if reminding himself of the macro and the micro.

Thirty-First Petal: Conciliation

Every day Janaki felt apprehensive of the fact that she could still be assaulted by Antony, even though she had escaped narrowly one night. What loomed ahead was a dangerous uncertainty. Rather, such had always been the state of her life. There was no one on the face of the earth to question or resist violence against a prostitute. The great souls around would only keep a polite distance, considering such an effort beneath their dignity. Where had the universe marked the place for a whore in its scroll of time?

Janaki could rely only on Roberto. Yet, she did not reveal to him any hint of the threat surrounding her. He was a scientist destined to scale the pinnacles of worldly acclaim, and his departure was imminent. The kind heart of the prostitute considered it would be a shame to distract the scientist's focus with distasteful topics.

Roberto had shared a secret with her, hitherto unknown to anyone. The world would make sure that he soared to the summit of glory one day. Even if he did not wish it, the force of the universe would descend to pull him upwards. It was Valiyammachi, after her near-death experience, who had told him what was in store. Separating from her body, Valiyammachi had travelled forward in time and seen the future. She had emphasized that there was a state of consciousness where, in a moment, one could see an entire lifespan. It was the infallible indication of the relativity of time, which his Valiyammachi, who had never studied science, had imparted to Roberto.

Janaki knew that Roberto wasn't in the least celebrating his existence as a man. She could easily read him, based on her knowledge of different manly traits. His life was geared towards ensuring that the arrow struck the bullseye. Many great scientists had vanished from the earth without savouring their lives. Or one could say that they celebrated life by immersing themselves in scientific inquiries.

It was good that Roberto remained a bachelor. He was 100 per cent dedicated to science. He might not be a good husband or father. He would live, unravel the mysteries of science and offer the solutions to the universe before vanishing into the void. If, before that final disappearance, Roberto was to reach the zenith of fame, Janaki wished to be alive just to witness that event.

Out of inquisitiveness, Janaki once tried to gauge the sexuality of Roberto the man. She purposefully directed their conversation to that subject. When Janaki claimed that she could assess a man's sexuality based on signs, Roberto was astounded.

'But how?'

'There is a science which can correctly measure masculinity.'

'Wow, what is that intimidating science?'

'You can read the face, the structure of the nose, the length of the fingers, the veins, the nails . . . all are indicators of a man's sexuality. Extend your hand towards me . . . let me take a look!' Janaki said.

Roberto unhesitatingly stretched out his hand.

'Just consider it a prostitute's clandestine science,' Janaki smiled.

Taking the spine of a coconut leaf, Janaki measured the length from Roberto's elbow to the tip of his fingernails. Then she measured the fingers and his nose, and snipped away some finger lengths from the *eerkil* in her hand. Afterwards she put out two pieces from the assortment. 'This one for the scientist's peaceful state. And this symbolizes his provoked state.'

Roberto laughed heartily, tickled by the measurements of that mysterious science. 'How did you do that?'

'Everything has a science behind it. You told me that science is what one gleans through observations. I took that lesson seriously, and the result before you is based on many observations. With true gratitude to my guru, of course . . .'

'Which guru?'

'Our guru . . . Vatsyayana, the author of the Kama Sutra! He was also a sage!'

'Admirable! You should be nominated for the Nobel Prize for this signs-based science. Now, this is the science of men. Is there an equivalent science for women too?' Roberto asked.

'Undoubtedly. Fingers, gaps between the fingers, the undulations of the palm . . . all are relevant. Show me a woman's hand and I will tell you more!'

'Janaki, let us explore your own hand.'

'That won't be proper. It will be a disrespect to the guru.'

Janaki had tried to analyse Roberto's smell when she was in his proximity. There was never a whiff of anything in his physical odour which indicated a sexual proclivity. On the other hand, Antony's body exuded something diametrically opposite. It was permeated with the smouldering, feral stink of sexual craving. As a hobby of sorts, in hindsight, Janaki had started dwelling on the odours of the men who had known her.

The sour smell of Bhaskaran, the exhilarating manliness of Damu's bodily scent, the jaggery-tinted bitterness of Chettiar . . . Janaki was sure of one thing: if anyone were to spread all the world's scents before her and ask her what turned her on, she would disdainfully disregard the talc powders and expensive perfumes and point at the odour emanating from Damu's perspiration. Janaki could recollect the different smells wafting from each part of his body.

While Janaki was engrossed in these thoughts, Antony appeared yet again before her. He was not alone but accompanied by Bhaskaran and Sahir. Since she hadn't seen Antony for a long time, Janaki was under the impression that his evil spirit had been exorcised forever. When the trio knocked at her door, Janaki was scared witless thinking about how she could fight off the combined strength of three males. As she stood bewildered, Sahir spoke.

'Don't panic. We are not here to pick a fight.'

Based on her previous encounters with them, Janaki could not take that at face value.

'Heard that Acchayan threw a fit after boozing that night. Janaki, please let it go,' Bhaskaran pleaded, pointing at Antony.

Janaki could not determine the intention of that roundabout approach. 'No issues,' she said. 'But what is this conciliation all about?'

Out of the blue, Antony attempted atonement. 'See, my nature doesn't allow me to apologize even when I am wrong. Maybe I am seeking someone's forgiveness for the first time in my life.'

Janaki was flabbergasted. Was this another of Nireeswaran's marvels? How else could hard-shelled masculinity melt before her like this?

The aged female help peeped in from the kitchen and, seeing the trio, pulled her head back in terror. Three wasps, one after another, buzzed around and vanished behind a photograph on the wall. The wasp family now lived there, having been made refugees when Antony broke the old chair during his last visit.

'Janaki,' Bhaskaran adopted a smooth tone, 'we have come requesting your help.'

'Ayyo! You three mighty ones seeking my help? All I could do was sell my body. But it was a business involving money exchange and not free aid! Now, if you are here for a cashless deal, let me warn you that there is no scope even with cash! Dear brothers, Janaki has stopped that business!'

Sahir intervened, 'Tut, tut! Janaki, you misunderstand us. What we want is another favour.'

'Can you speak straight?'

'You know that our pride has been bruised in this Nireeswaran matter, right?'

'Ah, you guys were banished from that site, weren't you?'

'Speak of sheer injustice! The stone that we installed to mock superstition has now been anointed as a god by the rest. We are hell-bent on destroying it.'

'Easy, isn't it? Just a stone. Why don't you seize it and hurl it away?'

'Are you making fun of us?' Antony scowled, losing the conciliatory expression on his face.

'Not at all. How can I help you in this matter?' Janaki asked.

'See, we cannot go near that place. Why can't you help us? You can enter the place without rousing any suspicion. We will pay you any amount.'

Janaki burst into peals of laughter. 'There is an idol of Nireeswaran somewhere. And the Abhasa fellowship assigns a village prostitute to destroy it. How funny! All right, imagine that I succeed in my assignment. But what if another powerful idol replaces it tomorrow? Will you be able to stop that?'

'No need for loud-mouthed philosophy. Can you do it or not?'

'No. It is better to sell flesh than to get paid for this! Not that I have any special affection for Nireeswaran. But I cannot.'

Janaki was intractable. The Abhasa was incensed at the rising hood of arrogance displayed by a mere woman, that too a prostitute. However, had they reacted, it would have been counterproductive. They could only retreat, fuming. So the trio issued a strict warning to Janaki before leaving.

'We will destroy it! If not you, someone else. Money can purchase devastation of even nations. This is merely a piece of stone.'

'Whatever you say,' Janaki replied.

'Beware! If you dare to betray us . . .'

'That won't happen. Not because I am terrified of you! I am actually curious to know whether the intrepid warriors can accomplish the mission. That will be the real test of your manhood. If Nireeswaran is so powerless that you can demolish it, what's the use of a piece of stone like that? Hurl it deep into the canal. I extend my full mental support.'

The speech of the prostitute, which hit hard at their self-esteem but had overtly seemed innocuous enough, confounded the Abhasa. They weren't sure whether she was laughing at them or extolling their virtues. As the trio walked away, Janaki watched three wasps accompanying them.

She instinctively knew that the hotblooded young men were not going to remain silent. They were yearning to proclaim something to the world at large. She wasn't interested in vivisecting the right and wrong of it. That would entail taking sides and justifying all the fallacious arguments from a particular viewpoint.

While watching a cricket match between India and Pakistan, it was a person's bias towards one side that made the game exciting. For a neutral person, viewing the match might be boring. Janaki felt that her state was that of an indifferent witness in the matter of Eswaran and Nireeswaran. If an Eswaran or Nireeswaran existed, they might bicker with her for that reason. Else there was a possibility that neither of them would feel any animosity towards her. If, by any chance, both were the personifications of the same entity, their attitude towards the poor whore who had escaped ensnarement might be positive!

Janaki did not give the slightest intimation to Roberto about her meeting with the Abhasa. She was careful that Roberto's mind should not get tainted by the implication of violence in the trio's plan. She was adamant that Roberto left the village without a snarl of worry in his mind.

Roberto had already invested much in her loose, shoddy life. If Janaki did not feel disgusted about her erstwhile life, it was solely due to Roberto. Her self-loathing seemed to have left her now. Janaki would never sell herself again. But not because it was a wicked thing to do.

Shortly after, Janaki came to realize that every enforced decision had an equal and opposite reaction. It wasn't known, as Roberto had jestingly suggested, if Newton's laws of motion had come into play, but on that very day, Janaki ended up willingly offering her body to an unexpected person.

Thirty-Second Petal: Boon

Finally, on a Monday afternoon, Sudha stepped out for a walk. It had been decades since she had crossed the gate. Sudha had hacked away from her life an entire period equivalent to Indrajit's sleeping phase. She had chosen a life without any sights or experiences which were denied to the comatose man. Much like Gandhari, who wilfully covered her eyes for the sake of Dhritarashtra, Sudha had also turned a blind eye to the long years stretching ahead of her.

Sudha had limited her world to Indrajit's cot, unaware of her children growing up and not even paying attention to their studies; it was her in-laws who had taken up those responsibilities. Thus, the childhood of Arun and Akhil was moulded under the nurturing shade of their grandparents. Though they had parents, neither was actually present. None of their schoolmates ever saw their father or mother. Their grandparents accompanied them to PTA meetings and annual functions. With the passage of time the boys adapted to the situation, and a precocious maturity graced both of them. Before their demise, the caring grandparents had ensured that both the boys stood on their own feet.

Meanwhile, Sudha had been focused exclusively on Indrajit as if meditating on an '*eka* mantra'. She found herself wondering how she had crossed those long years.

'Sudha' should have been the title given to a sequel of implausibilities. She was born to a poor family. Her education was mediocre. The circumstances that could enable her to dream of a husband like Indrajit, who hailed from a prosperous family and held a top-notch job, had not existed at all. As far as Sudha was concerned, Indrajit was a boon bestowed on an undeserving person like herself. The statement 'my husband is my living god' captured the state of Sudha's mind, as if she were a character from the myths. Eventually, her life ended up like a mythical story.

While hoping that Indrajit would wake up at any moment, twenty-four years had passed her by. And when he woke up, more troubles were in store for her than she had faced in his years of slumber. Sudha could not understand who had decided and executed the series of events in her life. It was like wrestling with an equation whose solution remained out of reach. On the right side of the equation, a zero would be playing around tantalizingly. Zero held a humungous uncertainty. Sometimes it acted like a treacherous vortex, sucking lives into its depths.

On sleepless nights, Sudha brooded over escaping that uncertainty altogether. After many rough calculations, Sudha arrived at a hard decision, unbearable for any wife. It was a strategy devised by her female mind, which involved stepping right into the centre of a problem.

It was like plucking out her own heart, sundering its roots and handing it over to another. Since the commodity of exchange was her most beloved, afterwards Sudha would have to retreat to an impoverished existence. Only laments and darkness would await her there.

Though she tried to muster the necessary courage, Sudha could not confront Megha. It was not an easy matter which could be written down on a slate and erased later. She was unsure which spaces would be rendered to cinders from the lethal power of words.

But when a do-or-die situation arose, one had to choose either the devil or the deep sea. When life came to haggle shamelessly with her, she could only surrender without uttering a word in protest.

The next time Megha visited her, Sudha tentatively introduced the subject, as if tottering on a precipice. She was terrified of toppling due to a misstep or strong breeze. Megha's reaction was as unpredictable as she feared. The girl looked scorched, her expression as if something heavier than the earth had dropped on her head.

'He is my father's age, and I have always considered him in that light. Just because of evil gossipers . . .'

Sudha watched the wretched young woman before her. A girl wrecked by the arrows of slander. Her face made it evident that her nightmares were blood-hued nowadays.

'Age has not affected him. The mind is young. I request that you help him.'

'Even hearing all this is a sin! How . . . how can you talk to me like this?' Megha sobbed.

'You do not know what is going on between us,' Sudha said. 'It is nobody's fault. Things just happened so. If you try, you can save a good man. Had it not been for you and your family, that poor man . . .'

It was true—a man had spent twenty-four years imprisoned in coma, having tried to save her. It was a debt that would not be repaid even after many rebirths. Yet, any indebtment was also covered under clear moral guidelines. One should never demand such a payback. The only thing left for Megha was to leave the vicinity without bidding farewell.

And she walked away.

That gesture was an unmistakable answer. It was a death-like departure, cutting away all possibilities of another rendezvous. When she thought that Megha's footprints would not grace the house again, Sudha realized how much she adored her.

As she gazed at the departing young woman, who had cropped up as an obstruction in her life, her tongue murmured to the whimpering heart, 'Poor girl.'

Though the attempt had failed, Sudha experienced great relief. The revelation that Megha had never harboured a wrong notion about Indrajit imparted her with an ineffable lightness of spirit. Sudha knew, even when she was cajoling Megha, that a Shakuni inside her was surreptitiously longing for a 'no'. Female minds cannot help it, their feelings of attachment being more intense than that of men.

Megha stopped going to Sudha's house after that day. She retreated into a deep abyss within herself, hiding from others. Every look was like an arrow tip of derision darting at her. 'The slut who wrecked a family' was the allegation which every tongue sniped at her.

The public mind happens to be like that. It is indifferent to the soul-crushing agony of an individual. It promises only crosses to those who do good.

With immense grief, Roberto too observed how two different worlds were judging Indrajit and Megha with their own rules of justice. He was caught in a rabbit hole of helplessness, unable to disclose the truths he knew. On deeper analysis of Indrajit's state of mind, Roberto had understood how the subconscious mind held many secrets.

The mind was like a monstrous iceberg floating in the sea. What was visible was only a tiny portion of the whole. And since the rest was submerged in water, it appeared non-existent. One could not gauge the secrets of the depths by just scratching the surface. Only those who consciously undertake a deep dive into the sea come to realize the marvellous treasures beneath the surface.

Though consciousness connects to the subconscious in sleep, it forgets all on waking up. Somehow, Indrajit could visit the subconscious intermittently and retain the memories in his conscious mind. However, one had to be careful while exploring secrets. They have an inherent tendency to remain secrets and follow the law of inertia—where objects continue in the state of stability. Even the most brilliant scientist would not be able to decipher the secrets with the exclusive power of his wisdom, as in doing so he would be attempting to interpret the subtle cause of intelligence, depending on the very same intelligence.

The only way to comprehend the minuscule is to turn into the minuscule itself.

The disbelief caused by what one has heard can be removed only by seeing for oneself. In the same way, only with one's own direct experience can the secret of subtlety be understood. Except through practice, there is no other recourse to mastering cycle balance and floating in water. A mere 4 feet of water is sufficient to sink an expert on the science of buoyancy whereas someone clueless about science might easily swim across even a deep sea. If out of practice, even an ustad of momentum theory can topple down from a bicycle. And an unschooled country bumpkin might exhibit amazing feats on it! Similarly, only those with mastery recognize that control over the mind is the doorway to a true wonderland. Roberto knew that he could not reveal these interpretations verbatim to anyone else. What he did not know was how he could solve the problem at hand.

While many minds were seeking solutions in diverse ways, one day, unexpectedly, Sudha stepped out of her house. She walked through the paths lying forgotten for years, searching for some remnants of her past. Since the years had exhausted her, even former acquaintances failed to recognize her. The woman who had kept awake for twenty-four years was passing through the same experiences faced by the man who had woken up after twenty-four years of sleep.

Sudha widened her eyes like a newborn in an intimidatingly immense world. The old path to the Mahadeva temple had undergone a sea change. Massive walls had risen on both sides of the way. Such fancy walls were unheard of two decades ago. Back then, fences made of stems of the *veliparuthi* plant and *poovarasu* were ubiquitous; there were also a few tiled houses scattered in the vicinity. Now, tiled houses had become extinct. Instead, there were concrete houses with false tiles paved for style, a trend that appeared to ridicule the old ways.

Since the village had expanded around Nireeswaran, Sudha found the side paths unfamiliar. They stretched antagonistically, like formidable trails belonging to some strange country. Yet, Sudha was sure that she would reach Nireeswaran's abode on following the track. It had become the confluence point of all the paths.

The peepal and the mango anxiously gazed at the woman walking towards them. Like one soul recognizing another, the trees could connect with the woman who had once experienced oneness with another being, like themselves. The trees sensed the radiance emitted by the devoted wife. As they readied for the meeting, for which they had been preparing since their birth, the peacock screeched from the top. Sudha looked up and saw the bird. The handsome creature had frequently visited her yard and pecked around. The charming one was fed by Sudha's own hands.

Sudha noticed that the stone platform around the gigantic trees had been recently spruced up. It was a place about which many people had waxed eloquent. She eagerly looked at the stone idol which was waiting for her.

Nireeswaran.

The one who existed before the origin.

The one who had woken up a sleeping man and returned him to life. Sudha wondered whether it was true. Would a simple stone have such powers? To reject the thought without prejudice did not require much erudition; a nursery child's intelligence was sufficient.

So, Sudha perceived the stone just as a stone. She glared at it with disdain. Then she asked the unclear form a question: 'Why did you wake him up?'

Nireeswaran remained silent. How could a mere stone break its silence?

'When he was asleep, he was my own,' Sudha's voice choked. 'I could touch him, hug him, kiss him . . . And now? You made my husband a stranger to me, didn't you?'

Nireeswaran did not respond. How could a mere stone respond?

'Nothing to say, eh?' Sudha unwittingly raised her voice. The onerous pressure inside her, escaping her control, leapt out. The onlookers heard the tirade, but the protagonist was oblivious of her surroundings. For her, only she and Nireeswaran existed in the world at that moment.

'You are acclaimed to be a great power, aren't you? Then, I am also asking for a boon.'

Sudha's voice and face became hard. She did not know that Sumitran and Sudharman were standing right behind her. They had felt that something was amiss in Sudha's loud monologue. Never had they witnessed such a scene where someone challenged a deity, except in a few melodramatic Tamil films.

'Fulfil one and only one task for me,' Sudha demanded, forgetting the surroundings. 'I want my Indrettan back. In his old form, asleep. I don't need an awakened husband.'

While the listeners stood dumbstruck, Sudha swooned and collapsed in a heap at the platform.

Thirty-Third Petal: Return

The Abhasa never had any feud with the woman called Sudha. They only had respect for the way she had sacrificed her life for a comatose man. Still, when they heard that she had fallen unconscious at Nireeswaran's abode, they relished the news. The power that had awoken Indrajit was being censured, and it was natural that they would receive the news with pleasure. Two contrasting prayers regarding one man had reached the same place.

A young woman had pleaded for the awakening of a sleeping man, and now his wife had arrived with an entreaty against it, triggering widespread gossip. It was solid proof of how a deep chasm had opened up between the husband and wife. If, one by one, events turned against Nireeswaran, the tide would shortly turn in favour of the Abhasa. Their new strategy was to be furtive. After Janaki's refusal to go along with their plans, the trio was wary about approaching anyone else.

On the other hand, Sudharman was intensely discomfited. Indrajit occupied the top slot of the Niprasa's marvellous accomplishments. The news had boosted the association's fame by no small means. When enquiries arrived from far and wide about that miracle, how many times had Sudharman narrated the story in his own inimitable style! Now, after witnessing the heartfelt entreaty of the poor woman, Sudharman's own heart was bruised.

How much pain was Sudha enduring that she ended up praying that her husband be made comatose again? Sudharman ruminated that each prayer expressed the selfish interest of short-sighted people.

Unable to decipher the cause-and-effect connection, people projected their wishes as prayers. Those who prayed for someone's awakening, could not fathom the consequences of that prayer.

Sudharman was in the motley group which helped Sudha after she collapsed. Lying on her side, she watched the canopy of the Athmavu towering above. Sudha caught a glimpse of the peacock hiding in the foliage, peering at her. And she recognized the affinity, spanning many past lives, in its eyes. When someone suggested that they shift her to a hospital, Sudha struggled to a sitting position, saying she was all right. It was not to end up in a hospital that she had, after decades, stepped out of the house. When someone yearned to die, medical care appeared like a garish joke.

It flustered her to see people jostling around her. Having spent long years without seeing the outside world, she was suddenly trapped in the middle of a horde and felt like a wild fawn caught amid the city lights. She simply wanted to go home. In that bustle, Sudha forgot Nireeswaran, forgot the Athmavu and forgot the peacock.

As she hurried home without a backward glance, Sudha bitterly cursed herself for losing control and yelling gibberish at a piece of stone. She had forgotten the surroundings in a tumultuous moment, and it was shameful! The news would spread like wildfire in the village. A tongue of fire scalded her innards, as the dread grew about Indrajit and her sons getting to know of this utterly foolish act of hers.

When she had set out for the temple, nobody had been around. Both her grandchildren had left for school. Arun and Akhil were in their offices. Ranjini, her daughter-in-law, had caught the morning bus to visit her ailing mother. The only person left was her husband. And Indrajit, trying to evade the discomfort of being alone with Sudha, had left home too.

Indrajit preferred to spend the long days in Rose Villa. Since Janaki would cook lunch for Roberto, he would partake of it and avoid going home. There was hot coffee, made with milk from Annamma's house, in a flask filled to the brim. Roberto was addicted to coffee, and Indrajit too started relishing that habit.

He found it difficult to request Sudha for even a glass of water. The face-to-face meetings had ceased almost completely. Ever since Megha's arrival in their lives, there was a question mark over the relationship between the husband and wife, and Indrajit was reeling under that burden. How long could he continue under the same roof, his head bent low like a wrongdoer? That his lacklustre life, bereft of any purpose, was stretching ahead endlessly was nothing short of banishment to hell.

Whenever Indrajit felt dismayed about the emptiness of his present days, memories of his old office days came rushing to him. Though he wished to revisit the place, it hadn't worked out yet. There were no familiar faces waiting for him there. Yet, in his imagination, the seat towards the left of the west-facing room tugged him to the past. Indrajit yearned to see the giant mango tree that used to sporadically knock against the windowpanes. Would all that even be there today?

Though he had crossed the age for retirement as per official records, Indrajit wished to take up some job to while away the frustrating hours. But who would provide him with employment? Occasionally, he thought about accompanying Roberto to Bangalore and trying for a private-sector job. He had had enough of life in the village! Indrajit wished to move away from everyone and everything for a while. However, he did not share his thoughts with Roberto, deciding that he would do so at an opportune moment. The only person in the world who would understand him was the scientist.

Lethargic and exhausted with sitting throughout the day, Indrajit got up to leave at sunset. Since Roberto was deeply entangled in his research paper, Indrajit preferred not to disturb him. At a simple request, Roberto would have gladly freed himself from his studies and accompanied him home. Indrajit thought it would be unfair to him, since the young man was immersed with such focus in his work. Such interludes, where the creative juices flow, are rare.

'If you can wait for some time, I shall come with you,' Roberto offered when Indrajit got ready to leave.

'No worries. Go ahead with the work.'

'Just a moment, I will join you,' Roberto insisted. 'Don't go alone.'

'No need! I will manage fine by myself today.'

There was a reason he wanted to leave alone. Megha's absence had been shaking the very foundations of Indrajit's existence for the past few days. Not knowing if it was intentional or whether she was unwell, and unable to control himself any longer, he had visited the *Anganwadi*. On being told that she hadn't been there for a few days, he had become panic-stricken. When he went to the house where Megha lived as a paying guest, he was informed that the young woman had left without revealing details about her destination.

A flight from this world to some other, without leaving a single clue behind . . .

Nevertheless, Indrajit visited Nireeswaran's abode many times and continued his wait like a *dwarapalaka* who was denied even a camphor wick.

Today, he started from Roberto's place alone, carrying within himself a slowly dying flame of hope. Indrajit did not know then that the journey would rewrite his life yet again. Had Roberto received the slightest hint of the impending danger, he would not have allowed Indrajit to travel by himself.

Someone was lying in wait for him, like a hungry predator. A cunning beast named Madhavan, who knew the exact trail of the prey he was hunting. Ever since the slander linked his daughter to Indrajit, he had been waiting to confront the man responsible for smearing Megha's reputation.

The father and daughter were not close to each other. Madhavan was a father in name only. Megha's childhood and adolescence had gone by without knowing any fatherly affection. When her mother passed away, Megha began to consider herself an orphan. With the meagre income from the Anganwadi, she sustained her life without depending on anyone else.

Her father being an unbalanced man, it was better for Megha to keep her distance from him. Forget about favours, with certain people it was enough of a blessing if they abstained from doing any harm to one.

The gossip spread by wagging tongues had reached Madhavan's ears. His mind became a riot-stricken zone. An urge to set fire to anything in front of his eyes possessed him. On conveniently encountering his enemy en route the Nireeswaran temple, the assailant within leapt out with flaring vengeance. First act, then think' was his twisted motto.

The attack was unleashed from the rear.

Bludgeoned at the back of his head, Indrajit lost his balance and fell heavily. Before he could recognize what was happening, his white shirt was coloured red with blood. Blood oozed from his nose and merged with the mud. His life oscillated, clinging to a still centre between two states of existence.

By the time Roberto heard the dreaded news and frantically rushed to the spot, the locals had shifted Indrajit to a hospital. Roberto saw a single slipper lying face down on the side of the path. He was filled with unbridled fury at the thought of that animal attempting to tear Indrajit's life into shreds once again.

The poor man was just beginning to reclaim his shattered life. The thought that Madhavan had trespassed into that piteous life again was unforgivable. Had the blasted man strayed into Roberto's path at that moment, he would have lost his self-control. The scientist was overwhelmed by the strength of his vehement emotions.

In front of the ICU, Dr Amir told Roberto that Indrajit needed emergency surgery. Sensing the doctor's urgency, Roberto asked worriedly, 'Doctor, is it serious?'

'He has suffered a brain haemorrhage once already. There was the possibility of a recurrence. But now that he has been bludgeoned . . .'

Dr Amir stopped abruptly. Observing Roberto's despondent look, he said, 'To be frank, the scan has detected something serious. He is still unconscious. Let us try . . .'

Roberto could gauge that the percentage of hope in that statement was dismal. The fact that the man who was chatting with him just a while ago was now immersed in silence made Roberto feel deeply guilty. He should have accompanied his friend! Then, such a tragedy would not have unfurled in front of Nireeswaran.

The research paper had caused him to let down his guard. With his extended leave ending, Roberto had very few days left before returning to the lab. He had been in a hurry to finish his work. But the price had been too heavy. Roberto felt a stab of self-loathing thinking that all his research-related efforts had turned out to be futile. A thought started ticking in his mind that Indrajit would never talk about those unheard-of incidents again. Neither would he confront problems unknown to others.

The whole village floundered in the throes of the tragedy. Acquaintances and strangers poured into the hospital unceasingly. Zaid and Embrandiri stood forlorn among the crowd, unable to utter a single word. After Arnos's departure, their group had lost an essential element. Now Indrajit, too, was bidding farewell in another way. He was in a serene slumber, unaware that his friends and relatives were thronging nearby. Only two remained of that group of four friends. They stared silently at each other in that uncertain, overwrought atmosphere. Speechlessly, they parted ways, and retreated to the uncertainty of their own remaining lives.

Indrajit was shifted from the ICU to the ward after a fortnight. Sudha wept on seeing the unconscious man, silent and still like his previous form. It was as if the man was bound down to the earth with multiple tubes.

'What a despicable sinner I am,' Sudha wailed bitterly. 'The one who prayed for something she should never have! My poor Indrettan . . .'

Roberto noted the implosive power of those words.

The house was relinquishing its sights and sounds yet again. It was not known how long his festering inner wounds would make Indrajit sleep, even if his external wounds were healed. Perhaps he might make another miraculous recovery. Otherwise, though tied to the earth with life-giving tubes, he might continue travelling to his parallel existence without any disturbances. Would he be enjoying the endearing presence of his loved ones right now in such a life—the presence of the woman who had left without bidding goodbye, who hadn't yet paid him a visit in the hospital?

Whatever the answer, Roberto was determined never again to experiment with Indrajit's consciousness using his own. It was better to let nature take its own course. Every dam built across a roaring current invited many disasters. As he wordlessly wished Sudha, who was setting out on another phase of caregiving, Roberto decided that it would be his last visit to Indrajit. He did not wish to see him in that immobile state again. It would be enough if some day he could encounter the sleeping man in a world where he was active.

Roberto unobtrusively touched Indrajit's feet and stepped out. He then spoke to himself, 'Dear friend, who is like my own father, please accept this as my farewell.'

Thirty-Fourth Petal: Explosion

Janaki appeared in front of Roberto the next day with the voluptuous allure of a woman in her prime. On seeing him, a peal of laughter erupted from her and flowed uninterruptedly, as if a fissure had occurred in an earthen dam.

Roberto gazed at the laughing woman quizzically. 'Hey, what's this?' he asked.

'This is called joy,' Janaki replied. 'Today, I experienced what joy truly is. I am the happiest woman in the world right now.'

'And pray, what miracle occurred in the universe overnight?'

'Miracle . . . a real miracle.' Janaki giggled ceaselessly.

'Please stop laughing and tell me about it. Then help me pack my bags. It is time for me to gather my bundles and depart.'

Momentarily, the laughter dried up and Janaki descended to the world of reality. 'Good! Before you leave, I will make you listen to one new story about smells. It happened last night . . . like a marvel.'

'What marvel?'

'Janaki sold her body again last night.'

'You said that you had stopped doing that.' Roberto's voice echoed his disappointment. He was under the assumption that Janaki's deeds were immaterial to him. Now, though he pretended to be indifferent to it, Roberto was taken aback by his own reaction.

'Actually, I could have stopped last night only. Otherwise the body would have haunted me for long. You know for us Hindus, if there is even a smidgeon of karma, salvation is not possible,' Janaki smiled.

'Do you need Vedanta's support for selling the body?'

'Okay, let me leave aside Vedanta and resort to the language of the body,' Janaki responded. 'Rather, I will explain in the language of smells that the scientist is keen on.'

'Smells?'

'Yes, let me educate the scientist today on the different smells of the same body. Not guesswork, mind you! Experience! Possibly a newly sifted insight obtained by selling my body for the final time.'

Janaki told Roberto about an incident that had occurred five years before. She was a prostitute much in demand. A stranger knocked at her door one day. At first glance, Janaki recognized that the man was in extreme distress, his body a quivering mass of nervousness. The repulsion which welled up within her at his body odour made her averse to engaging with him intimately. The distraught man was clearly naive when it came to carnal negotiations.

He was a college professor working in the city, and had fought with his wife and come searching for a whore to get over his indignation. Sex was not for purging anger but for the appeasement of lust. But for that man, sex had become the means of paying back his wife rather than a way to fulfil his desire. Janaki's lone goal became to wrap up the deal quickly and get the money, since the miasma around the client was daunting and abhorrent. Janaki knew that a body-seller had to be dispassionate when it came to smells, good or noxious. Hence the thought that she was not being fair to her customer niggled at her. When he paid her generously, Janaki felt remorseful: she should have cooperated with him in a better way. It was unwarranted for a third-rate prostitute to show sincerity in earning her pay.

Even so, the realization that the client's body odour had been the reason for her disdainful behaviour was disturbing. The episode was forgotten, and she continued with her drudgery-filled life. Until another event occurred, deepening the old remorse.

On days when she was out of work, she realized that for a prostitute penury was very close at hand. Stricken with a serious ailment, when she was unable to work with her body, she couldn't find money for treatment or even for a single meal.

One day, Janaki dragged herself to the government hospital, wheezing and heaving. Ridden with fatigue, she felt her journey would terminate midway. Janaki sat on the edge of a stone bridge, seeking respite. The earth seemed to revolve around her at that moment. With nobody to help her, she stared at the barren landscape ahead, meditating on death. She surmised that the death of a prostitute would not cause even the flutter of a dropping leaf in the world. She felt she deserved to die. Those were the days when neither Damu nor the old woman were part of her life.

The exuberant flow of water beneath the bridge tempted Janaki greatly. As she gazed at the river, Janaki felt that it was coursing its way through the lapsed years of her life. The yearning to cover the miseries of the present, in the rush of the past, washed over her.

Such yearnings spring unexpectedly on people, luring them to catastrophe. Janaki felt the thrust of an ineffable force, swallowing all reason, instigating her to climb atop the culvert and peer into the depths. Bundling up all the muck and grime of her existence into a single moment, Janaki climbed the edge. And just at that moment, a car, trundling its way through the road, swerved into her life. The same college professor was driving the vehicle. Any man respected by society would have stayed away from such a worthless life like Janaki's. But this man, whom she had once been unfair to, stopped his car, recognizing her plight. Some inner prompting must have triggered that benevolence.

The professor arranged for Janaki's admission to a decent hospital. Janaki, who had long stopped trusting the world, looked at the man in utter disbelief. It was like fuel to the fire of guilt burning within her. It was on that day that Janaki realized that certain godly messengers came searching for whores too. They were destined to arrive without fail, at the exact moment when one reached some critical juncture of life.

Janaki could only pledge to herself that after her body regained strength she would spare no efforts to delight the man, treating his insufferable odour as fragrance. That was her plan of atonement. But the professor did not wait for a word of gratitude and, after giving her some money, left the premises. He also informed her that he had patched up with his wife and they were happy together.

After many years, Janaki had met that man near Nireeswaran's abode, a day before her visit to Roberto. The professor's wife, stricken by cancer, had passed away two years ago. He was planning to migrate to Canada the very next day, since his only son was settled there. Perhaps the universe had arranged such a meeting because that would be their last. The professor looked more handsome than before. Indeed, there was a rare dignity on his ageing mien. Perhaps the sincere love surging inside Janaki had made her think so. The only means to express her gratitude was her body.

Now, the body was no longer that of a prostitute. She was nature incarnate, ready to accept her man. It was when trying to repay her debt that Janaki became aware of a stunning truth. The loathsome stink of the professor's body, which had repelled her all those years before, had changed into an alluring, manly smell. It wasn't the fragrance of any perfume but that of the physical body. How could such a drastic change occur in a human's odour? Janaki had reached Roberto's side armed with that wondrous knowledge.

As she animatedly described the curious encounter, Roberto watched a radiance, never seen before, spreading across Janaki's face—the sort of radiance that diffuses to the face directly from the mind. Very seldom in a lifetime did such a radiance grace a human being; it suggested that one had paid off all one's debts and acquired a sky-like lightness of spirit.

The initial stab of disappointment which Roberto had felt after listening to Janaki's confession, that she was selling herself again, vanished. The woman was brimming with serenity and joy, as if she had indulged in some virtuous deed. Even prostitution could turn to virtue.

'It is quite natural, Janaki,' Roberto elucidated. 'The professor, when he approached you while enraged with his wife, exuded the dreadful stink of hatred. Yesterday, what he emanated was the fragrance of unconditional love. Each emotion is a smell.'

'Yes, each emotion is a smell. What, then, will be the smell of a perfect man?'

'I have heard that the body during transcendental experiences exudes the fragrance of musk. No idea if that is correct.'

'Perhaps! But there is something beyond. A state devoid of smells, when one overcomes all emotions.'

On hearing that, Roberto marvelled at the utter ease with which the woman presented arcane secrets which he had never ever contemplated. He moved near her, trying to sniff whether Janaki had attained the state of being that is devoid of smells. But restricted within his own ability to smell, Roberto could not pick anything up. Impulsively, provoked by mischief, Roberto asked, 'Janaki, any idea which is most important sexual organ of the human body?'

'Oho!'

As Janaki squirmed in mortification, he continued, 'I will tell you.'

'Hold on a bit! Let me cover my ears,' Janaki pleaded.

'No need to cover your ears. The name of that organ is the brain.'

'What?'

'Nothing but the brain! Every sexual experience happens in the human brain. All sight, touch, sound and smell, which we were searching for, all actualize there. These sensations don't happen in the eyes, nose or ears. Now, if one can stimulate the centre of the brain where all these senses are amassed, one can experience pleasure a million times more than the sexual gratification or the ecstasy produced by any drug.'

'God! I can hardly understand anything.'

'There is only one thing to know. The last word in pleasure is neither intoxication nor sex.'

Janaki wondered whether it meant that Roberto had overcome the sex drive by experiencing realms beyond that. However, Janaki preferred to keep that thought to herself. The man was bidding her goodbye. Though Roberto assured her of his return, Janaki's mind murmured that she would never see him again. Rare phenomena scarcely repeated themselves. That made them all the more precious.

Janaki could not ponder over this for long, since there was an unexpected explosion outside. The sound, which appeared to have arisen near the Nireeswaran temple, was followed by loud shrieks.

When Roberto leapt towards the door, Janaki stopped him by bolting the door.

There was a flurry of running feet, followed by sounds of screeching vehicles.

'What . . . what has happened?' Roberto became fraught with worry.

'Something has exploded,' Janaki replied.

'What?'

'If I have guessed right, Nireeswaran.'

'Eswara!'

Thirty-Fifth Petal: Apocalypse

Many, like Janaki, had suspected that the youthful trio would attempt to destroy Nireeswaran at any opportune moment. It was evident that they were simmering with rage. A whole village had witnessed them being struck by the lightning of ridicule and condemnation. After that, the Abhasa began to view Nireeswaran as their enemy incarnate rather than just a tiny piece of stone. Its growth had been like that of Frankenstein's monster, venturing to annihilate the creator himself.

Certain sprouts had to be snipped off while they were unformed else they burgeoned into menacing wild trees. By sinking their roots into the foundation, they might topple the home itself. The stone at the foot of the peepal and mango trees was no different. The Abhasa had wanted it to become a little popular before executing their plan; they had wanted to relish the egregious sadism involved in the whole process, like a cat teasingly playing with a mouse, delaying its death. No one had foreseen that the mouse would transform into a tiger. Indeed, Nireeswaran had spread its roots and branches more profusely than the peepal and the mango. There was no alternative other than slashing the mother root with a sharpened axe.

'We should destroy it, even if we have to adopt the most nefarious route,' Antony would often say. The fury in those words was sufficient to render Nireeswaran to ashes, had they landed on the deity.

'But how?' Bhaskaran and Sahir would ask.

Recently, Bhaskaran's confidence had been shaken. His fiancée Veni had cautioned him that he was going through an 'inauspicious phase'. Though he tried to laugh it off, the repeated warnings started giving him the creeps. Conscious that Bhaskaran did not believe in astrology, Veni's parents had surreptitiously collected his horoscope from his mother and matched it with their daughter's.

When Veni murmured that they matched in eight aspects, including *yoni porutham*, knowing that it pertained to sexual compatibility, Bhaskaran had breathed against her ears and asked lasciviously, 'And what is yoni porutham exactly?'

'Sssh . . . !' Veni blushed at the question as his breath tickled her ears.

Neither of them knew that there was nothing embarrassing about that *rajju* porutham, the sixth and the most important aspect for an auspicious marriage.

Yet, as per Veni, Bhaskaran needed to be wary about a malevolent planet glaring unblinkingly at him. That was why she called him often, requesting him to be cautious.

It might have been the influence of that evil planet gazing balefully at Bhaskaran that had made the terrorist within Antony start his strategic manoeuvres against Nireeswaran.

'An act of insurgency, no less.' Antony was resolute.

'What do you mean?' Sahir gasped, worried to the hilt.

'We shall climb over the boundary wall of the temple one night. A crude bomb will travel with us.'

Sahir was terrified by the suggestion. Never had he gone to such extremes, even in his dreams. 'Bomb' was a term he had encountered only in newspapers and television broadcasts; it was a word that he feared would explode even if he uttered it! Sahir felt a million splinters shatter inside his mind at the very thought of handling such an item.

'Acchaya, are you sure? If anything goes wrong . . . ?' Sahir croaked fearfully.

Sahir wasn't alone in this. Neither Antony nor Bhaskaran had ever harboured violent thoughts in their lives. They had only righteous intentions behind the pointless consecration of Nireeswaran. They had conceived it as a joke, and the innocuous thrill in executing something novel, never attempted by anybody before, had been their prime motivation. The 'high' of scripting a boisterous drama for the temple festival and enacting the heroic roles! The success of their endeavour egged them on further. But they were wrong to presume that they were the master puppeteers.

The young men could not effectively counter the myriad tales, both false and true, linked with Nireeswaran. When Indrajit relapsed into coma, they felt a temporary respite. With sad faces, the Abhasa too visited the house of the intriguing man who had fallen asleep again. Though they felt pity for Indrajit's condition, an inhuman gloating also accompanied their sympathy.

If the resurrected man had gone back to the dead, it was to be seen as the powerlessness of the one who had awakened him. The thunderbolt that had hit that particular household would soon land on Nireeswaran too. Then the deity would be relegated to the back burner of history, merely as a farcical character to be sniggered at, on reminiscing.

At Nireeswaran's abode, it was the creator's freedom to design the destiny of his creation which had been assaulted. Had they dumped the idol in a garbage pit without waiting for anyone's consent, it would have ended then and there. But that stage was long gone. The villainous character had acquired a life beyond the control of its creator.

'History has always witnessed such annihilations,' Antony unearthed the philosophy from his coffers of historical knowledge. 'If someone we created and fostered outgrows us, he should be immediately destroyed. Every country in the world practises that strategy. Not only nations, but even political parties do the same.'

Antony had an intransigent nature, and wishy-washy approaches left him cold. Even if they disagreed with him on many occasions, the duo of Bhaskaran and Sahir would usually concede to Antony's overarching confidence.

Antony, used to making unyielding decisions, had the strength of character to easily turn his back on both drinks and women if he so wished. However, never had such an exigency cropped up in his life.

As per his current beliefs, sex and liquor were markers of manliness. If he became convinced that control over such urges were true masculinity, he could renounce those without batting an eyelid. Because they knew their friend's nature, Bhaskaran and Sahir lost their initial trepidations. Once the argumentative inner voice against violence was banished, a different mood took over, and they became convinced that they should demolish Nireeswaran.

Antony was acquainted with someone who considered manufacturing crude bombs an art. He swore that the man would never betray them, even at the cost of his life. Hearing that, Sahir once again felt as though a storehouse of firecrackers was being set alight in him. Even from afar, he could see the canopy of the Athmavu caressing the sky. He felt stirrings of nostalgia at that sight. It must have been the poet in him that stoked such emotions at inappropriate times. The romantic inside Sahir whispered that even though it was faraway, the Athmavu could listen to their conversation. Though he tried to shrug away that thought, castigating himself that 'there was no place for poetry amid bomb-making', he could not manage to divert his mind. The sporadic screeches of the peacock emanating from the pinnacle of the Athmavu pulled him towards the trees.

The Athmavu watched compassionately as the trio, on a mission to question belief, became entrapped by the same entity that they had set out to destroy. The peepal and the mango adored the three. How could they not have a fondness for the youths who consecrated the beautiful notion of Nireeswaran, over whom they offered a reverential shade? But the rumination of the trees did not reach the humans. More than anyone, the Athmavu knew that they would scale the walls and reach Nireeswaran on the fateful night.

A new-moon night had been selected for Nireeswaran's consecration, and so the Abhasa chose another Amavasya to end it. Every act of violence has a predilection for darkness, because violence is darkness's own progeny. In this case, the advantage of pitch-darkness was that no one could espy what was unfolding in the vicinity.

After crossing the boundary wall, the trio soundlessly edged near the deity. As there were stone walls surrounding the temple and there had been no recent uprisings against the deity, there were no security guards in the compound. A solitary lamp kept watch near the idol, like an alert soul even as the body slept. In the light of the lamp, Bhaskaran retrieved the crude bomb from his bag. He had volunteered to destroy Nireeswaran with the same hand that had created it.

Similar to Perunthachan, the legendary temple architect who gazed at his son before releasing the deadly chisel, Bhaskaran glared at Nireeswaran, whom he had given life, one last time. When the light of the lamp fell on the idol, it seemed to be looking back at him through its single eye, the 'Ekanetra'. Bhaskaran castigated himself for thinking thus. He could never imagine eyes except as a pair. To confirm it was only a hallucination, Bhaskaran looked carefully again and again. He told his mind that what appeared as the single eye was the sandalwood mark applied on the idol by the eccentric priest.

How could an eye appear in a stone otherwise?

That too, a single eye!

Even if it exists, let the lone eye shut forever!

Without a moment's delay, he aimed the Agneyastra, the divine fire arrow, at Nireeswaran.

However, the mind can waver at critical junctures.

When this happens, the body also wavers.

Bhaskaran realized that the sight of the single eye had thrown him into a frenzy. Meanwhile, even as the weapon was hurled, it ended up accomplishing its objective.

The peacock on the Athmavu shrieked desperately.

The roosting birds scattered, cawing raucously.

The bull in the vicinity, offered to the deity, bolted for its life.

After the explosion, which shook the universe, plumes of suffocating smoke billowed around.

Sahir and Antony saw Bhaskaran fall, clutching his bloodied right hand.

There are moments when all amassed courage drains away. When unexpected things happen, the intelligence get short-circuited, comes to a standstill or commits some fatal error. Even to those who are arrogant about their intelligence, it will be revealed that they are not the owners of their own intelligence. Facing such a moment, Antony and Sahir bolted, driven by the instinctive impulse to escape.

Bhaskaran, writhing in immense pain, his sight fading slowly, watched his friends running away without stopping to help him. Seeing his fleeing friends, his mind suffered more than his body. He lurched to the ground, and the single eye's look seemed to pierce him like a sharp arrow. His consciousness had turned topsy-turvy by then, befuddling him, making him think that *this* was the truth and whatever had happened earlier was a mere illusion.

Thirty-Sixth Petal: Immersion

Life, at critical junctures, can tie a noose around anyone's neck. Even divine avatars cannot elude the laws of nature. So, how could the Abhasa be any different? The fact that Sumitran, someone they had always scorned as a halfwit, had taken the lead in trapping them mortified the trio greatly. It was a demeaning experience over which death seemed preferable. They earnestly wished for a bolt of lightning to descend from the skies to split open the earth. How wonderful that would be! For in those moments, there wasn't even an inch of the earth where their egos had a foothold.

When they were surrounded by a bloodthirsty mob, the final dredges of self-worth seeped away. Maniyan, sleeping in his shop nearby, was the first to wake up at the commotion. When he saw his acquaintances being manhandled, the bewildered Maniyan attempted to restrain Sumitran and Sudharman. By that time, more people had joined the melee, shining torches in the dark. Annamma and her daughters stood petrified by the side. Janaki and Roberto were the last to arrive. All the onlookers who had once witnessed the hunter's climbing escapade, including Sadananda Panicker and the butcher Moosa, were part of that crowd.

The same lot had witnessed the consecration of Nireeswaran by the light of the flambeaus. The stark difference was that the trio, who had been the cynosure of all eyes, now stood in their midst humiliated and shamefaced. The Abhasa had planned to celebrate the ceremony of Nireeswaran's dislodging with pomp and show. However, Kalapurusha, the Lord of Time, who enjoyed kicking the sun and moon around in the vast playground of the skies, had dragged the Abhasa into a deadly whirlpool. And it landed them in zones they hadn't seen in their worst nightmares.

Manacles, police, jail . . .

Jail was like an odd planet. The sun, which rose for everyone, the stars, which shimmered at everything, the light of the day and the ubiquitous winds never peeped into that place. Once they ended up there, the Abhasa felt that their identities had been shattered, that they had morphed into someone else, losing something essential from within and without. On the first day, they gloated that their contacts and a good advocate were enough to get them out. But all such endeavours proved to be fruitless.

'We are dealing with an act of terrorism,' the khaki-clad inspector said gravely.

'Terrorism?' those who had gone there to sort out the matter asked with trepidation.

'Of course! They were trying to destroy the Nireeswaran temple with a bomb.' The word 'bomb' being inseparable from the word 'terrorism', this was not surprising in the least.

The insignia on his police uniform popped out like eyes that investigated secrets. In the eyes of the law, the Abhasa had turned into terrorists who had to be kept away from society, though the truth was far from it.

Cognizant that they had crossed a line and were stepping onto treacherous ground, Bhaskaran and Sahir became panic-stricken. Even Antony, who considered himself the epitome of masculinity, lost his poise and became embroiled in bitter worry. His tempestuous, rebellious spirit seemed to have been tamed!

Usually, when his mind was flustered, Antony would sit in a remote corner of a liquor shop and let the confusion seep away. Now, not a drop of alcohol was within his reach. The law decided what he should do and when he should do it. Even the time to urinate was fixed by the law.

In the initial days, he found it difficult to use the common bathroom as he was a stickler for cleanliness, and restrained himself from even answering the call of nature. Soon, he felt a loathing for his own body, thinking of the waste materials festering within himself. When his thoughts travelled to the liquor shops in pursuit of an imaginary aroma, his body and hands trembled with need. Antony wished to break the prison bars and dive into a bathtub filled with intoxicating bubbles.

But the law exerted its force on him and restrained him from indulging in any of his longings. There were strict rules for allowing visitors since the Abhasa were branded as terrorists. Only after arduous efforts were a few close relatives allowed access, and that too for a restricted period.

Antony's uncles came to shower him with abuses. Quoting from the Book of Ecclesiasticus, they said that whatever had transpired was God's punishment for his disobedience towards his parents. When Veni's father came to inform Bhaskaran that she was abstaining from even drinking water, he was devastated. Sahir's uncle embraced him, and both of them burst into tears. When his uncle warned that the matter was not as simple as he perceived, Sahir felt that his body was stinking like a corpse.

The Abhasa faced a groundswell of derision from all sides. Even their co-prisoners, comprising murderers and thieves, looked at them with deep contempt, as if the three criminals were more depraved than the rest.

With each passing day, more burdens of uncertainty were stacked on their heads. The last lamp on the crag of hope dwindled. They were totally at a loss, unsure of the next step and unaware if they would ever get respite. Had they been believers they would have prayed to an invisible force—even if the prayers were futile—and held on to the flickering flame of hope. However, since they'd renounced faith right from the beginning, even trying to sabotage it with a counterforce, their stint in jail was unbearable.

The Abhasa yearned for someone who would commiserate with them and come to their aid. If only an old acquaintance, even an erstwhile enemy, would visit them with few words of consolation!

As the days passed their condition worsened, and they were dragged into an abyss of helplessness. It was Sahir who languished at the very nadir, experiencing death-like suffocation. Though relying on his inherent fortitude, Antony had withstood the onslaught for a few days, soon even his self-assurance started abating. Finally, in frustration, he asked his advocate whether he could somehow escape, even if it involved selling his Mangalore plantation. His body craved a breath of the outside air. The three friends had become fragile like sand figurines, likely to collapse at a mere touch, losing the sense of self that had once forged them together.

One day, the jail warden came to announce that two people had arrived to see them. When the Abhasa eagerly went forward, they blanched at the sight of the visitors: Roberto the scientist and Eswaran Embrandiri the priest. Never had the trio considered the remotest probability of those two ever visiting them.

Roberto observed how the faces of the three friends transformed at seeing them, like three pictures bleached of colour. It was difficult to recognize the unshaved and unkempt Antony. On Sahir's face, a heavy cloud loomed. Bhaskaran was clutching his plastered right hand with his left, biting down agony which could not be assuaged with painkillers.

The bars of the prison, exuding the coldness and indifference wrought over centuries, separated the jailbirds from the visitors. As they stood on either side, like strangers who did not speak a common language, neither party knew what to say or where to begin.

Antony's state of mind prevented him from trusting anyone or anything. He suspected that there was something nefarious about Roberto and Embrandiri suddenly visiting them. His expression made it obvious. Probably noticing that, and in order not to push the three into further pangs of doubt, Embrandiri started the conversation with a well-aimed, light-hearted question.

'Having fought against belief in Eswaran, you ended up fighting belief in Nireeswaran too, didn't you?'

A simple question sometimes had the sharpness to lacerate every cell of the body. There was no recourse except to stand wordless in its blistering wake. Bhaskaran and Sahir were undergoing that sensation. Antony's face blazed; he wanted to burn down the whole world.

'Caught in a frenzy to oppose, you forgot one fact! Both belief and disbelief are fundamentally the same! The intensity of belief the devotee has in the existence of God is of the same magnitude as the belief a disbeliever has in the non-existence of God. But the truth is naked, devoid of the garb of either belief or disbelief.

'You can colour the belief with hues of a tribal god, a ghost, Eswaran or Nireeswaran. It is just like sketching the pictures of God and Satan on the same drawing paper with the same pen. Though they are both ink stains on the same page, your mind makes them appear different. It was the same mind that snared you. What is the difference between you, who set out to oppose superstitions, and hardcore terrorists now?'

Though multiple explosions were taking place within them, the Abhasa were not in a position to react to Embrandiri's words. It is easy to ambush vulnerable minds; and if bodies, too, lose strength, people become sitting ducks for any foe.

Averse to looking at the faces of the visitors, Antony fixed his gaze at some distant point. That lone dot was his refuge now. Unable to even flex a muscle in response, he ground his teeth to control the swelling fury within.

Roberto felt uncomfortable watching such a tenacious young man hapless and despondent. It was galling to see the king of the forests tamed inside a tiny cage. A feral energy, and a delinquent lifestyle, suited Antony better. The universe would be complete only if such people existed, questioning the world. It would be a boring world indeed if everyone stayed serene, reciting hymns.

Those were Roberto's views. But Embrandiri had very different opinions, as his ensuing words proved.

'Even a person who can grasp atheism in its entirety can experience pure spirituality. It is a state beyond form and name. Unfortunately, such searches do not happen among atheists. By chasing petty gimmicks, they are satisfied easily with skin-deep tickling. Most of them do not attempt to touch the deep possibilities beyond. That's what happened to you too! It was your strong belief that there was no god. And you ended up gifting a form to that belief of yours. Many people sincerely surrendered themselves to it, and in that union, extraordinary events occurred.'

'Miracles, you mean!' Antony, who had controlled himself till then, lashed out. 'There are no miracles! Anything which cannot be explained scientifically is unacceptable to us.'

Roberto felt admiration for the young man who reacted so vehemently even inside a prison cell. The blood of a revolutionary flowed through his veins, making him openly proclaim his beliefs. It was the ability to accept the truth, whatever it may be, that freed a person from all bondage.

His mind preoccupied with such thoughts, Roberto compassionately looked at the three friends and spoke gently. 'Quite right. Nothing indescribable by science should happen in the universe. But it has another side to it. Gravity existed even before an apple fell on Newton's head. Similarly, anything acclaimed as "extraordinary" exists only until it is scientifically clarified. Once proven, it ceases to be an amazing phenomenon. What worked here was the mind's power. There is nothing more powerful and miraculous than the human mind.'

'If that is so, what is the need for a god? Man is the god of the universe!' Antony was unbending.

'How right! But this should be experienced and not bragged about. Haven't you heard that the one who knows can never be arrogant? The self-conceit that one knows everything is the clear symptom of ignorance. That vanity itself will turn into an iron curtain, shuttering the person's knowledge. Consequently, he never experiences the true wisdom within himself,' Roberto said.

'Ah, the scientist came to point out the divine punishment for my haughtiness! I could have imagined this crazy priest spouting all that! Aren't you ashamed to say it after having studied science?' Antony fumed.

Respecting the smouldering embers within the young man, Roberto listened unperturbed and resumed, 'I didn't come to accuse you. Though you didn't intend it so, the consecration of Nireeswaran was a stupendous act. It is no small matter that every human being can enter the place, unstopped by any barriers of caste or creed. Only the religion of humanity exists in that place. In a sense, the world needs no consecrations. There is no need to proclaim that a non-existent entity does not exist either. Similarly, there is no need to prove that an existing one exists. It is akin to sticking a bill saying 'Stick No Bills'! The paradox of being forced to do something to prevent others from doing it!'

The Abhasa stood, unsure how to respond. They seemed discomfited by what they'd heard. Any idea can be bloodied and mutilated in a duel of words. But to replace any understanding, which is in one's very blood, is not so easy. True spirituality cannot be understood by merely listening about it but only by self-realization. The word's meaning itself was 'concerning one's own self'. Ripening in its own time, it should attain fruition within oneself. That is why spirituality becomes different for each person.

Since that clarity was deeply entrenched within, Roberto steered clear from the conflict zone and said, 'See, I did not come here to pontificate on anything. Neither do I intend to mediate for you. I shall miss my train if I stay any longer. You know, I just wanted to say farewell before I left.'

At those unexpected words, as if a blizzard had swept inside, the three friends froze. Roberto felt compassion for the youths gazing at him unblinkingly. His entry in the village had been unexpected. And his exit, too, happened to confound expectations.

The probability of his meeting the Abhasa again was remote. Yet, aching at that thought, Roberto said, 'I hope to see you some time. Even after reaching there, I shall keep in touch. And I shall try to help you in any possible way.'

Roberto stretched his hand through the prison bars.

Prodded by a subconscious compulsion, all his bitterness draining away, Antony extended his hand too. Roberto felt the flow of blood of that calloused hand in his own. It was indeed a realization that the barrier between minds was as thin as blood; you just needed a word or a touch to break it.

His hand met the softness of Sahir's palm afterwards. Since Bhaskaran's hand was covered in plaster, Roberto patted him on the shoulder.

'I liked you three and your so-called debaucheries. Shall see you soon, dear friends.'

On hearing that goodbye, the trio felt that in spite of all the misunderstandings, they too had always liked that man. When the very person whom they had railed against was making a sudden exit, it felt as if a significant character of a story was walking away. The atmosphere illuminated by his presence seemed to be getting blurred. Every departure without proper farewell was incomplete.

Embrandiri observed how the trio slipped into ruminations while gazing after the scientist. Sometimes, an edifice erected after many calculations collapses along with the scaffolding and foundation. But even then, the cornerstone needed for raising another structure lies somewhere in that same rubble. It has to be discovered first. Where was that cornerstone hiding now?

'He has left, and my time is approaching. Don't you want to get out of this place?' Embrandiri asked.

The Abhasa were not expecting that query. They wondered why Embrandiri had not accompanied Roberto. Then, Embrandiri said, 'You have one and only one way ahead.'

Perplexed about where the conversation was headed, the trio looked askance at him.

'Which way?' Sahir, who had been silent throughout, asked hopefully. He had foolishly assumed that some secret path would open before them, and he could escape from the prison pronto. His grip on reason had been lost to such an extent. His wan and pale face was the result of many tearful nights.

Turning to face him, Embrandiri enunciated clearly, 'You might feel contemptuous on hearing it. But my mind insists that I say it loudly! Only one can save you from this inexorable situation.'

'Who?' Bhaskaran asked eagerly, curious to know about the invincible one who could breach the prison.

'Nireeswaran, whom you created with your own minds.'

On hearing that, Antony, like a man possessing full faith in his intelligence, exploded in fury. 'Again, with his idiotic talk, this man is trying to fool us! Asking us to pray to a ridiculous entity which we created ourselves? We don't want to escape by submitting to any superstition!'

Embrandiri recalled the time when the Himalayas had come searching for him with their chilly silence. The days and nights that made him realize that in order to get rid of the ignorance of knowing it all, the ego had to bow before its origins. There was nothing more miraculous than melting pride that was harder than diamond. It was then, and only then, that the subtle rope for one's ascent became visible. Till that moment, every mighty man in the world experienced it as a mere folly, utterly incompatible with intelligence. That was the secret behind its very design.

'What do I gain by making you succumb to any belief?' Embrandiri asked. 'Son, everything is the strong imagination of the mind. Eswaran's existence and non-existence is also a matter of imagination. The attribute with which one's mind gets synchronized will be experienced as reality. The visible universe itself is the result of an individual's imagination! Is there any bigger miracle than the universe?'

'These are all sophistries of Vedanta followers! Absolute hogwash! Whatever you say, we will not compromise on that stone!' Antony was strident.

'Totally your choice! I did not want to feel any remorse later. Nobody cares if you languish inside the jail. Even if you are sent to the gallows, nobody will come to help you. It shall be considered as just deserts for trying to annihilate Nireeswaran. You alone are the sufferers. I have nothing more to say. Following the one who returned first, I am also departing now.'

Embrandiri turned to leave. As the saying goes, after delivering the message the emissary should not remain on the premises.

Antony was enraged that the old gaffer was exulting in his victory over them, having blabbered whatever he wished. The thought seared him, and Antony's suppressed rage went out of control. He suddenly stretched his hand through the bars and caught hold of Embrandiri's neck.

'You . . . you are the main reason behind everything . . . I will . . . !' he yelled, trying to suffocate the old priest.

Since Bhaskaran was aware of how recklessly Antony behaved in such volatile moments, he rushed forward and grabbed Antony's hand with his own left hand. 'Eda, let go now!' he hollered furiously.

The unexpected intervention by Bhaskaran, who had never opposed him, confounded Antony. For the first time Antony felt that the man who had aggressively shouted at him, addressing him 'Eda' disrespectfully, was a stranger. The strength drained away from his hand and the grip around Embrandiri's throat loosened.

Embrandiri, freed from the hand that was throttling him, started coughing. Never had he expected such an attack. Fortuitously or otherwise, his life had been spared. Stroking his neck, Embrandiri staggered away, breathing raggedly and leaving the young men behind the prison bars.

When the tense moments, where reason battled with passion, had passed, Bhaskaran called out with a tremble in his voice, 'Embrandiri . . . !'

That was the first time he had hailed the old priest thus. As the old man turned on hearing the call, Bhaskaran pleaded weakly, 'I want to get out of here . . . at any cost.'

It was an utterly disconsolate young man, devoid of hope, that the aged priest saw at that moment. Even if one were born in an aristocratic family, hunger could make one extend a begging hand. Then one's sense of pride attained the lightness of milkweed.

Bhaskaran continued, 'I don't know what is right or wrong! There is no more certainty about anything. I am willing to do anything to escape this wretched place! I want to be with my family and marry Veni. When she warned me that my time is not good, I never paid attention.'

The iron-clad resolve of Bhaskaran's mind seemed to have melted. It was as though his whole being had turned liquid; anyone could have poured him into a vessel of a desired shape. On solidifying again, he would turn into another form, a different human, with a different attitude . . .

'What drivel are you talking about?' Antony objected. 'Forgetting our decision, are you joining that old geezer? He is just trying to take advantage of our situation. Don't break away. We had stood together till now!'

Bhaskaran detonated like a human bomb at that. A scorching thought, more lethal than any bomb, which had been choking him since the moment he aimed the weapon at Nireeswaran, burst out.

'Who stood together? When I was injured, didn't you guys run away from the scene?' he snarled ferociously.

Shredded by the shards of that question, Antony became speechless.

Bhaskaran spewed forth. 'Had you both escaped that day, I would have been alone in this jail now! Seeing people run for their lives, leaving one behind, is something so terrible! Death would be a better option! If someone who cannot trust his friends decides to believe in an unseen Nireeswaran, who dares to point fingers? I escaped with some severe burns. What if my hand had been severed? What if I were to be shattered by that bomb? What loyalty are you babbling about? Else tell me, can you save me or this poor Sahir?' Bhaskaran's voice was brimming with the burden of unshed tears.

Antony was at a loss for words. Bhaskaran's impassioned overture overwhelmed him.

'You have no answers for anything. When we requested you not to mess around with bombs, you were rigid about it. Friendship is not a dictatorship where one person imposes on others. I don't need anyone's permission anymore! Whether I escape from here or not, I can console myself that it is an act of atonement. A man with nothing more to lose will attempt anything. Nireeswaran emerged from my mind and was shaped by my own hands. It contains at least the powers bestowed on it by an artist. In which case, I am relying only on my own mind's powers.'

Bhaskaran again remembered the single eye which he had seen before collapsing. Even if it had been an illusion, he was not willing to dismiss it as such. He was allured by the great possibilities within that single eye.

Watching his dear friend become disconsolate, Sahir, who was timid by nature, became extremely remorseful. He recollected that it was the animal instinct of self-preservation that had overwhelmed him during the crisis, and a sword of self-loathing slashed through his heart. Hadn't self-interest superseded the friendship at that moment!

Approaching Bhaskaran and leaning against him regretfully, Sahir pleaded, 'Forgive me please . . . I give you my word that I shall be with you from this moment onwards. Whatever you decide shall have my full support.'

Antony shuddered at hearing those words. 'Sahir, you too . . . ?' he asked, unbelievingly.

'Acchaya, I cannot help it. I need at least a straw to clutch at! After all, we are putting our faith in Nireeswaran, whom we churned out of our own selves! We stood together so far. Now . . . Acchaya, won't you also join us?'

A surfeit of emotions flashed on Antony's face. The friends had been a trinity till now. Each had stood up for the others always. Today, one was getting cut off. Antony came to realize that every union faces the crisis of a sundering and that he was standing in the middle of such a crisis now. He became aware that he was faced with the greatest dilemma of his life.

What had glued their three hearts together? Was it Eswaran, Nireeswaran or something else?

Sahir could attune himself to Antony's ruminations more than anyone else. Clutching his friend's shoulder, Sahir asked in a heart-rending tone, 'What are you hesitating about? Who is left to fight with? Our wretched lives can fade away if we catch a flu inside this damned jail! Acchaya, won't you stand with us?'

In a flash, Antony felt his old life dropping away, as if he was shedding skin. Some moments can suck away the mind as if into a dense emptiness. Then the body empties into the mind, the mind empties into intelligence and the intelligence into its quintessence. Antony realized that he was stranded in that inexplicable emptiness.

He said, to nobody in particular, 'If I had ever placed anything above all profits and losses, it was only my friendship. To be true to it, I poured my whole life into it. But from this moment on, I must strive for the strength to stand alone.'

Antony's voice broke and sounded strange even to his own ears. As he felt Sahir's warm touch on his shoulder and then on his right hand, he enunciated softly, 'I shall not oppose. Standing together means I become nothing.'

'I become nothing . . .' Embrandiri took a liking to that phrase. He could feel the waves of a breeze squeeze through the crevices of the prison. As his eyes darted a look at the trio, who had elevated friendship to a divine level, the old man recalled a sacred phrase he read long back: 'Whoever is not against you is in favour of you.'

What the inner voice reiterated was no different.

To cross the barrier, one moment is enough. One and only one moment.

Thereafter, the enthroned cornerstone becomes just an ordinary stone, vulnerable to being thrown away.

Restoration

Devout, blessed souls . . .

What remains to be seen are the ways of justice.

Since law is relative, it changes in every land, at every point of time. What is admissible in a foreign land might be punishable in ours.

But the universal law is unchangeable and is not affected by relativism. All we need to know is how it worked on the three friends.

When all godly ideas wax eloquent on the miracles of the past, here is Nireeswaran proclaiming what is yet to come.

Since he existed even before the origin of Eswaran, Nireeswaran is Eswaran's Eswaran, the Aadi Shakti. The One who shines the same light and wafts the same breeze over the believer and the non-believer, the sinner and the saint, the prostitute and the seer. He opens a door to an equitable space. Anyone can step inside.

Still, if there is any doubting Thomas around, who only believes in tangible reality, honour the place where you stand as the temple of Nireeswaran and seek a boon! By closing your eyes and fixing your gaze on the inner eye, you shall, if you imagine decisively, witness for yourself how the thought germinates and flourishes as a fruit-laden tree.

He who has eyes, let him see.
He who has ears, let him hear.
Even while alive, he shall be reborn.
Om Nireeswaray Namah!